Quest for the White Wind

Alan Black

Books
By
Alan Black

Fantasy
Quest for the White Wind

Science Fiction
Metal Boxes (book one)
Metal Boxes - Trapped Outside (book two)
Metal Boxes - Rusty Hinges (book three)

Chewing Rocks
Empty Space
Larry Goes To Space
Steel Walls and Dirt Drops
Titanium Texicans

Christian Historical Fiction
(An Ozark Mountain Series 1920 Trilogy)
The Friendship Stones
The Granite Heart
The Heaviest Rock
(An Ozark Mountain Series 1925 Trilogy)
The Inconvenient Pebble
The Jasper's Courage
The King's Rock

General Fiction
Chasing Harpo

Western
A Cold Winter

Non-Fiction
How To Start, Write, and Finish Your First Novel

This is a work of fiction. Names, characters, places, and incidents either are the product of the author's imagination or are used fictitiously, and any resemblance to actual persons, living or dead, business establishments, events, or locales is entirely coincidental. The publisher does not have any control over and does not assume any responsibility for author or third-party websites or their content.

Quest for the White Wind
Published by arrangement with the author.

Copyright @ 2016 by Alan Black

Cover Layout and Design: The Cover Collection at http://www.thecovercollection.com/

All rights reserved.

No part of this book may be reproduced, scanned, or distributed in any printed or digital form without permission. Please do not participate in or encourage piracy of copyrighted materials in violation of the author's rights. Purchase only authorized editions.

Copyright registration: 1-3280763811
ISBN-13: 978-1535026178
ISBN-10: 1535026170

Dedication:
This novel wouldn't exist in this form without my brother Steve Black or my wonderful wife Duann. It was their prodding that pushed me into converting an old story I'd written years ago into a fantasy novel. It wasn't as easy a task as they told me it would be, but the result is better than I could have wished for.

Acknowledgement:
Thanks beta reader team for your quality reads and feedback. Steven, Bennett, Melanie & Melissa, you make my books much better than they would be, if left to my own imagination.

I also want to thank my editors. Melissa Manes (www.scriptionis.com) has done her usual wonderful job. My chief editor has exceeded all expectations.

Quest for the White Wind

Alan Black

CreateSpace

CHAPTER ONE

Rough hands jarred Tanden awake, dragging him from the captain's bunk. Before he was fully alert, fists slammed into his stomach while someone struggled to pull a dirty, smelly sackcloth over his head. Before he could strike back, his arms were yanked behind him and his wrists tied with a rough cord. More hands grabbed at him than he could count. His attackers grunted as they fell about trying to get at him, climbing over each other, his small desk, and the trade goods stacked about his cabin. Other than a few guttural curses, no one spoke, leaving him no clue about his attackers.

The hits to his body were painful, but not enough to stop his struggle. His twisting and turning brought more blows. He shook his head trying to loosen the sackcloth, but it was looped tightly around his neck. The rancid stale odor of the cloth did little to block the smell of sweaty unwashed men and the acrid fragrance of smoke.

Falling onto his bunk a few hours earlier, he was certain he could sleep through a whirlwind. He had stripped off his shirt but was too tired to pull off his boots. Now, sharp fingernails raked across his bare back. Dragged to his feet, his boots saved him from injury when a foot stomped on his instep.

Clanging swords, loud voices, and the sound of running feet came from the deck above.

Tanden wasn't concerned about the insult to his person, the harsh binding of his hands behind his back, the sharp sizzle and pop of a magical spell, or the possibility of injury and death to him or his crew. He was alarmed about the smell of smoke swirling about his cabin. Smoke on board a sailing vessel was a bad sign, even in this modern age. Fire threatened his passengers, the ship, and his cargo.

He and his crew were aboard the White Wind by their free will—by their deliberate choice. The crew had selected his vessel as their best option for a successful, profitable voyage. Their lives were important, but not Tanden's primary obligation, at this moment. A ship's captain is the ultimate steward of her passengers, the ship itself, and her cargo. Stewardship was serious business to Tanden. Any losses would severely damage the rewards he worked hard to earn, rewards in this life and in the life yet to come.

His attackers dragged him down the short hallway passing by the passenger cabin. Lady Yasthera il-Aldigg shared the cabin with her maid, I-Sheera. Her bodyguards didn't stop them. Normally, anyone walking the passageway would have stumbled around one of them or the Lady's elderly, male cousin who acted as her escort and chaperone. All three men slept in the tiny corridor, however, this time the passageway was clear.

Tanden was thin and well-muscled for a man coming into the middle of his thirties. Many would describe him as wiry if he was a smaller man or bony if he was taller. Years as a warrior, a sailor, and a ready laborer on his adopted father's docks and warehouses had toughened his six-foot frame. Age hadn't thinned his wild mop of red hair, nor dimmed his clear blue eyes. He was strong, hard, and stubborn.

Struggle as he might, Tanden was well and truly bound. Trussed like a goat on the way to the market, they dragged him up to the top deck. The rough handling did not hamper Tanden's tongue. He called upon the wrath of the gods—all six of the planet's moons—though he believed their power was a myth and they certainly weren't listening. Unsure of who he was cursing, he threatened them with the vengeance of Emperor Monstantong who sat upon the blue throne in Tunston; the might of Warwall, the Red Wizard of Drohnbad; and the promise of a blood feud with King Krebbem, ruler of the Holden Kingdom and the green priests. His captors unceremoniously dumped him onto the top deck as he called on the shrill voice of his adopted grandmother to cause their ears to bleed.

The air on the deck was clear, but Tanden was still concerned about the possibility of fire. The ship and her cargo would be lost if a fire caught hold. He and most of his crew could swim or grab onto hastily constructed rafts, but the White Wind was a long way from shore. He might not be able to save his passengers.

Losing his passengers, even if he saved everything else, would be an unacceptable failure. Not living up to his adopted father's faith would shame Tanden beyond measure. Tanden had sworn to the memory of his long dead mother and the six gods that he would never fail. He no longer believed in the six gods, and the memory of his mother had long since faded, yet he steadfastly held to his oath with unflinching conviction.

The knife Tanden felt at his throat did not bode well. The blade's edge was sharp and held expertly against his skin, pressed by a skilled hand. The slightest shift would cause blood to flow. He rose slowly to his knees hearing the sounds of a scuffle around him. Recognizing Gadon's angry voice and the voices of others, he could not discern their words, because the sackcloth muffled the sound. The clanging swords and scuffling stopped.

Tanden shouted, "Cease! Release me."

Someone said, "Shut your mouth." Their response was punctuated by a slap to his head.

He was thankful the blow pushed his head backward away from the knife blade. He realized with a start that he recognized the voice. Heraclius was a crewman, a Glendonite who had sailed on the White Wind once before.

"Herry," Tanden shouted, hoping that calling the man by his common name might help calm the situation. "Let's discuss this before it goes too far and someone gets killed."

"It's too late for that, you arrogant bastard," Heraclius snarled.

Another voice interrupted, "He's right, Heraclius. No more blood, we have what we want." The voice was Gregin's.

Heraclius had enlisted and vouched for Gregin shortly before they sailed from Harkelle in the Kingdon of Holden. The man was small and pinched, in stature and personality. Tanden appreciated Gregin's small intervention. Although he was not really sure what was going on, he swore silently that Heraclius and Gregin would pay dearly for this, as would any others involved.

Heraclius shouted again, "Gadon, hold or we'll split the throat of this Surr cast-off bastard." If Heraclius could see Tanden's eerie smile under the sackcloth, he might have regretted his remark about Tanden's birth.

When he was younger, Tanden would have mutilated or outright killed anyone who insulted him in such a manner. His mother, a Nechepeg maid from the northern reaches of the Holden Kingdom, was raped by a Surr raiding party and left for dead. She lived to give birth to Tanden, only to die a few years later from a fever. A moderately well-to-do merchant family raised Tanden. He started his childhood as more of a servant than a ward, but grew to become family. Despite his adopted family connections and the passing years, he was still sensitive about his birth and the loss of his mother. He had studied with the great scholars of science in the secret Arius libraries in Allexia as a young man. There, he had become convinced that insults from ignorant men should not go unanswered. He believed the six moon gods were not deities at all and had no authority to punish, neither in this life nor in the next. Tanden would cut Heraclius's tongue from his foul mouth if the Geldonite lived long enough for justice and revenge.

Tanden heard no response from Gadon, but the knife retreated, and the sackcloth was yanked off his head.

"Fire?" He asked as his vision cleared in the gray of the coming dawn.

"What?" Gregin asked.

Heraclius answered, "We've taken the fool's ship, all his cargo, taken his passengers hostage, and he wants a fire to warm his frail old bones."

"Is the ship on fire?" Tanden asked patiently. Time would tell who was the fool if Heraclius and Gregin did not understand the dangers of a fire on board a ship at sea without a red magician present to control it. "I smelled smoke where there shouldn't have been any. Is there a fire?"

"No fire," Gregin replied. His voice was calm and relaxed, with a steadfast tone Tanden had never heard from him before.

Tanden decided he must have smelled a burning torch or lamp they used to light his cabin when he was taken. He took stock of the situation about him as his eyes cleared. Four of his men sat with him: Alton, a fair-haired citizen of Holden; Durrban, an older man, was a devout green magic acolyte; Tuller was Gadon's younger brother; and Seenger from Huzzuzz, was a dark ogre.

In the pale morning light, Tanden saw Alton and Seenger had bleeding wounds about their heads and faces, clear indications they had not been subdued without a struggle. It would have taken a magician or a priest to stop the ogre without more than a handful of men. Alton was a small man, easy to

4

knock down and tie up. Tuller and Durrban were bound hand and foot. Tuller would not have been taken without a fight unless captured by surprise.

Durrban was as small as Alton and well on his way to his sixth decade, with limited magical ability. This far out to sea, a green magic acolyte could not collect and condense enough magic to fight a blue magician who could draw strength and power from the winds and the movement of the six moons themselves. No acolyte stood any chance for success in a battle against a priest, magician, or wizard of any color.

Seenger's wounds would have been deadly on a human. His cuts were on the thick bony ridge along his forehead, well below his black straw-like hair. The ogre's upper and lower fangs were evident, showing his willingness to continue the fight, despite the danger of a magician or priest on board. A light dusting of blue swirled around Seenger's hands, binding them tighter than leather or hemp bonds. The ogre glared at Obert, another crew member armed with a short sword standing uneasily over the captives.

A glimpse at the surrounding sea assured Tanden no other vessel had come upon them in the night. All he had to deal with was a handful of mutineers and thieves.

Two other crewmen, Greeta and Tuba, had Gadon cornered on the aft deck. Gadon's back was to the sea. Holding a pike menacingly in his hands, Gadon slashed it through the early morning air. The pike was a boarding pike with a foot-long metal point on the end of an eight-foot wooden shaft. A sharp hook was welded on at the junction of wood and metal for catching mooring lines or dock pylons. Today, the metal hook caught the first rays of the sun. The sharp curved end succeeded in keeping the two men away from the first mate. Gadon's short, heavy frame made him look fat, but many a tavern brawl proved Gadon a difficult man to put down in a fight. As Gadon swung the pike before him, his face looked ready to explode.

Greeta and Tuba managed to keep him cornered from a respectable distance. Tuba was favoring one leg, a sure sign his respect of Gadon's fighting ability was earned the hard way. Nommer, the twelfth crewman, was nowhere to be seen, nor were the Lady, her maid, or any of her attendants.

Gregin shouted to Gadon, his voice commanding and imperious. "Yield now or you will be killed."

5

"I'll shit in your beard first," Gadon spat. "I'll give your body to the sea, where I sent that idiot Nommer. Then, I'll die a happy man."

"You misunderstand me, Gadon." Gregin's voice was calm and confident. "It's not just you, but all of you who side with Tanden will be tossed into the sea to drown. As a servant of blue magic, I must follow the commandments of my lord, the Blue Wizard of Tunston, who says, "Thou shalt not murder." Still, I'll not hesitate to have Heraclius and his companions toss you all overboard, here and now."

"And if I yield, then what?" Gadon asked.

"No promises, no promises at all to you," Gregin said. "If you continue fighting us, you shall be the last to go overboard. His high and mighty self, the great Captain Tanden, will go overboard first...with his hands tied and then all the others; each in turn. You last of all because I doubt even your strength against the five of us."

Gadon called, "Tanden, what say you?"

"Yes, Tanden," Heraclius snarled in a taunting tone. "Tell us. What say you; you imperious bastard. You lord yourself over us like you know it all. Tell us, in your genius, how you expect to get out of our hands."

Tanden said, though mostly to himself, "I will find a way, in this life or the next."

"Ha!" Heraclius shouted in triumph. "Then I still win. Gregin is a Tunston blue priest, sent by the Blue Wizard himself. He has assured me of my place in the next life."

"Enough, Heraclius!" Gregin interrupted. "We don't need to cast the Blue Wizard's wisdom before these swine."

"Tanden," Seenger spoke for the first time, his voice low and gravelly, "Let's take some of them with us if we're to die by their hand on this deck or in the sea. My god would enjoy a few blue sacrifices."

Like all Huzzuzzian ogres, Seenger was a pagan, never using magic of any color or form. Tanden doubted he worshipped any gods, though the jibe wasn't lost on Obert who was standing guard over him and Gadon's brother, Tuller. Seenger was as tough a creature as Tanden had ever met, doubly dangerous because he feared nothing and cared about even less.

Tuller, always the negotiator, said, "Gentlemen. Gentlemen. Surely, there isn't any profit in our deaths. We would die if we went overboard. Yet, I know for a certainty, we would take some of you with us. The five you have now is barely enough to sail this good ship and cargo back to Stantinstadt. It'd be wasting the quality goods on this ship for no man to claim them. Nor would you want our deaths on your souls. We can surely reach some accord if we calmly discuss your demands."

Gregin looked disdainfully at Tuller, then back to Tanden, "Your ship and cargo mean nothing to me. I'm afraid you mustn't live to tell of what has happened here today."

Tanden silently thanked Tuller for his intervention. Now he knew the intention of the mutineers. They were here to take or kill his passenger, Lady Yasthera il-Aldigg. She was bound for Holden, engaged in marriage to a younger member of King Krebbem's household.

Political tensions were thick enough to cut with a wooden kitchen spoon. Warwall, the Red Wizard of Drohnbad captured the Oggy Strait and the city of Stantinstadt a few years before. The strait bottled up access to the Black Sea. The narrow waterway was the only shipping lane from the Holden Kingdom to the Almodovar Ocean. Closing the strait strangled Holden's economy. Warwall pressured Holden's King Krebbem into an agreement to convert his realm to the red magic order. For Holden to survive as a separate kingdom, converting was their only political option. The forced agreement greatly disturbed Tunston's emperor, who blindly followed the Blue Wizard, the strongest member of the blue order and the head of their conclave.

Colorful magic ruled every aspect of Tanden's world. Everyone was affected by it, believers and pagans alike. Wind and the movement of the stars and the six small moons in the sky were the sources of blue magic. A follower gathered shifting winds into his hands, condensing it into blue power. The flickering flames of fire were the source of red magic. The order collected and condensed the power of rising heat and the dancing red blaze to wield their magic. The green magic order gathered their force from the growth of all living things. The minute movement of a single blade of grass as it grew without external compulsion generated magical power. Green magic could be

7

harvested from a grassy meadow, the bushes hedging the clearing, the trees growing near the clearing, and the small creatures that called the meadow their home. Their growth from egg to adult added to the green's strength.

The priests, magicians, and wizards of each order gathered their power from natural sources, teaching their acolytes age-old techniques.

Tanden was not a magician, priest, or acolyte of any color. He had been tested as a child, as a teen, and even as an adult in the Allexian science schools. He was as devoid of magical ability as a man can be and still have a beating heart. He had come to believe that a man must make his own way or die trying. Using magic was an easy way out.

Though he had no love for any magical order, he especially disliked the blue order. He believed they perverted their magic with a multitude of pagan rituals to lure converts to their ranks. They enticed pagans with little regard or belief in magic, regardless of color, to follow the Blue Wizard's sometimes bizarre commands, paying bribes for magical favors, and paying for the right to be magically transported to the next life upon death.

Each order of magic—blue, green, and red—scoffed at the others, claiming their magic was the true source of power and any other was—somehow—less clean. None but a few heretics still believed in the old white magic. Ancient myths said the white magicians were able to draw magic from any movement regardless of what generated the movement, as slight as the swishing of bare hands through the still air.

King Krebbem's conversion to the red order slightly disrupted the balance of power. When Warwall withdrew his magicians, priests, and army from Stantinstadt, Krebbem withdrew his conversion to the red, proclaiming that the citizens of Holden could believe whatever their hearts led them to believe. Warwall and Emperor Monstantong, the polical face for Tunston's Blue Wizard, barely tolerated Krebbem's reaction. Both threatened military action unless Krebbem converted to their order.

Balance came to the region only after King Krebbem, in his wisdom, converted to green magic, proclaiming green magic as the official magic of the Holden Kingdom. The conversion was a brilliant stroke of statesmanship. It firmly balanced the power of the three great political empires with the three orders of magic: green, blue, and red. In truth, Krebbem continued to allow any to believe and call upon any order of magic; a position the kindom had allowed for centuries before Warwall's capture of Stantinstadt.

Any marriage between the royal Holden house and Warwall of Drohnbad might once again shift the balance of power in favor of the red magic order. The Emperor of Tunston would most likely attempt to stop any shift of power not tilting in his direction.

Tanden thought Gregin's ultimate goal must be to stop the upcoming marriage and alliance. Although he could do so by killing Lady il-Aldigg, it would be more profitable to sell her into slavery. Many brothels or unprincipled rich men would pay dearly for such a beauty, and she would disappear from the face of the earth, as if she was dead. The lady would already be dead if Gregin did not have some profit in mind. Greed did have its own motivational value.

Tanden spoke, "Gregin, Tuller is correct. Neither you nor Heraclius can sail this ship back to Stantinstadt with less men than the five men you have now, even with good winds. Surely, the six of us would take at least one or two of your five with us—."

"With or without your magic, I can guarantee it," Seenger interrupted.

"And I, too," Gadon shouted, adding to Seenger's promise.

A chorus of agreement rang out from Alton, Durrban, and Tuller. Obert, who was still guarding them backed up a step. Heraclius growled and knocked Tanden over with a blow to the head.

CHAPTER TWO

Tanden struggled to his knees.

"Gregin," Tanden said, ignoring Heraclius and the thin trickle of blood he felt running down the side of his face. "I'm making an observation, not a threat. I want to live as much as the next man. Surely, the Blue Wizard wouldn't object to the profits of this ship and cargo—profits to pay your new crew, and as an offering to the emperor. Some agreement must be reached or more men will die here today."

He saw Heraclius's eyes light up at the mention of profit.

Gregin answered, "My purpose will be served whether we all die or not. Do you intend to surrender?" Gregin continued, his voice overriding the shouts of "No!" from Tanden's remaining loyal crew, "Captain, I will accept your word of honor for you and all of your crew. Surrender now and serve this ship until we reach Tunston. I will turn you over to the mercy of the Blue Wizard, a most noble and generous man. I have no wish to send any of these unclaimed men to hell."

Heraclius scoffed, "You'll take the word of a Holdenite? Everyone knows they change sides at a whim. What of Seenger? He's nothing but a filthy ogre. Everyone knows they have no honor. And Durrban? He's a green acolyte, nothing more than a blue order rejector. He should die on principle."

Gregin replied, "Yes, the word of this Holdenite. I know Tanden is a man who doesn't break his promises. These others will obey his command. Isn't that why we didn't approach each of them? I will kill here if I have to, Heraclius, but if blood isn't on our hands then we need not carry the guilt to our masters. Your place is set in the afterlife. You'll be carried there by the power of the blue, but don't continue to contradict me or your eternal seat will not be so assured."

Obert spoke for the first time, "Uh, Gregin, I, uh, Master Gregin, I uh, I wouldn't mind a little profit to last me through my old age."

"Yeah!" Tuba shouted. "Or a Tunston brothel, whichever comes first."

Tanden said, "Gregin, I can't serve you and I won't sail this ship to Tunston, however, it is a two-hour sail to the western shore of the Black Sea. We're near the land of the Hummdhars, who hate all who aren't their own, especially the men of Holden. If they don't kill us, the Coodhars will, or the forests, or the mountains. Ask Heraclius if he can find Stantinstadt without the coast to guide him. No? Then you must sail to the coast anyway. Put us ashore. We'll most likely die, but your hands will be clean. You have my promise we'll leave the boat peacefully if no more die here."

"No!" Gadon and Seenger shouted together.

Tanden shouted back, "Be silent. Do you dare contradict me?"

Seenger replied, "No, sir, my apologies." Any who knew Seenger understood his humbleness held no more sincerity than a thief protesting innocence to the authorities.

Tanden, still on his knees, twisted to face Gadon and said, "Well?"

"Well, what?"

"Do you follow me or not?"

"Now you're going to insult me as well as make me die at the hands of the Hummdhar? They're barbarians who like to tie a man to two trees and split him into two parts." Gadon smiled and looked at Tuller, "Well, my skinny little brother, Mother always said Tanden would be the death of us both with his wild ways. Of course, I follow you, Tanden."

Tanden said, "Gregin, as a gentleman of the blue order surely you will put the lady and her woman ashore with us?"

Gregin replied, "No. They are to remain aboard with me."

"Ha!" Greeta shouted. "Send the maid, I-Sheera with them. She'll kill them if the Hummdhars don't."

Gregin said, "Tanden and these four with him will remain tied. Gadon, retake the helm. Steer us toward the shore. Tanden and all who stand with him may peaceably leave this ship if there is no more violence."

Tanden said, "Gadon, do it! Steer the helm directly west by southwest for the best wind. Tuba and Greeta, reset the sheets."

Both men looked to Heraclius and received a confirming nod. Neither man turned his back on Gadon nor did they rush to their ordered station at the sails. It would take the two men a long time to change the sails, much longer than the normal crew of eight. It would take even longer because Tuba and Greeta were the slowest crewmen on board. The delay would prove his point about sailing with fewer men than Gregin and Heraclius currently had and, hopefully, make them think twice about more killing. A direct westerly track would be a slow sail into the wind blowing out of the west. Tanden knew this coast as well as he did the docks at Harkelle in Holden, having sailed along its edge on a dozen voyages. This tack should place the White Wind in a wide bay. Holden's troops had chased the hostile Hummdhar and Coodhar tribes back into the mountains west of the bay years ago. It appeared Gregin and Heraclius didn't know the region might still be uninhabited. He and his loyal men should only have to contend with the forests and rough uncharted terrain. Being set ashore along this coast might give them an opportunity to win back all that was being stolen, if they could survive long enough to reach shore.

Tanden nodded to the crewmen Obert guarded, "Obert isn't a harsh man and won't keep your bonds any tighter than necessary. Gregin?" He looked to the man he had thought a common seaman, "May I inquire as to the health of the women?"

Gregin replied, "Obert, when you finish there, bring the women on deck. They're cowering in their cabin. And Heraclius, the White Wind is yours to command. Watch Gadon carefully. Any tricks from any of you and none will leave this ship alive. It matters not to me if we all die, for with our deaths I'll become a martyr to the blue order and assure my place in the next life."

After Obert finished tying Seenger and Alton, he went below decks, followed by Tuba. Heraclius remained on deck with Gregin, guarding Tanden, Gadon, and the others, leaving Greeta to struggle with resetting the sails alone. Having caught the wind, the sails luffed badly becoming difficult to grab and control.

Tanden's eyes calmly followed the two men as they dropped out of sight down the ladder to the deck below. He knew the mindset of mutinous men could make them capable of anything. To mutineers and murderers, rape was a small thing. Tied as he was, he could not protect the women. Cursing the mutineers or swearing further vengeance was futile, after all, how many times can you kill the same man? You could do it fast, or slow, or even slower still, but they would die just the same.

Tanden thought, *"It's been a reasonably pleasant voyage, until now."*

The round trip journey between Harkelle and Drohnbad was long, but reasonably uneventful. He captained the White Wind, a fast two-masted merchant craft with a crew of twelve. Their course was south from Harkelle in Holden on the Uube River to cross the Dukos Sea. They sailed between the twin cities of Kalos and Fortin on the Mery Delta. They had smooth sailing down the Black Sea, through the Oggy Strait. The final leg of the voyage was across the mighty Almodovar Ocean to the port city of Gaudet. His cargo of skins and furs from the great northern forests and the eastern mountains of the Huzzuzz ogre tribes brought excellent prices in the bazaars of Gaudet and the Red Wizard's exchange rooms.

The negotiating skills of Gadon's wily brother Tuller overstuffed the holds of the broad, tall ship with trade goods for the return voyage. He was forced to fill the crew's quarters causing them to sleep on deck. Tanden even stored cargo in his own cabin. He attempted to stuff cargo into the passenger cabin, but Lady il-Aldigg threw a tantrum and demanded it be removed.

The return voyage was pleasant, except for the irrational demands made by his special Drohnbad passenger and her most irritating lady-in-waiting. Long ago, he had dismissed his first mate's assertion about women bringing bad luck to a sailing vessel on the open seas and how they did not belong. He might not like to admit it, but before this day was done, he might have to tell First Mate Gadon that the man was right. Such an admission would please Gadon immensely.

Gadon always followed where Tanden led. True to his nature, his fat friend grumbled loud and long about making this journey to Gaudet and the overland trip to Drohnbad, the red order's capital. Nevertheless, Tanden knew Gadon would join him when Tanden accepted the assignment from his adopted father to master the White Wind, even to swallowing the unintended insult of choosing his adopted son over his natural-born son to captain his best ship.

Tanden reveled at the opportunity for such a journey, sailing a good ship to collect and bring back the Red Wizard's niece, Lady Yasthera il-Aldigg for marriage to Tarran, the youngest son of Krebbem. There was great profit in a cargo of spices, silks, and precious metals from the Red Empire and the Far East trade routes. Profit was important to the family business. Being connected to this politically motivated alliance, however remote the involvement, was more important than the voyage or cargo. Such a connection would bring great value to his adopted father's household and business. For scores of years, the Holdenites kept the invading Surr tribes from the north out of the Almodovar Ocean and the Red Wizard of Drohnbad was a barrier to the far eastern hordes, keeping them from the Holden plains. This marriage would strengthen the bond between the Red Wizard and King Krebbem.

The return trip to Holden began pleasantly. The weather cooperated, the wind filled the sails, and the crew didn't suffer from sleeping on deck. The winds were so favorable the oars remained stowed the entire voyage. If the winds had not cooperated, making headway using the oars would have been backbreaking work. The ship was too overloaded with cargo and extra passengers.

The only sand in the ointment was Lady il-Aldigg. Unlike Gadon's good-natured jibes, the Red Wizard's niece delivered complaints with the nasty edge of threats. She demanded changes in everything. She challenged everyone aboard. She complained about the wind blowing in the wrong direction and the breeze not refreshing her cabin sufficiently. She demanded the ship only sail so the wind blew directly into her cabin's porthole.

Much to Tanden's distress, Lady il-Aldigg didn't deliver her complaints to him personally. It she had, he could have taken refuge in her beauty while she incessantly whined about not stopping in a port of call each night to stay in a decent inn. Yasthera il-Aldigg was plump and full-figured as a young woman should be with dark lush hair and pale ivory skin.

I-Sheera, her traveling companion and lady-in-waiting, delivered all complaints. I-Sheera's irritating whine came from a sun-weathered, labor-hardened, skin and bones body. She was a mid-twenties spinster wrapped in ill-kept robes. Her dark scraggly hair flew about in complete disorder in the constant sea wind. Even Gadon admitted I-Sheera's pretty eyes complemented her full lips, however, nothing helped offset the size of her hooked nose with wide nostrils that flared like a wild saurus. The giant lizards, wingless four-footed dragons from the northern steppes domesticated as carry beasts were noted for their ugly noses and short stubby tails.

Nostrils flaring, her wild-eyed tantrums brought gales of laughter every time she stomped her foot and demanded the sailors bathe or stay down wind of Lady il-Aldigg. Tanden and the rest of his crew found I-Sheera occasionally humorous. Bathing? Who ever heard of such a thing!

Tanden was barely thankful for I-Sheera's presence. A woman alone without a companion would have been trouble indeed. Even with two bodyguards and the lady's elderly male escort, the women were always underfoot. The lady never went among the crew without both a male and female attendant.

The White Wind sailed past Stantinstadt into the Black Sea without stopping, heading north toward home. For three days they sailed north by northwest to take advantage of the continuing westerly winds. The ship sailed off the western shore, near land the Coodhar and Hummdhar tribes constantly disputed with the Holden Kingdom, but they sailed beyond the sight of land, only catching glimpses now and again as reference points along their course.

Tanden asked, "What of the Lady's male escort and her bodyguards?"

Gregin flicked his eyes to the sea. The slight raise of one eyebrow showed how little concern he had for killing the three men.

A screech from below startled everyone on deck.

Tanden's head snapped around to the hatch opening, but from his angle, he was unable to see anything. A loud guffaw closely followed the screech. Heraclius's echoing laugh brought Tanden's attention back to the deck. Even from this distance, Tanden could see Gadon's knuckles turn white against the tiller.

A second throaty yell caused Gregin to move to the open hatchway, "Stop that and come up on deck."

Obert popped up through the hatch. Pushing him hard from behind, Tuba propelled him up the passageway ladder. Obert held one hand wrapped in a bloody rag.

"She cut me," he yelped. "That red harpy, I-Sheera has a kitchen knife and she cut me."

Tuba laughed, "Twice. She cut him twice. He was too slow to get out of the way and she cut him twice."

Obert wandered around showing the cuts to anyone who would look. "She's a harpy. That's what she is. Look. I'm going to bleed to death. That harpy has killed me." Looking at the cuts, the men could readily see Obert was in no danger of dying, much to the regret of half the men on deck.

Gregin asked calmly, "And the lady and her woman?"

Tuba answered, "Her majesty and Obert's harpy will be up directly. I-Sheera said we could try to drag them up, but we'd go home to our wives without our testicles. I may not have a wife, but I for one, am willing to let them come up when they're ready to come up."

Tanden doubted anyone would disagree. The top deck was tense enough without adding a pampered lady and a knife-wielding harpy to it.

CHAPTER THREE

The White Wind wallowed slowly to the southwest facing into the westerly winds. She slipped two leagues to port for each league forward. The slight southerly tack was what allowed them any headway.

The tides and currents in this part of the Black Sea were uncharted. Even experienced captains could be pushed off course by the tides faster than their forward movement against the wind. The closer they came to the shore, the more unpredictable the winds became as they swept down from the Erway Mountain slopes to the west.

Tanden believed his ship would sail deeper into a large bay. Science, not magic, formed the basis of his belief. The six moons made the tides difficult to predict—the Rose, the Potato, Lumpy, the Egg, Six Finger, and Deering—had much to do with where a ship sailed. Not because they were gods with divine powers or any magic harvested from their movements. The lunar orbits affecting the tides were as rock steady as science once a sailor learned how to calculate their movements.

Yasthera il-Aldigg and I-Sheera were sitting in the bow of the boat watching the shoreline inch closer. Their nervous glances at the mutineers were proof of their fear, although the lady affected an air of royalty and untouchability. I-Sheera tried to follow her lady's example, but the kitchen knife in her hand was evidence of her willingness to protect herself and her lady.

It took most of the morning to maneuver toward the shore, far longer than Tanden's earlier two hour estimate. They were slowed by the sails popping and snapping, luffing badly, not catching the light wind's full force. Tanden thought he could see some slight progress, but he didn't think the White Wind was any closer to shore than it had been an hour earlier.

The coast might have been no more than an hour's walk had they been on dry land. The ship was heading straight down the bay. Great cliffs rose on three sides, appearing to be somewhat closer to the starboard side, though the distance may have been an illusion.

Finally, Heraclius shouted, "Enough. Turn to port to catch the wind. We've stopped moving. Sail toward shore."

Tanden replied, "Rocks, Heraclius. Are you familiar with this coast? There may be rocks here to send us all to the deep."

Gregin said, "What would you suggest, Tanden?"

The man had changed into his blue order priestly robes; all white with a splash of blue from the elbow to the hands. Blue magicians wore white robes with blue arms and torso and blue wizards wore blue robes with a hint of white trim. The Blue Wizard, the highest and most powerful man in the order, wore an all blue robe.

Tanden wondered where the man had hidden his robe. Durrban kept his white acolyte robe with only a blotch of green color on the chest in the ship's stores, never trying to hide it. Still, there were cubbyholes all over the ship. He knew them all, but rarely inspected them. He allowed crewmen to buy and ship a few small goods of their own for extra profit. He had never given his crew any reason to hide anything brought aboard.

He answered the blue priest, "Continue down the center of the bay to the point. We may find good anchorage there."

Heraclius hissed, "He's just trying to lengthen his life."

"Maybe, Gregin," Tanden said, ignoring Heraclius. "But I'm also trying to save the lives of the women and this good ship."

Heraclius said, "I said enough. Gregin, you gave me the command of this ship. Gadon, turn to port. Now!"

Gregin asked, "Gadon, you're at the tiller. Are there rocks here?"

Gadon shrugged. "There may be, there may not. We won't know until we run aground on one."

"Heraclius," Gregin sighed, "I don't think it would be wise to sail too close in unknown waters. Yet, you may do as you wish."

With a sweeping gesture toward the captives, Heraclius said, "What I wish, is just to toss these over the side and sail back to Stantinstadt and then on to Tunston. Let's get on with it!"

Gregin moved to the hatch leading below. At the top of the ladder, he paused long enough to say, "Get on with it then. I'm also anxious to get back to Tunston."

Tanden's head whipped around when someone let out a whoop, but he wasn't able to identify who shouted. "Gregin, wait! As a priest of the blue way and an honorable man, you promised to put us peaceably on shore."

The priest halted on the ladder. "No, Tanden. You don't remember. My promise was to sail *toward* the shore. I promised to let you leave the ship peaceably if there was no further violence. It's of no concern to me if we haven't reached shore when you leave the ship." He continued over Tanden's objections, "And, if you wish to break your promise and not leave peaceably, then that's also no concern of mine. Heraclius, toss them over the side."

A babble of voices followed Gregin down the ladder until he was out of sight.

Tanden shouted to his loyal crew, "Hold. I promised to leave peaceably. Any man who follows my command will do the same. I won't break my promise, nor allow any other to cause me to lie. Heraclius, we will leave peaceably. Please untie me so I may try to swim to shore."

Heraclius said, "Slowly. I want to enjoy this. Greeta, you and Tuba untie and throw the ogre over first."

"Wait," Durrban cried. "Seenger can't swim. Allow me to go first so I may aid him."

"Do it," Heraclius said. "They can drown together; a dirty Huzzuzz ogre and a dirty greenie."

Greeta moved to loosen the bindings on Durrban's hands. Tuba stood warily watching for any hostile movement. Durrban stood slowly and stretched. Shaking his hands in the air and wiggling his fingers, he stepped to the starboard railing. He glanced back at Seenger, who firmly nodded to him. Turning, he quietly saluted Tanden and stepped off the starboard side dropping into the sea.

Tuba whooped and rushed to the edge. "Quick," he said, shouting back to Greeta, "Untie Seenger."

Untied, Seenger stood and without any fanfare or flourish, went to the rail and into the sea. Tuba whooped again. "Look. I'll wager that's the first bath Seenger has ever had in his life. An ogre in the water! I didn't think I'd ever see that. Look at 'em splash."

Heraclius said, "Get on with it, Tuba. Let's not take all day. Isn't there a brothel in Stantinstadt that you want to get to?"

Tanden thought, *Am I going to overboard with such style? Do I go like this or do I get tossed overboard kicking and screaming? No! If Seenger can step off with quiet dignity when he can't even swim, I must do no less. If he drowns, is it my fault? I hired him on as a sailor when no one else would take on any foreigner, much less an ogre. Is it my fault if any drown? I took on Heraclius and Gregin knowing they weren't of Holden. Alton is from Holden and it'll be my fault if he dies here. And Durrban. And Seenger. And Tuller and Gadon, too.*

Tanden clamped his teeth together in determination. *"No! I'll not die here. I will not. Damn Gregin and all these mutinous pus pockets. I'll go over the side with the pride befitting a son of Holden. I mustn't do less, or I won't be fit to be the messenger of vengeance on these children of the dark demons."*

Tanden watched while three of the mutineers advanced on Gadon at the helm to throw him overboard. "Gadon," he shouted. "Do not make me a liar. I've made promises and given my word. Go quietly. Wait for Tuller and try for the starboard shore. I'll be along shortly."

Unable to do anything Tanden watched while Heraclius, Greeta, and Tuba pounced on Gadon. Gritting his teeth, he saw flurries of kicks and punches rain down on the unnaturally docile Gadon.

"Obey me, Gadon," Tanden silently willed his friend. *"Damn me, my vow may get my oldest friend beaten to death."*

Tanden looked to Tuller. The man's face was strained with the effort of trying to break his bonds. A glance at Obert showed the man was more interested in picking at the small wounds I-Sheera had given him than guarding Tuller, Alton, or Tanden. Obert was muttering to himself and watching the women furtively out the corners of his eyes.

Heraclius, Greeta, and Tuba finally picked Gadon up and cast him over the port side of the ship. Tanden's peripheral vision registered Tuller as he ran straight toward the three men. His broken bonds lay on the deck. Quicker than Tanden could call for him not to fight the mutineers, Tuller crashed through the three men sending them scattering about the deck. He dived over the side out of Tanden's sight, obviously near his brother Gadon.

Alton quickly followed the others into the sea.

Tanden thought, *"None but these diseased mongrels are here to witness my embarrassment if I can't go to the sea with my honor intact."* He gave no thought of the women's opinion, after all, princess or slave girl, they were only women."

All three men attacked Tanden at the same time. Clamping his teeth shut, he tensed against the blows striking his exposed body. *"Cowards,"* he thought. *"Not one of them ever challenged my authority face-to-face. They're no more than animals. I won't expose my fears to such creatures."*

Tanden was lifted up and carried to the starboard side. He struggled with his thoughts and anger, trying not to fight back. Still tied hand and foot—and against his conscious effort—rather than be tossed bound into the sea, he kicked and struggled, to no avail.

Fortunately, he felt the ties ripping away as he was tossed into the sea like yesterday's trash.

Hitting the water felt like ripping a veil from his eyes. He realized he must have taken a blow to the head. Anyone would be fuzzy headed to even think of fighting back. Tanden knew in his heart it did not matter that he was unsuccessful struggling against the men. It only mattered that he tried. Tanden vented his frustration and anger on the water about him.

Hearing laughter from the ship, Tanden looked around him. Seenger and Durrban should be near him, but the slight rippling of waves blocked his view. From his vantage point, any of his men could have been five feet away and he wouldn't see them.

Tanden considered shouting, but every man in the water would need all of his breath to make it to shore. He hoped they would find a beach or a shoreline when they got to the water's edge. The verticle high rock walls did not look inviting.

"Hold. Damn it!" A voice shouted from above him.

Looking up, he tilted his head back in the water trying to see the edge of the White Wind's deck. He could not see who shouted.

"Throw the harpy over, too."

Tanden easily recognized Obert's whine.

Another voice echoed, "Yeah, yeah, let's do it. I've had all of her mouth I ever want to hear."

21

Tanden shouted, "*No! No! No! Women are to be protected, not drowned, you fools.*" He realized with a start that he hadn't shouted out loud.

"*Why?*" he asked himself. "*Why didn't I speak out loud? Am I that much of a coward? What more can these men do to me?*"

A voice from the ship said, "Might as well throw her overboard. She's too scrawny to fetch much of a price from any slaver I know. Besides, I wouldn't screw her with Obert's tool."

The crude laughter didn't die down until Tanden heard a woman's scream. He was unable to recognize if the scream was Lady Yasthera il-Aldigg or her servant, I-Sheera.

Tanden had already sworn personal revenge. Promising to bring further pain and suffering was futile.

I-Sheera was propelled over the rail from the shoulders of the mutineers. She screamed and flailed at the air on her way to the sea. Stark terror on her face was evident. Her layers and layers of flimsy clothing floated around her like a cloud.

The slow headway the White Wind was making hadn't taken the ship more than a short distance from Tanden. He momentarily thought she would hit the water on top of him, taking them both under to drown. He'd seen men drown before, dragged under by wet clothing long before they could strip it off.

She missed him. Her splashing and thrashing threw stale saltwater into his eyes, momentarily blinding him.

He thought, "*This is stupid. Don't do this. Let her drown.*"

Nonetheless, he immediately reached to grab her. Even reacting as quickly as he had, she was sinking fast. Tanden grasped a handful of cloth. He yanked upward toward the air and the sun. The action should have plunged Tanden downward below the surface, but that reaction did not account for his rapid descent. Her flapping arms and legs clutching at him dragged him underwater before he could gulp air into his lungs.

"*See,*" he told himself. "*I told you this was stupid. Let this creature go or we'll both drown.*"

Tanden pushed downward and away from I-Sheera, propelling himself up again into the air. As he broke the surface, he saw the White Wind turning, coming around to catch the wind. Indistinct faces were turning away from him toward the rigging. Tanden knew from personal experience it is one thing to send a person to their death and quite another to stand and watch it. The putrid walking dead did not have the courage to face what they had started.

Tanden spun around in the water to look for I-Sheera. She was nowhere in sight.

The Black Sea isn't like the great Almodovar Ocean. In many places of the Almodovar, Tanden could have seen I-Sheera sitting on the bottom, many fathoms under the water. Here, the water was dark, quickly hiding anything in its wet silty folds.

Tanden ducked his head under water and felt around. His fingers brushed against something. He clutched and found himself holding a mass of wild tangled hair. Raising his head, taking a deep breath, he yanked upward. Prepared this time against I-Sheera's panicked assault, Tanden was able to keep his face in the air.

I-Sheera's head popped up facing Tanden. She sputtered, spitting water in Tanden's eyes and raggedly gasping for air. Her arms and legs reached out to tangle around Tanden, trying to climb onto him. Without a shirt, his wet skin was slippery, making it difficult for her to cling to with any sense of permanence.

Tanden realized she was trying desperately to stand on him. He pushed her away again.

She whipped her arms around, churning the water into froth.

He shouted, "Stop fighting me or drown." Reaching forward, he gave her body a push to rotate her in the water.

Down she went.

Tanden thought, *"I'm going to tire myself and not have the strength to swim to shore if I continue wrestling with this woman. But damn me, I can't go to my death knowing I didn't try."*

He reached into the sea again. Once again, he grabbed a fist full of wet tangled hair. He pulled I-Sheera into the sun.

This time she spat and sputtered away from him. Not releasing his grasp on her hair, Tanden roughly pushed a fist into the small of her back, twisted her head backward, forcing her face to the sky. She gulped, more from pain and fear of drowning than lack of air.

Tanden said calmly, "Fear not. Relax and we'll both live." To emphasize his point, he pushed her head under water, but just as quickly, he pulled her up again.

I-Sheera had enough breath this time to begin cursing in a whining voice, "You foul camel dung eater—."

Tanden interrupted her curses by dunking and slowly raising her again. "Obey me or die. Now!"

"Yes, sir." Her voice quivered with fear, without the whine Tanden had come to expect. Her body relaxed and floated easily in his grasp. Her long eastern style robe swirled in the water about them.

"Trust me, girl. I won't let you drown, but you mustn't fight against me. Relax. Do all that I say. Don't fight me. Curse me again and I'll leave you to curse the fishes."

I-Sheera started to speak, but Tanden interrupted, "Don't say another word until I give you permission. I give you breath to live, not to corrupt the air with your tongue. Do you understand?"

Her head nodded slightly in acceptance.

He said, with more calm than he felt, "We'll live, but it's a long way to the shore. I must swim for both of us. Your robe is already tangling my legs. Remove them as best you can. Now!"

Tanden struggled against the sea, using one hand and his legs to keep himself above water. Loosely wrapping his other arm around I-Sheera's throat, he put as much upward pressure on her chin as he could.

His legs came free of the cloth. "Don't release your robe. Bundle and hold it. You'll need it when we reach land."

He thought, *"Or so is my desire. Am I such a coward that I fear drowning here or at the shore? Am I so dishonest that I will lie to a woman to bolster my own lack of courage?"*

He said, "Relax now. As I swim, let your feet float to the surface. Don't fight against me. I'll save us both."

Despite having his own doubts, Tanden thought it best for both of them to not worry about how much danger they were facing. He glanced at the sun almost directly overhead. He was able to see each shore, but the cliffs themselves gave him no clue as to which way to swim. North had been to the right. With a practiced sailor's eye, he struck out for the northern shore with more confidence than he truly wanted to admit, even to himself.

Handful after handful of water, Tanden moved closer to the cliffs. At least, he hoped they were moving closer to the cliffs. From his vantage point at sea level, he could not judge the distance with any accuracy. Their progress was far too slow to be apparent.

The woman allowed herself to be towed quietly, but it was not long before Tanden's breath become labored as he fought against even the small waves of the bay. Tanden's limbs had been tied all morning. The strain and stretch of swimming in the sea felt good at first, but now his arms and legs started to ache in the chilly water.

The Black Sea's temperature at this time of the year was survivable but still cold enough to sap his strength. Swimming kept his body heated, but he felt I-Sheera shivering where her body pressed against his side and hip.

"Girl, move your arms and legs up and down through the water. It'll warm you. Don't move in a forward and back motion as that will work at cross purposes to our movement to the shore. Do you understand?"

He felt her nod against his arm, but she held her tongue.

Tanden wanted to shout and look for his friends and crewmen, but looking would waste his time and shouting would waste his air. Stroke after stroke, he swam toward the shore, not sure he could swim that far, even without towing another person.

CHAPTER FOUR

Tanden's feet scraped something in the water. Salt eels or sea wolves! Involuntarily, he jerked his legs up and away. The reflexive movement snapped his mind into focus. He looked around, surprised to see the cliffs looming over him. Gingerly, he set his feet down onto the rocky bottom. On dry land, his wobbly legs would have collapsed, but here the water helped support his weight.

"Girl, can you stand? Try now, we are close to land."

As she complied, Tanden released his hold on her. He looked to the sky, not able to see the sun. He had been lulled into senselessness as he swam, having no idea how long they had been in the sea. His body ached from one end to the other.

The cliffs ended at the sea with a thin strip of rocky shore. The shoreline could not be called a beach. It was nothing more than big boulders gathering at the foot of the cliff face with smaller rocks between to keep them company. The largest of the boulders stood seven or eight feet tall. Most of the area was jagged and angular. Flat, dry surfaces were at a premium.

The accessible shore extended a hundred yards to the left. The cliffs touched the sea within a few feet to the right of where the two approached the shore. The rock wall shot almost straight up for two hundred and fifty feet. Tanden noted the cliff face was not as straight and unbroken as it appeared from the ship. A close look revealed gaps, gashes, and nooks where the weather brought down the boulders forming the shoreline.

From his angle so close to the cliff face, Tanden was unable to see beyond the crest of the cliff. No birds were here, not even the usual sea eagles or wyverns looping through the air. He put a hand on the small of the woman's back, pushing her forward, propelling her toward the shore. He followed I-Sheera's stumbling steps.

Standing in water up to his mid-thighs, he stopped and swung his arms painfully around his head, stretching back and forth. The movement caused shooting pains throughout all parts of his torso and down his legs. Stomping about as best he could with the footing available, he wanted to shout out in pain and anger, but clamped his jaw shut. He would not allow himself the luxury of such an outburst with a mere woman close by to witness his weakness. This woman, as obnoxious and irritating as she has been on this journey, was still his to protect. Showing weakness before her would be as unfruitful and damaging as showing weakness before a crewman. He was in command. He must remain in control of himself first to remain in control of others. If he could not do so, he did not deserve to be captain.

His aching, cramped muscles had begun to quickly loosen providing freer movement in all parts of his body, Tanden walked carefully out of the water to stand on the uneven rocks. He turned his back to the rock wall and faced the sea. The small strip of land was shaded by the cliffs. He saw no others on the rocky shore.

The woman collapsed on the rocks.

"Girl, are you all right?"

She nodded in reply, looking up at him wearily.

Tanden said, "You may answer me, but remember, I command here."

"Yes, Captain. I'm as well as I can expect to be. Thank you for my life."

The deep calm tone of her voice surprised Tanden, yet he was too tired to visibly react. She sounded like an entirely different woman than aboard ship.

He thought, *Almost dying can transform a person, but a contrary wind will return to its westerly ways as sure as a dog returns to its own vomit. She'll return to being nasty as soon as she's rested. I wonder if I can keep her exhausted until I find a place for her safekeeping.*" He shook his head in disgust, "*By my mother's eyes, I must be tired myself. That was an unkind thought. Well deserved, it's true, but unkind.*"

He said, "Take your clothing off. Then—"

The look on the woman's face turned to shock.

"What? Speak. I won't toss you back to the fishes this one time."

"You wish me to disrobe? Here? Now? I owe you my life. If you want me then, you may take me. I won't resist."

Tanden laughed until a short fit of coughing caused him to suck in gasps of cool air. "You eastern reds! Amazing! You cover up every possible part of your bodies, but your minds are always on sex. I think you'd have fewer problems if you uncovered yourselves." He continued despite her shocked look. "Holdenites are unashamed of our bodies. Even ogres have a saying that it's better to see what you can't have, than to not see what's yours to take. You don't agree? Let me ask you, you know adultery exists in your culture, yes?"

"Not often among the women. But it does occur with some men."

"Ha! Some eastern men pervert themselves with beardless boys, but adultery and fornication takes two. The red order teaches against it as it's contrary to forming concentrated magic. It prevents a person from focusing their attention on harvesting magic. Among Holdenites, the Hummdhars, and even the uncivilized Huzzuzz ogres, adultery is rare in comparison to your country. We have no punishment for adultary, except for what passes between a husband and his wife. We aren't ashamed of our bodies."

He sat on a waist high rock. Pulling off his boots, he dumped water from them. "Girl, my intention isn't to ogle your flesh or partake of your delights. I'm concerned for your comfort and health. You're enough of a problem already. If you grow ill because you're wearing wet clothing, I'll be obligated to doctor you back to health." Tanden put his boots on, speaking slowly and distinctly, "I don't have time for such nonsense."

"I'm ashamed in my ignorance. I didn't understand. Forgive me, master."

He liked this version of the woman much more than the previous. He spoke gently, "Unless I miss my guess, we have more to deal with than wet clothing. Get up, wring the water out of your robe and put it on. It'll still be damp, but not as wet and cold as what you have on. Move down the shore behind a rock to change your clothing. Dry what you can as quickly as you can." Tanden gestured around. "I can't offer you any more privacy than that."

I-Sheera stood and turned to move, but halted. Pointing at the sea toward the other end of the beach, she shouted excitedly. "Look. There's something in the water."

Tanden looked, but from where he sat, he saw nothing in the bright white light across the waves. "What? Where? Where?"

I-Sheera jabbed her finger in the direction she wanted Tanden to look. He still saw nothing where she was pointing. He clambered to the top of a large boulder, then leaped to a small ledge on the cliff where he was able to get a toehold on the cliff face. Scanning the sea from this higher vantage point, he saw a darker blotch in the water surrounded by dancing white waves. Was the shadow his crew reaching the coast or some giant sea beast hunting for an evening meal?

Tanden said, "Change as I have commanded. I'll go down the shore for a closer look."

He glanced down at I-Sheera to see if she was going to comply or give him another argument. If Tanden was a betting man, he would have wagered on hearing an argument. He was surprised to see the slave girl beginning to remove her clothing.

What he saw pleased him. I-Sheera was thin, but not skinny. Her flowing eastern-style robe hid her true form. Her breasts, smaller than most Tanden had seen, jutted strongly from her smooth chest. Her dark, hardened nipples thrust outward. Broad, straight shoulders, with a flat, well-muscled stomach and strong legs were proof of a life of hard work.

"*Good*," Tanden thought to himself. "*Very good. She'll need strength in the times to come, and she's much more comely than I'd have guessed.*" His gaze traveled to the dark triangle between her legs and swept back up enjoying the overall proportions of the figure before him. "*Ah, Tanden, you're a fool to be thinking such ideas, today of all days. First things first. Certainly not so recently after a lecture on nudity. My good man, lust doesn't allow a man to make good decisions.*"

Shaking his head from side to side, he tore his eyes away from I-Sheera and looked down the shore. Carefully, he charted a route along the rocks that should put him near the object in the water. He could not afford to break a leg on the slippery rocks any more than he could afford to drag a sick woman across unknown and probably hostile territory. From his point of view, the large boulders appeared to be small cliffs in themselves, blocking his view of the shore ahead and I-Sheera behind.

Still weary from lack of sleep, hours of bondage, and the long swim to shore, he wound his way around and over rock after boulder after rock. He scanned the sea at every opportunity, but saw nothing more than water, sky, and stone. For every foot he moved forward, he moved two feet sideways and one up—or two feet down and one back.

"By my father's ears, I don't know if I have the strength to do all that's laid before me."

A voice spoke, "Quit whining about it and get your lazy butt over here. And next time you get us tossed off a ship, would you do it near a comfortable place to set down. These rocks are anything but comfortable."

Tanden whooped when he recognized the complaining voice of his longtime friend, Gadon. With renewed vigor, he bounded around the rock. Gadon and Durrban were sitting on the rocky shore. I-Sheera had seen his crew.

Both men had collapsed on the rocks, dripping wet from having just come out of the sea. Alton, Tuller, and Seenger were nowhere in sight.

Noticing Tanden's glances, Gadon said, "I think we have lost my brother and Seenger."

Durrban silently nodded in agreement.

Tanden asked, "Did you see them go under? How do you know they're lost? How did you two end up together?"

Gadon replied, "I'm tired, cold, and hungry. Don't badger me. I don't often lose my brother to the sea."

To stop his complaining, Tanden interrupted, "Tell me exactly what happened. Both of you. Durrban?"

The man shrugged and said, "As the green power wills."

"No!" Tanden said. "I'll not hear that. None of the magical orders condemn good men to drown at a whim. It's the dark demons who will the death of men; it's their will and the will of those who serve them. Alton, Seenger, and Tuller may yet live, that is my will. Gadon, speak."

Gadon spat back, "Oh yes, pick on the short guy. We almost drowned a few short yards from the shore, but the waves and tides must have lifted us from the nice soft water and set us upon these hard boulders. I've got water in my ears and every other opening of my body. I'm perched on a sharp rock that pokes at my delicate behind and you want me to tell you stories? Well, by mother's beard, I will then."

"Tell me first of Nommer. You killed him?" Tanden asked.

"I cut his gut from crotch to throat and sent him to sleep at the bottom of the Black Sea. The fool thought to attack me alone."

Nommer was a lazy crewman and none too bright. Tanden doubted if anyone would be sad or troubled at his death. He was where he belonged if he was part of the mutiny.

Gadon continued, "After being tossed overboard, I no sooner splashed into the sea than Tuller came in after me. We both went over the port side near the stern. We began swimming around the ship to the starboard side." Gadon looked up at Tanden. "That was your command, wasn't it? Swim to the starboard shore?"

Tanden sat next to his friend. "Yes, Gadon, to the starboard shore. What happened?"

Gadon continued, "Tuller and I went over the side near the stern. Durrban and Seenger went over larboard amidships. The forward progress of the White Wind was so slow that when Tuller and I reached the starboard side, we found ourselves face-to-face with them."

Durrban nodded in agreement.

"Did you see Alton go overboard?" Tanden asked.

Gadon replied, "No, nor later in the water. I heard you both go overboard, but I couldn't see anything."

Alton was a quiet man, but a good one.

Tanden said, "All right, go on, Gadon."

Gadon continued, "Seenger was floating as best he could and Durrban was towing him along by his tunic. Seenger looked like he was trying to relax as much as any ogre in water could, so as not to hamper Durrban. We could hear yelling from the ship, but we couldn't see anything. Not that it mattered, we couldn't help you anyway. We decided to stay together and swim to shore taking turns towing Seenger. I really hate swimming and I like seawater less than Seenger, but even I took a turn at pulling him along."

Tanden sympathized with his men. He would have gladly shared the task of towing I-Sheera. They didn't have long to rest. Time was short in more than one way.

"Somewhere out there we lost them while Tuller was towing Seenger. He was the strongest swimmer and he took more of the burden. When Durrban and I next turned around, they were out of sight. We shouted and searched as best we could. Tanden, by my own hairy balls, if we'd searched one minute longer we wouldn't have had the strength to reach these rocks. I'll miss my brother. He always was a pain, even as a little one, remember Tanden? What will I tell Mother?" Gadon hung his head in his hands.

Tanden said, "Men, we've all had losses this day. Can you get up? We must be about our business."

Startled, Durrban said, "What business? Please, Captain. We're tired. Look at what we've already done this day. Look at what we've been put through. Let us rest, then I'll try to gather what magic I can, though there be little green here on this rocky shore."

Tanden said. "We must move now. It's my intention to retake the White Wind."

"What?" Both crewmen exclaimed in unison.

"It's my father's ship and I intend to retake her."

Gadon looked at Tanden and shook his head. Again, Tanden knew Gadon would do as he asked. Where Tanden went, Gadon followed with gusto, not without complaint, but with zeal and zest.

Gadon had been with him as his friend for as long as he could remember. When Tanden went to the libraries and schools of Allexia, Gadon went with him, where he complained of being bored. Later in years, when Tanden fought the Hummdhars in the Western Wars, Gadon went with him, complaining about the lack of food and beds. When Tanden traveled to the Geldonite States on a trading mission, staying in taverns and brothels, Gadon went along. Even there he complained the women were too pretty for his tastes, the drink too strong for his head, and the food too rich for his stomach.

"Yes, Gadon. It's my goal to retake the White Wind. Do you remember this coast from the charts?" Tanden continued without giving the man a chance to reply, "To the south of us is a large peninsula. If I'm correct, we're near the isthmus. Heraclius is a poor sailor at best. He'll have to hug the coast all the way back to Stantinstadt or face missing the city altogether. He'll not want to sail out of sight of land, nor too close to the rocky shoreline. The winds are with him as he sails east, but the tides are contrary right now. His westward course will be very slow as he sails into the wind. It may take him three or four days to reach the south coast of the isthmus. We can cross the peninsula by land, gaining an advantage and retake the ship. We must not delay on this shore. We must be up and moving now."

Durrban spoke, "I still follow you, Captain Tanden, but I beg you to let us rest awhile. I see no way off these rocks except straight up these cliffs or back into the sea."

The men looked up at the rock walls around them. The cliffs looked imposing, but not impossible to climb.

Gadon said, "These rocks are uncomfortable, Tanden, but I was on helm watch as we sailed north last night and I was on helm all morning as we sailed west. We all swam for what? hours? When we're rested is time enough."

Tanden replied. "Time enough is the problem, my friends. We have little enough of it on these rocks. We must forget what's past. We must move forward now and rest later. How is it we all reached the coast at the almost the same spot? Luck? I think not. Gadon, tell me, where is the watermark on these rocks for high tide?"

Glancing up at the watermarks on the boulders and cliffs, Gadon looked startled.

Tanden said, "That's right. The tide pulled us to the same spot and now sets upon us. In a very short while, if we stay, we'll be taking our rest crouched upon the largest boulder here and we'll still be in two or three feet of water."

He shook his head, looking pointedly at Durrban, "I know you're an acolyte to the green order and have been studying their magic, but can your green skills hold back the ocean?"

Durrban shook his head, "There's little growing here to gather magic. I haven't got the power nor the skills to harvest and store enough power to even aid our ascent up the cliff."

Tanden said, "All four of us must be up and moving quickly."

"Four?" Durrban asked.

Gadon said to Durrban, "The poor man has water leaking into his brains. Oh, woe to us! We're led by a man who can't count to three."

Tanden said, "The lady's servant, I-Sheera is with us."

Durrban moaned, rolling his eyes to the heavens, "Oh my aching ears! What have I done to offend the six gods in such a manner? Let the green magic take me to the next life now."

Gadon's jaw clenched at the news, "If there be any power in the six moons, they have a sense of humor. I swear she's the last woman in the world I want to be with. Leave her here, Tanden. She's more trouble than she's worth."

Tanden commanded, "Up now. Look for a way up. Do it quickly. I'll fetch the woman." He turned his back on the men and began making his way back to where he had left I-Sheera.

About halfway back, Tanden realized he had miscalculated the rate of the incoming tide. The sea now covered most of the lower rocks. Even though the waves of the bay were small, the tides were causing them to rise, spraying mist and foam across the rocks, making the already hazardous terrain more difficult to traverse. The six moons seemed to conspire against sailors and fishermen alike as their movement across the heavens often made the tides almost unpredictable.

Tanden stood facing a large, irregular boulder. He distinctly remembered going seaward around it. The cliffs and the rising sea now blocked Tanden's path in every direction. Looking about him, he noticed handholds were plentiful on the boulders, so he climbed up.

CHAPTER FIVE

Perched high on a rough rock, he looked back and saw Durrban and Gadon on a boulder. They waved at him and pointed upward. The available light made it difficult to see the path they were trying to point out. A shallow ledge from where he was standing angled back and upward to a point midway between them. Tanden couldn't see a way to make progress beyond that point. Unfortunately, he also couldn't see another alternate route from where he stood.

He turned back to continue to where he had left I-Sheera. Looking down, he saw her standing below him patiently waiting to be noticed. She had gone back to her flimsy skirt and loose flowing top. She tied the top closed with a strip of cloth torn from around the waist. The cloth held it firmly in place. She carried her bundled robe tied on her back, leaving her hands free.

"Well?" he asked.

She pointed at the water already lapping at her toes. "I was running out of dry places to stand. I didn't know what else to do, so I came looking for you." I-Sheera seemed to want to say something else, but she refrained.

"And?"

"Sir?"

"And what?"

With a deep breath, she said, "And I was afraid that you had left me to drown. Please, Captain Tanden, help me up?"

I-Sheera thrust her hands up to Tanden with an imploring gesture. Squatting down, he grabbed her by the wrists and pulled her up beside him.

He said, "We must climb, or we drown."

I-Sheera nodded in acceptance, turning to face the rock wall before them. She gingerly reached forward and grabbed a small outcropping of rock with her right hand. She gave the rock a quick tug and swung forward to jam the left toe of her dainty slippers into a small crevice. Scanning the area above her head, she put her left hand on the rim of a ledge. With a fluid motion, she put her right foot on the same small rock outcropping as her right hand and shifted her right hand to the ledge above. Without pausing, she pulled herself upward until both feet had small toeholds on the same rock. Pushing upward with her legs, I-Sheera kept her body close to the rock wall and her palms flat against the face of the cliff. Her fingers danced across the rock, looking for a handhold anywhere above the ledge she was on.

Her agility and strength surprised Tanden. He expected to see her flimsy skirt hamper her movements or become twisted and end up bundled around her waist. He noticed the servant girl had transformed the skirt into pants by ripping long slits up the front and back. Smaller strips of cloth tied the front and back edges together forming billowy leggings. Her ingenuity pleased him, though the result somewhat disappointed him as it afforded him less to look at than he would have liked. He continued watching as I-Sheera's hands found a much larger handhold above the ledge. She slithered upward until she was standing on the ledge above Tanden. She glanced down at him.

He smiled and gestured upward along the ledge toward the two crewmen who were even now beginning the ascent up the face of the cliff.

"Ah!" I-Sheera cried in obvious delight at seeing the other two men."

"Gadon and Durrban survived also," Tanden said.

"Good. I like Gadon. He's a funny man."

Tanden was surprised. I-Sheera seemed to take a perverse pleasure in seeking out the heavyset first mate for many spectacular verbal barrages. Without further comment, she began working her way easily along the ledge. Her slippers moved quickly in a sidestepping motion. Tanden looked at his thin-soled shipboard boots. They had hard uppers and thin flexible soles as opposed to the thick-soled boots he normally wore when he was ashore. His boots were too bulky for the task ahead, but he would need them once he reached the top of the cliff.

He thought, *If I reach the top. I've spent the last few years letting others climb the rigging of my ships and while I do occasionally load cargo, I'm not getting any younger. I'm strong enough, but I'm not as limber as I used to be. Would it be better to drown here without the effort or climb almost to the top and then fall backdown to drown? No, the fall on the rocks would probably kill me.*

He shook his head as if shaking away unwelcome visions. *"If anyone ever heard my self-doubts they wouldn't follow me to the dinner table. Look at the girl, you fool. She has more courage than you. Get up and get moving."*

As he berated himself, Tanden sat down and removed his boots. He tore a long strip from the bottom of one pant leg to tie the boots together and placed them around his neck so they hung down his back. He stood, flexed at the knees, leaped upward, and grabbed the ledge I-Sheera stood on with both hands. Using his momentum from the leap, he pulled himself up to get a foot on the ledge. Balancing on one leg and pushing upward, he found himself standing upright in short order.

Being taller than I-Sheera, he found the hand holds above the ledge quite accessible. The ledge was wider than it looked from below. He was able to put the length of his feet on it. He looked over to see the girl traveling quickly along the ledge, scooting her feet along without raising them off the ledge except to step gingerly over rough spots or an occasional gap. She only slowed to search for new handholds.

Below him, he saw the tide was rising fast. The water was almost halfway up the boulder he had just quit. "No going back now," he said to himself, "as if there ever was."

Tanden shivered, certain it was due to the chill settling over him, because he was wet and in the shadows of the cliff. He hoped it did not indicate the coming of night air. He had lost track of the time. They needed to reach the top of the cliff before nightfall to survive. They were all too tired, cold, and hungry to have the strength left for such a task. Tanden was sure Durrban could list more reasons than being tired, cold, and hungry. After all, he was close enough to listen to Gadon's constant complaints.

Despite it all, Tanden would make every effort to succeed until he died. He could not face his adopted father if he lived and failed. The guilt of failure was too great a burden to carry even into the next life.

Tanden attempted to twist around far enough to look out over the bay. From this vantage point, he hoped he might be able to see Tuller, Seenger, or Alton. There was a possibility they might still be alive. If they were late in reaching the coast at this point, the incoming tide would probably push them against the rocks and pull them under before they could gain a handhold on the cliffs. He also hoped to see the White Wind. Her tall sails might not have gone over the horizon due to the high incoming tide in the wide bay. He could not twist far enough. His broad upper torso prevented him from turning without unbalancing his stand on the narrow ledge.

"*Gods,*" he asked in supplication, "*protect my men.*" Almost as an afterthought, he added, "*and me.*" It was foolish to pray to six lifeless rocky moons, but where else could a man without magic send his supplications? He had been a pagan long before he heard of science and old habits die hard.

Following I-Sheera along the ledge, he imitated her movements. In no time at all, he was warmed by the exertion. The mixture of sweat and the seawater from his damp trousers formed a cloud of steam around him.

"*At least,*" he thought, "*it'll take the chill out of my body.*"

Tanden looked down at the surf crashing onto the rocks below. The incoming tide raged against the half-submerged boulders.

His arms were tired.

His feet hurt.

His back ached.

He was almost too physically tired to continue climbing the sea cliff, but inside he was boiling mad. His ship had been stolen, her cargo taken, and his passengers killed or kidnapped. He, his loyal crewmen, and a passenger's maid were tossed into the sea to drown or swim to the distant shore to face an uncertain death by savages or wild animals.

Tanden climbed, forcing his tired body forward.

The skinny servant girl outdistanced him. They were still moving along the thin ledge, an outcropping wide enough to stand on, but so narrow it forced them to move along in a sidestepping shuffle. She reached a peak in the ledge that reversed direction slanting downward. She moved like a veteran sailor climbing aloft in familiar rigging. Tanden followed as fast as he could, though he felt like he was lumbering along like a ship's lad going aloft for the first time.

Reaching the midway point on the upsloping portion of the ledge, Tanden looked up to see I-Sheera looking back at him. She had reached a wide place on the upper ledge. "Keep going," he commanded the girl. "Find and follow the path Gadon and

Durrban took. If you rest now, you might not get moving again. You have the strength and speed, girl. Gadon will help you to the top when you catch up to him." Without hesitation, she turned and continued climbing.

Tanden noticed I-Sheera was moving slower, possibly from fatigue, but her pace was still faster than he could manage. His boots were rubbing a raw spot on his back as they swung freely with each move. Quitting now would mean falling into the raging sea and certain death. Tanden wasn't ready to die yet, so he climbed.

Tanden reached the point where the ledge reversed direction, forcing I-Sheera to traverse back as she moved to the slightly wider place on the upper ledge. He did not see any readily available handholds to climb vertically. He would have to follow the girl's downward slanting path. If reaching the top of the sea cliff was the goal, moving back down did not make sense, but there was no other path.

Moving downward should have been much easier physically, but strangely, down was just as difficult. Tanden wasn't able to see each foothold or handhold. He found each purchase in the rocks by touch alone.

Finally, he reached the wide spot on the ledge. The small shelf was large enough for two men to stand closely side-by-side. He stretched and twisted, not daring to sit, afraid his muscles would cramp up before he drew his first breath.

He looked out over the empty sea to see the shadow of the cliffs racing eastward as the sun was setting. He, and what remained of his crew, had only a short while before they lost all light. This climb was difficult enough in the daylight. It would be impossible in the dark.

Tanden remained standing on the ragged shelf for several seconds easing the knots out of his weary muscles. The shelf was not a cave exactly, just a place where a chunk of the cliff had broken off and fallen into the sea. I-Sheera had passed it by. Tanden could do no less than to keep moving after her. Climbing up a short distance, he followed along another ledge, little more than a crack in the rock face. With his greater strength and longer stride, he should have caught up to her, but her smaller size enabled her to move easier and faster. Tanden forced himself to stay focused on his task. He constantly strained to watch every step, every handhold, to double-check every rock and piece of ledge. I-Sheera was only half his weight. What held her might send him crashing into the sea below. He was careful not to step with his full weight until he was sure there were no sharp pebbles under his bare feet.

Looking down again, he saw the water now fully covered every rock below.

He continued forward. His downward slant shifted and he began ascending again. By the time the upward slant of the ledge brought him to about a quarter of the way up the cliff, his forward progress put him about two-thirds of the way to where he had last seen Gadon and Durrban. Tanden glanced upward toward I-Sheera, surprised again to see she was still quite a distance ahead of him. Due to the ever-increasing upward slope, she was in an area a bit higher than he was on the ledge.

"Girl," he shouted. "How close are you to Gadon and Durrban?"

Before she could answer, Gadon said, "You're closer than she is."

Tanden looked straight up to see Gadon leaning over a ledge, staring down at him about thirty feet above.

Gadon said, "I wish you'd hurry. I'm not liking this cliff at all, even if we have found a shallow gap to rest on for a bit. You've been lagging behind all day." He looked behind him and said, "Durrban, someday we need to find a captain to follow who isn't so clumsy and slow."

Tanden replied, "Ha. I beat you to the shore with a woman in tow."

"Sure," Gadon said, "now he's going to brag that he's so irresistible to women that they'll follow him anywhere. But Tanden, my valiant captain, it looks to me like you're following the woman, not the other way around."

I-Sheera shouted, changing the subject, "We can't move forward too much farther. This path becomes too steep."

Tanden said, "Hold on a moment, girl. Gadon, are you able to move upward from where you're resting on your fat butt?"

"Fat, he says!" Gadon said to no one in particular. "That's gratitude. I risk my life to sail the world with him. I could be home with a big bowl of my mother's goat stew and one of Uncle Rollen's beers. But where does he lead me? I'm here on a cold, hard rock. I'm only resting because I'm waiting on you. You going to take all day?"

Tanden said nothing and Gadon continued to complain. He could tell by the way Gadon's voice faded, grew stronger, and faded again that his friend was searching the rock face above them.

Durrban was out of sight. He said, "Here, Gadon, then there, and there and then there."

Gadon's answered, "Yes. I see it, then, across to that crack, from there we should be able to climb up that chimney looking thing. Yes. That's best. Tanden, are you still there or have you fallen off?"

Tanden said, "I was just napping."

Gadon responded, "I knew it, Durrban. Here we are doing all of the hard work and Tanden is relaxing again. Tanden, if you can reach this location we can point the way to the top."

Tanden shouted, "I-Sheera, can you see a way to reach Gadon's perch?"

"Yes, sir. We'll have to leave this ledge. If we climb straight up from here, we can go above where they are now and then angle back toward them. That is, if it pleases you, Captain."

At this last phrase, Tanden looked up to see both Gadon and Durrban staring down at him, eyes wide as if to ask, "What have you done to that girl?"

Tanden tried to ignore their looks. "Don't wait for us. This light may fade fast. We may not reach the top if we don't get there before last light." Tanden cut off Gadon's complaint, "Do it, Gadon. Get up and get going. Stopping is failing. You know that as well as I do. Move, now!"

"Yes, sir," Gadon said with a mock salaam.

Tanden instantly regretted snapping back at Gadon. He had been talking as much to himself as to the men. He wasn't able to bring himself to call out to them and explain. His weaknesses were his own to bear. Gadon would forgive and forget far quicker than Tanden would forgive himself.

Taking his own commands to hand, Tanden moved again along the ledge to where the girl had stood. It became steeper as he edged sideways. His bare toes began to cramp as he tried to clamp them to the ledge to hold his footing. When he reached a spot directly below I-Sheera, he started his vertical ascent. He could see the path the others had taken, following it with his eyes to the bottom of a long crack shooting vertically to the cliff's top. Durrban was right. They had not been able to see it from below, but it looked like a chimney.

Gadon and Durrban had already reached the bottom of the chimney and were beginning a slow ascent. The chimney looked easier to climb than what they had accomplished to this point, but they were tiring and slowing. They needed to reach the top before their bodies gave in to the strain of the day. Tanden believed his men would make the top with daylight to spare if they kept up their pace. I-Sheera, with her greater speed, would reach the top shortly after them. Tanden's pace was too slow, he would not make it to the top before dark.

He could backtrack and try to spend the night at the wide spot on the ledge or reach the shallow place where Gadon and Durrban had sat. However, even if the night was warm, he was fifty-five or sixty feet above the sea. The dampness would set into his fatigued muscles and he would be too stiff to move in the morning. Instead of backtracking, he continued upward.

After a few steps, he realized this area of the cliff was not as steep an angle as it appeared. It slanted back away from the sea. His balance wasn't as precarious as before. He found the few degrees off vertical quite refreshing. He was no longer forced to constantly struggle for balance. Climbing with increased speed and vigor, he raced to beat the setting sun.

The path laid out by Durrban was easy to follow once you knew where you were going. Tanden did not have any trouble moving from handhold to handhold. He continued to be careful not to slip, but he realized he no longer needed to test every handhold as carefully as before. Each of these rocks and crevices had held Gadon, Durrban, and I-Sheera, so they should hold him, or so he told himself until a handhold gave way as he grasped it. Fortunately, Tanden had not yet put his weight it. His emotions cried out to slow down, but logic told him he must continue on even faster, or he would die alone in the dark.

The bottom of the chimney came none too quickly to suit Tanden. There was no place to rest at the bottom, but he could see the uneven handholds going up the crack. He looked up, fully expecting the men to be at the top. All he could see was I-Sheera silhouetted against the dark rock—she was not moving.

Tanden shouted up to the woman, "Girl? Why have you stopped?"

"Gadon has stopped above me."

Gadon called out, "And Durrban above me."

Tanden shouted, "Durrban. Move it. We don't have time to dally. Can't you see we're losing the sun?"

Durrban's voice floated down to him, sounding frightened and overly tired, "I can't go higher, Captain. There's a ten-foot gap above me with no handholds."

Gadon added, "It's true, Tanden. I can see beyond him. The crack is as smooth as a skinned salt eel. Oh, what a life I've led. This isn't where I want to die. We have to turn back. Maybe we can pass the night in that little cave. I know it would be uncomfortable—"

Tanden interrupted. "No. There isn't time to get back before we lose our light. Prepare yourselves to let me climb past you."

He began to climb. The chimney was thin enough that the best speed he could make was climbing with one hand and one foot on each side. He climbed crab-like, moving from side to side, with his back to the sea.

He was still twenty feet below I-Sheera when a shower of small rocks pelted him. Caught in mid-shuffle, he allowed himself to twist sideways, letting his back fall against one side of the chimney. Bracing with both feet against the opposite side, he brought his hands up to protect his head from any larger stones that might be breaking loose.

A scream jerked his head upward just in time to see I-Sheera lose her grip. Tanden grunted and pushed hard with all his aching muscles against the rocks. His legs and back screamed in concert with I-Sheera as she dropped toward him. He braced with all his might, knowing that if she hit him squarely, they would both die. Tanden thought frantically, almost as a chanting prayer. "*She's going to miss me, to miss me, to miss me.*" Without thinking, he reached an arm up and out to her. He slapped at an ankle and missed. He grasped at a shoulder and missed. He felt a touch of her arm and clamped on tight. He closed his hand around a wrist as she shot past him. Rock slid under his bare feet and back. His body cried in agony, but he held.

Tanden swung the girl in and under him. Still holding her by the wrist, he called to her, "Find a new handhold. Hurry."

With the numbing jolt to his shoulder and arm, he could not hold her for more than a few seconds. She swung outward again, her legs and free arm beating the air around her. She tried desperately to grab at anything, even grasping at him, stark terror in her eyes.

He shouted frantically, "Don't grab me. Reach for the crack. Do it now." He swung her under him and out of his sight again. He felt weight easing off his arm. It was now or never, he could not hold her any longer. If she died, then she died. He saw no use in both of them falling into the sea. He released his hold on her wrist.

CHAPTER SIX

Tanden could not hear anything over his own ragged, harsh breathing. Grabbing the girl had dragged him ten feet down the rock ladder. He had escaped jutting rocks that would have sliced him open, but knew he would suffer badly for his efforts later from seriously strained muscles and torn flesh on his feet and back.

He heard an uneven sob below him.

Bracing his legs and torn back against opposite sides of the crack, he worked his way up a few feet until he could change his position to straddling the open air to release the strain from his back. His legs were beginning to quiver with the constant strain of the day.

Again, Tanden found himself with his arms and legs spread across the crack in the cliff with his back to the sea. Confident he could hold his current position for a moment, Tanden looked down the chimney at I-Sheera. She was only a few feet below him and in the fading light he saw tears streaking down the dirt on her cheeks.

Tanden said gently, "Listen to me. I know you're scared. I also know you're a courageous girl. Take heart. You're strong enough to save your life. We need you to save our lives as well. I need you. I need you to save my life now. Do you hear me? I need your help."

Stifling another sob, I-Sheera looked up into his face. "Yes, Master. I'm here."

Gadon shouted from above, "Tanden! What's going on?"

He answered, "Not now, Gadon. Hold your peace."

Gadon shouted back, "I would but I can't reach it and I don't see that this is the right time for that anyway. Maybe later, but thanks for the suggestion."

Noticing I-Sheera's robe looped around her neck, Tanden asked softly. "Girl, I need you to unbundle your robe and pass it up to me."

Without answering, she worked her way up the chimney, squeezing between Tanden and the chimney wall. She stopped when Tanden's feet were level with her midsection. Careful not to brush against him, she carefully braced both feet and one hand. Removing the loop from her neck, she put the robe into Tanden's open hand, then leaned back against the rock wall. She began to shiver.

Tanden put the loop around his own neck before reaching down to stroke her cheek. "Thank you. Be brave, girl, you've saved us all. I can get us the rest of the way to the top. Are you with me?"

Tanden could see she was making an obvious effort to control her trembling, but the tears continued down her streaked face. She nodded and gave him a half-hearted smile.

Amazed at her change, he easily recalled that dozens of times he wanted to toss her overboard into the sea. Her brutal, biting, bitter tongue had lashed at everyone, time and time again. Her demands for her mistress to be pampered and waited on day and night grated on the nerves of every crew member. I-Sheera still looked like the same crude, vicious harpy, but she certainly wasn't the same woman.

Living on the edge of life and death changed many a person, he mused. During the war against the Hummdhars, he'd seen his share of battlefield transformations. Good men changed to bad, bad men to worse, and the worst of men turning to the six gods or, if their magic prevailed, to one of the orders. With a mental shrug, Tanden brought his focus back to the present.

"Follow me as best you can. Do you hear?"

"As you command."

Tanden climbed, not stopping until he was a few feet short of where Gadon sat perched on a ledge barely wide enough for his heavyset body. I-Sheera was just below him.

He thought, *She looks about ready to quit. We're all tired. I've got to drive them forward.*" He said. "Gadon, are you all right?"

Gadon said, "All right? The man asks if I'm all right. My stomach has left me to look for a master that'll feed him. I'm cold. I'm sitting on the hardest rock on the face of the earth and you have the gall to ask if I'm all right? What kind of brother are you, to torture such a sweet tempered man as me?"

Tanden replied, "Good, I'm glad you're well." He ignored Gadon's snorted response, in better times Gadon would have broken wind in his face and laughed the night away.

"Durrban, how about you?"

"Captain?"

"Yes, Durrban?"

Durrban asked, "Captain, can you get us out of here?"

"Yes, I can. Trust me."

Durrban said, "Then I'm as well as can be expected. Tell me what to do."

Tanden took a breath before he said, "Listen to me. This chimney isn't wide, but we have to change positions." Over Gadon's protests, he continued, "We need to be cautious passing each other. I need to get above Durrban. I'm tall enough to brace myself across the chimney and I can work my way above the slick spot without handholds. I have I-Sheera's robe with me and I believe the cloth is strong enough I can tie one end above us then lower it down so each of you, in turn, can use it as a rope to climb up the rest of the way."

Gadon asked, "Tie it to what? I can't see anything to even grab on to."

Tandon answered, "Something. I'll find something."

Without a hint of complaint in his voice, Gadon said, "Hand me the cloth, let me do it."

Tanden said, "Thank you, Gadon, but I don't think you have the height to make the climb, nor does Durrban. But, I have to ask you to give I-Sheera your seat. She needs to rest before climbing further."

"What!" Gadon shouted. "Let the harpy fall. Haven't I been brutalized enough these past weeks? Tanden, this's too much, even for me."

Tanden could tell Gadon was truly angry and rightfully so.

"Do it for me, Gadon. Please do it because I'm asking, not commanding, but asking." Without waiting for a response, he spoke further, "Durrban, move to a place where I can pass you to go higher. Gadon, once I'm above you, trade places with I-Sheera. I want you below her. Try not to touch one another, we need to keep from increasing the chance of someone slipping. We need to be quick, but also very careful."

Climbing past Gadon was much easier than Tanden expected. Many small holes and rough chunks pockmarked the general area, so hand and footholds plentiful. As he slid past his friend, he heard the man cursing under his breath and chuckling as he broke wind in Tanden's face.

When they were face-to-face Gadon whispered, "Tanden are you all right? I see blood on your back."

Tanden said, "I'm as well as I can be expected. I'll live. It's over and done with. We need to keep moving forward, my friend. We'll overcome each obstacle in its turn." Tanden spoke with more conviction than he felt.

He had made a commitment to his father back in Harkelle. He must keep moving forward. To stop was to fail. He might not be able to get started again if he stopped.

Durrban braced himself as deep into the back of the chimney as possible. He was small and did his best to become smaller, giving Tanden as much room to pass him as possible. Tanden smiled at his crewman as he went past.

There were no handholds above the men. Tanden twisted sideways letting his tortured back fall against one side of the chimney while bracing both feet against the opposite side. He dreaded putting his savaged back in contact with the rock again. Strangely, the cool wall felt comforting as it drew out the sting.

Working with his back and shoulders on one side of the chimney, pressing his hands hard against the slick wall, he walked his feet up the other side until he reached a choke point that was wide enough for Tanden to squeeze through. Just above the narrow spot, the chimeny opened wider providing easy access to the top. He could clearly see the open sky above. Handholds were plentiful, but there was no place to tie the cloth.

Taking the robe from around his neck, he unwound it. He braced his legs across the crack, just above the choke point where if formed a seat-like ledge on each side of the chimney. He tied the cloth around his right thigh, leaving enough cloth to reach the others.

Lowering the cloth down, he called, "Durrban, can you reach the robe?"

Durrban said, "Yes, Captain."

"Good. Use the robe as much as you need to, but try to brace your feet against the sides as much as possible. Try not to put all of your weight on the robe."

Tanden felt a quick tug on the robe, then a hard pull yanked his thigh against the rock. He was braced well enough to keep his position. Reaching under his thigh, he grabbed the cloth with both hands. Locking his elbows, he clenched his teeth and leaned back.

In short order, Tanden heard Durrban's voice from just below, "Captain?"

Releasing his grip on the robe with his left hand, Tanden leaned forward, thrusting his open hand down between his legs toward the climbing sailor. Durrban grabbed the offered hand and scrambled up through the opening. The pressure release on Tanden's thigh was a welcome relief, however short-lived. Still below was the girl, light as she was, but just below her was heavy Gadon.

Durrban stood over Tanden with his legs spread across the opening. He removed his shirt. Folding it carefully, he bent down and slipped the padding under Tanden's thigh.

He said, "Thank you, Captain. The green order blesses you."

"You're welcome, Durrban. Now finish the climb. It's getting dark fast and you'll need to help the others as they reach the top."

Durrban nodded and climbed.

Tanden re-grasped the robe, braced and called down, "Girl, it's your turn."

He closed his eyes, enduring gentle tugs and soft jerks on the robe. Quickly, the servant girl climbed up through the gap. The light was fading rapidly. Tanden saw the determination on her face as she climbed past.

Tanden heard Durrban from above say, "Oh crap!"

Tanden looked upward. Durrban had reached the top and climbed on through. He couldn't see anything that caused the concern in the sailor's voice. It wasn't in the man's nature to utter even a mild curse. They had to hurry, he didn't want to be climbing after dark and called up, "Durrban, I-Sheera is coming up, you need to help her. Gadon?"

"Yes, yes, yes, I'm ready. Hurry the woman. I can barely see the rope, not that it matters, I doubt it will hold a man of my healthy proportions."

"It'd better hold. It's all we have. Climb fast, my friend, but be careful or you'll drag us both down. I'm not ready to die quite yet."

A taut strain on the robe caught Tanden by surprise. His butt slipped toward the hole. He rapidly flexed his legs and pressed his back toward the rock wall behind him. After re-seating himself, he grabbed the robe tightly with both hands. He resisted the urge to call Gadon and ask him to move faster.

He clenched is eyes tightly shut and clamped his teeth in a hard grimace. His jaw muscles working in sympathy with his body as he strained to support Gadon's climb.

Gadon's hands grabbed at Tanden's legs as the man pulled himself up to the shelf just above the choke point. Tanden sighed and released his hold on the robe, letting the tension ease from his body. He flexed his hands to get the blood moving back into them. Opening his eyes, he was surprised to see that is was almost full dark. He could barely make out Gadon's face anxiously studying his own.

Tanden's mouth was dry and his voice raspy from the strain. "Shit! Oh, sorry. Gadon, up!" He was too exhausted to say more.

Slowly, he slid Durrban's shirt from under his leg and tucked it into his trousers for safekeeping. After he pulled the robe up to his lap, he unknotted the loop around his leg and tied the robe into a long loop, dropping it over his neck. With his boots and the robe bundled around his neck and shoulders, he was beginning to feel like a pack animal.

He turned and looked out to sea for the first time in what seemed like hours. Night had fallen in earnest with the stars shining brightly in the small section of the sky he could see. A bright moon wouldn't rise for a few hours. If he remembered his charts, only the Potato, the Rose, and Deering would be in the sky this evening. Even if the Potato and the Rose were up, they were the two smallest moons and would not provide enough light to continue climbing. Deering was the largest of the six moons and would flood the area with its light, but it wouldn't rise until after midnight.

Tanden vigorously rubbed his legs. He was beginning to wonder if he was trying to get the blood moving or stalling for time. He looked up at the small patch of visible stars. Gadon had achieved the cliff top. The chimney was completely dark now as he worked his way upright from his sitting position. He needed to move. not moving was not a viable option.

He said to himself, "Well, the hard part was past. I can do this last part with my eyes closed."

Smiling in the darkness, he climbed with his back to the sea. His only measure of distance was glancing at the small patch of dark sky above him that grew ever larger with each upward thrust. He could hear the others talking and moving about on the cliff top, but not enough to make out their words clearly. He wondered if he had trouble hearing them because he was too tired to focus on sounds or if he was still far enough below them that the rocks muffled the sound.

A cool wisp of sea breeze ruffling his hair was the first sign he had gained the top of the cliff. He threw his arms out before him over the still warm rock. Locking his hands into a small crack, he swung his legs up, levering his body up and over the cliff edge to lie flat out on the rock. He wanted to lie still, sucking in the cool night air and let the heat from the stones warm his aching, scraped, bruised body. He was frustrated even in that simple pleasure.

Before he could draw a second breath and long before he thought to look for the other three, Tanden heard Gadon shouting, "Get up, Tanden. Hurry! Come on, hurry!" Durrban and I-Sheera were also yelling at him to move quickly.

Tanden got to his feet. The night air cleared his head enough to wonder why all three were perched on a large flat rock a few feet away. He took a step toward them, placing his foot down on a pile of rocks that seemed to move on its own, slipping over and under his feet. Tired or not, Tanden jumped forward to land sprawling on the rock with his friends. Rolling to his feet, he looked around.

Gadon, Durrban, and I-Sheera stood with their backs to each other, along the edges of the large flat stone. Even in the dark, with only the starlight to see by, all around them were dark shadows slithering in the darker shadows. As far as he was able to see in the dim light, rock upon rock, stone upon stone into the darkness beyond, thin shadows moved on the ground. The three were busy kicking at any shadow attempting to crawl up on the rocks with them.

CHAPTER SEVEN

"Snakes," Durrban said unnecessarily.
Tanden asked, "You were the first to reach to top with some small measure of light left. What did you see?"
"Green help me! I saw snakes everywhere. I hate snakes." He accompanied each phrase with a kick at a shadowy snake, some imagined and some he sent flying off into the darkness. "There isn't any green near enough for me to gather enough magic to keep this rock clear. A magician or a priest might, but I don't have the talent or the training. These spawn of the dark demons don't offer any green movement for me to harvest magic from."
Their conversation was sprinkled with shuffling feet punctuated by kicks at shadows.
Tanden gingerly sat on the stone in the middle. He hurriedly untangled his boots and pulled them onto his bruised aching feet. The feeling of snakes squishing between his toes was one he was sure he would not soon forget. He handed Durrban his shirt, then unwound I-Sheera's robe and handed it back to her, with a quick suggestion that she wrap it around her shoulders to keep her legs free.
Gadon said, "This is a great finish to a really foul day. These things make my skin crawl. Tanden, remind me to put a knife through my heart if I ever sail with you again."
I-Sheera spoke, "Snakes aren't so bad if you cook them right." Over the sounds of Gadon's disgust, she continued in a familiar, whiny voice, "I'd think that you of all people would appreciate such a wonderful delicacy. Catch us a juicy one, Gadon, you great man of valor. Let's see how they taste raw."
The whiny, nasal tone she used was the voice that made the hairs stand up on Tanden's neck. Everyone on the ship was accustomed to this voice. It was one Tanden wished he would never hear again.
Before Gadon could spit back a retort, Tanden said, "Enough, girl. You too, Gadon. Problems don't go away by

themselves, so we have to deal with it, or we can't retake the White Wind. What else did anyone see? Gadon?"

Gadon replied, "Me? What did I do? By my blind sister's eyes, I'm truly mistreated. Tanden, sir, great captain, this area looks like the ground during a drought, full of big, flat, squarish stones with deep gaps between them. Most of the rocks looked to be the size of this one or bigger, maybe half again as long as you're tall. It looked that way for as far as I could see and that wasn't very far."

"Girl?" Tanden asked, "What did you see?"

Gadon interrupted, "Why ask the harpy anything? Command her to be quiet or throw her to the snakes, I don't care, but I truly don't want to hear her voice again. Ever."

I-Sheera answered, "I don't know what Gadon is so upset about, when I came up there were snakes all over the place. And they're still here. Great big man afraid of skinny little legless crawlies!"

Tanden could see snakes squirming in knots in the faint starlight. Long, fat ones and quick, darting, skinny ones slithering in an angry orgy, each fighting for a space on top of the rapidly cooling rocks. There were so many snakes it looked like the rocks were moving.

Occasionally, he could hear the shrill cry of some small dragonette caught up in the turmoil.

Tanden shook his head to clear his thoughts as he kicked at a shadow crawling up on the rock. He sent the snake flying back into the spaces around the rocks.

"Girl, speak with a civil tongue, or I'll do as Gadon suggests. I have other things to do than to umpire your verbal battles."

"Yes, sir. It's as Gadon says, except before the light faded, I could see the edge of a forest that way." Pointing inland, she continued in a calm and definitely non-whinny voice. "I don't know how far away the trees are from here. A ten minute walk maybe, they were a ways away."

Tanden said, "We're stuck here at least until Deering rises. By then these rocks should be cool enough that the snakes will return to their warmer holes. They only come up to catch the warmth of these stones. We should be able to keep this small area clear until then, but we also need to rest. Gadon, you and the girl find a clear space together in the middle of this stone and rest as best you can. Durrban, can you help me keep these vile creatures off our rock for a while?"

Durrban answered, "Captain, I couldn't rest knowing there's a snake within a league of my bed. I'll keep this rock clear, I swear to the green order I will."

Gadon said, "I couldn't sleep either, Tanden."

"Gadon, you were on helm watch last night, plus it's been a hard day. Yes I know, it's been a hard day for a hard man, but you have to rest. We'll need your strength later."

"Sir?" I-Sheera asked.

"Yes, girl?"

"I can help Durrban. I did nothing all morning but float in the sea. You did all the swimming for both of us. You should rest now, too."

Tanden thought to argue, but realized she was correct. "Durrban, wake me immediately if you or the girl tire. Otherwise, wake us at moonrise. Do you understand?" Unlike Durrban, Tanden was sure he could sleep even if the snakes were crawling all over him. He sank down onto the middle of the stone next to Gadon, who was already asleep.

Tanden did not like snakes, but sleep was sleep. Over the years, he had learned to take sleep where and when he could. He had slept in worse conditions. During the war with the Hummdhars, he had been the only survivor of an ambush in a blind canyon. All around him were piles of dead men and sauruses. Carrion eaters and insects of all kinds came in swarms. When the Hummdhars gathered to capture and torture any Holdenite left alive, Tanden gutted a dead saurus, crawling inside to hide. Despite the heat, the stench, and the danger, he slept. This night, he dreamed of snakes crawling from a dead saurus to pluck at his paralyzed flesh.

Tanden woke at Durrban's touch to relieve him from snake duty. The first sight of Deering's moonlight was visible. The older sailor and the girl sank down to rest on the middle of the stone. Tanden felt refreshed from the short rest and his memory of the nightmare faded fast in the reality of their situation. A light boot against Gadon's backside woke him.

Tanden noticed the night was getting colder and there were fewer snakes. The moon had risen to a full bright globe, lighting the night and deepening the shadows. The Rose was still in the sky, but her dim light only emphasized Deering's glory. Many of the stones were almost completely clear of snakes. The shrill cry of a sea wyvern caused Tanden to search the night sky. This snake pit would be a hunting paradise for a small, hungry winged dragon.

Movement at the corner of his eye brought Tanden's eyes back to the cliff's edge. He saw larger, darker, moving silhouettes against the sea's backdrop. Uncertain of what he was seeing, he looked behind him. The angle and line of sight would not silhouette his group. Their shadows would blend into the rocks behind them. There in the distance was a forest edge, dark, and foreboding.

CHAPTER EIGHT

Tanden asked, "Gadon?" He pointed questioningly in the direction of the shadows.
"It's a man." Gadon yelled, "No! Two...I think." He began waving his arms.
"Gadon, they must have heard you shout. Call them."
Almost immediately, the smaller man began shouting.
Durrban and I-Sheera got to their feet and looked toward the cliff's edge. They began babbling, questioning whether it was Alton or Tuller—because of the size, they were sure one of the shapes was Seenger—and whether they had been there all night, and if there were snakes where they were. Tanden set their focus back to watching their own stone for any late coming slitherers.
"Gadon, can you hear them?" Tanden asked.
Gadon replied, "I might if you'd all be quiet. You three are loud enough to wake the snakes up again. We don't want that, do we? No? Then let me listen, I'm getting older and my hearing is getting worse, you know." He shouted into the distance, "Hello the rock."
A voice floated back, faint but clear, "Gadon? Is that you? I knew you wouldn't drown while you still owed your favorite brother enough money to buy a fat pig."
Gadon danced a quick little jig at hearing his brother's voice, hooting with glee. His belly jiggled with unrestrained relief and joy.
Tanden let out a sigh of relief, "Gadon, we're heading toward the forest. We'll angle back toward them on a southerly heading. We must leave now. Have Tuller and Seenger angle toward us to meet us as soon as possible."
Gadon shouted the instructions to his brother and the ogre.
Turning to Durrban and I-Sheera, Tanden said, "We could wait until it becomes colder and all the snakes are driven below ground, but I believe we must move now. We aren't going to starve for days yet, but we'll weaken quickly if we don't locate drinking water. It's well past time to leave this snake den behind us."

57

Without waiting for an agreement, he continued, "We'll move from rock to rock, staying on top. Avoid any darker shadows and stay together as much as possible. Don't lag behind or we may unknowingly lose you in the dark. We won't head straight to the forest's edge because we'll be able to move farther and faster here than in the forest. By moving south, we'll angle away from the sea towards the trees. We need to move as fast as possible so we can reach the forest's edge before moonset."

Tanden noted that Tuller and Seenger were already moving along the rocks, jumping from one to the other. He wondered how Tuller felt about snakes. As for Seenger, in the time Tanden had known him, the ogre had never shown any fear. Tanden was exceedingly glad they were still alive and would shortly be back with him. They were excellent crewmen and Tanden would need them when the time came to retake the White Wind. First, they must get off these rocks before the warmth of the morning sun brought the snakes back. It saddened him that Alton was still lost, maybe alive and maybe dead.

Tanden commanded, "Follow along. Gadon, you bring up the rear."

As Tanden leaped to the next stone to the south he heard Gadon start complaining, "Last again. Why me? I have such short legs I should go first so everyone goes at my pace."

Tanden let him jabber on knowing from experience that he would soon tire. He had heard Gadon talk and complain for hours on end in many a tavern, but here, without water and exerting himself jumping from rock to rock, he would stop talking before too long.

Normally, moving along the top of the stones would not be difficult. Well rested, in daylight, having eaten and having had plenty to drink, it might be a pleasant diversion. Running two steps in the dark, then leaping over a crack in the earth to land hard on another stone caused all of Tanden's overused muscles to cry out in protest. Fortunately, the night air was cool on his scraped up back and his boots protected his bruised feet.

Stone after stone, they jumped. Tanden heard the others following behind him, their feet slapping and pounding across the rocks. Their movement became repetitious: two running steps and jump. Two more running steps and jump. Two more running steps and Tanden froze. Coming to a sliding halt, he found himself barely inches away from a deep crevice too wide to jump across.

He shouted. "Stop. Stop. Stop. Stand where you are." His warning came too late. I-Sheera crashed into his back. He started careening into the open air and the jumbled rocks below. If Durrban had not been close on the girl's heels, he would have fallen. The acolyte grabbed his trousers, yanking him upright.

Tanden looked back at Gadon on the rock behind them. He was unable to read the man's expression in the pale moonlight. Gadon shrugged and flung an arm out questioningly in a westerly direction.

Tanden said, "Gadon, maybe you're right. Maybe I should have let you lead the way."

Gadon grunted, sucking in air, and waited with his hands on his knees.

Looking back across the crevice, Tanden saw Tuller and Seenger just twenty feet away. "I'm truly happy you didn't drown. You're well?"

Tuller spoke for both. "We are well, but tired, like you, I'm sure."

"Good. I plan to head in a southerly direction as much as the terrain permits, but this crevice blocks the course." To the left, the gash in the rocks angled toward the cliffs by the sea. To the right, the gash ran another forty or fifty feet before branching off in two directions. In the faint moonlight, Tanden could see both branches curving toward the west, one farther west than the other. It possibly circled back toward the north, though its full course wasn't clear in the dim moonlight.

Tanden continued, "It may take too long to go around. We need to find a way across. I have no desire to climb down into a snake pit at night."

Tuller's voice had a puzzled tone, "Snakes? We haven't seen any snakes. Seenger and I made the shore near the cut in the cliffs from a dry streambed. Apparently, rain in the forest causes flooding and this channels the run off out to the sea. We climbed up the cut last evening. Access to the top of the cliffs was easy, but we didn't see any snakes. We moved to the edge of the cliff, watching for you while we rested from the swim. There's no fresh water in the channel. We were just about to go looking for water when we heard Fat Boy shout to us."

Gadon snorted, "Fat Boy? You young pig turd, where's your courage? You wait until there's a great canyon between us before you insult me? I'll get you for that, you slimy pile of maggot droppings."

Tuller laughed, "And what are you going to do, Old One? Tell Mother on me? Besides you lazy tub of goose fat, this "great canyon" is only a five or ten feet deep." The moon had risen high enough to cast a glow into the streambed.

Before Gadon could respond, Tanden said, "Then, even in this poor light, we should be able to cross here. Trying to go around this great canyon might take us too far off course. South is the way we must go, if possible. Changing course too far to the right or the left will take us farther away from our goal. We need to focus our attention on finding the White Wind." He went on to explain to Tuller and Seenger his plan to retake the ship.

"South, then," Seenger grunted.

Tuller agreed, "Without a doubt, south. You can cross here as easily as any place. This crevice is a jumble of rocks turned every which way, but I suggest you stay out of shadows if you can."

"Why?" Durrban asked. "You said you hadn't seen any snakes."

Tuller said, "True, but Seenger and I spent the time between sundown and moonrise fighting off running hordes of dragonettes. Any snake near us would be dragonette supper by now."

Dragonettes along this area of the Black Sea were tiny, no larger than a man's hand. The two-legged, wingless lizards seemed to be all neck and tail, except for the wickedly sharp teeth that filled their over-sized mouths. These were not the grazing dragons like the tame saurus, but meat eaters. As small as they were, running in packs they could easily swarm over an unwary man, bringing him down, and eating him while he yet breathed.

Gadon wondered, out loud, "Dragonettes?! Hunh! We're swarmed with snakes and you're overrun with dragonettes."

Tanden said, "It may be this crevice presents a natural barrier or a buffer zone. Any creature foolish enough to wander over to the other side becomes a meal. Nonetheless, if we're going to reach our goal we must overcome this obstacle and get moving."

Without further discussion or comment, Tanden chose a largish, flat-looking rock bathed in moonlight below him in the streambed. He jumped, landing squarely in the middle. The shadows tricked his eyes into thinking the rock was much farther below than it really was, resulting in his landing sooner and harder than expected. His breath whoofed out of his chest, his knees jarred, and his teeth rattled, but no harm was done. The rock teetered briefly, but remained in place and he kept his footing.

"Watch my path across, then follow me," he said to the three behind him.

Choosing another rock, Tanden leaped. The rock skittered sideways as he landed. The last rush of water had undercut its base and it scooted out from under his feet sending him rolling into the shadows. He rolled across smoothed rocks adding to the bruises of his already aching body. He briefly rolled into a ball of scaled legs, tails, and necks that broke apart and scattered for deeper shadows. They chittered madly and rushed back to see how much they could grab of this large meal that had dropped into their hunting ground.

Before he became a meal, Tanden jumped up and grabbed a nearby stick. He stomped his feet and swung the stick at every beady-eyed dragonette he could see. Stomping and turning about he spotted another rock and leapt up. He held his stick in front of him, ready to swing at any dragonette attempting to follow him into the moonlight. He looked down at his hands and realized in horror that he was holding a dried out piece of half-eaten dead snake. With a shiver, Tanden tossed it back into the shadows.

From his angle in the streambed, Tanden could see bundles of snakes and piles of dragonettes in a free-for-all melee of eat or be eaten. Farther downstream, he spied a dragonette start to scurry across a large flat moonlit rock. In the blink of an eye, a sea wyvern snatched the dragonette airborne, its huge leathery wings snapping in the cold night air.

Gadon called to Tanden, "Good guiding. I think I'll try a different stone if you don't mind. Mother always wondered why I let you lead me around and now I begin to wonder too. Dragonettes, snakes, and running around in the middle of the night. I'm probably going to break my neck before I get home. And it'll be your fault, Tanden. Tuller, if I break my neck here tonight, tell Mother it was Tanden's fault. And by the way, Tanden, I'm getting hungry. Water I can do without, but a man of my physical prowess and boundless energy needs food to survive."

While Gadon spoke, I-Sheera jumped down to the first rock Tanden had used. Watching her from below, it looked to Tanden like she floated. The moonlight fluttered through the flimsy, flowing garments and her wild hair flowed about her face. Her clothing did little to cover her body. The robe wrapped around her shoulders billowed around her like a mist. It was a pleasant vision, one Tanden knew he would be able to trade for a drink in any tavern in his old age. That is, if he ever entered another tavern or if he even lived to old age.

Durrban followed her quickly to the next rock and then the next. Tanden turned back to Gadon, who shrugged and leaped down to follow. All three teetered on unstable, uneven rocks, but continued to move across and up to the top of the crevice.

Tanden moved in a different direction, quickly, but carefully. It would be easy to break any number of bones, just as Gadon had complained of breaking his neck. He had not broken anything yet, so he put it out of his mind.

Moving forward had always been Tanden's best method for not dwelling on the past. Once an incident was over and done with, he chose to forget it and move forward. Now he set his mind on retaking the ship. All else was of no long-term consequence unless he allowed it to cause him to deviate from his goal. This single-minded focus had stood him in good stead his whole life. Tanden didn't have a one track mind as many men did. He was able to see the other tracks to follow, but once a valid course of action was set, he could and would follow it to its logical conclusion. For Tanden this often meant success and continued life. He had set his current goal on retaking the White Wind. He would succeed or die trying.

Tanden reached the upward bank of the dry streambed. An overhanging ledge jutted out at eye level, so he placed both hands on the rock to pull his body to the top. The rock broke free from its weakened hold tipping back toward Tanden, sliding and rolling down the bank to crash within inches of his feet. The rock dislodged a shower of screeching dragonettes that rained down around Tanden. Many scurried off into the darkness, more swarmed over Tanden. They grabbed and bit at him from all directions. He felt them climbing all over him. Twisting and turning, flailing his arms, Tanden tried to free himself. There were more dragonettes than he could reach. Knocking dragonettes off in sweeping motions only cleared a spot for other dragonettes to clutch at him. He realized he only had seconds before he would be swept under and eaten alive.

Suddenly, he was clear. Seenger vaulted into the streambed behind him and swept dragonettes away from Tanden's back and shoulders. Tanden reached up both hands to grab at the bank's edge. He might survive if he could get out of the gully. Hands grabbed at his wrists and arms, jerking him up through the air. Almost before his feet hit the ground, hands plucked dragonettes from his body. Dragonettes flew away into the darkness in all directions.

Tanden spun around to the crevice to see Seenger leaping up beside him.

Gadon said, "I know I said I was hungry, Tanden. But if you're going fishing for dragonettes, I think you could find an easier way to bait them. Besides, I don't think I'd like dragonette on a stick. That is if I had a stick and a fire to cook them."

Seenger said, "Dragonettes are fine, even raw, but these are too skinny even for a good stew." He turned and began moving southward without another word. They all watched him move away. Tanden was unsure, was Seenger joking or not? The ogre had never shown a sense of humor, or if he had, no one understood his jokes.

I-Sheera asked, "Are you all right? I was so frightened. I'm sorry, I tried to help, but I couldn't."

Gadon sneered at the woman, "Yes, she cowered away from you, leaving the rest of us to do all the work. Typical, pampered woman."

"I'm fine," Tanden said. Feeling about his arms and chest, he could tell there were more cuts, scrapes, and bites than before. He couldn't do anything about it now. "It's done. Seenger is right, let's move. We have a long way to go."

They reached the edge of the forest in good time while Deering was still high in the night sky. They had about an hour before it set. The Rose and the Potato were long gone. The stones had given way to a sparse, grassy clearing, with a scattering of shrubs and scrub bushes. Larger animals scurried off through the grass and bushes before them. They stood before large tangled knots of trees.

Tuller asked, "What's next, Tanden?"

Gadon said, "I don't like dragonettes and snakes, but I really hate going into a strange forest at night. Who knows what evil demons lurk there. No sir, I'd rather be at home in a warm comfortable bed than here. Maybe we should wait here until sunrise. Or maybe Durrban could use his green magic?"

Durrban shook his head. "I'm not that good with protection spells yet. Not for a group this size. Maybe I can harvest and collect enough magic if you give me a few hours."

"No," Tanden said, "We need to find water and food. Sitting still and waiting won't help us. We need to keep moving forward while Deering gives us any moonlight. There'll be time enough to stop when it gets totally dark."

"It looks dark enough to me, right now," Gadon commented.

The others stood by quietly waiting for directions. They were all battered and bruised, dehyrdated and hungry, exhausted and sleepy. He wanted to rest too. Now was not the time or place to rest. A forest's edge is prime hunting ground for many predators of all types and sizes. They should be reasonably safe if they stuck together. Few carnivores would attack a group of men. Even now, he saw the shining, yellowish eyes of a large creature of some type, watching them from the deep forest foliage.

CHAPTER NINE

Tanden watched as a second pair of yellow eyes joined the first, then another. They would soon face a pack of dire wolves. This would not be a hungry, desperate, unorganized rabble of animals. They would be facing a well-fed, strong, and organized pack. The plentiful supply of dragonettes and other small animals living in the area provided daily nourishment for many predatory carnivores. Such an abundant food supply would feed a larger than average-sized dire wolf pack. While most packs would avoid groups of humans, a hungry dire pack was capable of chasing them down and tearing them apart one by one. They should be safe as long as they stayed together.

Tanden saw no reason to call anyone's attention to the watching eyes. They would find out soon enough. He noticed Seenger watching him. Seenger's eyes flicked to the dire wolves and back again. Tanden shook his head slightly, receiving a shrug of acceptance from the ogre.

"We're a strong group. I know we can all keep moving for a little bit longer. While Deering is up, we can look for water and find a safe place to rest. Just stay together."

Tuller asked, "Wouldn't it be more reasonable if we spread out a bit? In this forest, we might pass by freshwater and not know it. If not singly, then maybe we should walk in pairs."

Tanden responded, "That's a valid point, Tuller, and a valuable suggestion. However, I think that in the dark we might also lose one another and walk in circles. Daylight may give us the opportunity to spread out more effectively. Does anyone have a flint with them to start a fire?"

No one answered, but from the looks they gave each other Tanden knew the answer was no.

Durrban said, "I'll start a fire if someone has a string or a length of cloth. It'll take longer than a flint, but it'll work."

Gadon snorted. "Surely you can condense enough magic to start a little fire. There are enough trees and grass here to set the whole coast on fire."

Durrban shook his head. "I will not make fire. Encouraging red magic by sparking a fire will muddle my green magic. Fire itself is okay, but I can't bring it to pass by magic. The old way will work just fine."

I-Sheera tore a length of cloth from around the bottom of her robe, then she sat, watching in fascination as Durrban moved about fashioning a small bow to build a fire by friction.

Tanden said, "Gather some short limbs, knot grasses and vines for torches. Deering's moonlight might be sparce inside the forest. And men," Tanden tried to make this sound like an afterthought and not as important as it really was to their survival, "we might as well see if we can find clubs or staffs. You never know when you might need a weapon."

Gadon looked quizzically at Tanden as if to ask, "*What are you talking about*?" He said, "Oh my aching back. I'm tired and this man wants me to carry firewood through a forest."

As he spoke, Gadon kneeled down and grabbed a young sapling at its base. Without even a grunt, he straightened his legs, ripping the small tree from the ground. He knocked the dirt from the rootball and stripped the small limbs away from the trunk. A quick snap took off the top section. He then tossed the ready-made four-foot long club to Tanden and stepped over to a second tree to make a weapon for himself.

The other men followed suit, each finding a weapon of some sort. Tuller found a long staff for himself and a club for Durrban. Seenger armed himself like Tuller, although his staff was double the length and twice as thick.

Durrban's fire didn't leap to life or roar into tall flames. It flickered slowly and grew larger as he fed it small leaves and grasses first, twigs next, and then the larger sticks handed to him by the girl. Tanden saw the watching yellow eyes blink out. The dire pack silently withdrew at the first flicker of flame.

Seenger's eyes never left the forest's edge. Tanden looked everywhere but at the fire, knowing he would lose any ability to see at night if he let the fire get into his head.

Tanden had studied the four elements of the world in his schooling at Allexia. Of the four—earth, water, air, and fire—he was sure fire was the most dangerous to man. Water was dangerous, but Tanden made his living on the water and had learned to make it his friend. Not like a blue wizard would make friends with the wind driven waves, collecting, condensing and storing the magic hidden there, but friendly enough that the oceans didn't try to kill him more often than a couple of times each sailing season.

He had seen fire act all too often like it had a mind of its own. He knew it could get in a man's mind to drive him crazy. It was that power that drove the red order to seek their magic from the flames.

Tanden said, "Gadon, Tuller, Durrban, each of you carry a torch and a second unlit spare." He watched the men light their makeshift lamps. Durrban and Tuller then kicked dirt over the fire. As soon as the fire was out the eyes of the dire wolves reappeared as if out of thin air.

"Girl," said Tanden. "You needn't carry a weapon, but stay close to me."

She stepped close to Tanden and opened a tiny bundle she had made from part of her robe. Inside she had a dozen sharp shards of rocks and a two-foot strip of heavy cloth, "I'm not very good with a sling, but, I can use one if you need me to. I'll stay close to you."

"For now, everyone stay close together and watch one another," Tanden said. He motioned Seenger to lead them into the forest. He was startled when Seenger tilted his head back and bellowed like a raging, angry bull, his fangs and tusks glittering in Deering's pale light. The watchful eyes in the forest darted away noiselessly.

Seenger moved forward without a backward glance. The others followed closely behind him, each with a questioning look to the others about Seenger. Tanden brought up the rear, pushing I-Sheera ahead of him.

The foliage was thick and hard to walk through at first, but the deeper they moved, the thinner the underbrush became until they found themselves in the forest proper. The thick canopy blocked out all of Deering's glow. The three torches now provided all their light. Seenger forged ahead just at the edge of the light.

The group moved away from the bay in a southerly direction. Tanden had no clear knowledge of area's interior. Farther to the west, he and Gadon had fought the Hummdhars near the banks of the DuVall River, chasing their enemies back into the mountains.

He believed they were crossing the isthmus of a large peninsula. Only to himself would he admit he was not positive of their location. He knew little of the terrain beyond the Black Sea's coastal shores. He would have to trust the ogre to locate water and a place to rest. He hoped Seenger would find it sooner than later.

Durrban's torch flickered and died out. Rather than re-light it or light his spare, the man kept walking. The little sailor was almost asleep on his feet. Time was short, but they could not afford to stop yet. Without water and an easily defensible position, they would not last the night against the forest's predators, whether dire wolf pack, fellosaur, or giant sloth.

Without missing a step, Gadon reached across relieving Durrban of his torch, tossing it to the ground. Taking Durrban's spare torch, he lit it from his own light. He turned and thrust it into the hands of the servant girl. I-Sheera took the light without comment and followed Gadon as he turned again to follow Seenger.

Suddenly, Seenger was gone. He dropped out of sight before anyone saw him leave. The group rushed forward at the sound of crashing bush and breaking tree limbs. They heard the ogre cursing strange gods and thrashing about, but they could not see him.

Tuller was the first to reach the edge of a small downward slope. Stopping, he waved his torch high above his head to light the area below him. Trees were sparce along the slope and the brush grew thicker. The others joined him quickly. There were no sounds coming from down the hill. Gadon and I-Sheera's torches lit up the area, still, they could not see Seenger anywhere.

Tuller, cursing his own foolishness, dashed down the hill, following the path of crushed bushes and broken limbs. His feet churned to keep up with his headlong rush. There was nothing for the others to do but chase after Tuller and Seenger.

A small stream ran through a clearing at the bottom of the slope. In the middle of the stream, Seenger stood surrounded by the dire wolf pack. The ogre was barely keeping the wolves at bay by swinging his great staff in wide circles.

The wolves danced in the waning moonlight, splashing and spraying water everywhere. They snarled at the ogre, seeking an opportunity to leap forward and take him off his feet. The water was only mid-calf deep on the tall ogre. It was enough to slow the wolves, yet not deep enough to give Seenger an edge against so many dire wolves. He was already running out of time as the pack circled closer.

Tuller plunged barehanded through the pack without hesitation, having lost his staff running down the hill. He kicked the side of one wolf and jammed his torch into another, burning hair and scorching flesh. The wolf he kicked whirled around snapping at him. Tuller thrust the flaming torch into the wolf's open mouth. The flame went out, but the wolf knocked two others down in an effort to escape the searing heat inside its mouth. Others in the pack raced after the wounded wolf, obviously not hungry enough to continue attacking the pair.

The remaining wolves ringed Seenger and Tuller as they stood back-to-back. Seenger waved his staff in the faces of the animals while Tuller brandished the remains of a torch in one hand and held a hastily grabbed rock in the other. It was a toss up whether or not the two could withstand a coordinated attack. The animals turned to flee at the sight of more humans rushing into the clearing.

One dire wolf wasn't fast enough as it sped past Seenger. His staff slashed down across the neck of the wolf, snapping it cleanly with one stroke. The dire pack whirled about, ready to protect one of their own. Seenger bellowed a challenge, his fangs and tusks flashing a grim warning. He set himself to charge the wolves, but a rock whizzed past his head striking a large male wolf on the nose. The wounded animal yelped, snarled, and bit at the air. A second rock flew into the pack sending another wolf yowling into the dark, limping on three legs. The large male spun about and raced after the injured wolf. The pack followed closely on his heels.

Seenger looked back at I-Sheera, who had loaded her sling with a third rock and was swinging it about her head looking into the shadows for another target. He nodded to her and put a hand on Tuller's shoulder as if to say thanks.

Gadon stared at the woman, "Very good aim. You'll have to show me how you do that."

I-Sheera looked at her feet sheepishly. "I've only seen them used by shepherd boys. I've never used one before. I don't know how to aim."

Gadon smiled as he said, "Well, damn my own eyes! You'll have to show me anyway. And you," he turned to Tuller, "what kind of idiot stunt was that? Racing off on your own! You're sure one pitiful excuse for a younger brother. It's not as if I don't have enough to do without having to come along and save your sorry butt. Hey, Seenger! Thanks for finding water." Gadon spread his arms wide and slapped both Tuller and Seenger on the shoulders, stretching tall to reach Seenger's shoulder.

I-Sheera jammed her torch into the bank and flung herself down by Durrban at the water's edge. Tanden knelt upstream, near them to drink. Both the green acolyte and the woman sucked greedily at the water, gulping great quantities to quench a day old thirst. Tanden slowly lifted the water to his lips one handful at a time, always keeping his eyes on the others and the forest's edge.

Gadon sank his torch upright in the bank on the other side of the creek. He stretched out beside his brother to bury his face neck-deep in the cool running water of the stream.

Tanden watched Seenger as the ogre knelt by the carcass of the wolf he had killed. Seenger lifted the water to his lips as he watched and listened to the night about them. Tanden nodded to himself. There was more to this Huzzuzz ogre than he knew.

Tanden said, "Seenger. What are you planning for that wolf?"

"Supper, I think, or breakfast, maybe both," Seenger replied with a shrug.

Gadon lifted his head. "I wonder if dire wolf tastes anything like dog."

Seenger said, "Somewhat, but tougher to chew."

Tanden said, "Enough water for now. Too much at one time and you'll make yourselves sick."

When the others looked up at him, he continued. "This close to the coast, if we move downstream, we could end up back at the bay. We'll move upstream for a while and locate a defensible place to rest before continuing south."

"Uphill?" Gadon complained. "I swear, my whole life has been spent walking uphill. Are there no downhill paths in this wide world?"

Seenger stood and shook himself like a wet dog. Reaching down, grabbing the carcass of the wolf, he draped it across his shoulders. Using his staff as a walking stick, he stepped to the far shore. Ever watchful, he stood quietly, waiting for the others to gather themselves together.

Tanden helped Durrban to his feet and up the bank. The little man was almost at the end of his strength, yet, at no time did Durrban complain.

Gadon and Tuller rebuilt the three remaining torches with new grass and vines. Once all three were re-lit, Gadon handed the woman a torch, a bit more gently than before.

Staying together as much as the terrain permitted, the small group moved upstream. Tired as they were the water revived their spirits, with the exception of Durrban. Gadon and Tuller took up a two-decade-old argument as to who had stolen whose wooden toy sword. Unasked, Gadon moved to put an arm around Durrban as the older man stumbled sleepily. I-Sheera quietly followed on Tanden's heels.

Tanden moved to position himself next to Seenger and asked, "What happened back there? How did you get separated?"

"I got foolish," Seenger said. "I was tired and didn't watch where I stepped. One minute I was fine, the next I found myself tumbling down a hill, crashing through the brush. When I came to a stop, I heard the wolves about me. I ran to the middle of the clearing, jumped into the stream. The rest you know."

"It's my fault, Seenger. We're all too tired. I should've tried to find a place to rest sooner. But it's done and I can't change the past. I'll try not to let it happen again. We only have a few days to gain the coast or we'll miss the White Wind, but I shouldn't throw our lives away needlessly. We'll retake our ship if we have to follow her to Tunston itself."

The group hadn't gone far when they came to a rocky outcropping where the stream cut through a hillside. A small, three-sided canyon would provide protection for them through the remainder of the night.

Durrban sank to the ground, snoring before the dust settled around him. Tanden could not put the man on night watch, nor the woman. He looked at her. Her eyes told him she was almost asleep on her feet. He motioned her to lie down where Durrban lay. Quietly, she slid to the ground next to the sleeping man.

"Seenger, stand watch for a moment while the rest of us gather some wood for a fire. We can build one across the coanyon opening. It may provide us some small protection and warmth.

The ogre tossed the wolf's carcass onto a ledge along the rock wall. The other men gathered a small pile of firewood. Soon, a fire burned in the middle of the canyon opening warming the air about them and heating the rock walls.

They had allowed the torches to burn down to nothing, so Tanden had them rebuilt before any of the men rested. His plan was to remain in the comfort of the fire until daylight, but he wanted to be prepared if they had to move quickly.

Tanden said, "Tuller and I will take the first watch. We'll wake you halfway to daylight. You, in turn, can wake all of us at daylight. Allow Durrban and the woman to sleep all night or they'll slow us down tomorrow."

Seenger moved silently to the rock wall. He sat upright with his back to the wall, bracing his staff across his knees. Nodding his head to his chest, he fell asleep.

Gadon lay with his back to the fire, complaining of having to sleep on the cold hard ground, rather than a warm, comfortable bed with a warm, comfortable woman to warm and comfort him. He fell asleep in the middle of his next complaint.

CHAPTER TEN

Tanden woke with the sun in his face. Rolling onto his back, he sat up with a start. The morning was at least an hour old and no one had come to wake him. He looked around their camp. Durrban was asleep, Seenger and Tuller were squatting by the stream doing something with an animal skin, while Gadon and the servant girl stood by the fire.

The girl was turning great chunks of meat cooking over the fire with a sharp stick. She was also attempting to show Gadon how her sling worked. In increasingly louder hushed tones the two were arguing over something. I-Sheera was smiling happily and that seemed to frustrate Gadon. The angrier he became, the wider she smiled as their voices grew louder and louder.

Tanden didn't know whether their voices woke him or the smell of the meat roasting over the fire. He stretched and felt better for having slept longer than expected. All thoughts of chastising his crew for not waking him vanished. They had to take care of their bodies or they wouldn't reach the south edge of the isthmus to find the White Wind. Even if they reached their destination, they would not be able to retake his ship if they were too tired to fight.

The camp voices quieted causing him to pause his reflections and to look up at his friend and the girl. Both were looking at him. The girl looked sheepish.

Gadon turned to the girl and said, "See there. That's what your stubbornness has done! Now he's awake. I don't know what we should do with you." He turned his back on her and moved to sit next to Tanden.

"Well, Tanden?" Gadon asked. "I was beginning to wonder if you were going to sleep all day." At Tanden's questioning look he continued, "I know you wanted to leave at daybreak, but I decided we all needed a bit more rest and some food before traveling. I didn't see the need to wake you up just to tell you to sleep longer. You and I are strong men, but we're dragging this woman with us, and that baby brother of mine is so worthless we'll have to lead him around by the hand any minute now."

"You're right," replied Tanden. "I was pushing us too hard. We'll make better overall time if we're rested. Next time wake me up to tell me when you contradict my instructions. It may not make sense to you, but I'm responsible and I must know. We should be moving soon."

Gadon nodded and shouted to the woman by the fire. "Girl, bring us food. Durrban, time to eat. Wake up, we have work to do. Tuller, drag your lazy butt back here and eat as soon as you're finished."

I-Sheera handed each of them a piece of smoking dire wolf meat. Tanden nodded to her and asked Gadon, "What were you and I-Sheera arguing about? It looked like she was getting the best of you."

"Never!" Gadon snapped. "This girl doesn't know her place. I wanted the sling and pouch of rocks. She can make herself another, but she refused to give them to me."

The woman smiled while dropping the pouch and sling at the man's feet. She moved off to take food to Durrban who was sitting up rubbing the sleep from his eyes.

Gadon continued, "Besides, slaves don't own property, and they sure shouldn't argue back with a free man."

Durrban, hearing the conversation, said, "I thought she was a servant to Lady Yasthera il-Aldigg, not a slave."

Tanden called the woman back to sit and eat with them, "Well, girl. Which is it? Are you slave or servant?"

I-Sheera looked puzzled and asked, "Does it matter which?"

Durrban said, "Well, in the case of the sling, a servant can own property, but a slave is property."

She shook her head and said, "I've only had what was given to me and I kept it until someone else took it away."

Tanden looked puzzled, "You don't know whether you're slave or servant?"

She said, "I know, but I truly don't see that it matters."

Gadon snorted, "Just like a woman to not know the difference."

"No," she said. "I know the difference. There just isn't a speck of weight between the two stations."

Tanden said, "Of course it matters whether you are bond or free."

Joining them, Tuller and Seenger sat cross-legged on the ground. Each held a double-fist sized piece of wolf roast on a stick. Tuller looked thoughtful, spit out a large piece of gristle, and said to I-Sheera, "I can understand what you say. To Tanden, Durrban, and even myself, slave or free would make a big difference. But to a woman? Yes. I can understand that."

I-Sheera asked, "If I was a servant then I'd be free to leave my master?"

Tanden and the others nodded.

She continued, "Fine, but where could I go? Without a protector, where in this whole world can a woman go alone and survive? How would I eat? What would I wear? Where would I sleep? A man can make his own way in the world, but a woman can't." Her questions held no hostility or anger. She made her point as if knowing she could not change the world. "Can a woman in your country carry money? Can she go alone to the bazaar? Even in my enlightened homeland a rich woman must have male servants do for her what she, by law, can't do. A poor woman starves or is taken by another master. I truly know the difference between free and bond, better than all of you, but it doesn't matter. I do as I'm told and I live."

Tanden said, "It matters to me."

I-Sheera shrugged and said, "My mother died when I was a tiny child. Although, I have no memory of her, I've heard whispered rumors she was taken away for consorting with demons. My father was a free man. The Red Wizard gave him a position in his army as compensation for losing his wife. He died quickly, far away in some long forgotten war. I grew up in Warwall's household as a free woman, but what difference it made, servant or slave, I don't know."

Tanden asked, "Girl, can you answer me one more puzzle?"

"If I can."

"Why aren't you acting like you did on shipboard? You're pleasant and helpful now. I don't mean to offend you, but on the White Wind, you were less than pleasant and not a bit helpful."

She smiled, "I do as I'm told, remember? My mistress, Lady Yasthera il-Aldigg, commanded and I obeyed. It would've been beneath her to speak to common seamen. I spoke in her stead, and I might add, in her true manner. To survive and succeed in a servant's world, you must be all things to all people.

When I spoke for her, I spoke as she would speak. That's why I was rude. Gadon, what's your excuse?" She poked the heavyset man in his side with the stick that had held her breakfast.

Her sudden change of tactic caught the men by surprise, Gadon more than the others. He sputtered, choking on a piece of meat. Laughing with the others, Tanden slapped him on the back until he started to breathe again.

Tanden said, "If we knew the answer to the age-old question of why Gadon complains, Tuller and I could die as happy men."

Gadon made as if to jump up and thrash someone, but looked like he couldn't decide who to start on. He sat back down, dusting the dirt off his piece of wolf. Continuing with his breakfast, he mumbled under his breath about how unappreciated he was in the world.

After the laughter subsided, Tuller said, "Seenger and I made a couple of water bags." With obvious admiration, he pointed a finger at the ogre, "Seenger was able to skin his wolf in one piece with just a fire-sharpened stick. He sewed up one end and tied a cord around the other end. The skin should hold enough water to last us the rest of the day. I stretched out the wolf's bladder. It's two-thirds the size of Seenger's waterbag, but it increases our supply." He tossed a handful of sharp flat bones into the middle of the group. "These might work better than sharp sticks."

Seenger and Tuller had set sharp bones into their staffs. Seenger's staff resembled a heavy spear. Tuller's new staff was fashioned like a boarding pike or a docking hook. Tanden picked out a dire wolf shoulder bone with the leg still attached. It had pieces of flesh hanging on it and it was discolored by blood. He believed it would substitute very well for a hand ax. He jammed the makeshift tool in the waistband of his trousers while the others chose short blade-like bones.

"Time to move?" Tanden asked. No one took what he said as a question any more than he meant it that way. He stood up, stretched painfully and walked slowly to the stream where he seated himself on a flat rock by the water's edge with his back to the others. He could hear them moving about the campsite chatting good-naturedly with each other as they prepared to leave.

After Tanden pulled his boots off, he sank his feet into the cooling water. His bruised, scraped feet were sore from climbing the cliff. It seemed like days ago, not just yesterday evening. He wiggled his toes in the clear water. He had not broken anything but skin and that would heal. He tore a small strip of cloth from his trouser leg, rinsed the cloth in the water, and dabbed at the cuts, abrasions, and bites covering his upper torso. He winced as he cleaned each wound until it bled cleanly.

I-Sheera and Durrban knelt next to him. Each took a small rag and cleaned the wounds on his back and shoulders. The scrubbing was painful, but Tanden believed it necessary. He did not allow himself to dwell on how he had become injured. That happened yesterday. Today, he needed to press foreward.

Gadon shouted, "Aren't you ready yet, Tanden? Here we are standing around waiting for you to get done primping. You're as pretty as you're ever going to get. Let's get moving."

Tanden sighed. It was somewhat pleasant to have others attending to him. He thought *"Time enough to relax when I get old, if I get old. Without Gadon's prodding I might sit here and do nothing until I become dinner for a pack of wild squirrels and rabbits."*

He pulled his boots onto his bruised feet, maintaining a stern face. He was unable to allow the others to see the pain it was causing him. Suddenly, he remembered I-Sheera wore only light slippers. He looked down at her feet. She had wrapped strips of cloth around them as padding before putting her slippers back on. Her feet must be almost as bruised as his, but he couldn't see any damage. Tanden turned his face rather than let his crew see his shame at having been so selfish in only thinking of his own physical comfort.

He gained control of his thoughts and checked over his crew. They were almost ready to leave their campsite. Seenger had a large wolf skin slung over his shoulders and held his spear in his hand. Tuller had a water bladder tied around his neck, plus his makeshift boat hook. The smell from the bundle I-Sheera carried told Tanden she had collected the pieces of uneaten wolf roast. Gadon had his club and the small bundle holding his newly acquired sling. Durrban picked up Tanden's wooden club as well as his own. Only Tanden was empty-handed. His only weapon was the ax-like bone in his waistband.

The fire still smoldered. Tanden knew that without a red magician to hold fire in check, an unattended flame could soon spread and overtake a walking man. He had seen what an unchecked fire could do when he, Gadon, and others had come upon a band of Hummdhars hiding in a stand of trees. The commander of the Holden forces decided to drive the barbarians out with smoke rather than fight. They burned a pile of green trees and leaves, but the fire refused to cooperate. It escaped their planned stack of wood, spreading and leaping from tree to tree roaring into the Hummdhars, burning men and sauruses to death. To their dismay, they later found that the group also contained Hummdhar women and small children.

Tanden currently had enough concerns without having to worry about running from a forest fire, so he lowered his trousers and emptied his bladder. Gadon and Tuller joined him. Quickly, they extinguished the fire. He shook the last few drops off his penis. Turning as he stuffed himself back into his trousers, he almost burst out laughing at the shocked look on I-Sheera's face. Both embarrassed and shocked she was unable to turn away. When she noticed Tanden looking at her, she turned away red-faced.

Without another word, Tanden took his makeshift club from Durrban and began striding upstream. Rather than backtrack, he decided they would move westward along the stream going uphill until they could locate an easier path to turn southward. He planned to stay banded together for now, if possible. not knowing what lay ahead. There was safety in numbers.

The sun was high and warm when Tanden turned away from the meandering stream to move southward. The small group climbed up the hillside through the dense, thorny underbrush along the stream banks. They picked and ate small berries growing in great abundance along their path as they walked. The juicy blackberries supplemented the remainder of their morning meat.

The brush gave way to more and more clear spaces as they moved back into the forest. The light dimmed noticeably as it filtered through the trees.

Gadon shouted suddenly, "Dragon!"

A bone-chilling roar filled the air and the ground shook.

CHAPTER ELEVEN

Tanden spun around in time to see a monstrous, black-scaled dragon rear up on its hind legs to three times the height of most men. He had once seen a chained dragon at a festival in Harkelle, but there was no comparison between that creature and this. The chained animal was submissive and comical with its huge leathery wings clipped and tied, and teeth and fangs blunted. This dragon was neither submissive nor comical looking.

It shook and bellowed in rage at Tanden's puny band. Its teeth and fangs flashed in its gaping maw. Hot frothy steaming saliva dripped from its mouth. Dropping again to all fours, the ground shook with its bulk. Again, it rose up on its hind legs, roaring in blistering rage. It unfurled its massive wings in fury with a snap of air that blasted the group with a hot gust of wind. Its wings, only partially unfurled because of the density of the trees surrounding them, were twice the length of the dragon's height.

The half-believed stories told by drunken old men in taverns of hunting such beasts had not prepared Tanden for what stood before him. Someone screamed, but Tanden could not tell who it was, nor could he tear his eyes away from the towering beast before him.

For the third time, the dragon rose up with a quick pop of its thick, rigid wings. It lifted its huge body off the ground. Still, it could not completely unfurl its wings to take flight and it slammed back to the ground. Rushing forward, it crashed through a tree before stopping a short twenty feet from Tanden. It rose on its hind legs thundering an angry challenge.

Tanden was struck dumb. He wanted to run, in fact his thoughts were screaming at him to do just that, but his body was locked in place, refusing to move a muscle. The dragon's bellowing froze him in place. All he could think was, *"It went through a tree. Not around it, but through a tree. Oh, the six gods be damned, I'm a dead man!*

He squeezed his eyes shut and waited for the jaws of the beast to rip him apart.

The dragon dropped to all four feet again and rocked back, preparing to charge. Everything else in the forest grew ghostly quiet. The great dragon's rage shocked all to silence. Gadon grabbed Tanden by the arm, yanking him to the side. Screaming at his captain to run, the sailor pushed Tanden hard.

Tanden ran, but he didn't believe he would escape the death behind him. He heard nothing beyond the pounding of his own heart in his ears. He swept up his crew before him as he ran. His sincere desire was that, for once in his life, Gadon could push his short legs to run fast.

A bellow and a crash of brush stopped Tanden short. The sound was farther away than he expected. He whirled around noticing Gadon was not with them. He spotted Gadon standing alone, facing the dragon. The dragon reared over Gadon and he fell to the ground. The dragon dropped to all fours, its body engulfing the man.

Tanden started to run back to aid his friend, but Tuller and Seenger stopped him. Each grabbed an arm, pulling him along, almost dragging him away from the scene. Durrban and I-Sheera ran ahead of them. Tanden tried to wrench free, but they held him tight.

Struggling for breath, Seenger shouted, "We must run or die." Ogres were known to be afraid of little, Seenger even less than most. No sensible creature faced a dragon.

Tanden cried out, "But Gadon's my friend, we must—"

Tuller interrupted, his voice ringing in Tanden's ears. "He's my brother, damn you! This is his choice. We must get away or he sacrifices himself for nothing."

They were right and he knew it. He tried to regain control of his mind. As frightened as they were; they ran southward. Even in rout, they must stay together. He could not bring himself to look behind him; even long after Gadon and the dragon were out of sight.

None of them knew how far they ran. A wide, sloping hill brought them up short. Everyone was breathing raggedly. I-Sheera dropped to the ground, panting and heaving. Durrban leaned against a tree and vomited dryly into the air. Tanden and Seenger watched Tuller drop tiredly to his knees. Seenger turned away as Tanden watched tears streaming down Tuller's face.

Tanden thought of his lost friend, "*His death is my fault. How can I comfort Tuller when I'm to blame. I lost vigilance and let death move in among us.*"

"*No!*" he screamed in his mind. "*I will not blame myself for this. Gadon's death falls on the heads of those mutinous son's of the dark demons who stole our ship. Without their treachery, we wouldn't be here. I call upon the six gods to help me mete out justice for a good man's death and not because of the anger in my heart.*"

Summoning gods that were nothing more than lifeless rocky moons reflecting the light of the sun caused Tanden to calm himself. He put a hand on Tuller's shoulder and gave him a gentle squeeze. He knew nothing needed to be said now. Both men would talk later over a drink to honor their lost one.

Seenger said, "My water skin didn't hold. Its seams rent as we ran."

Tanden said, "Tuller, your water bag is still full. Hand it to me and I'll give water to Durrban and the girl."

Tuller shook his head, "I'll do it. You first."

Tanden shrugged and drank. He handed the bag back to Tuller, who in turn passed it to Seenger. Moving off, Tuller stood over Durrban and I-Sheera where they collapsed on the ground. He retied the water bag after Durrban and I-Sheera drank their fill.

Tanden said, "We move up and over this hill. Where one dragon lives, there must be others. We've lost one good man here. I have no desire to lose any more."

He walked to I-Sheera, took her arm and lifted her to her feet. Climbing the steep hillside caused them to breathe in gasping gulps as they had not taken the time to recover from their long run. Small stones rattled and slipped beneath their feet. He increased his grip on I-Sheera's arm and pulled her up behind him. Without complaining, the woman scrambled to keep up with Tanden's longer legs. By the time they reached the top, he was almost dragging her behind him.

At the top of the hill Tanden stopped to get his bearings. In front of him was a hundred foot escarpment dropping to a river below. Across the river was a wide valley cluttered with clumps of trees and rolling hills before turning into a forest in the distance. On the far side of the valley was a series of high, rugged-looking ridges.

He saw no signs of human habitation. He was not aware of any Holdenite villages in this region, but the Hummdhars and Coodhars may have filtered down from the high mountains in recent years, to resettle near the coasts. Both tribes had warred with each other and Holden for years. The Holdenites drove them back to the mountains time after time.

Tanden thought to himself, *"Can I do this? Do I have time to reach the sea before Heraclius and Gregin pass me by? Is this even right? Maybe I should leave vengeance to the fates. Look what I've done, I've killed my friend in this mad rush to regain a ship, a silly pile of floating wood."* Though he doubted himself, he could not deviate from his course.

A stifled whimper caused him to look down. He still held I-Sheera's arm in a tight grasp, holding her at his feet. In horror, he released his grasp on the woman. Welts were already sprouting on her skin. He turned and strode to the edge of the escarpment. He wanted desperately to apologize, but could not bring himself to speak.

Durrban dropped to the ground next to I-Sheera and spoke gently to her. She nodded quietly to him and responded, but Tanden could not hear their words. He tried to think of what to do or what to say. He had abused these people for his own goals. Now he had lost his best friend and he was sure he was beginning to lose his own mind. Unable to formulate even the right questions in his mind, Tanden found himself at a loss of what to do.

He felt a presence beside him. It was Durrban. The man put an arm around Tanden's shoulders and turned him to face south across the valley. Durrban said, "We should move on, Captain."

Fiercely, Tanden flashed back at the man, "Do you command me now?"

Durrban responded softly, "I saw my mother and father die before my own eyes at the hands of the Surr. I know that's no comfort to you. But listen, Captain; I lost the ability to think for a long time. The ache in my heart clouded the thoughts of my mind. We all follow your lead. We need you now. We're all lost here without you. There will be time enough later to grieve for our lost comrade. He was a good man who'd want us to go on."

82

Tanden calmed himself. "Yes, Durrban. We should go on. Delay won't bring him back." He tried to say Gadon's name, but couldn't bring himself to do it. "I hurt the girl. She was fond of Gadon and I treated her so rough, she probably hates me for it."

"No one here hates you, Captain. She'll be fine. You'll see."

Tanden could not bring himself to speak to the girl. Calling Seenger over to join them, he told Durrban to stay with Tuller and I-Sheera. He pointed to the left and instructed the ogre to look for a way down to the river below. He moved off to the right, carefully searching for a path off the ridge.

CHAPTER TWELVE

Staring down at the river from the hilltop, it appeared deep and slow, though looks can be deceiving at a distance. They could not turn and go back, there was nothing behind them. To move on they must cross the river somewhere. Around a small grove of trees, Tanden saw a rugged path angling down to the river, apparently a deer or goat path.

He called to the others to join him. Tanden sighed and stepped onto the steep path. He was able to keep his footing as long as he moved slowly. The others called to one another as they began to follow him down the path. A tumble here would send him crashing down the rocky escarpment into the unknown waters below. His sailor's balance held him in good stead all the way down to the river's edge.

The muddy water gave no clue to the river's depth. It flowed faster than it appeared to when they first saw it. Their best course of action was to swim across the river. Tanden would have preferred to build a raft, but they had neither the tools nor the time.

Swimming in the sea was difficult enough, but the uncertain currents of a river could quickly pull them under or sweep them away. The speed of the water would be tough for a strong swimmer and they had two non-swimmers among them.

Tanden formulated a plan. It wasn't a good plan, but it was all he had.

Seenger, the last one down, sent a small shower of loose rocks splashing into the water. Tanden laid out his plan.

He set Seenger to re-sealing his wolfskin waterbag. Sealed tight, it might hold air and give the ogre support in the water. Tuller drained the wolf's bladder of all remaining water. Blowing hard into the opening, he stretched the bag and tied the end closed. With a long strip of cloth from his tunic he tied the ballooned bladder to I-Sheera's chest where she could grasp it with both arms.

They tore the rest of Tuller's tunic into two long strips to use as straps. One end of each was tied around I-Sheera's torso.

The other end of each was tied to Tanden's and Durrban's ankles. This was an awkward task due to the short length of the straps. They accomplished the goal by having the woman sit at their feet as they were tied together.

Tanden planned for them to tow I-Sheera across the river first. The straps would keep their hands free for swimming. The air in the inflated wolf bladder would help her float and keep her head out of the water. Once across, Durrban and I-Sheera would wait on the other side while he swam back for Seenger.

Tanden commanded Tuller and Seenger to make the wolfskin as air tight as possible and wait for his return. The current looked so strong Tanden believed it would take two strong swimmers to help a weak one across the river. Though Durrban was not a strong swimmer, I-Sheera was much smaller and lighter than Seenger. His plan should enable them to successfully tow the woman across to safety. Then Tanden would return to help Tuller tow Seenger across.

Tanden said, "Durrban, we must synchronize our strokes as much as possible. We can't allow the river's current to pull us away from each other."

Durrban nodded his understanding and the two men stepped to the water's edge with I-Sheera scooting along between them. Tanden noticed the man and woman exchange glances of assurance. He was still unable to look the woman in the face, so he focused on the river. He felt her warm hand on his leg, just above his boot top. Her hand squeezed lightly sending a shot of heat through Tanden's body. He stepped forward into the water with Durrban at his side and I-Sheera slightly behind them. Tanden chose a spot far up river as a point of reference. As they swam up the river, the current would carry them downstream. He was sure this would allow them to reach the other bank almost directly opposite Tuller and Seenger.

The water was warmer than the Black Sea had been yesterday. The early afternoon sun warmed them as they stepped into deeper water. The river tugged and pulled at them, testing their strength. Tanden believed they could beat the river as long as they stayed united. If they separated, one or all of them would fail to reach the opposite shore.

Tanden lost sight of his reference point almost immediately. The current was far stronger than he guessed. It tugged and yanked in every direction except toward the other side. At first, Tanden thought they were making no forward progress. The current swirling around them kept pushing them back toward the bank they just left. Glancing behind, he saw they were already farther downstream than he had planned.

I-Sheera passively floated behind him, her eyes wide with fear, her clamped jaw clenched in determination. Tanden instantly regretted not speaking to her about his roughness. He would not be able to forgive himself if she drowned in this river before he healed any rift he had caused between them.

Drowning was becoming a possibility for each of them. He longed for Durrban to cut himself loose so he could swim free, the man might survive without I-Sheera's weight dragging behind him. Tanden choked back his command realizing he could not save the woman from drowning single handedly.

He shouted to Durrban, "Try to swim straight across to the far bank. We're wasting our strength fighting upstream against this current. We'll make shore where the river takes us."

Changing directions was easy enough as an individual, but swimming in tandem was more difficult than Tanden had anticipated. He was a much stronger swimmer than Durrban and neither man could use the full power of their legs without kicking the woman.

A large ripple washed over the swimmers, rolling them over and over one another. Durrban and Tanden grasped at each other. It rolled them over again. Both men sputtered and spit out muddy river water to gulp in air. I-Sheera was gasping for air behind them. Her tether pulled hard at his leg, the current pulling her in the opposite direction, but the strap held. Tanden grabbed the collar of Durrban's tunic, swimming for shore with his free hand. He kicked as best he could with his free leg, driving at the water, trying not to kick his companions.

Tanden released his hold on Durrban once the man regained his swimming stroke. Together they pulled at the water; hand over hand, crossing the river. Tanden tried to synchronize his swimming to match the other man stoke for stroke. Suddenly, they shot forward as the current let them go. Tanden's feet struck bottom. Looking up, he was disappointed to discover that the far bank was still a long way away. Below them, underwater, was an unseen sandbar, blocking the stronger current. Tanden pushed against the shifting sand with his free leg, calling for Durrban to do the same. They were unable to stand on the sandbar, because I-Sheera's tethers were too short—doing so would pull her head under water.

He said, "Keep moving forward. This sand may shift enough to take hold of our feet."

I-Sheera smiled weakly. She pushed forward through the churning water clutching the float to her chest. Not having to pull her weight was a relief to both men. Tanden looked back at the bank for Tuller and Seenger, but they were out of sight. The three had been carried much farther down the river than he expected.

Again, the current grabbed at Durrban and Tanden, yanking them downstream. The sudden jerk pulled I-Sheera off balance into the swiftly moving current. She was sucked under water before she could draw a saving breath. The water ran quickly in the channel between the sandbar and the bank. Barely able to stay afloat and continue breathing, neither man could reach the woman.

Partially pushing against the bottom and partly swimming, the two men quickly reached a calm backwater near the far bank. Reaching back to grab I-Sheera, Tanden was startled to see her head bob up out of the water right before his eyes. Coughing and gasping for air, she continued to clasp the inflated bladder to her chest. Tanden noticed it was beginning to lose air and she would soon sink, but he knew they could now reach the bank safely without it.

Grabbing Durrban's ankle, he untied the strap and pushed the man toward the nearby bank. Putting his own head underwater, he untied the strap from his ankle. A few stokes moved him close enough to the shore he could stand on the bottom. He pulled the woman through the shallow water a few feet closer until she was able to put her feet down on the river bottom. Still clutching the float to her chest, she followed Durrban up to dry land.

Tanden stood for a few seconds, staring into the reeds flourishing along the side of the river. The unseeing eyes of a dead man stared back at him. A chill crept into his bones and raised the hair on the back of his neck. He splashed over to the bloated, pudgy body, pulling it free from the entangling weeds. An arrow protruded from the man's neck. Pushing the body into the river current, he watched it swirl and bob away. Then waded his way to the bank and climbed up beside Durrban and I-Sheera.

He said, "You both saw?"

They nodded quietly.

"Good." He continued, "I know we're tired, but we must stay alert. This river is the least of our concerns now. Tuller and I will be able to bring Seenger across to this side. I must leave you two here. From the man's clothing, he was either a Hummdhar or Coodhar. Any arrow that long definitely came from a long Hummdhar bow. The poor bastard ripped open his own throat trying to pull the arrow out before dying."

He shook his head "I don't know what's happening in this valley, but we shouldn't take any chances. Let's get you out of sight and then you stay that way as much as you can."

A small grove of trees edged up to the river. Tanden led the two into its shadows. He detected no evidence that anyone had been in or near the spot. Indicating the two should stay hidden in the grove and watch the river, he reminded them to keep an eye on the area around them as well. He reluctantly agreed to let Durrban make a small fire to dry their clothes, warning him to keep it as smokeless as possible.

After leaving the two in the grove, Tanden moved cautiously upriver from one cluster of trees to the next. He glanced at the other bank, watching for his crew, but his true concentration was on the valley around him. He had no desire to be taken by either tribe. He, like most Holdenites, considered both tribes barbarians.

He began to think that in his caution he had passed where Seenger and Tuller waited for him. Then, he spied them. Both lay asleep in the shadows, propped up against rocks. If he had not specifically been looking for them, he would not have seen them against the escarpment rocks. He thought to shout, but changed his mind, thinking it was better to let them rest, they would need their strength for the river swim.

Continuing upriver, Tanden watched the terrain around him finding no indications of hostile tribes. Moving back into the river without hesitation, he refused to think about another swim or the one after that. If he had, he might not have been able to get back into the river.

The water tugged and pulled at his body. He felt he was being pulled in all directions at the same time. One swirling eddy twisted him around to face the way he had come. He locked his thoughts on the far bank, driving his mind to drive his body through the water, ever watchful for his crew.

He reached the foot of the escarpment, but there was no bank to climb. He was sure he had not passed his men, so he allowed the current to float him down river. Each time the current threatened to push him back toward the middle of the river, he swam a few strokes to keep himself in easy reach of the bank.

He soon spotted Tuller and Seenger. Two swift strokes brought him to a good handhold. He pulled himself out of the water into the sunlight. Shaking like a wet dog, he remembered I-Sheera complaining on ship that his crew did not bathe often enough. His group had spent so much time in the water lately, they were beginning to slosh when they walked.

Tanden wanted to rest beside the two men, however, he didn't want to leave Durrban and the woman alone any longer than necessary.

He said softly, "Tuller. Seenger. Time to go."

Awakening with a start, Tuller said, "I was beginning to think you'd decided to drown and leave us here." He yawned, stretched, and stood. "We watched you shoot out of sight in the current. The river runs faster than it looks."

Seenger said nothing, but he got to his feet and began tying the inflated wolfskin to his bare chest. Seenger had used his shirt to make straps and both sailors had torn their trousers from ankle to thigh to give them enough material to tie the float to the ogre. There was just enough cloth left over to tie Seenger to Tanden and Tuller.

Tanden noticed they had turned the skin inside out and some kind of pitch or resin had oozed out and dried around the seams. Tanden was sure no profession in the world made a man more self-reliant or adaptable to the tools at hand than a sailor.

Tanden said, "That looks like an excellent float. I'm certain if we had more skins we could make a boat to carry us across the river. Seenger, finish tying us together, let's get on with it."

Tuller looked down at his own barely covered body and said, "I hadn't thought of needing more wolf skin. If we need more cloth than we have, Seenger and I'll be as naked as the day we were born, but so far we seem to have what we need when we need it."

Tanden said, "Let's get going. I'm uncomfortable leaving Durrban and the girl alone." He told the men about the dead body he found.

Tuller tsked loudly when Tanden said he had freed the body and let the river take it away. "Wasteful. I could have used a new shirt and some pants, from a dead man or not."

Tanden said, his voice dripping with sarcasm, "Next time I find dead bodies lying around, I'll leave them for you to scavenge."

Tuller responded, "Thanks, I'd appreciate it. You never know what you'll find."

The three slid into the water in unison. Again, the current tore at Tanden, but this time he was ready for it. Swimming in unison was much easier with Tuller.

Seenger rode high in the water on his airbag straining his neck to keep his face out of the water. He kicked awkwardly with his feet trying to mimic the kicks of the men. He had no rhythm to his strokes. His actions resulted in splashing water, but his powerful legs propelled him forward with enough momentum that Tanden and Tuller had little to do with him other than guide his direction.

A strong current yanked and jerked at the three swimmers like it was purposely trying to separate them. A sudden jerk snapped the tether between Tanden and Seenger. Before Tanden was swept away, he felt Seenger's hands grab his ankle and squeeze. He continued pulling at the water though his swimming was much more difficult. Seenger's hand on his ankle jerked back and forth with the ogre's uneven kicking motion. The jerkiness caused Tanden to sink and rise, gulping air and water with each forward stroke. Tanden stretched each stroke trying to reach the sandbar he had found earlier.

Tanden's ankle popped free of Seenger's grasp. Before he could reach back for the ogre, he was hit from the side, the air forced from his lungs. Twisting and turning in the rushing current, he was pushed underwater and rolled. He felt like he was being pummeled and beaten. Fighting to the surface, he gasped air. Something struck his back and pushed him underwater again.

Just as suddenly as he was hit, he was free of the current. He gulped air, thrashing in the water looking for, but unable to see either crewman. Floating near him in the shallow backwaters was an uprooted tree. Unseen, they had collided with it and it had torn them away from each other.

Tanden pushed himself through the shallow water and up onto the bank. He raced back along the bank searching for Tuller and Seenger. Finally, he found them sitting half out of the water. Seenger was working to untie the straps from around them. The wolfskin float was tattered and torn to rags.

Seenger looked up at Tanden, looming above them on the bank and said, "It isn't natural. If ogres were meant to be in the water, we would be able to breathe water."

Tuller looked up silently, as if he agreed.

Tanden said, "I thought I'd lost you both. Thanks to the six gods you're safe."

Tuller replied, "You thank those useless gods, my friend. I'll thank Seenger. I don't know how we got to shore. Something hit me on the head. The next thing I knew we were here. I think Seenger may have learned to swim at last."

Seenger shrugged, "I saw the log and shouted, but you didn't hear me. I grabbed the log and towed Tuller along by the strapping. I floated on it until we came to where I could walk on the bottom. If that's swimming, then I have indeed learned how."

Tuller shook his head and spoke to no one in particular, "I think I'll take up farming."

"Come on," Tanden commanded. "We need to get out of the open. We can rest when we get to the grove where I left Durrban and the girl." Tanden looked about and realized that he didn't know whether they were up or down river of the others. He sniffed the air. With the wind blowing from the west, if they were down river he should be able to catch the scent of Durrban's fire. Tanden pointed downriver. The two crewmen followed him as he moved from the open clearing into a clump of concealing brush. He moved eastward looking for the grove hiding his missing people. With a half-concealed smile at himself, he realized he had just included I-Sheera as part of his crew. For the first time he had not thought of her as someone else's servant.

CHAPTER THIRTEEN

Tanden stood before his crew. The small, half-naked band was scattered around a tiny smokeless fire in the shade of the riverside grove. "We still have a few hours before sunset, but we're in unknown and unfriendly country, so I don't believe we should go stumbling blindly forward. We need to rest, eat, and heal. We may be safe here for the coming night, plus we have a supply of fresh water for all our needs. Other than our dead friend in the water, I haven't seen any signs of Hummdhars or Coodhars."

Tuller asked, "What about the White Wind? If we delay, we might miss her at the south point of the isthmus."

"Yes," Tanden said. "We might. But it won't benefit us if we're too tired to retake the White Wind when we find her. Tomorrow will be soon enough to travel. We'll make better time if we're fresh and well fed."

Tanden could use the rest now, but he needed to make full use of the daylight they had left. He continued, "First, we look to our safety and our needs before resting. Seenger, follow the river downstream as far as you can go, but be back here by sunset. Tuller, scout up river. I'll range southward. Durrban and I-Sheera stay here and hunt for our supper. Squirrels and rabbits seem to be in abundance. See if you can find edible berries or roots, also. Above all, keep the fire small and smokeless."

Tanden sighed tiredly, "Everyone, be careful and watchful for any sign of men. I don't want to send anyone alone in this country, but we must be sure of our surroundings. I think it wise to arm ourselves as best we can."

For the most part, they were without weapons and tools. Seenger and Tuller patted the bone blades stuck in their waistbands, having abandoned their long staffs on the other side of the river. With quick nods, both moved silently in their respective directions.

Tanden slid his wolf bone axe blade from his trousers and handed it to Durrban, "This may help you make and set snares and dig. Don't wander too far from this location and be watchful of the girl. Both of you watch each other's back. Don't allow anyone to come up on you unawares."

Tanden ran from grove to grove, stopping often to study the land around him, fixing many of the points of land into his memory. He searched for any high point to give him a better vantage of what lay ahead. Once, he thought he smelled smoke and heard the clank of metal on metal. Without checking farther, he turned aside and gave the area a wide berth.

The groves of trees gave way to broad woods surrounding grassy meadows. He traveled faster keeping to the shadows of the trees and away from the open areas. Many small streams and creeks crossed the terrain, so fresh water wouldn't be a problem.

Focusing his mind on the task was difficult. His thoughts returned unbidden to the events of the past two days. He allowed his ship to be taken from him. Crewman Nommer's death was his fault, though the man had given in to mutiny and murder. His leadership failures allowed Nommer to fall prey to evil. Alton was missing—probably drown in the sea. All because Tanden, as captain, had allowed evil to board his ship. His friend Gadon was dead, torn apart by a great dragon. Now, what remained of his loyal crew was wandering through a hostile land. Tanden told himself that if he had been a better captain, he would have chosen his crew more carefully. Other Holdenite captains warned him that he was courting disaster by adding foreigners to his crew, but he had ignored their warnings. Now Gadon was dead. He had lost his friend forever.

Every time Tanden realized his thoughts were wandering, he berated himself. Shaking his head, clearing his thoughts, he concentrated on the terrain around him. As before, pictures of Gadon and the White Wind creeped silently back into his active thoughts.

"Enough," he said to himself. "I must be too tired to concentrate. I'm being foolish and accomplishing little here." He turned and made his way back to the small grove by the river.

CHAPTER FOURTEEN

"I saw nothing," Seenger said.

Tanden nodded at the ogre while gnawing on a roasted rabbit haunch. He looked to Tuller with a silent question.

With dusk upon them, the three sat close by the fire in the chilled air of the grove. The dampness coming off the river chilled Tanden to the bone. Durrban and I-Sheera stood watch on opposite ends of the grove, out of the firelight, yet within hearing distance of the quiet voices.

"I wish I'd seen nothing," Tuller said. "We aren't alone. About fifteen minutes walk beyond where we crossed the river, I came upon a camp of men."

"Hummdhar or Coodhar?" Tanden asked.

"I don't know. Does it matter?"

"No, not much." When Tanden and Gadon had gone to war against the Hummdhars, Tuller had stayed home, his father thinking him too young to fight. Tanden said, "Go on."

"I didn't get too close, but I counted about twenty men with sauruses. That's too many for a hunting party and not enough for a battle. There were no women or children, except a couple of camp-following whores. It looked like the troops have been camped there for some time. Paths lead in and out from the camp in all directions. There was a river ford and a break in the rock wall across the river. It looked to me as if they were set there to guard the path."

Seenger said, "Maybe to protect a re-supply route."

Tuller nodded, "It looks that way and there were a few saurus-drawn wagons. I tried circling around to see what was farther north, but there was too much traffic coming and going along the paths, so I came back here."

Tanden said, "We have to stay together as much as possible from now on. Through the night, we need two on guard. Durrban and I will watch the first half of the night. Seenger and Tuller, you take the second watch."

"Captain?" I-Sheera's voice floated softly out of the darkness, "Let me watch, so you can sleep. I'm more rested than you."

"Damn it!" Tanden cursed. "Why are you questioning me? Do you think I'm incapable of standing a simple night watch?"

I-Sheera strode into the light to stand over Tanden. "No, sir." Through clenched teeth, showing her anger, she added, "I'm not as strong as you or any of these others, but I can watch, even though you question my ability." She took a breath, calming herself, "You saved my life. I can help. Please."

Tanden was taken aback. His temper had flared at her insolence, but her evident desire to help surprised him. She was just a woman and could not be trusted with much, but one watch should be safe enough.

"Stand watch then. If I catch you sleeping, I'll turn you over my knee and whip your backside until you can't sit down. Durrban, you and the girl didn't stand watch last night. Do so now. And Durrban, I must ask you to do double duty tonight. Seenger and Tuller will take the second watch. Tuller, wake me and Durrban for a third watch into the morning."

With no more questions or comments from anyone, Tanden lay back to rest. Staring up at the canopy above him, he thought, *"What is the matter with me? I just cursed at a woman for no reason other than she wanted to help. I better get control of myself. Gadon's council always kept me from becoming too full of myself."*

Tanden fell asleep with his thoughts on his dead friend.

CHAPTER FIFTEEN

"Move over," Gadon said.

Tanden drifted in sleep, not wanting to awake. Dreaming of Gadon was pleasant.

Gadon said, "You leave me nothing to eat and build such a small fire to warm these old bones that I practically have to lay in the flames to dry out. Then, like a lazy lay-about, you hog the best place to sleep. Tuller, wake up and help me roll Tanden away from the fire before he cooks."

A quick jab in the side woke Tanden with a start. Before he could move, he heard a whoop from Tuller. Two bodies pounced on Tanden, rolling over him and each other. He grabbed a head in the crook of each arm and yanked the two apart. In the dim firelight, he could see it was not a dream. Gadon was here and he was alive.

Tanden squiggled loose from Tuller and grabbed Gadon in both arms. He hugged him tightly, rolled on top of the heavyset man. Tanden locked his hands onto Gadon's ears and kissed him on the forehead. "I thought you were gone forever. Thanks be to the life after this one that you're alive."

"You can also thank my old Uncle Gall. When I was a child, he told me about hunting dragons. He said that if you fall down and play dead, the dragon will leave you alone. He claimed the large dragons aren't carrion eaters and only eat what they kill. It worked. The old monster pushed me around for a while and sniffed at me until I thought I would die from his bad breath. But I'm alive. Now, I'll thank you to get off me. Tanden, you smell like an old goat—that's fitting since you look that way. Tuller, get away from me. You don't smell any better. The way you two act, you'd think that no one had any confidence in me to outsmart a dragon. Then you run off and leave me to track you down through the night across wild country. I'd have passed you by altogether if Durrban hadn't seen me moving by the river's edge."

Tanden sat up beside his friend and pulled Gadon to an upright position. Gadon's clothing was torn and twisted, but the man looked healthy enough. Tuller sat beside his older brother, grinning like a sailor on a three-day drunk, overjoyed at the resurrection of his favorite sibling.

A crash of brush around them jarred Tanden's attention away from Gadon to the grove surrounding them. Durrban stood before him, his grin frozen on his face. The night shadows around them moved and formed into armed men stepping into the firelight.

A dark-haired youth stepped forward from the men circling them. He spoke the guttural language of Hummdhar, with a sneer to his voice, "Hold! Don't move or you'll die. I do hate to break up such a tender reunion, but it's late and I miss my warm bed. I would just as soon kill you now rather than take you back to Father."

Tanden was familiar enough with Hummdharian to understand the boy, but none of his crew could speak that language. Gadon and Durrban only spoke Holdenish. Tuller also spoke Eastern and Geldonite. Seenger only spoke Holdenish and his own tongue. As for I-Sheera, he knew she spoke Holdenish well enough to be understood, but he had no idea what other languages she understood and spoke. Tanden couldn't see Seenger and I-Sheera.

Tanden didn't dare translate. He was sure they would understand without being told. They had fallen into the hands of an enemy tribe.

The youth turned to a man near him, "Build up that fire, Seekin. Let's see what we've caught."

The man tossed handfuls of wood on the fire until it blazed. Tanden looked at the young man. He could not be more than nineteen or twenty, yet he spoke with authority. He had long, dark, greasy hair falling in the long braids of a Hummdhar warrior. The boy had the evil look of a one who enjoyed hurting others for the sake of the hurting.

The man called Seekin was older, a warrior wearing old battle scars across his twisted face. He was thin but had the look of strong leather. His eyes blazed in the firelight as a man whose life was fueled by long smoldering anger. A half dozen other men stood around them weapons at the ready.

Tanden decided the older man was much tougher than his size indicated. The major cut scaring his face would have killed a lesser man. The twisted slash had been poorly sewn shut many years ago. Even in the firelight, Tanden could see it had not healed properly, it oozed even now.

One man hit Durrban in the back of the head, knocking the little man to his knees. Surreptitiously, Tanden looked around for Seenger. He still could not see the ogre or the woman. Maybe they got away.

"Seekin," the youngster in charge sneered, "we have all four."

"Yes, Bransch. There were three here before this fat fool led us right to them."

Seekin stared at Tanden with glaring recognition. Tanden could not remember ever having seen the gnarled face before.

Seekin said, "You don't recognize me do you, Holden dog?"

Tanden didn't reply. He thought it best not to let on that he understood their language.

Seekin said to Bransch, "Well, Nephew, we've done well this night. Before you is one of the Holdenite cowards who killed your mother and little sisters. This is the very pile of pig shit that reformed my face."

Looking into the face before him, Tanden saw nothing he remembered.

Bransch grabbed Tanden by the hair and twisted his head back to light his face better. "Are you sure, Seekin? It's been many years."

"I swear by my sister's cold grave. I'm as sure as this scar across my face. Rather than fight like men, this was one of the cowards who burned the forest hiding our women and children. We caught up with them and in the fight to slaughter them, I stood face-to-face with this dog. Had I not lost my footing, I would have gutted him then and there. Instead, he gave me this." Seekin jabbed a finger at the scar on his face. "Your father and the others tracked down and chased the Holden cowards into a blind canyon and slaughtered them. How this one escaped is beyond me!"

Seekin said to Tanden, "I'm glad you've survived until now. The gods have smiled on me this day. You'll die once for my sister and once for each day I've felt pain because of your blade."

Tanden held his face as passive as he could make it. He remembered the incident clearly, but in the heat of battle, he did not take time to study the face of every man who challenged his sword. He had not commanded the group who burned the forest that day, but if he had, he would have made the same decision. Risking your own men is foolish if another method is available to kill the enemy. The women and children who died in the fire were no more dead than the Holdenite women and children killed by the Hummdhar raiders who started the war.

"Seekin," Bransch said, "Father will want his revenge as well. Let's take these scum back to camp where we can treat them as they deserve. Tie these foul creatures up and send someone ahead to tell Father about our catch. He'll be pleased with us this night."

The smile on Bransch's lips did nothing to hide the look in his eyes. Tanden could readily see the boy was happier to have someone to torture than he was to take prisoners back to his father. Tanden held a dispassionate face as two men roughly tied his hands with strong leather cords. The Hummdhars dragged the four bound men from the fire to sit in the shadows.

Seekin grabbed two Hummdhar warriors from around the fire and thrust them into the dark. Propelling them toward their camp, he instructed them to run fast, the rest would soon follow.

The Hummdhars stood around the blazing fire warming themselves with its heat and the warmth of their self-congratulations for capturing an old enemy without suffering any casualties of their own. Tanden, his back to the fire, listened as each man bragged about how he followed Gadon stealthily to the grove and snuck up on the band.

Taking a burning stick from the fire, Bransch walked to Tuller and began slowly burning the hair away from the sailor's scalp. He took no particular care whether he touched the burning brand to hair or skin. Tanden smelled the burning hair and flesh, yet Tuller made no sound, though he flinched involuntarily. At each twitch, Bransch snickered to himself, the bulge of an erection visable in his pants.

"Enough, boy. Let's get back to camp. There's time enough to deal with these vermin tomorrow."

"No. Leave me this one and Pugh to stand guard. I'll return to my father's camp in good time."

Pugh was a huge beast of a man, larger than any Hummdhar Tanden had ever seen. The man had a blank look in his eyes and a loose enough lip that he drooled a bit down his chin.

Seekin hesitated.

Bransch shouted in a whiny voice crackling with anger. He punctuated each phrase by striking Tuller on the head with the burning stick. "Go on, old man. Uncle or not, I'll tell my father you refused to follow my commands."

Seekin and his tribesmen dragged Tanden, Gadon, and Durrban to their feet, moving them into the darkness away from the light of the fire. Seekin led the way with another. The two remaining Hummdhars followed closely behind. One held his short sword in hand ready to prod the captives should they lag behind the group. The other strung his bow and notched an arrow to cut down any man who ran.

Before they had gone a hundred paces into the moonlit night outside the grove, they heard a scream cut through the night. Gadon turned as if to run back to aid his brother. The rear guard thrust his sword into the man's face as a warning to move. For a moment, Tanden thought Gadon would challenge the two armed men, even with his hands tied behind his back.

Slowly, Gadon turned back, walking quietly beside Tanden.

Tanden said quietly, "Our time will come, Gadon." He wanted to say something to comfort the man, but no other words came to mind.

Seekin called back, "No talking there. Amdar, keep them quiet or you can join them."

Amdar ran to Gadon and shouted into his face to be silent or die. Though Gadon didn't understand the words, he understood the message. Gadon clamped his jaw shut, but his eyes glared back.

Tanden's mind outraced his steps, searching for a way out of their predicament. Taken by Hummdhars under any circumstances meant death. He was sure his death would not come quick. No solutions came to mind, try as he might.

In the dim light, Tanden recognized the slope of the escarpment across the river. They were opposite where they had started their swim. A call from Amdar caused Tanden to look behind them. For his trouble, he got the point of an arrow jabbed into his backside. His look was worth the pain. He saw Tuller trotting toward them with his hands behind his back. Bransch and Pugh were prodding him along.

In front of the column, Seekin turned about without slowing his forward progress or losing a step. He grunted in surprise and spun back around. He said something to the man next to him that Tanden was unable to hear. The Hummdhar guard looked over his shoulder. Turning his eyes back to the front, the man shrugged in the age-old motion of a foot soldier who obeys without question. Commenting on the peculiarities of those in command was a bad and dangerous habit.

A moment later, rushing past the Hummdhar rear guard, a wild-eyed Tuller plowed silently between Tanden and Gadon pushing them sideways. He carried a Hummdhar short sword in his hands. A step behind the two lead Hummdhars, Tuller thrust his sword at the back of Seekin. A shout from behind alerted the warrior.

Seekin spun about with his sword at the ready. He parried Tuller's thrust with his sword, then using his left arm and shoulder, he pushed Tuller away from him. With catlike speed, the grizzled warrior fled toward his camp.

Tuller spun sideways from Seekin's push and fell against the other Hummdhar tribesman. Using his momentum, he pushed the sword through the man before he reacted to protect himself.

Tanden turned to throw his body at the Hummdhar guards behind him, but instantly recognized Seenger dressed in Pugh's clothing. Seenger had already run a spear through the chest of the archer. The ogre closed in to finish off the dead man before the Hummdhar could even fall to the ground.

I-Sheera, wearing Bransch's clothing, was backing away from Amdar's sword. The Hummdhar was swinging cut after cut at the smaller girl. It was her startled shout that alerted Seekin, allowing him to avoid Tuller's first killing stroke.

Gadon's shoulder connected with Admar's back sending the guard sprawling to the ground. He rolled away from the armed guard barely dodging a sword stroke. I-Sheera stood over the Hummdhar with a double handful of sword at the ready and drove the point through the startled man's chest. With a shout of victory, she gave the sword a twist and yanked it free.

Running away quickly, Seekin was almost out of sight. When the man reported to the Hummdhar camp, they would have many more men to deal with than a small night patrol.

CHAPTER SIXTEEN

"Cut me loose," Tanden commanded.

He leaped to the body of the archer as soon as he was cut free. Untangling the bow and arrow, sighting carefully at the running man, he loosed a shot. A normal bow wouldn't reach the distance, but Hummdhar bows were longer. The unusually strong pull of the bow gave him hope the arrow might reach its target.

The arrow sailed harmlessly past the running man, causing Seekin to dart into the shadows of some nearby trees.

Tanden snarled, "Damn me!" Calming quickly, he added, "Sorry. I guess that was a waste of a good arrow."

Tuller cut Gadon and Durrban free. Gadon turned to hug his brother while Durrban stood quietly beside Tanden.

Tanden said, "We must get out of this area before Seekin returns with reinforcements. Gather up the weapons. Hurry, we need to move now."

Tuller said, "Time enough or not, this one has less need for his clothing than you or I." He, Gadon, and Seenger stripped the three dead men in short order. Gadon tossed a tunic and an over vest to Tanden. The tunic was still warm from the dead man's body. The warmth was a comfort in the night air, so Tanden ignored the warmth's origin just as he ignored the wet spot around the gaping hole just under the right arm made by Tuller's sword. They also handed him a leather shield with a metal buckler and the archer's quiver with a dozen arrows

Tuller put on Amdar's shirt and leather overcoat. Gadon could not find anything to fit his girth, but found a fur hat. It perched above his ears like a second head of hair.

"These blasted Hummdhars probably have bugs crawling in their clothes. This hat will undoubtedly make my hair fall out. At least, it will keep my head warm." He turned to I-Sheera and said, "The next time you kill a man, make sure you kill one that's not so scrawny. This bunch is nothing more than skin and bones."

Tanden looked at the woman. She was dressed in the Hummdhar youth's clothes, holding a short sword still dripping blood in the moonlight. She was breathing heavily, but she appeared resolute and ready for whatever came her way.

"Well," he asked Seenger as his men stripped the bodies of anything useful, "what happened?"

Seenger looked at I-Sheera and shrugged, "I couldn't sleep with a woman on guard, so, I watched the watcher. I saw her step out of sight and I got up to follow. If I'd stayed behind I would have seen these vermin slipping up on us." He tugged at Pugh's leather garments, trying to stretch them as they barely covered his torso. The pants were so tight their sides had split open at the seams.

I-Sheera said, "It's my fault. I had to urinate. I would've rushed back and been captured if Seenger hadn't followed me. He grabbed me and held me quiet."

Tuller looked up from pulling on a second pair of trousers, "I'm glad you didn't wait longer. That little piss hole already had me bent over and was about to rape me in the ass, when Seenger came rushing in like a lion to the hunt. He killed the guard with his bare hands and held the young pervert until I-Sheera cut me loose. We stripped them both and came after you three."

"And the boy?"

Tuller shrugged and said simply, "He won't rape anybody again."

Durrban said, "This is my fault, Tanden. I was so excited to see Gadon I missed these men sneaking up on me."

Tanden put an arm around his shoulders and said to everyone. "This is no one's fault, understand? It's over and done. We're tired, but we must move now. Southward is as good a direction to go as any other, as long as it's away from here. Plus, southward is toward the White Wind. We move in pairs. I-Sheera, you're with me. Gadon and Seenger, follow Tuller and Durrban. Stay close behind. Don't lose sight of each other. Be as careful as possible to not leave tracks."

Tuller interrupted Tanden with a fit of coughing and cursing before dropping to his knees. Everyone gathered around him with concern. Sputtering, he looked up with tears in his eyes. He handed a water bladder to Gadon that he had taken from one of the dead men. "Drink this easy, brother. This stuff'll make you think Grandma is a pretty young maid."

Gadon drank. Then in a raspy, hoarse voice, he said, "This is watered down, little brother. It doesn't do much more than tickle my tongue." It was apparent to everyone, the drink was stronger than Gadon expected. He handed the bladder to Seenger. The bag passed from Seenger to Durrban and then to Tanden. Each in turn drank a few swallows to warm their inner fires. Lastly, Tanden looked down at I-Sheera standing beside him, dressed in the leather and rough cloth of a Hummdhar raider.

He said, "And you, Little Warrior, deserve this as much as any of us. I know your red magic creed doesn't allow you to take alcohol, but this will warm you for the night ahead."

"What creed?" she asked. Her tone made it clear she did not expect a response. Taking the bladder in both hands, she drank long and deep. With a ragged sigh, she tossed the bladder back to Tuller, turned on her heels, and walked straight south.

The men quickly gathered their collected equipment and followed the woman. Tanden caught up to I-Sheera before they reached the first grove of trees. He guided them around the trees, staying as much in their shadow as possible while avoiding large clumps of brush. In Deering's fading moonlight, he looked for clear areas they could pass through without leaving a trail for the Hummdhars to follow. They would have a few hours of complete darkness before the Egg and Lumpy rose high enough in the sky to shed their moonlight over the night.

Even a skilled tracker could not follow them in moonless darkness. The moon waned and the darkness deepened. In half an hour or so, it would be fully dark. The Egg and Lumpy's reflected moonlight would barely shine enough to throw lighter shadows. His crew could not travel well without light. Morning would come too soon and any village idiot could track a group of six people in daylight.

Picking up his pace, Tanden began trotting at a ground-eating pace. He maintained a steady measured pace he could have kept at all day in his youth. Now, only time would tell when his body would quit. His crew stayed with him, silently moving as fast as possible.

Tanden splashed into a small creek with only a sliver of the moon left. Turning downstream, he quickly waded through the water. He needed to find a way out of the water that would not leave tracks for the Hummdhars to easily follow. The stream swung wide around a hill, but in doing so, it cut into a high, rocky bank.

Tanden spied a ledge leading to a wide plateau. It was beyond his reach. He stopped and without a word, bent down to take hold of I-Sheera by her lower legs. He easily lifted the woman high enough to grab the ledge and scramble up. He handed her his newly acquired bow, quiver, and shield.

Tanden waved Seenger over to him. Clasping the ogre's hands in his own he commanded Gadon to climb. Gadon, achieving the ledge and laid down with his arms stretched to those below. The ascent was a quick matter for Tuller and Durrban to step into Tanden and Seenger's grasp, then be lifted up by Gadon's strong arms and pulled up onto the ledge. Tanden grunted as he lifted Seenger into Gadon's hands. Once Seenger was up, he turned, and with Gadon, stretched out his arms to Tanden.

Tanden leaped upward, making a quick grab at their hands. Catching him, they pulled him up and dragged him onto the rocky ledge. Deering had set and the night was dark. Clouds swirling across the sky from the west obscured the stars.

Tanden said, "We must wait here until we have enough light to see. I-Sheera and I will keep guard." He backed away from the rim of the ledge until he could not see or be seen from the stream. He sat cross-legged on a rock and told the others to find resting places behind him.

I-Sheera sat on Tanden's right, close enough he felt the heat from her body. She quietly handed him his bow, quiver, and shield. In the faint light of the night, he watched her lay her short sword before her, close by her hand.

Tanden sat upright, trying to adjust his eyes to the night. Try as he might, all he could do was distinguish dark shadows from darker shadows. In the sky above, the twisting clouds blanketed the stars. He sensed a coming storm, both hoping it would miss them, as they had no place to weather out a bad blow, and hoping it would come on them hard enough to cover their tracks.

The air was quiet and still, feeling heavy, thick, and ominous. As a student of the sciences, Tanden learned that none of the world's four elements were stable and only foolish men trusted them. Like all children, he learned fire was the most dangerous and deadly. As a sailor, he learned the air and water were always changing. He also learned to employ them, bending them to his will, not like a blue wizard or magician who claimed the air's magic, but like a partner, working with the elements. Fire, air, and earth were the elements whose magic could be harvested by those with talent and training.

Tanden once met a man who claimed to have felt the ground move beneath his feet. The man described how the dirt itself opened up and swallowed an ox. The man used his experience as an argument trying to convince Tanden to worship his pagan earth gods.

The dark demon and his minions had caused the earth to quake, just as the dark demon was even now brewing up a storm to hamper Tanden's efforts to reach his goal. Without a blue wizard or even a lowly acolyte to help control the coming storm, it would slow his march toward the White Wind. Durrban, as a green acolyte, had an abundance of grass, trees, and forest to gather his magic, but he was a new student with limited talent. He had no control over the weather or the dark one.

Tanden was firmly convinced he had made mistakes, but they were over and done with, to be forgotten. Though he was past his errors, they kept returning to his thoughts. Nothing would stop his doubts, but he believed he had the presence of mind to continue rejecting those thoughts of worry and doubt. Nothing short of his own death would keep him from reaching his goal.

In the stillness of the night, Tanden heard a grating noise like an animal in the throes of a painful death. Feeling about him on the ground his fingers closed around a small round pebble. Turning slightly he tossed it at a dark shadow he was sure was Tuller, sleeping near Gadon.

The pebble thumped softly on flesh and rattled away on the rocks. Tuller grunted softly as he woke. He sat upright, leaned over to Gadon, and rolled his brother onto his side. The snoring stopped as quickly as it began. Without a word, Tuller slid closer to his brother and lay back down to sleep. Tanden's thoughts turned to his crew.

I-Sheera and Tanden sat in silence, but he was sensitive to her presence. They were sitting close with thigh touching thigh. The heat from her body warmed him from head to toe. A rush of excitement suddenly flooded his loins. He was surprised at his body's reaction her. He decided she was no longer a burden to his life and that sometime in the last couple of days he had grown fond of her. He considered her an asset. Tanden silently chuckled, he was a man fast approaching old age and the end of his life, not an adolescent to be excited at the slightest touch of a woman.

He had seen a lot and done much in his life and realistically he had no reason to expect to live beyond another ten or fifteen years. He truly doubted he would ever see his grandchildren, that is, if he ever settled down long enough to gain a wife and have children. Gadon and Tuller were from a long-lived family. Their grandmother and Uncle Gall both lived into their seventies. Their grandmother's father was still alive, although he was frail and had to be spoon fed and carried everywhere. The old man was a fountain of wisdom. Whenever they were back home in Harkelle, Tanden and Gadon joined Tuller as he listened to the old man's stories. The family often said Tuller inherited the old man's wisdom and sharp mind. In truth, Tuller was who he was because he loved his great-grandfather and listened carefully to the old man's teachings.

Durrban had lost his parents to the invading Surr when he was young and his siblings had all died of disease and bad water. As a young man, he married a girl who also alone in the world. Together, they bore ten children. Durrban was proud that half his children lived to have children of their own.

Tanden suspected Durrban was on his final sea voyage. The older man would probably stay in Harkelle to live his last years surrounded by his grandchildren, enjoying his newfound studies as an acolyte to the green order. His share of the cargo from the overstuffed holds of the White Wind would have made his last few years comfortable, despite the high fees charged by the green priests for their magic lessons.

Tanden swore that the White Wind's cargo would still be his to share with his crew.

Seenger had no family. Beyond the crew of the White Wind, he had no friends in Holden. For all Tanden knew, Seenger thought of the crew as his family and the White Wind as his home.

As for himself, Tanden did not know if he had any living blood relatives. His mother had died when he was so young he could not remember her face. How could a man know his future if he did not know his history?

A change in I-Sheera's breathing told Tanden the woman had fallen asleep sitting upright. She twitched and mumbled so softly in her sleep he could barely hear it. No clear words escaped her lips. He should not tolerate sleeping on watch and should wake her. He realized now was not the time to be unbending. She had done more than he had any right to expect from a woman. He rationalized that they would travel faster tomorrow if the girl was well rested. He did not want to admit to himself that he just did not want to wake her. He wanted her rested and happy.

Tanden was not aware of how much time had passed while he daydreamed or how long the others had been asleep, before he realized being alone on watch was foolish. If he fell asleep, they would be unprotected. He located another small pebble. Twisting easily, he spotted Seenger's shadow—no one else cast as large a silhouette. He tossed the pebble at the ogre missed entirely. It clattered in the silent night, but the sound, as loud as it was, blended in with nature's serenade.

The shadow rose to a sitting position and waved. Tanden caught the motion as darkness against a black backdrop. He was certain Seenger was now on watch. He would stay on watch a little while longer and wake his replacement when he grew too tired to be alert to new noises.

Without conscious awareness, Tanden's arm reached out to the fitfully sleeping woman. He drew her head down to his lap, letting her rest there. Gently, he stroked her hair. During the day, her hair looked thick and tangled like the end of a frayed, blackened hemp rope. Here in the night air, her hair felt soft and smooth. Stroking her hair quieted her sleep. It also soothed Tanden. He smiled as she quietly moved closer to him in her sleep, resting a hand against his leg.

Storm clouds continued to blot out the sky. Without the stars, Tanden had no way to estimate the passage of time. Had eons passed since he was dragged from his berth aboard the White Wind? He knew he should sleep soon. The entire group was close to the point of exhaustion. Whom should he waken? Gadon had gone without extended sleep longer than any of them, having been on watch the night of the mutiny. Durrban was older and had less stamina than the rest. Tuller and Seenger had slept by the river earlier in the day, but they stood watch most of the night before this one. How much longer could he continue to rely on them to carry the burden of sleeplessness?

Tanden worried the problem through his thoughts. He added the hours of sleep each man had gotten in the last two days, trying to match that man's capabilities to go without rest. Tanden remained on watch, as he was unable to calculate that anyone—man, woman, or ogre—was more rested than he was. The truth of the matter was that he enjoyed I-Sheera's touch and he did not want to move. He continued stroking her hair, listening to the night around them.

Tanden noticed Tuller rise. He found a smooth place on the rocks to sit, facing upstream with his back to Tanden. Tanden leaned against his crewman, laying his head on Tuller's shoulder and slept.

CHAPTER SEVENTEEN

The pre-dawn hour was cold and gray when Tuller placed his hand softly on Tanden's arm to waken him. The dim moonlight flickering down from the Egg and Lumpy was doing less to light the sky than the sun, still hidden by the horizon. Tanden raised his head slightly, but otherwise, he didn't move. From where he sat, Tanden could not see Tuller. Shifting his eyes, he looked at Seenger. The ogre raised an index finger, pointed at his ear and then pointed upstream. Tanden listened. Finally, he heard it, the scrape of rock on rock coming from upstream, then a second noise, a small splash.

Tanden nodded to Seenger, raised a finger to his lips, and pointed to the sleeping forms of Gadon and Durrban. In silent obedience, Seenger moved to where Gadon lay, remaining hunched over to stay hidden from the stream below. He put one hand gently over the sleeping man's mouth and one hand lightly on his shoulder. Gadon awoke wide-eyed and alert. Seenger patted him on the shoulder and moved to awaken Durrban in the same manner.

Taking a cue from the ogre, Tanden reached down to place a hand over I-Sheera's mouth, but she sat upright silently before he could touch her. Tanden felt an empty chill where she had pressed against his body. He shook his head to clear his mind from invading sexual thoughts. Picking up the bow slowly and quietly, he notched an arrow from the quiver. Checking around him, he noticed the entire group had noiselessly re-armed themselves. Even I-Sheera picked up her short sword without as much as a scrape against the rock.

Gadon and Durrban sat quietly where they had slept. Seenger moved to the far side of the ledge. His flanking movement was as wide as Tanden could have hoped for here on their little plateau.

Tanden looked at Tuller. He was stretched out flat, close to the edge near a patch of scruffy weeds. He was able to see the stream without being seen. Tuller returned his look and raised two fingers. He slid one finger down across his cheek in a slashing movement. The position of the slash told Tanden that Seekin was one of the two men in the stream below them. Tanden nodded and deliberately made eye contact with the other members of his group. Each silently acknowledged they had seen the signals.

Tanden turned to focus on Tuller. This time, Tuller pointed at himself then at Seenger and pointed two fingers at the stream. Slowly, Tuller drew a finger silently across his own throat, with a question in his eyes.

Tanden shook his head slowly. Tuller nodded his acceptance. Tanden recognized that neither crewman agreed with his decision. Everyone held their breath while the two men tracking them passed by in the stream below.

Tanden was beginning to believe he had made an error by not killing the two Hummdhars, when he heard another splash from upstream. Then, he heard another and another. A full five minutes passed before the men following the two advance scouts waded along the stream below the group. Tuller signaled with a flash of fingers that he counted a dozen men leading their sauruses.

Tanden realized if they had killed the two advance scouts, the larger body following would have swarmed over them like hungry ants on a dead bug. He had counted on there being a smaller force. His original hastily developed plan was to attack the second group, using the element of surprise, but there were more barbarians than they could effectively kill without receiving unacceptable losses of their own.

CHAPTER EIGHTEEN

Tanden wanted the Hummdhar sauruses, but he shook his head and with an open hand, patted downward, signaling his crew to stay put and not attack. Tanden was thankful he had worked together with these men for a long time. Effective communications didn't always require words.

A tense five minutes later Tuller looked over the side and pointed downstream indicating the barbarians had all gone that way.

Tanden whispered, just loud enough his men could hear, "Then we will move upstream, quickly and quietly."

Tuller and Seenger gathered their weapons and slipped over the side of the ledge in tandem. Even this close, Tanden heard no more than a gentle tinkling of water. Staying low to the rocks, Gadon and Durrban moved forward. Swinging their legs over the edge, they slid off the ledge to hang by their hands before dropping into the waiting arms of Tuller and Seenger, who eased them noiselessly into the stream.

From the ledge, Tanden signaled the men with a fast flash of hands. Following his signs, Gadon stepped quickly with Seenger a few yards downstream. They watched the curve of the hillside and the bend of the stream for any Hummdhar returning their way. Durrban carefully waded upstream as an advance guard. Tuller remained below to assist Tanden and the woman.

I-Sheera swung her legs over the edge. Tanden, who was lying next to her on the rocks, grasped her wrists and lowered her down to Tuller's waiting arms. Tanden dropped his weapons down to the woman and followed as fast as he could. The six waded quickly upstream through the swift water. Gadon and Seenger keeping a constant watch behind them.

Tanden signaled for Tuller to catch up to Durrban. Durrban halted at a bend in the stream where trees and bushes obstructed his view. He peeked cautiously around the corner then nodded to Tuller, who swiftly continued past him, moving on upstream. Durrban waved to Tanden and the others, signaling all clear, silently calling them forward. He dashed out of sight after Tuller.

Tanden and the others came upon Tuller and Durrban waiting quietly hunkered down in the cold water after two or three more bends in the stream. Durrban was washing in the cold morning water. Tuller splashed water over his head—droplets clinging to the clumps of his hair not burned away by the young Hummdhar.

Looking to the east, Tanden judged they had a few moments before sunrise. The clouds overhead were dark and threatening so the sun would not shine brightly this morning. A stiff breeze from the west caused more than one of them to shiver.

Tuller said, keeping his voice low, "This is where they entered into the stream. Look. I guess twenty or thirty men riding sauruses split up here. Half went upstream and the other half passed us by downstream. It looks like they dismounted to scan for any footprints we might have left when exiting the water."

Tanden said, "Or to come on us quietly and catch us unawares."

Hoofprints and boot prints of numerous men trampled both streambanks. Tanden's group could leave the water here with virtual impunity. They must still hurry. No one could guess how far the Hummdhars hunting them would travel in each direction before turning back.

Tanden said, "Watch your step getting out of the stream. Try to walk backward so our prints match those who entered the water here. Tuller and Durrban, forward. Seenger and Gadon, behind."

Tanden watched their footprints as they left the water. It did indeed look as if a small band of men had entered the water. They should avoid recapture as long as no one recognized his group left different prints than Hummdhar boots. I-Sheera was wearing boots taken from Bransch, but the others still wore their soft soled, shipboard boots.

They continued walking backward for twenty yards before turning to run south toward another grove of trees, falling easily into pairs as Tanden instructed. Tuller and Durrban ran ahead quickly. Gadon and Seenger covered their rear, ever watchful of the stream behind them. The cold morning air pulled their breaths from their lungs, leaving wisps of vapor that blew away and disappeared as they ran. The exercise warmed them faster than any morning fire would have. Tanden signaled his lead men to run straight through the first grove of trees. He was unwilling to go around, believing the loss of speed they would experience running through brush and around the trees would outweigh their need to be hidden from sight before the Hummdhars doubled back.

Tanden was of two minds on the Hummdhars hunting them. On one hand, if the barbarians remained in large groups, as they had been, he and his small band might miss detection. His group could not survive a running battle against a sizable force. On the other hand, if the Hummdhars split up, their chances of discovery rose dramatically. Still, they might survive an encounter with a smaller force.

The grove proved to be more difficult than Tanden anticipated. The trees grew in tight clumps, with tangles of thorny nettles weaving through almost every open space. Each runner faired according to their size and agility. I-Sheera fairly sped through the tangle, she was small enough to slip easily through spaces that forced the larger men to go around. The leather garments she had taken from Bransch protected her from thorns and stinging nettles. Gadon's size and the torn, flimsy clothing he wore seriously slowed him down.

Gadon was running close behind Tanden, cursing and puffing heavily, yet Tanden could only hear about every fourth word. "...dog vomit...flat...butt-licking...overfed donkey...kiss my...pile of...egg stealing..." Tanden did not try to figure out who or what the heavyset sailor was railing about. Gadon sometimes cursed just to be cursing, or he cursed to get a laugh, and at times, he cursed to cover his own fears and worries.

A cloud-covered sunrise broke the horizon just as Tanden's crew ran into the clearing beyond the tangled grove. Another grove stood a hundred yards to the south. The grove behind them blocked the view of the stream. The time for stealth had passed and was yet to come. Distance was of prime importance now. The group ran onward as fast as they could.

Durrban's stamina was waning noticeably. Tuller slowed his pace to match the older man's, causing each pair to slow down to maintain their rough formation. It was obvious to Tanden that I-Sheera, Seenger, and Tuller could quickly out distance the others. Making the situation worse, a light mist began to fall. The air was thick with moisture and taking in enough air became difficult. They would have to seriously slow their pace down soon, but for now, they continued pushing on as fast as they could.

They ran through the next grove, across another clearing, and into the grove after that. They covered a mile or more in just a few minutes. Durrban and Gadon were both gasping and coughing. Their pace slowed to a fast trot. Their forward progress ceased when Durrban, tired and out of breath, attempted to jump over a fallen log. He hooked a toe and tumbled face first into a tangle of thorny nettles. As painful as the thorns poking the man must have been, he lay there, face down, sucking air.

Tanden and the others stopped in various conditions of disarray. Gadon dropped to the log to sit with his head between his knees. Tanden put his hands on his knees and resisted the urge to try to empty his already empty stomach.

Durrban recovered his breath enough to say in a deadpan voice, "Ouch."

Laughing, Tuller and Seenger stepped over to Durrban and lifted him from his bed of nettles.

Durrban looked solemn and said, "I haven't had so much fun since my youngest son had diarrhea for a week. Captain, the next time you decide to sail around the world, please don't forget to invite me along, I want to be able to laugh in your face."

Gadon laughed with the rest of them and added, "If there is a next time."

Tanden smiled and said, "There will be a next time, my friends. We'll quit this land and once again stand on the deck of the White Wind. Believe what I say. Just think of it. Can't you just see it? Gadon standing at the helm. The ship running before a stiff breeze with the wind at our backs and the sun on our faces. Seenger standing at the bow with the salty seawater spraying his face and a cargo hold full of Tuller's trade goods. Each of us with a belly full of Durrban's world famous seafood stew holding a mug of ale. And a soft, warm bed for our beautiful, young lady here. Just think on it! Are we going to let barbarian rabble keep us from this? I think not. The White Wind is out there. She's ours, let's go take her back."

Gadon looked at Tanden and said, "Who are you trying to convince? You or me? If you're talking to me, you're wasting your breath. I'll set foot on the White Wind before any here or I'll buy the next round of ale."

Tuller looked at Durrban and said in mock amazement, "Oh my, Durrban! We must hurry. That's a promise I've yet to see filled in all my days. Let's move. I can taste Gadon's ale even now." The two men moved on through the grove feeling more refreshed than either should have.

Tanden noticed I-Sheera looking at him. He smiled at her. She could have easily stepped over the log lying before them, but he placed his hands on her slender waist and exaggeratedly lifted her high over the log. He set her gently down on the other side. Tanden vaulted over the log and motioned Gadon and Seenger to follow. Tanden did not look back, but heard Gadon berating Seenger for not lifting him over the log and for not respecting his elders.

Tuller and Durrban surveyed the clearing ahead of them. A hard rain was falling and a cold wind was blowing out of the west. There were no signs of Hummdhars in pursuit. The silhouette of the next tree line lay across the top of a long hill more than two hundred yards away. Both men charted a course straight up the slope. They moved at a slow trot with Tanden and the others following.

Tanden recognized the slope ahead of them from his scouting trip the night before. The trees at the top marked the end of scattered groves and the beginning of the forest. Rolling terrain was before them as they moved farther from the flat of the river basin. Numerous creeks and streams crisscrossed the area. The next hill beyond was where Tanden heard the voices of men in the distance.

Tanden thought, *"Once we enter this forest, we should be able to cover our tracks and still move quickly to the south, circling around to those ridges and high hills in the distance."*

Halfway up the slope, Tanden felt the heavy beats of saurus feet on the ground long before he heard them. He whirled about, looking through the morning rain, scanning the area around them. No riders were in sight, but the hoofbeats were growing closer. There were no hiding places on the slope or the clearing behind them. He prodded his crewmen to run for their lives.

Pushing I-Sheera before him, he said, "Run. Get under cover."

A triumphant shout from behind them told Tanden they would not reach shelter before the Hummdhars caught them. Even well rested, a runner could not outrun a man riding a saurus. Halting, he spun about to face their pursuers.

Four Hummdhar barbarians rounded the grove his group had recently quit. In the lead was scar-faced Seekin. At his command, a rider wheeled about, racing back toward the stream. The remaining saurus riders whooped as their sauruses pounded up the slope toward Tanden's troop.

Tanden pulled three arrows from the quiver strapped to his shoulder. He stuck two arrows in the ground before him and notched one arrow to his bowstring. He stood, waiting for the riders to come into range.

Seenger stepped up on Tanden's right. He hefted a spear in his hand, testing its balance. Tanden felt sure the ogre would be more comfortable using the spear as a pike rather than throwing it at a moving target. Seenger returned his look with a shrug and set his feet.

Durrban stepped up next to them. He dropped his sword and stretched his hands out, palms down. He was a new green order acolyte having barely begun in his studies of magic, but the grass wavered around them as he used what little talent he had. The air shimmered slightly. With a sudden push, he thrust the magic he had just gathered back down the sloping hillside.

The sauruses were moving up the slope faster than Tanden hoped, but the ground was already slick with rain. Normally surefooted, the giant lizards' paws began slipping in the wet grass as if it was ice. The beasts, struggling to keep upright, faltered and stumbled.

Durrban shrugged and leaned down to pick up his sword. A fully trained green wizard or magician could have drawn enough magic from the grassy slope and the surrounding trees to throw up a barrier to block the advancing Hummdhars. Even a green priest could have gathered and condensed enough magic to splash the saurus, confounding the creatures, causing them to bound away in panic.

The older Holdenite had done as much as he could with his magical talent and the few lessons he had received. That small bit was enough to cause the sauruses to stumble and the riders to lose their seats. Tanden was pleased with any advantage he could get.

Raising the bow, he drew it to its full strength. Setting his aim on Seekin, the middle rider, he let it fly. A gust of wind pushed the arrow off course, yet it sunk a full third of its length into the broad chest of the saurus to the right. The saurus crumpled. Its head sunk slowly to the ground. Its broad body followed, somersaulting noiselessly over the Hummdhar rider. Neither saurus nor man moved again.

Tanden was unaware he had done any more than hit a target. He re-aimed and again let fly at Seekin. His third arrow was airborne before his second arrow passed harmlessly by both riders and sauruses. He set his feet and braced his body against the coming blow from the charging sauruses. He had tightly strapped his shield, with its pointed buckler, to his left hand for defense. His bow held in his right. Neither weapon was an appropriate close range defense against the saurus thundering toward him.

Tuller stepped next to him, gripping a short sword tightly in his hand. Durrban wore a grim look on his face. He gripped his sword tightly in his fist. Seenger cocked his arm back ready to throw his spear at the last possible moment.

At the sound of a whirring noise behind him, Tanden glanced over his shoulder. Gadon and I-Sheera spun slings above their heads. Both let loose their rocks at the same time. Gadon's rock shot straight up into the sky, thumping harmlessly back into the soft dirt. I-Sheera's shot slapped hard into the nose of the saurus on the left. The startled saurus shied sideways into Seekin's saurus. Dirt and mud on the slippery slope gave way under their feet. Tangled up with each other, they slid and tumbled to the ground, spilling their riders into the wet grass.

Seenger, Tuller, and Durrban rushed forward as one, weapons at the ready.

Tanden shouted to Gadon, "Flank them."

Tanden circled to the right and I-Sheera followed him. He pulled another arrow from the quiver and notched it to the string.

Seekin rolled quickly to his feet, sword in hand. The other rider was half a step too slow and found Seenger's spear pushed through his midsection. Durrban's quick stroke finished the man. They turned to see Tuller and Seekin standing face-to-face, sword-to-sword.

"Cowards," Seekin taunted them, "It takes six of you against one lone man? Don't you have the courage to face me one-on-one?"

The sauruses, unhurt, rolled to their feet.

"Grab the sauruses," Tanden called without taking his eyes off Seekin. The Hummdhar feinted a lunge at Gadon as he darted toward the sauruses. Tuller, Seenger, and Durrban had him corralled, but they did not move forward because the little barbarian's sword seemed to flash everywhere at once.

Gadon grabbed the halter of one saurus, holding the beast steady. I-Sheera managed to get one hand on the halter of the other saurus as it shied away from her. Refusing to release her hold, it tossed her through the air, swinging the woman's feet in a wide arc. She held on tight. Her feet hit the wet grass and slid as the saurus backed away. The woman balled her free hand into a fist and slammed it onto the nose of the wild-eyed lizard.

"Stop it," she shouted. The saurus stopped in its tracks, shivering, but it obeyed.

Tanden wondered where she had learned to control the giant lizards with such authority. He shook his head, clearing the thought. Now wasn't the time.

"Come on, cowards," shouted Seekin. "Who will be the first to die?"

Tanden cut short further taunts as his arrow burrowed deep into the man's chest. Seekin looked down at the arrow fletchings protruding from his chest. Tanden walked up to him and took his sword from his hand as the dying man waved it weakly at him.

Tanden said, "Coward or not, I don't care what you think of me." Placing his left hand on the arrow shaft for stability, he slashed the sword blade deeply against the Hummdhar's throat. As the barbarian's weight fell to the ground, Tanden's grasp on the arrow shaft drew it from the dead man's body.

Putting the arrow back into his quiver, Tanden said, "That'll teach me to finish a job the first time. We don't have time to spare, my friends. The rider he sent back will bring more Hummdhar warriors. Gather what we can quickly."

Tanden untied the sword sheath from Seekin's waist and strapped it on. Neither Seekin nor the rider Seenger killed were archers. Tanden trotted over to the third dead man. He was disappointed to find a broken bow, but satisfied he was able to add more arrows to his quiver. There was nothing else of any use on the dead man.

Durrban mounted the saurus Gadon captured and moved to hold the head of I-Sheera's saurus as she awkwardly climbed aboard. She held the reins tightly in both hands. Durrban talked quietly to her in a calming tone as they rode over to Tanden who was looking around the dead saurus for any weapons the rider had dropped.

Gadon and Tuller trotted up to the group. Tanden turned to look for Seenger. The ogre was already lumbering up the hill toward the edge of the forest. Gadon whipped out a short knife and without hesitation, slashed into the flank of the dead saurus.

I-Sheera turned her eyes away from the butchery.

Tanden asked, "What in the names of the six moons are you doing?"

His arms already bloody to the elbows, he looked up at Tanden. "Fixing a fine midday meal, if we ever get a chance to build a fire."

"Or even if not," Tuller added. Tuller stripped the tunic off the dead man and tossed it to Gadon.

The heavyset man wrapped two large bloody chunks of saurusmeat in the shirt, tied the shirt securely, and tossed the bundle up to Durrban.

Tanden said, "Two of us should ride each mount. The remaining two can run. As the runners tire, they can trade places with a fresh rider. We won't travel as fast as our pursuers, but it's the best we can do with what we have available."

Tuller said, "I'm fresh enough. Seenger and I can run. But first, we have a small message to leave for those who follow us." He stepped over to the dead man, raised his sword high and chopped through the man's neck, severing the head.

Tanden looked away from the grizzly scene. Butchering a dead saurus for dinner was one thing, but to mutilate a dead man, even an unredeemed barbarian, seemed particularly gruesome.

"Gadon," Tanden commanded, "Up with Durrban. You'll form a trio with Tuller. I-Sheera, slide forward. I'll ride with you and we'll trade off with Seenger. It's a good enough plan for now, though we may change it quickly as the situation changes."

He vaulted up behind the woman. Wrapping his arms around her, he took the reins from her hands and buried his heels into the sides of the mount. The saurus moved forward in a quick walk, a motion Tanden found reminiscent of a rolling ship. He wanted to spur the saurus into a run and just keep moving, but I-Sheera obviously was not used to riding saurusback. He thought it strange that she had shown such a sure hand with a half-wild saurus, yet obviously had never sat astride one. Now was not the time for personal histories. He needed to keep Seenger close, in order to change riders when the ogre grew tired. Ogres were strong and did not tire easily, but running was no more their strong suite than swimming.

Near the top of the slope, he stopped the saurus next to Seenger. The ogre had chosen three saplings standing apart from the forest. Using a short sword, he stripped the limbs and topped them, to form sharp pointed stakes about five-feet tall.

I-Sheera stared at the scene in fascination. Tanden watched in surprise and shock as the ogre picked up Seekin's severed head from the grass at his feet. With no fanfare, he drove the head down onto the point of one of the saplings. Seenger twisted the head around until the lifeless eyes stared back down the slope facing the direction they had come, and more importantly, the direction any pursuit would come. Seenger drove a second head onto a point and twisted it around. The eyes were closed, so he poked at the eye lids until they stayed open, staring across the clearing.

Tanden had witnessed the brutality and barbarism of war. He had seen men do things that a reasonable person would deny men were capable of doing. This casual mutilation of a dead body was more than he had ever witnessed. It did not seem right. He was not all that surprised at Seenger, who was little more than a barbarian, could do such a thing. He was shocked that Tuller would willingly participate in the mutilation of dead bodies. He was also surprised by I-Sheera. She had turned away from the butchery of a saurus, yet now watched human butchery with interest.

Tanden struggled to keep the quiver out of his voice when he asked, "Seenger, is this your idea?"

Tuller said, coming up behind them, "No. This is Grandfather's idea." Tuller tossed the third severed head to Seenger. It spun blood through the air, its black hair flopping.

Seenger caught the head and calmly set it in place beside the other two.

Tuller continued, "Grandfather told me of seeing heads on pikes at the gates of a Surr village in the far north. He said that to a man, none of the Holden warriors would enter the village. He said the lifeless eyes staring back at them were Holdenite and Nechepeg warriors. Behind the village wall stood only old women and young children. They were all brave men, but they passed by the easy pickings of that village. To this day, Grandfather swears the village was inhabited by devils in the shape of women and children. I don't know about devils and evil spirits, but if this gives the Hummdhars pause, then it's time well spent. Besides Tanden, these men have no more use for their heads."

Tanden said, "Truly, I must spend more time talking to your mother's grandfather."

"Besides, this one," Tuller patted Seekin's head, "left me to that young animal back by the river. He deserves no better."

Tanden agreed, but found it difficult to be as casual as Tuller.

Gadon said, "My butt is already sore from sitting on this oversized goat. Are you two going to stand in this rain and cold talking about something that's already an accomplished fact or are we going to get moving? You two old women would stand around gossiping all day if it weren't for me."

Tanden was about to tell Gadon to shut up when the thundering sound of running sauruses cut through the air. Without looking back or waiting for a command, the group headed into the forest. Tuller and Seenger ran ahead while the others following closely on saurusback. Tanden was immediately frustrated at their slow pace, but additional speed was not possible. To his amazement, the runners were easily able to stay in front of the mounted riders. A saurus had to maneuver around objects that a man on foot could make his way through and over. Still, at this pace, the running men would tire soon and have to trade places with riders.

He felt sure this was the first time I-Sheera had ridden a saurus. She grabbed the bony ridges along the saurus's neck, holding on tight with both hands. She slid precariously from side to side as the saurus moved at a fast walk. A trot would have unseated her in a breath's time.

Tanden said to I-Sheera, "Grip with your legs, girl. No, higher. Bend your knees more. Move when the saurus moves." Tanden gripped her tightly around the waist with one hand, holding the reins with the other.

The group moved down the reverse slope. Reaching the bottom, they crossed a creek before they heard shouting from the hill behind them. Twisting around Tanden could not see beyond a few yards. He pointed up the forward slope and Tuller and Seenger scrambled to follow his gesture. The sauruses took a different route, picking their way around trees and boulders.

Tanden looked behind him at the rocky forest floor covered with dead brush, limbs, and leaves. A good tracker would follow his group with little difficulty. However, in doing so, any pursuer would move slower. The sauruses and runners reached the top of the slope at the same time, crested the hill, and began down the other side. Seenger and Tuller were breathing hard. Each man needed and deserved a rest, even if it was short.

They had barely gone far enough to drop below the hillcrest when Tanden called a halt. "Durrban, you two go over there." He pointed at the top of the next tree-covered slope. In the small valley between the next two hills was a large open clearing, if he remembered correctly. "Straight down here. Circle around the clearing. Stay to the edge of the forest and then angle to the right up the next hill. Move, we're right behind you."

"Down. It's our turn to run. Follow Durrban." He said to the woman. Grabbing her upper arm, he swung her free and dropped her to the ground. "Tuller, come here." He tossed the saurus's reins to him and slid off the lizard's back.

"I'm fine," Tuller said. "I can run farther."

Tanden flared at the man, "Don't argue with me now, damn it. Ride or find your own way." He instantly regretting speaking harshly to the man, but wasted no time apologizing. Tuller and Seenger mounted and without a word followed after I-Sheera.

Rather than follow right away, Tanden ran back to the hilltop they had just crested. Standing against a large tree so as not to silhouette himself against the sky behind him, he stared through the rain-darkened gap between the hills. He caught the movement of milling men and sauruses on the hill where they had left the three heads. He heard shouting and arguments from the group, but in the poor light, through dense trees and with Hummdhars spread out below the crest of the other hill, Tanden could not tell how many were following them.

Suddenly, a group of seven or eight riders wheeled onto the top of the hill, fanning out as they crashed through the forest toward the creek below. Some of the riders appeared to be heading straight for Tanden's hiding place. Before turning to run, he saw another half dozen Hummdhars crest the opposite slope, turn their sauruses westward and disappear out of his sight, moving at a full gallop.

Tanden turned away and followed after his crew. His sped downhill so fast his feet were barely able to keep up with his body. Crashing through the brush, he passed Tuller and Seenger with a bound, leaping over a boulder and a fallen tree the two riders were going around. In a shower of mud and wet leaves, he slid to the bottom at the same time Durrban, Gadon, and I-Sheera reached it.

A risky plan came together in his mind. If they were successful, they would be free from immediate pursuit. He signaled them to hold up until Tuller and Seenger reached their position.

Catching his breath, he told them what he had seen of the Hummdhars. "Tuller and Seenger," he continued, "have cut their forces in half with that trick of putting the heads on those poles. Thank you, men. I doubted it at the time, but it was good thinking."

Gadon said, "Good thinking, unless the ones coming after us are twice as angry as they were before."

He replied, "Well, Gadon. I'm counting on their being so angry their hearts overrule their heads." He went on to explain his plan.

CHAPTER NINETEEN

Cold rain was driving across the open meadow in sheets as Tanden lay on his back in the middle of the open meadow. Hastily positioned brush concealed the shallow, muddy depression he was using for cover. Holding his bow tightly across his chest, he stacked the remaining arrows around him within easy reach and notched an arrow on the bowstring. He set his sword off to the side, as he would not need it right away if his plan worked. He had given his shield with the pointed metal buckler to Gadon.

He listened to the shouts of the Hummdhars riding toward Gadon and Durrban. The two sailors were afoot and racing across the center of the clearing toward the forest's edge. Try as they might, the two men were too far away to reach the safety of the trees before the riders overtook them. They stopped and stood alone, armed with sword and shield. Tanden could picture what the barbarians were seeing—a pathetic, little old man and a fat man dressed in tatters.

The last he had glimpsed of the pair, Durrban was trying to draw magic from the surrounding grass and bushes as he ran. Collecting and condensing what he could, Tanden doubted the man could focus and concentrate on his magic with armed Hummdhar soldiers rushing to ride them down.

Tanden hoped the group would not trample him as they rode forward to kill Gadon and Durrban. He also hoped I-Sheera was able to hide and Tuller and Seenger were safely clear with their two sauruses. The urge to jump up and run to his two men was strong, but he resisted. He did not dare give his position away. In any event, the Hummdhar riders were so close at this point, he could not run the hundred yards fast enough to reach his men without being killed.

The sauruses pounded past him, their wide padded feet slapping wetly across the muddy terrain. Rising quickly to one knee, he snapped an arrow at the back of the rearmost rider. It pleased him to see the man crumple and drop to the ground. Rather than revel in the success of his first shot, Tanden picked up another arrow and let fly. His second arrow found its mark in the back of a second Hummdhar saurusman. As he notched a third arrow, he saw the lead saurusman flip backward. The man did not release the reins and his weight dragged his saurus's head backward. Saurus and rider went down in a tangle, scattering the others, causing another saurus to stumble and spill its rider.

He knew I-Sheera's sling and rocks had caused havoc again. Her aim was true to the mark. He saw her standing in the meadow to his front left. He had positioned them to give his arrows and her rocks the best crossfire possible against the Hummdhar saurusmen.

Tanden let fly his arrow into the mass of riders without aiming. He looked to the forest's edge to his right rear. Charging full tilt across the field in a flanking movement was his cavalry. Seenger held his spear at the ready. Tuller held a long sharpened pole.

Tanden let another arrow sail into the riders. When he saw a rider splinter off from the group, he thought he had wounded the man or saurus. But the Hummdhar sat firmly on his saurus, riding straight for I-Sheera.

Tanden grabbed another arrow and put it to the bowstring, but before he could shoot, a yell caused him to turn. He ducked quickly and felt the swoosh of a long sword cut through the air above his head. The rider pounded past him turning his saurus in time to catch Tanden's next arrow. The injury unseated the man. The arrow shaft was protruding from his thigh. The Hummdhar still held the reins in one hand as he lay screaming on the ground.

Tanden grabbed another arrow and notched it to the bow. The riderless saurus blocked his view of where I-Sheera last stood. Tuller and Seenger crashed into the flanks of the two remaining mounted Hummdhars sending riders and sauruses sprawling in every direction. In the pouring rain, Tanden could see only two men still seated on sauruses. He could not tell if they were his men or not. Gadon and Durrban should be moving together to take on any Hummdhar knocked off his saurus. He believed they had the sense to avoid a fight with any mounted opponent. They should encounter enough unseated riders to keep them busy and win any fight if they watched each other's back.

Tanden held his bow with a notched arrow in his left hand. He swept up two extra arrows and put them across his mouth, biting down on the shafts. His clutched his sword in his right hand. Leaping out of the mud hole, he ran toward the injured man. He looked down at the two riders he had shot earlier, as he passed. The first man lay unmoving, an arrowhead protruding from his chest. The second man was clawing his way toward the forest, pulling himself through the mud and grass using only his arms. An arrow was stuck in his lower back just above his unmoving legs. Tanden ran by without stopping. His concern was for the living. He would deal with the dead and dying later.

The wounded man Tanden was running toward had dropped his sword as he fell from his saurus. He attempted to reach the weapon, but could not stretch far enough. The man had tied his saurus's reins around one wrist and the saurus drew back as Tanden ran directly at him, keeping the reins taut, jerking the injured man's hand away from his sword.

Tanden sank his sword into the man's throat, the dull blade jamming against bone. Blood spurted from the wound, but washed away quickly in the rain. He left the sword where it struck, with the hilt pointing skyward. He stepped forward, drawing his bowstring taut. Sauruses and men lay tangled and twisted around him. He was not archer enough to shoot into a melee without hitting one of his own men, even if he could determine who was whom.

Shifting his gaze to I-Sheera's location, Tanden discovered the Hummdhar had not run the girl down on his first pass. He was turning his saurus for a second attempt. I-Sheera was on the ground and slow getting up, a short sword in her hand. Tanden knew he was not good enough at this distance in the pouring rain to shoot the saurusman. He watched as the rider heeled his saurus into a run toward the lone woman.

Tanden's heart cried out for her, as a breeze blew mist and rain in a curtain between them. She had become a valuable member of his small band of crewmen. Her loss would diminish them, him most of all. Just as he was about to shout, the wind blew a small hole in the clouds and a flash of sunlight highlighted the girl. He could see her clearly again.

At the last possible second, I-Sheera jumped sideways, ducked low to the ground and spun around. Her clothing and long black hair spun rain and mud in a wild arc following the stroke of her sword. She reached out slashing across the tendons of the saurus's hind leg. A bone-chilling shriek filled the air as the saurus tumbled to the ground. Its fall threw the rider free. As he hit the ground, his forward momentum caused him to slide in the mud and muck of the drenched clearing, unable to regain his feet.

Running past the saurus, deftly avoiding its flailing feet, I-Sheera leaped onto the Hummdhar. She drove her sword into his back, pressing downward with all her weight to drive the point through the man.

Tanden tossed his bow to the ground and almost as an afterthought, spit out the extra arrows. He reached down, pulling his sword free from the dead man's throat. Grabbing the reins of the saurus in his left hand, he cut the reins free from the dead man's wrist. The saurus sidestepped away from Tanden, but he was able to grap a handful of neck and threw himself onto the animal's back.

Turning the saurus toward the melee in the middle of the field, he rode toward the center of the mass. The battle was over by the time Tanden's saurus skidded to a halt. He looked around him at the remains of the Hummdhar tribesmen. His crew had taken them by complete surprise. Their focus had been on the two unimposing men. The three-pronged attack from the rear and both flanks had thrown them into utter confusion. I-Sheera's sling sent them into complete disarray unseating the two foremost riders. Tuller and Seenger had ridden into the two remaining saurusmen.

The saurus Tuller had ridden lay on the ground unable to regain its feet with both of its front legs shattered. Tuller reached down with a knife and mercifully cut through the saurus's throat. Seenger remained mounted. His spear was deeply imbedded in the midsection of a body on the ground. Tuller's homemade lance lay in pieces near another body.

Through the thick rain, Tanden saw Gadon and Durrban leaning against each other, resting on the ground. Around the two men were two dead bodies. One of the dead had a sword jammed in his ribs. The other man lay at odd angles to himself, his back broken and twisted.

"Tuller. Seenger," Tanden called out. "Gather as many sauruses as we need." Looking around he saw two of the animals milling about, oblivious to the death around them, munching casually on the abundant grass. Some of the sauruses had bolted, but they had not run far. They should be able to catch a saurus for each of them.

Tanden turned his saurus toward I-Sheera. Through the driving rain, he could not see her. His saurus splashed through the meadow, making muddy puddles in the standing water. He spotted the woman sitting in the grass, cradling a wounded saurus's head in her lap. Riding up to her, he looked down at her in amazement. A small cut on her scalp caused a thin trickle of blood to flow across her face. It washed quickly away in the rain, mixing with her tears.

He did not know what to say to her. This girl, who had killed two men in two days and watched three men being decapitated with curiosity and without flinching, sat in the mud and cold rain crying over a wounded saurus.

"*The easterns breed strange women,*" he thought.

The wounded saurus grunted at his approach, looking wild-eyed, and starting to kick, but it calmed as I-Sheera stroked its face. She shushed the animal and rocked its head gently in her lap. She looked up at Tanden, her face streaked with blood, tears, and mud. Her eyes pleaded with him to do something. A small cry escaped her lips as Tanden shook his head slowly from side to side.

Tanden prepared to dismount, but she stopped him by picking up her sword. She laid it against the saurus's throat. With a stifled sob, she yanked the blade deep, across and out. With a little shiver, the saurus lay still, its life's blood flowing out across the woman's legs.

Gently, she slid out from under the saurus, laid its head in the wet grass and with an open palm closed its eyes. Tanden watched as she walked over to the dead Hummdhar. She jerked at the man's tunic, stripping him to the waist. Without a word, she walked back to the dead saurus and covered its head with the clothing. She stepped to Tanden and offered her hand to him.

Gripping her wrist, he lifted her up behind him. She wrapped her arms around his waist and buried her head against his back, hugging him tightly. He felt, more than heard, a ragged sigh. He turned his saurus back toward his crew. Tanden stopped when he realized only one man was standing in the middle of the battlefield. From the bulk he knew that the lone man was Gadon. Turning to look about him through a break in the rain, he saw

Tuller and Seenger on sauruses heading toward them. Each man had another mount in tow. He could not see Durrban anywhere.

"Where is Durrban?" he called.

Gadon pointed to a small body crumpled on the ground and said simply, "He used his magic to deflect a sword meant for my back. The blade turned aside, but he didn't have enough power to protect both of us."

Tanden nodded without saying anything to Gadon. The outcome was better than he expected. He wasted no wishes on Durrban. He had been a good man and would have to find his own way to the afterlife, as they all would. Maybe his green priests would use their magic to speed him on his way to the world after this one once they learned of his death.

Tanden looked down at his friend, "And you?"

"Alive," Gadon said. He looked back at the dead sailor and shook his head. "Best I could do for Durrban was to take revenge on the son of a snake who killed him." Gadon pointed to a Hummdhar lying in the grass.

He continued, "I broke his back with my bare hands. He still lives." Looking up to Tanden in defiance, he said, "I intend to leave him that way. Alive and helpless."

Tanden nodded, "It isn't my concern."

Gadon looked at I-Sheera and then gave Taden a questioning look. Blood was obvious as it mixed with the rain and ran off her body from her waist to her boots.

Tanden shook his head. "Most of it isn't her blood. Climb down, girl. Let Gadon look to your head wound."

"No!" she shouted. Calming noticeably, she said, "Sorry, Captain. Would you do it?"

Tanden looked at the woman in surprise then looked at Gadon, who shrugged back. He said to her, "I'll do it. But, I thought you liked Gadon?"

"Never mind. Just forget about it," she said. "I'm fine." She slid off the back of his saurus and went to sit in the mud next to Durrban's body.

Tanden shook his head, baffled by the woman.

Gadon said, "Women are more problem than they're worth, Tanden. I've told you that a hundred times but you just don't listen. As a matter of record, you don't ever listen to me. Remember that time in Allexia? I told you not to go down that back alley, but would you listen? Oh, no! And who had to follow after you and save you from that angry crowd of Eyyians? Me, that's who!"

Tanden leaned over the man and said, "As I recall, my friend, they'd come looking for you. Something about improper advances to the wrong man's daughter?"

"Oh, that's gratitude. I save your life and you blame me?"

Tuller and Seenger cut off Tanden's reply as they rode up to him. Each man had gathered weapons as well as sauruses. Seenger tossed a small bag to Tanden. He looked inside and saw a jumbled pile of smoked meat and dried fruits. He pulled out a large slice of meat and handed the bag down to Gadon. The four chewed quietly as Tanden looked around at the carnage.

Tanden bit into another piece of the smoky meat and chewed. He was unable to identify the type of meat they were eating, but he was hungry. Anything would do. He looked skyward, blinking as the rain pelted his eyes. The sky showed no sign of clearing. If anything, the wind looked to be moving the clouds around more than ever. Everything was so wet they would be unable to find dry wood to cook the hunks of butchered saurus meat still hanging on Seenger's saurus. Besides, as stringy and tough as the smoked meat was, Tanden thought it might be saurus anyway.

Finally, he spoke, "We must move on again. What happened here is done! We put it behind us and once again move toward the White Wind."

The men nodded, although Gadon looked over his shoulder at I-Sheera still sitting next to Durrban's body. No one wanted to leave a comrade's body to the scavengers. Tanden would not be able to face the man's wife and children unless he rightly cared for Durrban. They would have to find some safe resting place for the man.

"Search these men for anything we might find useful. Gadon, find something to wear before you're so undressed you embarrass us all. I'll deal with the girl and Durrban soon enough." Tanden wheeled his saurus around and rode back to where he started the battle. Alighting from the saurus, he retrieved his bow and arrows from the ground near the dead man.

Pausing only briefly to take another bite of smoked meat, he squatted down and searched the man's clothing. He found a small knife and sheath. Digging deeper, he found a small pouch of beads and a worn piece of flint. The flint was useful and the beads might make nice trade goods. He stashed the pouch in his shirt and the knife into his trouser's waistband.

Tanden picked up the man's long sword. Without a sheath, it would be awkward to carry, but he stuck it under the leather strap holding the sheath for his short sword.

He walked to where he had last seen the wounded man with paralyzed legs. His trail through the wet grass was easy to follow and he found him lying face down only thirty feet away. The arrow's fletching in his back pointed skyward. Tanden rolled the Hummdhar over onto his side. The man had driven the point of his own knife through his heart. Tanden pulled the knife free. It was rusty and of poor quality, so he tossed it into the weeds. Stepping around the man, he grabbed the arrow and pulled. The arrowhead grated on bone and the shaft snapped.

Tanden shook his head at the loss. *"Maybe the others will find more arrows."*

He took another bite of the smoky meat and began searching through the man's clothing. He had just about given up when he found a small pouch hidden in the top of one boot. A polished emerald set in carved ivory inlaid with intricate patterns of gold dropped into his hand from the pouch. Tanden was unable to fathom why a man would kill himself with a rusty knife on a muddy battlefield when he carried such a precious item that could have bought him a wife and a home. He placed the jewel in the larger pouch with the beads and stashed it back in his shirt.

He walked over to another dead man and grasped the arrowhead protruding from the man's chest. Pulling steadily, the arrow came through and popped loose with a sucking sound. Tanden swished the arrow in a puddle and calmly placed it in his quiver. He found nothing else useful on the man. Last of all, leading the saurus, he walked back to the depression to retrieve his quiver containing half a dozen arrows.

Tanden finished the slice of smoked meat on the walk back to the others, leading his newly acquired saurus. The meat only slightly eased the hunger in his belly and its saltiness brought his thirst to the forefront. Leaning his head back, he opened his mouth wide allowing the cooling rain to fall into his mouth, doing little more than wash away the salt, but it would do for now.

Tuller tossed him the food bag as he walked past the three men. He continued on until he stood next to the girl. He tucked his saurus's reins under a rock and sat down next to her. Setting the bag of food between his legs, he reached in, pulling out two pieces of dried fruit. He popped one into his mouth. The other he put into her mouth.

I-Sheera leaned against him, turning to put her hands on his chest. Tanden put his arms around her. He was not used to comforting women, but it seemed like the thing to do. He was not sure his arms were a help to her, but it felt good to him. He searched through her scalp as she leaned against him. When he finally located her wound, he dabbed carefully at it with a small piece of cloth he tore from his tunic. The rain mixed with the blood to flow freely, making the cut look more serious than it was. He cleaned it up as best he could, straightening the matted hair away from the wound. It would leave a scar when it healed, but he was sure no one would see it hidden in her mass of hair.

He swished the cloth in a puddle near at hand. Wringing out most of the water, he tilted her head back and wiped her face clean. When she lifted her eyes to him, he smiled and gave her a quick wink.

She smiled back, sighed, sat upright, and reached for the food bag.

Tanden stood up and stepped over to speak to Durrban's body. He said, "Thank you for saving Gadon. I swear I will take care of your family. You've done service to me for years and even now. Good-bye, my friend."

Tanden looked up from the dead man, into the eyes of the Hummdhar warrior with the broken back. Hot, angry eyes glared back at him.

Tanden said in the man's own tongue, "You still live then?"

"I'm a dead man. Still, I'd take you with me if I could."

"I don't doubt you'd try. Hummdhars have tried to kill me before, but I'm here and you're there."

"You!" the man spat. "You're the one? The killer of women and children?!"

"And worse. I hear you were looking for me? Well? Here I am."

"Coward!"

"That's a matter of viewpoint. And from where I sit, there doesn't seem to be anything you can do about it, does there?"

"I swear by any life left in me, my son will take my vengeance on you."

"That would be Bransch?" Tanden asked. At the man's surprised look, he could see Seekin had not told this man the whole truth. "Oh, maybe you have another son? No? Well then, I'm sure Bransch won't cause me trouble in the least, certainly not in this life, and I don't believe I'll see him in the life to come."

The energy seemed to drain from the Hummdhar. "Kill me then and be done with it."

Tanden said, "You aren't mine to kill, or you'd already be dead." He turned his back on the man. He bent down and picked up Durrban's body. He draped it over his saurus and turned to his men gathering around him.

"Gadon, why are you still barely dressed?" Tanden asked. Before the heavyset man could respond, he continued, "I imagine we'd have to sew two sets of clothing together to make one to fit you. Or we could catch and skin an oliphant."

Over Gadon's shouts of protest, Tanden asked, "Tuller, did you find any more of that strong wine among these men?"

"No," replied Tuller. "We do have a few swallows left from the bag we had last night."

Tanden smiled, "Good. Pass it around while it lasts."

The Hummdhar croaked, "Kill me, I beg you."

Gadon asked, "What's he saying?"

Tanden shrugged, "Nothing important. He asks to die."

Gadon said, "He will. Oh, he will die, in good time. From thirst, or hunger, or eaten alive by animals. But not by my hand."

Seenger tapped Tanden on the shoulder and handed him the wine bag.

"Girl?" Tanden gestured with the bag for her to join them. When she stood by him, Tanden handed her the bag. Each in turn took a swallow and passed it around. Gadon got the last swallow. Before drinking, he raised it in Durrban's direction.

Gadon said, "To Durrban. A good man. May he get to the next life on favorable terms!"

Tanden said, "Pick a saurus. Let's mount up and get moving. I want to find a resting spot for Durrban soon."

135

With five sauruses and five people, Tanden was sure they would be able to make good time to the south coast of the isthmus. He helped I-Sheera mount while Seenger held the saurus's head. She still looked uncomfortable, but she reached down and stroked her mount's neck.

Tanden grabbed her leg in both hands and bent her knee. He slid it forward onto the saurus's shoulder. Once in place, he patted her on the thigh. "Squeeze here."

She smiled down at him. She put her hand over his as it rested on her thigh.

"Thank you, Captain," she said. She gave him a quick wink, reined her saurus about, and headed after Gadon and Tuller, who were already halfway to the forest. Tanden mounted his saurus, holding Durrban's body before him, and followed. Seenger brought up the rear.

They put Durrban's body in a small crevice on the side of a rocky hill. It only took a few moments to cover the opening with stones. They left no marker and said no words, it was quickly and quietly done.

CHAPTER TWENTY

A whoop, a shout, and the whiz of an arrow passing his ears persuaded Tanden to dig his heels into the ribs of his mount. He shouted a warning to his companions riding ahead of him. Branches whipping around his face prevented him from saying more.

His saurus was not fond of him and for most of the past hour took an inordinate pleasure in running under the lowest branches it could find. The dense forest would keep their pursuers from getting a good shot at him. He ducked and twisted, lying as low on his saurus's back as possible. He grabbed a handful of neck and urged the saurus on to its greatest possible speed.

Tanden saw two riders on his right. The men wore clothing like the Hummdhar warriors, but they shouted in a language he could not understand. They turned toward him. He pulled his long sword from his waist and angled away from the riders. There was another rider to his left. The man shot an arrow at Tanden. It thumped into a tree missing him by inches. He heard his people ahead of him crashing through the forest. As the rearmost rider, Tanden's task was to keep the enemy from the backs of his men.

Tanden hauled in his running mount. Reining hard, he rode straight at the archer to his left. The man was unable to notch another arrow and loose it before Tanden sped past him. Tanden slashed the long sword across his body as he sped past. There was a slight jerk on the sword hilt, but no solid contact. He missed both man and saurus.

He spun his saurus about again. Driving his heels into its ribs, he shot forward, directly at the archer. The man had thrust his wooden bow at Tanden's long sword on the first pass. The bow, now useless, was the contact Tanden had felt. Tanden looked into the man's face, seeing only a frightened boy's eyes. This was not a warrior to be put to death easily, but a child sent to do a man's duty.

At the last possible moment, Tanden angled away and slashed through the reins on the boy's saurus. The startled saurus shied sideways into a tree, spilling the boy on the ground before bolting off through the forest. Before Tanden could pull the sword back to his side, he brushed a tree and lost his grip on the sword as the blade sank deep into the bark.

Tanden looked up and braced himself for contact with the two riders bearing down on him. Unable to pull a new weapon before he crashed into the two men, he grabbed a double handful of neck and sat as upright as the mast of his ship. He faced his mount at the two riders. He would only have to fight one man at a time if he could maneuver his saurus to one side at the last minute.

He reined his saurus violently at the last second. His saurus leaped to the right, putting both riders on Tanden's left. A blade sang through the air at his head. Tanden ducked backward. The blade slipped past his nose. Kicking to the side and upward, Tanden's foot connected against the midsection of the swordsman. The recoil almost unseated Tanden. His kick did not knock the other rider off, but did send him reeling against the other man, sending that man crashing to the ground.

Tanden pulled his short sword from its sheath and spun his saurus around for another pass at the two men. The unseated man rolled on the ground, cradling his head in his arms. Tanden could see the mounted man clinging desperately to the back of his saurus, bounding off through the forest.

Tanden wheeled his saurus again to the south, urging the animal to a run. Holding tight with his legs drawn high, he flattened his body against the running saurus's back. Limbs and branches slapped and scratched at him. Tanden and his saurus broke into a small clearing near the top of a hill. The sight of his friends rewarded Tanden.

They had stopped and turned to face the forest. Tanden shouted the command to get moving over the hill. He was not concerned about the three men he had fought, but where there were three, there might be more. He raced past them. Tanden crested the hill and saw why his men had stopped. The downward slope looked almost vertical. His saurus, unable to stop, continued over the edge. Tanden clutched at the saurus's neck. He leaned as far back on the saurus's haunches as he could stretch while remaining seated. Sliding down the hill, the saurus appeared to sit down as it braced all four legs against the slope. Loose muddy dirt and rocks sprayed every which way showering them.

Motion seemed to slow until Tanden felt as if he and his saurus were sitting still and all the world was sliding backward, up the hill, moving past them and not the other way around. Tanden glanced over his shoulder to see I-Sheera's saurus leap over the edge. Tuller and Seenger quickly followed her. Gadon's saurus slipped over the edge as if it was moving forward against the will of its rider.

Tanden looked at the valley in front of them. Surrounding a village in the center of the valley were large, cultivated fields. Although the rain had stopped, no one was working in the fields. All the villagers stood at hastily built defensive walls. He was unable to tell if the villagers were Hummdhars or Coodhars, nor did he know which tribe had chased his little band over this hill, though he assumed they were Coodhars because of their language. Not that it mattered which group was which. An old Holdenite saying stated: the only way you could tell a Hummdhar from a Coodhar was to ask and then you could expect them to lie.

To the right was a shallow river splitting the visible part of the valley by one-third. A large concentration of men sat at the far edge of the river ford, huddled around their noon fires. A few men stood guard facing the village. Both sides of the conflict were bundled tightly against the biting wind blowing from the northwest out of the mountains.

To Tanden, it looked like a standoff, equal forces taking time out from a battle to huddle down against the changing weather and partake of a midday meal. He realized the group of Hummdhars they had encountered earlier in the day must be reinforcements for one group or the other. Those reinforcements might have changed the balance of power in the fight for or against this village. Those reinforcements were now less than half their expected strength. Undoubtedly, this village was the key to controlling the whole peninsula.

Tanden felt, more than saw, the slope changing angle, beginning to curve outward, giving them less and less of a downward angle. He looked behind. Gadon's saurus was coming down the slope, skidding along without a rider. Gadon clung to its stubby tail with his legs churning through the soggy dirt.

I-Sheera had almost caught up to Tanden. Her saurus, completely out of control, looked like if it was flying. The woman had thrown herself forward around the saurus's neck. The top-heavy animal finally lost all balance and began tumbling head over hoof, throwing the girl forward. She landed on her feet, running downhill. The saurus tumbled behind her, its feet churning through mud, wet grass, and air. Any second she would be rolled over and crushed.

Tanden released one hand from the saurus's neck. Stretching for the woman, he grabbed a fistful of leather bunched at her chest. She jumped toward him as he pulled her up behind him. Tanden felt his saurus gathering control of its legs again as it leaped forward and away from the tumbling animal.

The sauruses were now running more now than sliding down the tree covered slope. Gadon had somehow vaulted onto the back of his saurus. I-Sheera clung to Tanden's back, refusing to watch as her saurus crashed to a stop against a tree. Tanden saw her saurus rise again to all four legs and shake itself free in a cloud of flying mud.

Continuing their momentum downhill, Tanden did not stop for I-Sheera's saurus. He was sure both armed camps in the valley below saw them. They were five riders on four sauruses now.

The hillside flattened to the valley floor just at the tree line. Not slowing his saurus, Tanden jerked the reins, steering a course straight to the river ford. The others followed closely.

A group of eight or ten mounted men from the village dashed after them, trying to cut them off or cut them down before they could reach the river camp. The village riders shouted curses and showered them with arrows. Tanden knew, as did everyone in that valley, that shooting an arrow from the back of a running saurus and hitting a man on a racing saurus was nothing but chance or luck, good or bad, depending on your point of view. Ignoring the arrows that fluttered harmlessly about them, Tanden and his group raced to the ford.

Shouts of encouragement from nearby men urged Tanden's people toward them. Gambling that he read the situation right, Tanden shouted a common Hummdhar greeting, calling for help. Half a dozen mounted Hummdhars thundered out of their camp, running their sauruses straight at the pursuing Coodhars. Tanden did not swerve from his course.

He heard a clash of swords and sounds of battle behind him. He guided his saurus at a full run through the river, sending water splashing in every direction. One of the men standing guard by the river, looked strangely at Tanden, but ducked and turned away from the spray caused by the saurus. The other men in camp focused their eyes on the fight going on in the middle of the valley. A large group of Hummdhar warriors quickly armed themselves and ran past Tanden's group, heading to assist their comrades.

Almost everyone in the Hummdhar camp ignored Tanden and his men. In turn, Tanden's group ignored the men in the camp. They continued on, urging their running mounts through the middle of a hostile force. One man shouted at them to slow down, but he quickly turned his back to the wind and re-focused his attention on a leg wound, daubing it with river mud to help stop the flow of blood.

The angle of their flight across the valley turned them to the west. Tanden wanted to be out of sight before he turned south again. They might be able to avoid further pursuit by either tribe if they could get out of the valley without being recognized. Just inside the tree line, Tanden rode into a group of men riding the opposite direction. Not slowing, Tanden shouted at the men in Hummdharian.

He said, "Full attack from the village. Circle north to flank. We'll circle south." He did not slow down for a response, not offering them the opportunity to recognize his group. He reined his saurus to the south. Rather than circling around, he continued to drive his mount up the side of a hill and down the other side.

Once out of sight of the valley, he pulled up to a stop. The saurus beneath him was blowing hard. He asked I-Sheera, "Are you all right?"

The woman nodded against his shoulder. She was almost as out of breath as the saurus beneath them.

Tanden said, "Seenger, look behind us to see if we're being followed." He signaled the other men to watch around them.

Tanden believed the village was a Coodhar settlement, under siege by Hummdhars wanting to move into the peninsula. The three men he had fought on the hill were Coodhar, probably working their way around to flank the Hummdhar camp. If there was one group of Coodhars in the forest, there may be others.

He also believed the group of riders he spoke to at the edge of the valley was the remnant of the Hummdhar replacements. He did not know whether they had turned aside at the sight of

Seekin's severed head or because they were under orders to reach this camp without delay. However, he did know it would only be a matter of time before the fighting wore down and someone in the Hummdhar camp put it all together, figuring out who had run through their camp.

Seenger came back from the hilltop behind them. He said, "I can see no one following, for now."

Gadon said, "Good. Now Tanden, just what it the name of my great aunt's saggy tits was that all about? We could've been cut to pieces down there. I plan to live a long time yet, and I don't see how I can do that with you running around jumping off cliffs and running through a troop of armed barbarians!"

Tanden said with a smile, "It looked to be the quickest way south. It would've taken us too long to ride around such a little bump of a hill and then to stop and kill everyone in that valley. Remember, I have somewhere I want to be. Besides, I don't know what you're complaining about. Your saurus did all the work."

Gadon snorted, "Maybe. But I did all the worrying."

Tuller said, "Should we try and make a deal with the Coodhars? From what I could see, it looked as if that village blocked access to most of the open land of this whole region. They may provide us the easiest access to the south coast of the isthmus."

Tanden replied, "Maybe they can. But, right now they don't look like they're in the mood for opening negotiations. Back on that other hill, Coodhars set upon us. Unless poking holes in strangers is their way of saying "Let's talk." I don't think we have time to work out a deal for passing through these lands. Remember, we're racing for the White Wind."

Tuller nodded, "True." They could still hear the sounds of the fighting from the valley. He said, "Besides, it sounds like we started a little fuss back there."

Tanden said, "Good. The longer they're busy with each other the longer we have to hide in these forests and the hills ahead."

Gadon added, "And the more of them that kill each other, the better for Holden. I don't care who lives on this wretched spit of land, but I do know a lot of men back home won't be happy to have Coodhars or Hummdhars living this close to our trade routes. They're more pirates and smugglers than settlers and that's bad for business."

None of their sauruses had caught their breaths, but Tanden decided not to delay any longer. He wanted to put as much distance between them and the warring groups as possible. Gesturing with his hand, he reined his saurus southward and worked his way down one hillside and up the next. As the group crested the hill, the found themselves silhouetted against the sky. The wind had blown the clouds clear leaving a bright blue sky beneath a hot early afternoon sun. The day turned suddenly from cold and wet to hot and humid.

A shout from behind them to the west jerked their heads around in unison. A dozen armed men were angling up the hillside towards them. From that direction, Tanden believed they were Coodhars who were circling around behind the Hummdhar camp, like the first group he fought north of the valley. Hummdhar or Coodhar, it did not matter. These men were ready to ride them down and kill them.

Tanden wheeled his saurus southward. Followed closely by the others, he fairly flew down the slope, putting distance between them and the men chasing them. Once they started up the next slope and the men behind started down this one, the gap would close. It could fatally close. Two people on his saurus severely hampered them and they would not be able to outrun any hard pursuit. They skidded to a stop at the bottom.

Gadon shouted, "What way, Tanden? Up, right, or left?"

Seenger said, "Or do we fight the bastards right here?" He grinned in ogre-like anticipation of another good fight.

Rather than answer, Tanden turned to the right and began working the saurus through the small gap between the hills. They moved in and around rocks, boulders, and trees. They weren't able to see the men chasing them, but they could hear them shouting to one another. He was sure they would send out flanking riders to each side. As long as they kept moving, any rider moving up the slopes of the hills should not be able to catch them.

Tanden kept pushing to the left, always striving to keep their direction to the south, constantly attempting to swing around the hill on their left. Shortly, their direction was to the south and a choice of courses lay before them. The next choice was between two high hills with south directly between. The two steep-sided hills would force their pursuers to follow the same path. The other way appeared to circle back toward the valley.

Without hesitation, Tanden moved into the gap between the two hills. *"Maybe,"* he thought, *"the Coodhars will think we went the other way."* Soon, they heard sauruses and shouting behind them. Tanden was surprised the Coodhar's had not caught up with them yet. His saurus was all but finished. Carrying two people at a run for so long had all but worn out the poor creature. It stumbled often but kept moving. The heat and humidity were like steam, tearing at all of them.

Tuller shouted, "Tanden, I think we're being herded."

CHAPTER TWENTY-ONE

Tandend looked at the high walls around him. They had been well and truly funneled into a canyon. He caught the sight of a Coodhar rider's shadow across the rock walls, pacing them on the rim.

Tanden called back, "Herded or not, we must keep moving. Look for a place to defend ourselves."

Gadon yelled, "Let's fight them now. In this canyon, they can't get at us more than a few at a time."

Seenger shouted his agreement.

"No," Tanden called. "Keep moving."

Tuller added, "Tanden's right. We're in the open here. They won't have to close in on us. They can shoot us from the rocks above."

"Great!" Gadon called. "What does it matter? I'm going to die of hunger and thirst before they catch us. That is, if the back of this pile of walking bones doesn't do me in first."

The canyon twisted and turned, becoming more and more pinched. They were riding single file, as there was barely room for two sauruses side-by-side. The afternoon sun's heat was coming at them in waves off the rock walls.

Tanden knew dehydration was setting in. He had stopped sweating. I-Sheera clung limply to his back, her head hanging in the muggy air. The saurus's tongue hung long and limp from its mouth as it gasped for air.

"There!" Tanden shouted. He pointed to a jumble of rocks ahead of them. A cluster of caves and depressions in the cliff wall should give them temporary shelter from arrows fired from the canyon rim. They had to take refuge now. None of their sauruses could carry them much farther, even if the canyon had an outlet ahead of them.

"Get into the caves. If they want us, they'll have to dig us out face-to-face." He grabbed I-Sheera by her arm and swung her to the ground.

She scrambled up the hill, ducking into a cave mouth closest to the canyon floor. Three or four smaller openings surrounded the cave entrance. Gadon and Tuller followed her closely, running toward the same cave. Both men's hands were filled with weapons and bundles. They ran up the side of the pile of rocks, with the practiced, sure feet of veteran sailors, a trait learned from years of climbing rigging on the rolling deck of a ship at sea.

Before Seenger could follow them, Tanden said to him. "Seenger, let's get these animals turned around. If we send them back out the way we came in, it may slow down our pursuit. Also, I don't want any saruses killed here. I don't have any desire to be stuck in a cave in this heat with a dead saurus within nose range."

Dismounting, the two quickly had the four saruses turned. They were standing two-by-two with their sides almost scraped the rough rock—effectively blocking the canyon. Tanden waited a moment until he was sure the Coodhars were right behind them. Shouting, he and Seenger slapped the rumps of the four saruses. Three saruses shot forward, running easily without the weight of riders. Tanden's saurus just shivered and stood.

Tanden pulled the small knife he had taken off the dead Hummdhar warrior earlier in the day. Apologizing softly to the saurus, he jabbed it deep in the saurus's flank. Startled, the saurus jumped forward from the pain and ran after the other saruses. Tanden wiped the blade on his trouser leg and re-sheathed it.

Seenger looked from Tanden to the canyon where the saurus had disappeared and back to Tanden. The ogre nodded his appreciation and turned to climb into the caves. Before he reached the opening, an arrow shattered on a boulder next to him.

Tanden squinted up at the high canyon rim. He could not return an accurate shot from his own bow, even if he could clearly see the archer. Both he and the ogre bolted into the cave without looking back.

Transitioning from the bright light of the canyon into the darkness of the cave blinded Tanden for a moment. He tripped over something and found himself lying on the cave floor with great puffs of dust settling around him. He shook his head to clear the dust away and looked into the eyes of Gadon, lying beside him.

Gadon said, "Oh, this is just wonderful. We're being led around this wilderness by a man who can't walk upright on his own two feet. Here I am, Tanden, parched with thirst, roasting in an oven and you decide to shower me with dust."

Tanden replied, with a smile, "My friend, I see you aren't so parched that you've lost your voice."

"True, true, all too true," Gadon said. "But everything else is wasting away to nothing. I'm going to be down to skin and bones before the sun sets. And hiding in this cave is going to do nothing for my skin. Why, in here I'll turn as pale as a newborn baby's bottom!"

Tuller laughed, "When have you ever seen a newborn baby's bottom? I've yet to meet a woman who would take you for a husband. Certainly, I've never met a woman who'd want to have your children. I shudder to think of what your offspring would look like."

"Me? My children?" Gadon sputtered. "You impudent young pup. By mother's beard, I've known more women than you've ever seen in your short life."

Tanden said, "It's true, Tuller. He has known many women in his life. And if he had all of the money back that he paid for them, we'd all be wealthy beyond our years."

Gadon looked at Tanden with mock pain on his face, "Ganging up on me now? Yes, I may have paid for a wench or two in my time, but they both gave me my money back. They said they couldn't take payment from a man of my talents. So, what have you two to say to that?"

Tuller glanced outside, squinting into the sunlight, "My eyes must be deceiving me. It must be a moon in the night sky and not the sun, because you, my big brother, and I do mean *big*, must be dreaming."

I-Sheera hesitantly spoke, "I think Gadon is quite a handsome man. I know many women who would consider themselves lucky to have such a man as a husband."

"Ha!" Gadon shouted in triumph.

Tanden and Tuller looked at the woman and then at each other. Both men watched Seenger move next to I-Sheera. The ogre put a huge hand on the woman's forehead. He wore a puzzled expression as unmoving as stone when he announced, "She has no fever. Must be delirious from lack of water."

Tuller roared with laughter. He said to I-Sheera, "Now you say something about wanting this uncouth brother of mine for a husband, when it's a little difficult to leave you two alone?"

"Wait. No, no wait," she said, "I didn't mean...I meant that. I...no, I didn't mean *I* wanted to have his children. I just said I knew women who *would* want Gadon for a husband."

Tanden was relieved everyone was joining in on the good-natured banter. It meant that in spite of the difficult position they found themselves in, they were in good spirits and still had more strength left than he would have imagined.

Tanden said, "Girl, you must have strange friends. When we get home, you find one of them for Gadon. He hasn't found a woman yet who could put up with him for longer than one night."

Gadon crawled back to the entrance to the cave and peered out, "I might as well go back out and face the barbarians. You, who are supposed to be my friends, will have me married to a fishmonger's widow before the day is out. What about my children then? I suppose they'd look like carp."

Tuller said, "Well-fed carp, by any standards."

Gadon waved a hand, cutting the conversation short, "We have visitors coming to call."

Tanden's eyesight had adjusted to the dimmer light of the cave. It was not large, but bigger than it appeared from the canyon floor. All the openings they had seen led to the same small cave. It was about eight feet high at its tallest point. For the most part, a man did not have to stoop to move around. To the rear, the cave narrowed and a tunnel disappeared into the darkness.

Standing up, he moved to the right. Stepping up a small rise to a higher opening in the cave wall, he untangled his bow and quiver. Looking into the bright light reflecting off the rocks, he counted only two men moving toward them. He could not see the canyon rim from his vantage point.

He said, "I see two. One by the rocks below and one sliding along this side of the wall."

Gadon said, "I see two also but they're in the rocks below. I can't see your man along the wall." He turned to I-Sheera who had come up next to him, "Girl, get back. I don't want you getting hurt."

Tanden said, "Leave her be, Gadon. She's stood us in good stead to this point."

Gadon nodded acceptance and gestured for her to take a place at the opposite side of the opening.

Tuller said quietly from another opening, "I can't see anyone below, but I can see half a dozen above us on the rim."

Seenger stood quietly in the shade, gripping his sword at the ready.

"I think," Tanden said, "we have Coodhar after us. They must've known about this canyon and drove us in here to bottle us up, so they can pick us off from above. Those we see in the canyon are the few they used to chase us in here."

Gadon replied, "Fine. Their three against our four—"

"Five," I-Sheera interrupted.

"Five," Gadon corrected with a nod in her direction, "Their three against our five is no contest. We kill these few and get out of this oven."

Tanden said, "Sorry, my friend. You forget the archers on the rim. They're in good shooting positions. We couldn't go ten feet before we'd have arrows raining down on our heads. No. I think we're well and truly cornered. We're under siege, all they have to do is wait for thirst to drive us out into the open."

Gadon said, "Fine. But tell that to these three here. They're getting ready to charge."

Tanden agreed, the men were working themselves up to rushing the opening. He notched an arrow to his bowstring and took aim at the man along the wall. The man's position was only partially exposed, but he was more accessible to Tanden than the other two. The man would expose himself fully to rush the cave opening.

Tanden heard Gadon and I-Sheera's slings begin to whirl awaiting a shot.

"Patience, people," Tanden said. "Wait for them to come to us."

The men were so close he would not be able to get more than one or two arrows away before they reached the cave entrance. He glanced sideways. Tuller and Seenger had braced themselves, with swords in their hands, ready when and if the men reached the mouth of the cave.

All three Coodhars began shouting and cursing. Tanden heard shouts of encouragement from the rim above, but held his shot.

Tanden said quietly to himself, "How thoughtful of them to announce their intentions."

Gadon, overhearing the comment, replied with sarcasm, "Oh yes, we must remember to thank them later. Maybe we can invite them over for dinner and a beer."

Suddenly, all three Coodhars rushed toward the cave. Tanden let his arrow fly sending his target sprawling on the ground. Tanden knew his shot missed the man's torso, but he could not see where he hit him. Instead of wasting time looking, Tanden notched an arrow and fired at the other man he could see. As he let his second arrow go, Tanden saw his target get pelted with stones. The man turned and sprinted toward his fallen companion.

Both uninjured Coodhars lifted up the wounded man who had an arrow stuck in his leg. He was unable to run unassisted, but the three men scooted quickly away on five legs. They ran out of sight around a bend in the canyon. Tanden's shot may not have been immediately fatal, but he saw there was damage enough. Depending on the angle of the shaft, the man could die from any number of causes. Tanden had seen men with similar wounds die from loss of blood within minutes, or from broken bones that did not heal, and some whose legs went numb. He had even seen men with lesser wounds die from decay, simply rotting from the inside.

"Tanden," Gadon called. "Do you want to tell them they're supposed to just wait for us to die of thirst? I'm sure that'll be any time now."

Tanden said, "They were just testing us to make sure we weren't going anywhere. I don't believe they'll rush us again for quite awhile. They'll let the heat work on us before they risk any more of their people. Tuller, you're on look out. The rest of us should move farther back in the cave. It'll be cooler the deeper we move into the dark."

"Oh, better and better yet," said Gadon. "For all we know this cave is inhabited by trolls, or maybe goblins, or maybe this is the opening to a dragon's lair. And you want me to walk blindly into the dark?"

Tanden replied, "Well, Gadon. If you're afraid, we can have the girl hold your hand. Besides, goblins live in forests and mountains. This cave is much too small to house a dragon of any dangerous size. And trolls, well, you should be able to smell them long before they attack. Do you smell any trolls?"

Gadon looked askance at Tanden. He was apparently unable to determine whether or not Tanden was joking with him. He said, "No. But I've never smelled a troll before. Have you?"

"Certainly not. But how many times have I told you that you should read more? Why I've read several books that talk of the smell of trolls! By all accounts, they smell like rotting cabbage and burning stinkweed."

Gadon said, "All right. If we get eaten by any creature of the night, I'm never going to listen to you again." He snorted, "Books! Ha! Waste of good drinking time, if you ask me." Gadon walked toward the tunnel at the back of the cave. Everyone noticed that he walked cautiously, with his sword at the ready.

Tanden smiled at his friend's back. He propped his bow and quiver against the wall near the cave mouth so anyone could reach it in a hurry. Turning to Tuller and said, "We'll spell you out of the heat before too long. If any of those men out there speak Holdenish, maybe you can talk them into letting us walk out of here."

Tuller said, "Not very likely. Any trade involves a fair exchange. At this point, we don't have anything to offer." Watching the others retreating, with a sly smile and a wink he said loudly, "Maybe you can bring me some troll or dragon skins, then we might have something to offer."

From inside the cave tunnel, Gadon's voice echoed, "I heard that."

Tanden walked carefully along the uneven floor of the cave, hunched over and stooped inside the tunnel. Gadon and Seenger were already sitting with their backs to the wall. The tunnel was noticeably cooler, but neither man moved farther back than the light traveled directly from the cave mouth. I-Sheera was standing near them looking for a comfortable place to sit. Tanden walked past them.

Tanden had long since stopped believing in trolls, goblins, and other monsters that come out of the dark—still, he quietly drew a deep breath before stepping around a sharp bend in the tunnel. Standing still, listening in the darkness, Tanden released his breath. The light was much dimmer, but it was considerably cooler. Little light and less heat reflecting off the canyon walls reached this part of the cave.

Tanden's eyes adjusted quickly. He could see quite a distance. He sat down on a rock with his back to the cool rock wall, wincing as his bruised and torn skin touched the hard rocks. It seemed like such a long time had passed since he climbed the cliff by the sea and been gnawed at by dragonettes. In the constant rush of events, he had almost forgotten how bruised, battered, and tired he was. The cool temperature of the rock comforted his aches and pains.

He sighed, mentally berating himself, *"What have you done? By your stubbornness, you've not only trapped yourself, but you've trapped the others with you. Why am I such a fool? Do I really think I'm something I'm not? Maybe if I'd never been born, these people wouldn't be cornered here with me and Durrban might still be alive to see his grandchildren again. Maybe if the midwife had bashed my head in when I first arrived, none of this would have happened."*

"No!" he argued with himself, *"No, no, no. The alliance between King Krebbem, leader of Holden and the Red Wizard would have happened anyway. Another captain would've mastered the White Wind. Maybe the others would've died sooner. No. I'm not a fool. I know there's a way out of this."*

Quieting his thoughts, Tanden closed his eyes to the dim light. Full of hope, he set his thoughts on the task ahead, thanking the six gods for helping him get this far. Even if the moons were not listening, a little wishful thinking could not hurt. He focused his thoughts on solid believing images of victory. Not fantasies or daydreaming but clear mental pictures of success that could only do good, helping him to keep his goals clear and his path toward those goals as straight and narrow as he could plan them.

A rattle of stones and the shuffle of feet startled Tanden back to alertness. He was not sure whether he had been thinking or had fallen asleep. He was not even sure how much time had passed, although the sunlight reflecting on the opposite wall did not look like it had changed at all.

I-Sheera stood before him. Tanden gestured for her to sit next to him.

They sat for a few moments not speaking. Tanden could sense she wanted to talk, but he decided not to press her. She would speak when she was ready. Whether she spoke or not, he was enjoying the cool rest and being near her.

Gadon called, his voice echoing down through the cave, "Tanden. Are you hungry? I'm starving and I've decided to eat."

Tanden replied, "Do you plan on chewing your own nose? Or have you decided to go troll hunting?"

"Ha!" Gadon shouted in triumph, "That shows what you know. Any child could tell you that you can't eat trolls, the meat is too tough to chew. Well, ogres might, but not humans." He poked Seenger in the ribs.

Tanden laughed, "Then don't joke about food. I'm hungry enough to try troll meat."

"Me too, my friend. But our good ogre companion here has reminded me that we have a fine cut of saurus rump just ripe for eating."

Tanden had forgotten all about the saurus meat Gadon had butchered in the morning. He thought, *Was it only been this morning? It must have been.*" He had only eaten a few bites of smoked meat and dried fruit all day. He said, "You don't have a fire to cook over, Gadon."

The heavyset man sounded far away. "Seenger doesn't care if it's cooked or not. Neither do I. Go hungry if you're so finicky."

"No," Tanden called. "Don't eat it all, I'm on my way." Tanden started to rise.

I-Sheera said, "Sit, Captain. I'll bring your share."

Tanden nodded and settled back onto his rock. Tilting his head back against the tunnel wall, he closed his eyes. He was tired, but not as sleepy as he should be. He rested quietly until the girl brought him a handful of sliced saurus meat. The meat was not as raw as he imagined. Hanging next to the heated side of a running saurus for most of the morning had warmed it.

I-Sheera seated herself next to him and began chewing on her meal. She looked up at him twice as if to speak, but said nothing.

Finally, Tanden said, "Speak, girl. You have a question?"

Between bites, she said, "Yes, Captain."

"I think you should call me Tanden over such a fine meal." He was no longer surprised at how much he had come to like the girl. She was certainly not the most beautiful girl he had ever seen, but she was more attractive than conventional standards dictated. She had proven herself in more ways than he could remember in the last two days. His feelings toward her had started changing with the stabbing of the mutinous dog Obert back on the White Wind.

"Captain, I can't call you by name. It isn't proper."

"Why not?" he asked. "Maybe in your country a girl wouldn't call a man by name, but we aren't in your country, or mine, for that matter."

I-Sheera said quietly, "I'm just a maid and you're a master, it wouldn't be right."

Tanden shouted into the cave, "Does anyone here look on this girl as a servant or a slave?"

A chorus of "no" echoed back to them.

Tanden said, "Neither do I. Whether you've been a servant or a slave in the past, from this day forward it doesn't matter. I give you your freedom."

I-Sheera said, "I'm bonded to Lady Yasthera il-Aldigg. I'm not yours to set free."

Tanden said thoughtfully, "You were on a Holden vessel under my command. Did your mistress do anything to save you from being cast into the sea to drown?"

I-Sheera shook her head, "No."

Tanden continued, "I thought not. She probably sat there and peed on herself. By Holden law, any master who doesn't protect and care for his property doesn't deserve to own property. Besides, Yasthera il-Aldigg is a woman, if I'm not mistaken, in your country, women can't own slaves, land or even hold the bond on a servant. You weren't given to King Krebbem or his kin. Therefore, the moment you left your country, you stopped being a slave. You're a servant girl by your own desire, if you choose to be a servant, but you aren't property."

"Please, Captain, don't tease me. I don't want to be a maid or a servant, but I don't know what else to be."

"Call me Tanden, girl. That's my name."

"Why? You've never called me I-Sheera. That's my name."

Tanden thought for a moment and then said, "I-Sheera. It's a nice name. I like it. Call me Tanden and I'll call you I-Sheera. I'll even set you free from being a servant."

"Stop teasing, Captain."

"No, I-Sheera. I'm telling the truth. Say my name and prove me."

"Tanden. There I said it. Tanden. Tanden. Tanden."

He laughed. Reached into his tunic, he pulled out the small pouch he took from the dead Hummdhar. He dangled it in front of her, holding it over her hands.

She placed the remainder of her meal in her lap and with a questioning look, gently took the bag. "What is it?" She asked.

"It's yours. Look inside, see what it is."

The girl loosened the drawstring and peered inside. The light was too dim to see what was inside the bag. Shaking it gently into one hand, out spilled a few of the worn beads into her palm. She held her hand out to catch more light.

A small "oh" escaped her lips. She said, "They're pretty. Are they valuable?"

Tanden laughed and said, "No. Not particularly. All the beads in this bag strung together wouldn't buy you more that two pigs and a goat, at best, and skinny pigs at that."

I-Sheera's eyes grew wide with awe, "Two pigs and a goat? Don't tease me. I've never had that much. They are mine? Really?"

"Really. Everything inside that bag is yours to do with as you please. Look farther."

She looked at him quizzically and emptied the bag's contents into her open hand. A few more beads dropped into her palm along with the green, ivory, and gold jewel he had taken off the dead man. It caught the light, sparkling and shimmering even in the dimness of the cave. Her mouth dropped open. She tried to speak, but nothing escaped her lips.

She cupped both hands around the bag, the beads, and the jewel. Scrambling to her feet, mindless of the remainder of her meal, she scooted around the corner, moving back into the main cave. She carefully cradled the jewel in her hands all the way to the light.

Tanden picked up the dropped saurus meat. Dusting it off, he bit into it and chewed. Rising to his feet, he followed the woman up the tunnel. As he drew next to her, I-Sheera opened her hands revealing the green gem surrounded by a handful of beads. The inlaid gold reflected shafts of light across the roof of the cave. The polished ivory glowed deeply, reflecting the colors of the old worn beads, as if in envy.

I-Sheera said, "I've never seen such a jewel. Not even in the courts of the Red Wizard. It must be worth a magician's ransom."

Tuller said, "May I see?"

I-Sheera looked to Tanden and asked, "Can I show him?"

Tanden snorted in mock gruffness, "Why ask me, girl…I mean, I-Sheera? It's your bauble. Do what you want with it. Gadon, come on up and take your brother's watch."

I-Sheera offered her open hand to Tuller like she was afraid to touch the jewel with her fingers. The light refracted across the cave roof in whirls, winking in and out with each movement. Tuller gently took her hands in his and carefully twisted them, moving the light around the cave.

Gadon glanced at the jewel on his way past, raising one eyebrow at Tanden in question. He shrugged and moved on to the cave mouth, settling down to watch the canyon.

Tuller said, "May I?" He poised his fingers over the gem to pick it up, looking questioningly into I-Sheera's eyes. At her nod, he laid it in the palm of his hand, rolling it gently with a finger. With a practiced eye, he evaluated its value, both practical and artistic.

After a moment, Tuller said, "Tanden, this is a work of beauty."

Tanden replied, "Aye. I thought so. Such a beauty should go to buy I-Sheera her freedom from any man's service. Do you think it's worth enough to support her?"

Tuller stepped closer to the cave entrance and squatted down next to Gadon in the bright light. "What do you think, brother?"

Gadon said, "I think it would support all of us for a lot of years. I also think our good Captain Tanden has been holding out on us. We've been his good and loyal friends for more years than any of us can remember. Yet, he doesn't give us gifts. What do we get for our troubles? Raw meat and hard rock. Tanden, Mother always said that you were no good."

Tuller didn't take his eyes off the jewel. "Yes, she did. Fortunately, neither one of us ever listens to Mother. If we'd listened to her, we'd be in the manure and farm tool business."

Gadon said, "Oh? Like that would be worse than this day's been? Ha!"

"Tanden," Tuller said, finally looking up at him and the girl, "The emerald is nearly flawless, the gold is some of the purest I've ever held, and the ivory isn't from an oliphant. It's from a giant sea beast. I've only seen this ivory from traders in the very far north. See how it glows? That's just the value of the parts. The jewel is worth far more than the parts alone. It's been carved, molded, and polished by a master jeweler. Gadon, this is the business for us, not manure."

Tuller continued, "I-Sheera. This little trinket won't just set you free from serving others, but you'll be able to have servants of your own. If we ever get out of here, I know people who'd buy this. I can get you a good price."

Gadon said, "We can get you a good price, for a small fee, of course."

"Of course," Tuller agreed. He offered the jewel to I-Sheera.

She shook her head and backed away waving her hands. "I can't take it. It's too much. I wouldn't know what to do with it. Please, Captain."

Tanden said, "No. It's yours. It's a gift." He took the jewel from Tuller and dropped it back into her hand. As he spoke, he turned her hands and poured the jewel and beads back into the pouch he was holding. He pulled the drawstring closed and folded her fingers around the bag. "You can't return it. I won't take it back. You do what you wish with your gift. This jewel can set you free from servitude, but freedom takes work. You decide. You can leave it here in the dust. You can keep it and do nothing with it for your entire life. You can save it. When you marry, you can give it to your husband and marry well."

Gadon said, "In that case, I may change my mind about letting you have my children."

Tuller turned, heading toward the back of the cave. Over his shoulder he said, "I-Sheera, if you decide to ever sell your prize, let me know, I'll be more than happy to see that you get your best price." He walked past a sleeping Seenger, continuing toward the cave tunnel until he was out of sight.

I-Sheera looked up at Tanden, "Thank you, Tanden."

Gadon said, "Tanden, if you're giving out presents, I'd like a drink of water. My mouth is as dry and dusty as the corners of my grandmother's heart."

Tanden said, "I would that I could, but I have no water to give."

Gadon pointed at the bag in I-Sheera's hand and said, "Last I knew, you didn't have any riches to throw around either. You're always sending wishes to the six gods. Call on them now asking for water for your parched friends."

Tanden smiled, going along with the joke, "Ah, you mock me once again. You still doubt the power that confession of belief yields receipt of confession? That's too bad. One day you'll see that a man's own thoughts, determination, believing action, and the confession of his beliefs can accomplish as much as a few moments of magic."

Gadon shook his head and continued watching the canyon.

I-Sheera asked, "Captain...Tanden, can I watch you call upon the six gods? Or do you have to do that in private? I don't know anything about the six gods."

"Follow me."

They returned to their seats in the dim tunnel. Neither noticed that Tuller was not there. Tanden sighed as he leaned back against the cool rock. He only had one slice of meat left. He offered it to I-Sheera.

She shook her head, clutching the bag to her chest. "Can I ask you a question?" she asked.

Tanden answered, "Of course, you can ask. Whether I answer or not is yet to be seen."

"When you call upon your gods, how do you know they listen?"

Tanden smiled, "Gadon jokes. There's no one to answer. The six gods are a myth, the old beliefs of ignorant savages worshipping the six moons in the sky. I do it more as a way to focus my own thoughts than as a supplication or meaningful worship to any deity. It's believing action that brings about what I desire."

She looked at Tanden with wide eyes, "You must be a god yourself. You always know what to do, where to turn. We wouldn't be alive today it weren't for you. You never waver or doubt. You're always there to show us the way. You…you pull riches from the air, like magic." She held the pouch up as if it was proof of her statement.

Tanden laughed, "No, I-Sheera. I'm just a man like the others. I have doubts and worries like every man. Scientists and magicians alike have tested me many times, but I don't have any magic or magical skills. However, I know above all, I serve a goal that guides me forward."

I-Sheera said, "In my country, no one speaks to a maid of their gods or their magic. They say their gods are too busy to hear the cries of someone like me. Everyone knows magic is useless in the hands of women."

"I don't know the limitations of the Red Way, or Blue, or Green for that matter. I do know that everyone has the ability to control their thoughts to help bring about their own desires."

"Even me?"

"I-Sheera. Good thoughts don't care whether you're a man or a woman, a slave or free, rich or poor. Control and focus work for everyone, they're required for using magic. They aren't any less necessary for controlling your thoughts."

"Teach me?" she pleaded. "Show me how to think."

Tanden took the pouch from her hands and hung it around her neck by its drawstring. He took both of her hands and folded them in his. He closed his eyes and spoke quietly, remembering how their lives had been saved over the past few days, how they had been saved from the hazards they encountered, and lastly, how they must find water to drink.

Tanden finished, "Water. We must find water."

I-Sheera was quiet for a second. Taking a deep breath, she asked, "Water? Yes. Where do we look for water?"

Tanden thought for a few moments but didn't have an answer. He was about to speak when Tuller shouted out of the dark tunnel. "Tanden? I've gotten turned around in the darkness. Call out to me."

"Tuller?" Tanden shouted. "Where are you?"

"Keep talking, Tanden. I can follow your…ouch…I hit my head. I can follow your voice out of the dark."

Tanden shouted, "Tuller, sometimes I don't know which of you is more of a problem: you or your brother."

From the cave mouth, Gadon's voice echoed back to them, "I heard that."

Tanden continued shouting, "Tuller, I would've thought you'd have enough sense to not go wandering around the dark in a strange cave. What's the matter with you? Have you lost your mind? And to think that your mother calls you the smart one."

Gadon shouted again, "I heard that, too. Keep it up and I'm going to have to come back there and thump someone."

Tanden shouted again, "Tuller, I can't come find you in the dark. Can you still hear me?"

Tuller stepped into the dim light where Tanden and I-Sheera sat. He said, "I can hear you quite well, Tanden. There isn't any need to shout in my ears." When Tanden started to speak, Tuller cut him off, "I know it isn't wise to explore too far into a dark cave, but I found water."

CHAPTER TWENTY-TWO

Tanden asked in surprise, "What? You found water where?"

Tuller rolled his eyes, an expression of exasperation apparent even in the dim light, "What do you mean where? Where could I have gone? You've been hanging around Gadon too long. That question is so stupid I would expect it from him." Tuller paused briefly. He cupped his hand to his ear, and said, "No, I guess he didn't hear that one."

Tanden prompted, "Water? Remember? Or am I going to have to throttle you to find out what you're babbling about?"

Tuller said, "When I stepped around this corner, I thought I would see how far I could walk into this cave before there wasn't any light. I moved slowly on my knees, with my left hand along the side. Once I had gone where I couldn't see the light, I thought I could go farther if I kept my hand along the side. Then, it looked brighter ahead. It was like the light was drawing me forward. I thought I'd gotten turned around and crawled in circles. Tanden, I hadn't gone backward. There was a crack above in the cave letting light leak into a small cave. There, in the light, was a spring, with cold, clear water bubbling up from the ground. It formed a little pool and flowed off through a tunnel back into the hill. Clean water truly more delightful than any wine I've ever tasted."

Tanden asked, "Can you take us there and find your way back again? I don't want us lost forever wandering around in the dark."

Tuller said, "I'm ashamed to say I became so excited that I did get turned around. I thought to follow the tunnel back using my left hand on the wall."

Seenger, having heard, came back. He crouched down next to them and said, "So?"

Tuller explained, "When I went into the cave I had my left hand on that wall." He reached out and patted the wall at his back. "But when I turned around, I followed with my left hand on this wall." He turned around and demonstrated what he meant patting the opposite wall.

Tuller continued, "Switching walls was foolish of me. We follow the left hand in and follow the right hand out. Tanden, there's enough water for all of us. I think the Coodhars outside will have a long wait for us. Better yet, we take everything with us and we move back to the pool. When they get tired of waiting for us, they may sneak down to look into the cave. They'll find us gone like we disappeared. I've heard the Coodhar are as superstitious as the Hummdhar. I don't believe they'll follow us into the dark for fear of Gadon's trolls or worse. They may believe that one of us is a wizard and he's transported us out of their reach. Once they see we're gone, they may leave, and we can escape."

Tanden felt I-Sheera squeeze his hands. He realized he still held her hands in his. Neither Seenger nor Tuller gave any indication they noticed, yet Tanden was sure neither man could have avoided seeing. He should let her hands go, but he did not release them.

He looked down at her with a questioning look, "Yes?"

I-Sheera whispered to him, "The water. You asked for water. It comes from your thoughts? You have made it appear like magic?"

Tanden said, "Almost, I-Sheera. All good things come to those who seek rightly and believe. I have no talent for magic."

He turned to Tuller and Seenger, "Gather up everything we brought into the cave. We'll leave no trace of our presence. It should completely baffle the Coodhar."

Seenger added, "Captain. We can rub out our footprints in this dust. If we're careful, it'll look as if we'd never been here. I fear little in my life, but I wouldn't go into a dark cave to follow a man who leaves no tracks."

Tuller nodded and patted the ogre on the shoulder, "Seenger, you're a strange one, but I like the way you think. If everyone in your tribe is like you, I wonder how Holden ever defeated your people."

Seenger turned to gather up their meager possessions and said, "I have often wondered the same thing."

Tanden followed his men back into the light. He collected his bow and quiver, sliding them over his head onto a shoulder to leave his hands free. Looking around the cave, he could not see anything they'd brought with them that had not been picked up by Tuller and Seenger.

Seated at the cave entrance, watching the canyon, Gadon glanced back occasionally at the three men. All the while, he berated Tuller for walking into the darkness and becoming lost.

Tuller cut his brother's tirade short when he said, "I found water."

Gadon hesitated, speechless for a moment, and then said, "Really?"

Tuller fixed an exaggerated frown on his face and said, "Oh, Gadon. I didn't want it to ever come to this, but Mother told me years ago that she found you under a rock, that you aren't my real brother. I've lied to you and to everyone else by calling you my brother. I wouldn't lie to you about finding water at a time like this."

Gadon replied, "Baugh! Under a rock indeed. Someday, someone will teach you to respect your elders, boy."

Laughing with Tanden and Seenger, Tuller said, "If I ever respect my elders, you'll be first in line, old man."

Tanden explained to Gadon their plan to hide by the spring beyond the darkness. Gaving him a hand to help him stand, they moved out of Seenger's way. Removing his tunic, Seenger dragged it around in the dust, effectively removing any trace of their passage.

Gadon jabbed Tanden in the shoulder with a stubby finger, "See, Tuller found water before your gods came to provide us any."

Tanden locked an arm around the shorter man's head, rapping him lightly on his forehead with the knuckles from his free hand. "Gadon," he said, "I know that you may find this hard to believe, but did it occur to you that the six gods put that spring there for Tuller to find? Or, that maybe Tuller is an instrument of their will?"

Gadon wriggled free and replied, "Tuller? An instrument of the six gods? Ha! Without me to guide him around by the hand that boy couldn't find the ground with his butt when he sits down."

Seenger called out, "Clear."

The four stood at the back of the cave looking toward the light at the entrance. It looked undisturbed.

Tanden nodded. "Tuller, lead us to the spring. Gadon, you follow close behind Tuller. We'll put I-Sheera between us. Seenger, continue sweeping the dust until our footprints disappear into the dark."

Tuller said, "Keep your heads low and crawl slowly. I banged my head once on this ceiling. Believe me; these rocks are as hard as any I've ever pounded my skull against." He crouched down and disappeared into the darkness.

Gadon crouched down, continuing after his brother, muttering, "Slowly, he says. I have shards of rocks poking my knees and scraping all the skin off my legs and he says go slow. I couldn't hurry if I wanted to. Wait! I smell rotting cabbage. Tanden, are you sure there aren't any trolls in this cave? I'm sure I smell rotting cabbage. No. Wait! Maybe not. That's just Tuller's butt. Move forward, boy. Wheeeee-ooooo! What have you been eating?"

Tanden crouched down to the floor imitating the three who disappeared into the dark before him. Putting his left hand on the wall, he ducked his head, and crawled slowly forward. He heard I-Sheera ahead of him and Seenger following closely behind. Gadon was rambling on about the temperature, the hardness of the rocks, and how generally miserable his life had become.

In spite of having his friends and crew surrounding him, Tanden was nervous. Trolls and goblins did not exist, but he had never experienced such blackness. Wiggling his fingers in front of his eyes, he could not see them. Even the darkest night had shades of dark and shades of darker. Here there were no shades at all. Tanden realized, for the first time in his life, he was not seeing the dark, but the complete absence of light. He noticed he was holding his breath, but spotting a dim glow ahead caused him to exhale in relief. He hoped no one heard his ragged exhale. It would be best for the others not to know he was afraid of the pitch black dark.

The dim light grew stronger and stronger until he could see well enough to follow the others into a small room. In the middle, lit by a shaft of light from above, was a clear pool of water. Tanden moved to the water's edge slightly to his left. Three of the others dropped to their bellies beside the pool. Gadon and I-Sheera sucked greedily at the cold water. Tuller drank only slightly less so.

Tanden scooped up a double handful of water, allowing it trickle through his parched mouth into his dry throat. He wanted to bury his face into the refreshing water, but refrained, struggling to be watchful and alert.

"Take care. We've been without water for too long. Too much, too fast and you'll get cramps. Don't come to me for sympathy if you make yourselves sick."

Seenger joined him at the pool's edge. Both slowly scooped water into their cupped hands and lifted their hands to their mouths. Both remained alert. The ogre stared back into the darkness behind them. Tanden's eyes flicked in every direction trying to see everywhere at once.

Light filtered down from a crack in the ceiling. Though they could not see the sky, it provided enough that they could see clearly. The room was ten or twelve feet high in the center and almost the same in width and length. The pool of water formed by a spring, was about a foot deep, and ran the full length of the cave, hugging the far wall. Tanden readily saw the water ripple as it bubbled up to the surface. The far end of the room split into three tunnels, each heading deeper into the darkness. The pool of water pinched into a small stream slithering down one of the tunnels.

Tanden placed a hand on Seenger's shoulder and said, "I think we're safe here for awhile. We should be able to hear the Coodhars long before we could see them if they try to follow us through the tunnel."

Gadon sat up and added, "If they could work up the courage to follow us." He hesitated and said, "Strange." The heavyset man jammed his hand into the pool and raised it again, dripping in the cool air. He moved it around a bit and repeated the process, all the while deliberately dripping water on Tuller.

Tanden quietly watched the man. He had known Gadon for so many years he knew now was not the time to distract the man from his thoughts. He watched as Gadon stood up and poked a wet hand into each of the tunnels leading out of the room. He dipped his hand into the pool again and stepped around Tanden and Seenger to reach out his wet hand into the tunnel they had just used.

Everyone was now watching Gadon move about, from curiosity or simply because he was the only thing moving.

Finally, Gadon said, "We may not have to go out the way we came in."

"What!" Tuller exclaimed.

Tanden said, "I think I understand, but explain it so we all know for sure."

Gadon reached over to his brother and slapped him on the back of the head, "Ha! I thought you said Mother called you the smart one. Not this time, boy. Any good sailor should be able to tell you which way the wind blows."

He turned to Tanden, "Airflow. I can feel the wind through the air in here. It doesn't flow from this crack in the top and down the tunnel to the mouth of the cave like you'd expect. The air flows from this crack, down the way the water flows. We should be able to follow the airflow out to another opening."

Tuller said, "You forget *big* brother. Air and water can squeeze through openings much smaller than you or me…especially you."

Gadon snorted, "That's what you think. I've been so starved and worn out for the last two days that I'm a mere wisp of my former self. I'm a puff of smoke. I'm the wind and light as air. Besides, I think I'd rather go out the way we came and fight the Coodhars than sit in this hole for two or three days until they tire of waiting on us and go away."

In a bare whisper, I-Sheera said, "The White Wind."

Gadon, the closest to her, asked, "What, girl? Speak up. You whisper so quiet you'll make me think that I've gone deaf."

She replied, "I said, the White Wind. Can we wait two or three days?"

Both Tuller and Gadon shook their heads.

Tanden said, "I don't think so. Heraclius is a poor sailor at best, but we'll miss him for sure if we wait longer than another day."

"Then we can't wait and do nothing, can we?" she asked.

Tanden nodded. She was right. He needed to regain his focus, to reset his eyes upon his goal of regaining the White Wind. Tanden reached out to her placing the palm of his hand on her cheek, cupping her face.

"Thank you," he said. "I-Sheera, that is a wise question. We haven't come this far to give up. Retreating is death. We lose the White Wind if we wait. We'll test Gadon's idea and follow the wind and water as all good sailors should." Tanden overrode objections and questions by saying, "I know it'll be dark, but we've just proven we can move from one point of light to the next. If we stay together, each person staying in touch with the one in front and the one aft, we can form a living chain to find another way out."

"Good," Gadon said. "There's no reason to delay. If we're going to do it, let's do it. Who goes first?"

Tuller poked his brother's belly and said, "Gadon should go first. The rest of us should have an easy path to travel if he can squeeze through every tight spot."

Everyone laughed. No one mentioned that Seenger was the largest.

Tanden answered, "That's a good plan, Tuller. But I think since you've already proven your success in moving about in the unknown darkness, I believe you should go first. The rest of us can follow in any order. I'll go last. If we find we can't move forward, then we can come back here and wait. We lose nothing by trying."

Gadon said, "We will too, have lost nothing! Just the effort and all the skin off my hands and knees."

I-Sheera leaned closer to Tanden and whispered in his ear.

He smiled and said, "This is no time to be shy, girl." He pointed to one of the tunnels they would not be taking. "Take your pick."

"Men, if you have to empty your bladders, do it now. I have no desire to crawl through your puddles."

Tuller nodded, "I guess this water did run straight through me." He turned and headed for the same tunnel I-Sheera had stepped into.

"Me too," Seenger agreed.

Tanden coughed loudly at the two. When they turned to look at him, he pointed at the other unused tunnel, motioning for them to use it instead.

Gadon said to Tanden, "When did you become such a prude? I can remember when you peed out the second story window in full view of a market street."

Tanden replied, "I was drunk that day, but it's not for me. It's for her. She's lived a different life than we have. You know how some easterners are about body parts."

"Crazy is what they are. They hide and shrink like they have something no one else has. What does this girl have that Tuller and Seenger haven't seen before?"

"Nothing different, my friend. Yet, I do find her special. Don't you?"

Gadon smiled, "You like this one?"

"Of course! Don't you see how different she is from other women?"

"Honestly, Tanden, I don't know what to think about her. Until a couple of days ago, I wouldn't have given a fart in a whirlwind for her."

"Me neither."

"Now...well, I just don't know. She's proven her mettle, but she changes too fast for me to follow. She's a fire-breathing warrior queen one moment and the next you'd swear she's a lost little girl. Confusing. I think I like my women a bit more simple. But Tanden, you never like anything simple. You never see anything for what it looks like. By all my father deems holy, if you want the girl, take her, and spare the rest of us from your adolescent love struck ways."

Tanden said, "Adolescent! You wouldn't know a real woman if she came up and bit you."

"Ha! That's what you think. I remember being bit once and I knew right away who did it."

Tuller exited the side tunnel. Quickly followed by Seenger.

Tuller said, "Remind me not to try that again."

"Try what?" Gadon responded.

"This tunnel is too short to stand up straight in. We had to pee bent over at the waist. Seenger practically wet his own chest."

I-Sheera startled them all when she stepped out of her tunnel and said, "Squat."

When Tuller looked baffled she said, "Squat. Next time, squat down. Your knees bend don't they?"

"Enough," Tanden said, cutting off Tuller's reply. "You can all discuss the merits of personal toilet habits at a later time. We have work to do. Before we go..." Without finishing his sentence, he pulled his knife from the sheath at his waist and sliced four wide strips from his tunic. He bound Gadon's knees with two of the leather straps and covered his own knees with the remaining strips.

Following his example, Tuller, Seenger and I-Sheera cut strips from their clothes. Each wore leather pants taken from dead Hummdhars, so their knees were protected. They bound their hands with the leather to protect them from the rocks as well. I-Sheera handed Tanden two strips of leather from her tunic. He passed one to Gadon. Cutting his strip in two, he wrapped his own hands for protection.

Tanden looked over the group as they prepared to move forward. They had been through a lot the last two days. He wondered whether he was doing the right thing by asking them to continue through the cave. They looked ragged. The strain was evident on each of them. Even the unstoppable Gadon was wearing down despite retaining his good humor. I-Sheera looked exhausted, but Tanden ceased being surprised by her strength and drive. Years of servitude and virtual slavery made her tougher than she looked. Tuller and Seenger were bearing up as well as could be expected of hardy sailors.

"Well," Tanden said. "No reason to delay. Everyone ready?"

Gadon said, "What're you asking us for? We're waiting on you. A man could die of boredom standing around 'til you make up your mind to do something. Tuller, get a move on, boy. We don't have all day."

One by one, the small band crouched down and moved into the tunnel. Soon they were on their hands and knees crawling slowly through the dark. The small stream wandered from side to side, sometimes filling the tunnel floor from wall to wall. The water had worn smooth any sharp rocks, but it was cold, adding to their discomfort.

Once again, in total darkness, Tanden thought to close his eyes. He reasoned if he could not see, then why have them open. Strangely enough, he was clumsy with his eyes shut. He bumped into I-Sheera ahead of him and even smacked his head on the ceiling. He opened his eyes again. Though he could not see a thing, he felt more in control, more coordinated. Experimenting a few times, he opened and shut his eyes at various intervals. After slipping face first into the stream with his eyes closed, he decided he would keep his eyes open, whether his vision worked or not. He pondered the complexities of the human body, a marvelously made machine.

As they crawled, he could hear Tuller, Gadon, and Seenger talking. Rather, he could hear Tuller talking, Gadon complaining, and Seenger providing a grunt or two for good measure. As close as he was to them, the distance was too far for him to follow their conversation. Tanden thought it was like a game of blind follow the leader.

Occasionally, Tuller would advise them of a low overhead to duck under or a boulder to slide around. Each person would pass the information back to the next. Tanden received his information from I-Sheera just ahead of him.

Tuller stayed close to the left wall of the tunnel. The right wall and the ceiling were sometimes close and sometimes out of reach. At times, Tanden felt sure they were in an open spot where they could stand and stretch, but they had no way of knowing in the dark without stopping to check, thereby slowing their progress. He believed, staying near the stream along the left tunnel wall gave them their best chance of finding their way to daylight and an exit. Even in the dark, cold water was an obvious road to follow.

Time passed or Tanden began to think of time passing. Without the sun, sky, or stars to give him a clue, he was unsure how much time had passed. He tried counting his paces, then realized he was not sure how far he moved with each crawl forward. He worked on counting spans of hands and counting seconds to calculate their rate of speed. When he crawled headfirst into a rock, he decided it might be better to try focusing what he was doing.

Tuller's voice rang out suddenly and then faded away from them. Everyone froze. A cacophony of voices shouted and called out to Tuller, echoing up and through the tunnel.

Tanden finally bellowed, "Quiet!"

It grew still, no one speaking. Listening closely, Tanden could hear the gentle splashing and rippling of the water, but nothing else.

"Gadon," he called, "where's your brother?"

"I don't know. We were talking and I had my hand on his ankle. He shouted for me to stop and then he was gone." Gadon's voice grew shaky. "He didn't fall, I'd swear to it. His voice faded away, but not down. His leg pulled forward out of my grasp. I've reached out as far as I can but I can't find him without moving after him."

Tanden said, "Don't move yet. Seenger, can you grab Gadon by the legs? Hold him tight."

Seenger answered, "Yes, Captain. I have him. Nothing will take him without taking me as well."

Tanden commanded, "Gadon, stretch out on your belly and see if you can reach Tuller."

After a moment, Gadon grunted and said, "I feel nothing but rocks and cold water. Wait."

Tanden listened impatiently.

Gadon called loudly, "Yes. I understand." His voice floated back to the others. "Could you hear him?" The relief in is voice was evident to all.

Tanden answered, "I didn't hear anything."

"Tuller is all right. He says we should move forward slowly. The rocks become very slick and smooth along the water. It's all downhill and he says we'll slide along unhurt until we stop. But he says we should go only one at a time or we'll pile up at the bottom."

Tanden said, "I've banged my head enough today. Did he say feet first or head first?"

Gadon's voice roared out of the darkness, "Feet first or head first?" A moment of quiet and then he said, "Your choice, I guess. Tuller said he doesn't know which is best. He went head first, so that's the way I'm going."

A wordless shout floated through the air, marking Gadon's departure. Seenger moved forward a few feet, followed by I-Sheera and Tanden. No one said a word, waiting with their own thoughts.

Seenger said, "My turn." He was gone with a splash of water.

I-Sheera moved up a few spaces and said, "Captain?" She paused for a moment, "Tanden, I'm frightened."

Tanden reached forward and patted her ankle. "It's all right. I'm here with you. Are you too frightened to go forward?"

Tanden felt her hand cover his own. "I think, I would be if I had any other choice," she hesitated, and added, "and if you weren't here with me. Tanden, I trust you. If you tell me it'll be all right, I'll go."

171

For the first time, Tanden heard Tuller's shout echoing through the cave. His voice sounded distant and hollow, but it was clear enough to understand I-Sheera's turn had come.

Tanden said, "Are you ready?"

Her voice shook, "No."

"All right. Listen. Turn around so your feet are facing forward." When she was in position, he added, "Check on anything you carry. Hold your sword close to your side so it won't catch on anything. Then scoot forward and slide."

"Oh, Tanden—I want to...I will if you tell me I have to. I'm scared."

"Hold on." Tanden twisted himself around. He heard more than felt something catch on a rock and snap.

He said lightly, "I sure hope that wasn't my neck that just broke."

I-Sheera agreed, "Or any other parts, useful or otherwise."

"Damn," he said. "Sorry. I broke the bow trying to turn around. Wait a moment."

Tanden quickly removed the string off the bow. He wadded it up into a ball and stuffed it into his shirt. He ducked his head under the strap of the quiver and set it down beside him. There was no sense taking the arrows when he had no bow.

He scooted forward, slipping his legs on either side of the woman until he could wrap his arms around her waist. He pulled her against his chest. She leaned back against him, relaxing in his grasp. Her warm back made him realize how cold and wet the tunnel made him feel. Her body heat comforted him.

"We'll slide together. Ready?"

"Not yet, hold me, please." She leaned her head back against his chest.

Tanden would have stopped himself if he actually thought about what he was doing. Sliding his right hand up, he caressed I-Sheera's left arm. Brushing his fingertips along her neck, he felt her shiver, but she did not pull away from him. He stroked her chin and then turned her head toward him. Tanden bent forward and caressed her lips with his. It was a gentle dance of lips on lips.

I-Sheera twisted sideways. She put her left hand flat against his chest as if to push away. Tanden held his place, not wanting to force his kisses on her, yet not wanting to let her go. She slid her hand across his chest and to his neck. Her fingers lay flat against the bare skin of his neck. Her lips darted forward to touch Tanden's lips and then she withdrew.

Tanden felt her warm breath against his face. His mind shouted, "*Stop this! Now is not the time. She's tired and vulnerable. Gadon is right. I'm acting like an adolescent boy in heat.*" Still, he held her tight. His lips searched again for hers. He kissed her softly, then harder. He wrapped his right arm in a cradle around her head, holding her lips captive with his passion. She kissed him back, matching heat for heat. Her tongue darted forward, flicking and probing to lie against his.

Tanden removed his arm from around her head, sliding his hand into her tangled hair. He twisted his fingers deeply into the mass of black hair, slowly pulling her lips away from his mouth. He felt her stretching toward him. Rather than release her, he dropped his head to kiss her chin, then her cheek and back to her lips.

He caressed her neck with his fingertips. Slowly and deliberately, he slipped his hand down along her chest. He cupped a breast in his hand, silently cursing the leather strap protecting his palm. Even through the leather, he felt her small, firm breast pushing up to meet his hand. His fingers flicked over her hard nipple.

His hand retreated to cradle her head, intertwining his fingers in her hair as he pulled her away from his lips.

I-Sheera sighed, "Oh, Tanden. I've wanted to kiss you since the first day I saw you on the docks. You stood there so handsome and confident with the wind blowing through your hair. I was sure you'd never even look at me." He started to respond, but she shushed him. "Let me say this, please, or I'll lose the courage forever. After a time, I knew you were a good man. No matter how nasty I acted, you always treated me kindly. No. Don't say anything. I know I was Yasthera il-Aldigg's voice and you treated me as you would treat the lady herself, but you didn't have to be so nice. I cried myself to sleep on the White Wind. The lady thought I was homesick, but I was sick because of how she made me treat you."

He interrupted, "Gadon and the others?"

She sighed and laid her cheek on his chest, "Gadon was fun to pick on. I think he enjoys the arguments, but you...all I ever wanted to do was please you. I know I'm not the prettiest girl you've known. I'm yours. I won't ever ask anything of you, just to be near you. Should you marry another, I'll serve her if it pleases you."

"I-Sheera, you please me." He cut off her reply by pulling her face to him and covering her lips with a kiss. He withdrew and continued, "You are much more beautiful than you give yourself credit for. You're a constant pleasure to my eyes. You please me in more ways than just your lush hair, deep eyes, and rich full lips. I've seen great compassion in your heart. I've seen fire in your eyes and iron in your arms. No man could ask for more than you have to offer. Yet, I can't give you any promises. I'm set on retaking the White Wind. I can't promise anything else until that's done."

"Tanden, I don't ask for a promise. I'll serve as you see fit and go when you tell me to go."

Tanden shook his head, "You have your freedom. Have you forgotten the pouch about your neck?"

"I haven't forgotten anything. I haven't forgotten it was you who set me free. I don't know much about freedom, but what good is it to be free if I can't choose to be with the man of my own choosing?"

"I-Sheera, you've set me on fire, but I can't turn away from the commitment I made to retake the White Wind. Right now, we have to keep moving forward. Kiss me again and we'll go."

He wanted the kiss to last forever. When she finally drew away from him, he could still feel the soft kiss against his lips. He would remember the feel and touch of her for as long as he lived, be it a day, ten days, or ten years.

He commanded, "Turn onto your back."

I-Sheera turned in his arms until she sat with her back against his chest. Before he could utter another word, she took his hands in hers and guided them across her body to her breasts. She pressed his hands hard to her and rocked back against him. Then just as quickly, she released his hands.

She said, "Let's go before I lose the courage you've given me."

CHAPTER TWENTY-THREE

Tanden was certain he had not given her courage. She was courageous of her own accord. He said, "Lean back against me and keep your head down."

He leaned back as flat as he could. Pulling with his heels and hands, he dragged them both forward until suddenly, they slid forward without any effort. I-Sheera's hands gripped his legs. Sliding downward, the water pulled and pushed at them trying to tear them away from each other. I-Sheera didn't utter a sound, but Tanden felt her body tense. She tighteded her grip on his legs the farther they slid and the faster they dropped.

Without thinking, Tanden shouted, not out of fear, but of exhilaration. His heart raced as it always did in a strong wind off the beam reach of the ship. The wind would drive them faster, as if to push them into the sea in one strong sensation of excitement. As on the ship, he was absolutely sure he would survive. He had proven many times he could overcome and master air and water. He was convinced he would overcome and master water and earth in his current situation. He had no need for magic, just the power of his thoughts, his strength, and his courage.

Tanden shouted to I-Sheera, "This is fun. It sure beats crawling on our hands and knees."

She didn't speak, but he felt her relax against him.

Tanden thought he saw a dim light ahead. He wondered if his eyes were playing tricks on him or if they had finally adjusted to the dark. The two shot around a curve and then quickly banked the other way. They slid with the water high up the wall of the tunnel. Light flooded the tunnel before them, hurting their eyes. Tanden squinted trying to dampen the bright light. Through the slits of his eyes, he saw an opening directly ahead. Faster than thought, the water pushed them out of the tunnel and into empty space. I-Sheera screamed as they dropped, splashing into a pool ten feet below.

The pool was only four or five feet deep. Tanden stood, shaking water from his face. He looked around and saw I-Sheera flailing about. She was slapping the water in an unsuccessful attempt to keep her head above water. Reaching to her, he secured a tight grip on her collar, then lifted her up until her head and shoulders were out of the water.

Gadon shouted, "Put your feet down, girl. The water isn't that deep."

Tanden said to her, "I guess we need to teach you to swim."

She stood sheepishly. She was short, but standing on her toes and balancing herself against Tanden, she could keep her face clear of the water. She hopped to the edge of the pool, bouncing through the cool water. She sloshed to the bank to join the others sitting there enjoying the scene.

Tanden stood in the pool where he surfaced, looking at the sky. It appeared to be only late afternoon. He would have wagered they had spent hours inside the earth, yet they had been underground for two or maybe three hours at the most. The sun was high enough to light the sky, but no direct sunlight reached the pool.

An unusual rock formation surrounded them. The area had once been a large, upside-down bowl-like cavern. The uppermost part of the roof had collapsed, opening it to the sky and flooding the area with light. Over time, dirt collected on the floor, seeds blew in, and a few stunted trees and bushes grew on the banks of the small stream. The stream angled around the wall of the bowl to disappear through in another opening.

The wind and rain had carved the walls into twisted inward curing spires making them utterly impossible to climb. Tanden thought it looked like he was standing in the palms of a giant's hands with the fingers curling around and over them.

A sneeze caused Tanden to look to his men. Gadon sneezed again. He shook himself like a large wet dog. "Curse this sensitive Holdenite nose of mine. There's enough dust in this hole to choke an oliphant." The large man sneezed a third time.

Tuller said, "You look a bit chilled, brother."

Gadon snarled, "When I get chilled, I'll let you know. I wouldn't be surprised if we all froze to death in this sink hole. We've spent more time in the water the last two days than we have in the last twenty years on the ocean. Some leader you are, Tanden. My skin has wrinkled up so much that I look like Grandfather. All my natural oils have washed off my body so I squeak when I walk. And there you stand in water up to your chest, without the sense to stand on dry land. Chilled! Ha! I wouldn't be surprised if all you puny, skinny looking people caught the croup and died. Hear me boy, I've never been sick a day in my life that wasn't due to bad wine."

Tanden waded out of the pool to stand over Gadon. "Or too much wine."

Gadon snorted, "That's what you think. There isn't any such thing as too much wine."

Tanden said, "Nevertheless, Gadon, Tuller is right. You do look like you've taken a chill."

"It's just cold here, Tanden. I'll warm up when we get out into the sun."

Tuller reached across to Gadon and put a hand against his brother's cheek.

Gadon slapped his hand away. "Tuller, don't you start pretending that you care about my well-being."

Tuller replied, "I only care because if you get sick, I'll have to drag your fat butt out of here, or Father will skin me alive for leaving his oldest son behind. Besides, you do feel feverish."

"Nonsense," Gadon said. "Your hands are just cold. Tanden, let's get moving before this young pup starts acting like Mother and tries to change my diaper. I swear, I may be wrinkled from all of this water, but I'm not an old man, Tuller. I'm still strong enough to slap you so hard that your children will be born dizzy."

Tanden nodded and said, "I don't see any way to climb out of this hole. Our best way out is to continue underground. The stream flows south toward the sea and the water has to go somewhere. We shouldn't rest until we reach the sea. I don't clearly remember the coastline along the south of the isthmus. Gadon, do you recall if these hills stretch to the sea?"

Gadon shook his head before suffering a sneezing fit.

Tanden could not decipher what Gadon's head shake meant. Did he mean the hills did not reach the sea or that he did not remember? Tanden decided it did not matter. Backing up would not help them reach their goal. Going forward was the only logical direction to go. Continuing onward while they were able was best even if Gadon had taken a chill.

Tanden looked to Tuller, "Do you want someone else to go first or are you still willing?"

Tuller said, "As you command, Captain. First or last doesn't matter. It'll be just as dark and cold whoever goes first."

Tuller stood. He held his hands out to Gadon and Seenger. Gadon slapped his hand away and slowly rolled to his knees, groaning as he stood. Seenger took the offered hand and allowed Tuller to pull him to his feet. Both Tuller and Seenger offered hands to I-Sheera.

She said, "Thank you, my good men." She took each of their hands and they lifted her lightly to her feet.

Seenger grunted. "That'll be the first time anyone called me a good man." He poked a big thumb against his own chest. "I'm ogre and proud of it, but I thank you nonetheless."

Tuller walked to where the stream poured into the rock opening. Without looking back, he dropped to his hands and knees and crawled into the darkness. Gadon, Seenger, and I-Sheera fell into line and followed. Tanden, last of all, took one more look around like he was trying to bodily draw in the light and heat to store it for the journey ahead.

For a sailor used to the open seas, the cramped space inside this cave network was more uncomfortable than just being cold and blind. Tanden shook his head to stop any thoughts of doubt. Analyzing his concerns would not prove profitable. Dropping to his knees, he followed his crew into the darkness.

Darkness seemed to ooze from the rock walls around him. As he moved into the cave, it wrapped him up, swallowing him whole. Rather than dwell on unbidden worries, Tanden began an old argument with himself, *"Air, water, fire, and earth are the four elements of the world. Why aren't light and darkness considered elements? Or rather just one or the other being an element? Is light the absence of darkness or is darkness the absence of light?*

"No. Darkness can't be an element of its own if can't exist without light.

"No, fire is paired with air. Air can exist without fire, but fire can't live without air. Light can exist without the dark and I've now seen dark without light."

He remembered his studies in the sciences at Allexia. A scientist, a man without magic, had been studying the myth of white magic. One day he invited Tanden into a darkened room. Lighting a candle inside a box, he then closed the lid. The candle light could only escape the box through a small hole covered by a glass lens tinted in red. The light formed a small circle of red light on a wall.

The man repeated the procedure with a second candle set in a box having a blue-tined glass lens. Facing the glass lens to the wall, a small circle of blue light appeared.

Finally, the man lit a candle in the last box, allowing the light to shine through a green colored glass lens, forming a small green circle on the wall. Once the man finished creating his three dots of light, Tanden thought he understood what the man was trying to explain about the three separate orders of magic.

Shining light through tinted glass was nothing new. He had seen it more than once in the homes of rich men who paid artisans to craft colorful windows with fancy scenes that would appear to play games when the sunlight shined on them. Even the three magic systems in the world used colored glass in their lanterns to advertise their training centers and businesses—at least they did in Holden where all three orders of magic were welcome.

In Drohnbad, the seat of red magic, the Red Wizard only allowed red light. Although he had never been there, he assumed Tunston was awash in blue lights at the command of the Blue Wizard. He wondered about the Green Wizard. If there was one great wizard who ruled over all the green wizards, magicians, and priests, he was unknown to Tanden.

Still, colored lights on the wall had not impressed Tanden until the man said, "All men believe that white magic is a myth and that the red, blue, and green cannot mix. Watch."

Shifting the boxes slightly caused the colored circles of light on the wall to converge, forming one bright circle of light. The single circle of light was brighter than any of the colored lights separately. The green, blue, and red colors blended to become white.

The man grinned, "This is just a child's illustration, one that I wouldn't dare show a wizard. As a scientist, it proves to me that mixing red, green, and blue light will make white light. Someday, I'll find a magician curious enough to test my theory. Does mixing blue, red, and green magic produce white magic? If so, then we can stop this silly stratification of man and be one once again."

Tanden thought the man was delusional about getting people to agree on anything. However, he might have had some valid arguments about combining magic. Even with cold water numbing his hands and knees, he reasoned, *"Okay. Red magic uses the movement and heat from the element of fire. Blue magic uses the movement of the sky and wind, the element of air. Green uses the movement of living things grown from the element of earth. Why isn't there an order of magic that uses the movement of water, not just the waves because that's just the wind and the moons moving the tops of the water, but the currents and tides? What color would that—"*

Tanden's line of logic shattered as he crawled headfirst into a rock.

CHAPTER TWENTY-FOUR

He sat back on his rump and waited for the dizziness to pass. A thin trickle of wet ran down his forehead. Running his fingers through his hair, he could feel the sticky blood, but could not locate any deep cuts or gashes. He reached forward, probing to find a passage around the rock before him, but there was none. He was sitting alone at the end of a blocked tunnel.

"Stupid, stupid, stupid. I don't know how many times I've told you to keep your thoughts on what you're doing. Well, no sense in getting your toga twisted too tight. Just back up until you hit the water." He sat quietly for a moment and listened. He could not hear his crew or the babbling of running water from the stream.

He turned around, keeping the rock wall to his right retracing his path. Before long, he heard the sounds of water and soon he was at the stream's edge. He paused briefly to splash the cold water over his head and face, washing away the blood. When his fingers could not feel any more blood, Tanden turned left continuing to follow the water downstream.

In the darkness, Tanden could not tell how he had become separated from his crew. A good excuse would be to claim that using his hearing as his primary sense was unusual. He needed to concentrate harder. He crawled forward.

He said aloud, "I need to listen more and think less. No, not think less. I need to think more but focus on the task at hand. Letting my thoughts wander is childish. Tanden, behave yourself."

A flutter of wings froze Tanden in place. He heard another sound coming from above his head. He realized he must be in another open area within the underground network. He crouched along the streambed listening. He could not tell how far away from him the winged creature was or what type of creature was hiding in the dark.

Tanden did not know of any animal that could fly in the dark and lived in caves, except dragons and demons. Demon spirits were not just stories to scare little children. The Dark One and its minions may indeed have wings and may move about the underground. Living without light would not hamper any demon. Holding his breath, he crawled downstream as noiselessly as he possibly could. He felt a flutter of breeze across the back of his neck. He squeezed his eyes shut and continued crawling forward.

After a few short yards, he drew a quiet breath and opened his eyes. Demon spirits or not, he decided he was not going to bang his head against another rock wall. Making as little noise as possible, Tanden crawled onward through the water. Hurrying as much as he could, he told himself he needed to catch up with the others quickly. Deep in his heart he wanted to leave this cave and any evil lurking within its darkness.

Shortly, Tanden heard Gadon's sneezing and coughing echoing through the cave. The noise came from in front of him. Hand after hand, with his knees following in rhythm, he crawled closer to his crew. Hearing splashing near at hand, he calmed his pounding heart. Trying to keep the edge out of his voice, he asked, "I-Sheera? Are you all right?"

"Tanden?" Her voice came out in a rush, "You were so quiet. You didn't answer when I called. I thought you were lost. I wanted to come back and look for you, but Seenger said to keep going. Where have you been? Are you all right? I thought real hard with my mind that you would return to us, is that all right? Oh, Tanden. I'm glad you're here. Listen to Gadon. He sounds very ill. This—"

Gadon's voice floated out of the darkness. "Enough, girl," he wheezed. "It's just cold in this hole. This is the only place on earth I've ever been that's both damp and dusty at the same time. I'm well enough."

Tanden smiled to himself, but he was concerned about his friend. They had all been cold and wet for what seemed like an eternity. Gadon had not been able to find any clothing to keep out the chill or fever. "We're all tired. Does anyone need to rest?"

Gadon snorted, "You don't fool me, Tanden. I won't have you thinking I'm a feeble old man that needs pampering. I say we keep moving." He would have said more, but a fit of coughing made him gasp for breath.

Tuller called out, "I'm tired and could use a break, but I think if I stop I might not be able to get started again. And I'm anxious to get into the sun again."

Tanden said, "Time may slip by us. We may lose the sun before we gain open air, but I do want to get out of this cave."

I-Sheera asked, "How do we know we aren't crawling in circles? We can't see our way."

"It's the water," Seenger replied. He spoke as if his statement needed no explanation.

Tanden said, "He's correct, I-Sheera. The stream we're following flows downhill. Water can't flow in an endless circle, at least, I've never heard of such a thing."

The group fell silent. As they crawled along in the dark, they listened to Gadon coughing and sneezing. Tanden lost all track of time and distance traveled.

Tuller called, "Hold your places. Tanden?"

"What is it?"

"The streambed drops off here. I'm at a ledge to a deep pool reaching from wall to wall."

"Do you know how long the pool is? Or how deep?"

They heard a splash. Then they heard a sputtering echo through the tunnel.

Tuller said, "At the edge it's about chin high on me. I make it about five feet, but the bottom is slippery and the footing is uneven. And Tanden?"

Tanden said, "I'm listening."

"The water is brackish. It's thick with salt."

"Does the water still flow?"

"No," Tuller said. "It's standing."

"Good." Tanden continued, "We may be nearing the sea." Tanden thought about what else thick brackish salt water might mean. The water could be salty because they had come to an underground lake with an inlet and no outlet. This pool might be like the Lost Sea that was so thick with salt a man could float without effort because the water didn't flow anywhere. He kept those speculations to himself.

Tanden continued, "Drink from the stream before we move into the pool. It may be our last fresh water for a time. Then Seenger, stay close to Tuller. We may have to swim to the other side if the pool becomes deeper. I'll take I-Sheera. Gadon, are you ready to swim?"

Gadon coughed a deep hack to clear his throat. "After all this time on my hands and knees, I'd enjoy the change."

Tanden heard the hesitation in the man's voice, "But?"

"Tanden," Gadon replied, "Wait, I do need to rest for awhile. I'm sorry, my friend, but I don't have the breath for swimming right now. Leave me here. I'll catch up."

"Gadon, I can't leave you here. Can you float if I tow you?"

"All I need is a rest without all of you jabbering around me. I'll be refreshed soon enough."

"No. I don't think so, Gadon. I'm speaking as your captain and your friend, you'll drag yourself out of here if I have to push you the whole way to get it done."

Gadon said, "I'm sorry, Captain. You can't tow me and the woman at the same time."

Tanden said, "I believe I can. I-Sheera is as light as a feather."

The woman spoke up, "I'll bet he can tow us both, Gadon. I'll wager my jewel. That is, if you've got as much courage as you have belly, old man."

Gadon shouted, "Old man!" He wheezed and coughed harshly to clear his throat, "Now I'm beset by a mere woman? I swear by the food in my children's mouths I'm truly the most maligned man in all of Holden."

Tuller said, "You don't have children, brother. Plus, we aren't in Holden. I heard a wager. What do you say, Gadon? Afraid to gamble with a woman?"

Seenger said, "Gadon, if you don't want the jewel, I'll take the wager."

Gadon said, "Wait. I'll take the wager. I-Sheera, what will you accept on the gamble?"

I-Sheera was silent for a moment, then said, "You have nothing I want with you right now, but I want a saurus of my own. When we get out of here, you buy me a saurus?"

"Done," Gadon said.

Tuller interrupted, "Wait. I've seen the jewel, Gadon. In Harkelle's markets, it's worth four or five good sauruses, plus a breeding stud saurus. You're cheating this woman."

Gadon said, "Mind your own business, Tuller. She set the terms, not me. I'll probably never live to collect, anyway. Tanden will most likely drown us both."

Tanden commanded Seenger to move past Gadon to link up with Tuller. He instructed the two to stay to the left side of the cave wall, if possible. He signalled them to begin moving through the pool, and warned them to stay within voice contact with him and the others. He slid up to I-Sheera. Reaching out in the dark, he patted her on the shoulder. He realized she had deliberately prodded Gadon's ego to keep him moving. He told her to stay close.

Together they crawled to Gadon, then the three moved to the edge of the saltwater pool. Tanden tried to ease himself into the water, but the edge and the bottom were as slippery as Tuller cautioned. He found himself thrashing for a foothold. Finally, he was able to balance upright on a couple of rocks sitting at opposite angles. He had become turned around in the dark and had no idea which direction I-Sheera and Gadon sat waiting for him until Gadon sneezed.

"Gadon? You first. Have you a strap?"

"Aye. It's not long, but it should be long enough for us both to hold."

"Come ahead, careful, it's slippery."

A moment later Gadon surfaced next to Tanden, having slipped and slid under water. The heavyset man came up coughing and gasping for air. Tanden braced himself against the rocks as best he could and held his friend's head above water. Standing this close Tanden heard the man struggling to breathe. His coughs raged from deep in his lungs.

Tanden held him close and whispered, "Hold on, my friend. We're almost out of this cave. We'll get you warm and well soon." Gadon didn't answer, but his coughing did grow quieter. Tanden reached for his hand and grasped the free end of the strap.

Tanden said, "I-Sheera. The rocks are slick, but both Gadon and I are here to catch you. Don't be afraid, trust us to catch you."

Without a word, she slid off the ledge into the water. She had not tried to reach the bottom and kept a firm hand on the ledge. Doing so enabled her to keep her head above water.

Gadon said, "Grab my leg, girl. Pull yourself along to us."

Tanden continued to brace himself against the tugging and pulling until he felt I-Sheera's arms wrap around his neck. She squeezed him tight, trying to draw herself up out of the water.

"Relax," Tanden said to soothe the woman. "We're fine. You need to relax and try to float in the water. I can't hold onto you like I did in the open sea. You must hold on to me, but hold me lightly. Here." He pried one hand loose and set its grip on the collar of his tunic. "If you hold here, then I'm free to swim, plus I can breathe if I feel the need."

Tanden raised his voice, "Tuller? Seenger?"

Tuller shouted back, "We're here, just ahead of you."

Tanden called back, "Now that we're in it, I feel the water flowing. We must be getting close to an opening."

Tanden pushed against the bottom towing his two charges along behind him. The bottom was slick and broken with loose rocks, but even so, he found it easier to continue to push along the bottom than to try to swim. He made almost no headway when he tried to swim. He had Gadon keep an arm stretched out to touch the left wall as a guide. Between Gadon's bouts of coughing and wheezing, he could hear Tuller talking to Seenger. They were discussing a future visit to a particularly rowdy tavern near Harkelle's wharf. Most taverns near the docks were rowdy, but few allowed ogres through the door. The one they were discussing did not. It sounded like they were planning a very rowdy evening indeed.

The darkness was frustrating to Tanden. He could not determine the size of the cave. He clenched his jaw, squeezing his lips tight. He knew if he spoke, he might say something he would regret later. No one could relieve the darkness. Cursing the surrounding rock seemed pointless. He tried to focus his thoughts but found his emotions were overriding his ability to control them.

"Tanden!" Tuller shouted. "We have a light ahead."

"Thank the six gods," Tanden said.

Tuller called, "It's not the air, but the water below is becoming lighter."

Tanden was not able to see anything for a few more minutes, but after a time, he could see a murky glow coming up through the water around him. He saw Tuller and Seenger ahead as dim shadows. Soon, he was standing next to the two men where the tunnel opened into a larger cavern filled with glowing water from wall to wall with no apparent outlet. The light in the water cast a glow around them. Ribbons of light and shadow chased each other across the ceiling.

Tuller flung out a dripping hand pointing to the other side of the pool. Tanden could see the light filtering through a hole lying under water. The pool itself looked bottomless with only the top layer highlighted in a murky whiteness.

Tanden said, "Gadon. Can you stand here?" Without speaking, Gadon let his feet sink to the bottom and stood. Tanden continued, "I-Sheera, hold on to Gadon." He took her hand and guided her through the water, putting her in contact with Gadon's shoulder. "Everyone stay here. I'll swim to the other side and look at the opening."

He pushed himself off the bottom, keeping his head up and his eyes fixed on the light. He swam to the other side in a few strokes. Not hesitating as he reached the other side, he took a breath and ducked underwater into the hole. His intent was to swim through it to gauge how long it would take before they could resurface. He felt the water sucking at him, drawing him along faster and faster. If he continued much farther he might not be able to get back to his crew.

He reversed direction and swam back, pushing against the current. In the murky water, he was not able to tell how much forward progress he was making. The water tugged and pulled at him, trying to drag him away from his crew. He was reaching the end of his last breath.

CHAPTER TWENTY-FIVE

Tanden rolled in the water onto his back and pushed himself up to the roof of the tunnel. Clawing for any handhold, he pulled himself against the flow of the water. His struggles against the current were sapping him of stored air. Suddenly, his face broke free from the water in a clear air pocket. The water gurgled around him as he sucked air filling his aching lungs.

He packed as much air into his lungs as he could manage. Pulling harder along the rocky ceiling, he fought his way upstream. Then with a kick, he shot into the pool. The surface of the pool was much calmer once he was away from the hole. Tanden swam a few leisurely strokes over to his crew.

He said, "Water is pouring out of the cave through that hole."

Tuller replied, "The water level in here is dropping. Right now it's only an inch or two, but it's definitely dropping."

Tanden said, "We may be in an area affected by the tides from the sea. We must be experiencing an ebb tide."

Seenger asked, "Will the cave entrance be clear at low tide?"

Tanden looked to Tuller, who shrugged.

Tanden answered the ogre, "I don't know, but I don't believe we should wait. We still have some light to swim by, but we don't know how much time we have remaining. This may be the dawn's light or the last piece of the evening sun. We must be through this tunnel before the tide comes in or we'll be trapped in here. This may be low tide. The outward rushing water will help us swim through quickly."

Picking a color at random to name a magician who could draw power from the fourth element, he thought, *"Where is that yellow wizard when you need him? A little water magic right now is exactly what we need."*

Tanden turned to Gadon and I-Sheera. "Are you ready to hold your breath for an underwater swim?"

I-Sheera swallowed hard and nodded.

Gadon looked pale, even in the dim light. Choking back a cough he rasped, "If I could hold my breath for nine months in my mother's womb, I can hold it here. Besides, if I drown what would you care? You drag me halfway around the world without so much as a please or thank you and now you pretend to be concerned about my safety? I ought to drown just to teach you all a lesson."

Tanden said, "Seenger?"

Seenger shrugged, "If you say to go, then I go."

Gadon coughed and said, "By my own aching butt, Seenger, you're right. What else can we do but follow where the great and mighty master leads! And follow we will and without complaint, because you all know with my sweet and gentle heart, I'd never complain. However, Tanden, should you ever ask, next time, lead us to a tavern with a warm fire and a busty wench to serve me my supper."

Tanden said, "Then let's go. Gadon hand me one end of your strap. I-Sheera, hold tight to Gadon. Stay with me as best you can. Take several deep breaths and hold it when I command." Tanden pushed off the bottom and swam across the pool using strong kicks, pulling at the water with his free hand. The surface of the pool was calm, so towing the two in tandem was slow, but relatively easy.

At the entrance to the hole, Tanden commanded, "Take one more deep breath, and hold it."

He ducked under the water and swam into the hole. After a few strong swimming strokes, he felt the stream tugging at him, sucking him into the tunnel. The current yanked at him and threatened to separate him from Gadon. Tanden tightened his grasp on the strap, silently willing I-Sheera to strengthen her hold on Gadon.

The water drew them faster and faster along the tunnel. As they rushed along, Tanden kicked furiously with his legs, trying to avoid Gadon. He thrust his free hand upward to the top of the cave searching for an air pocket. He wasn't yet short of breath, but Gadon's lungs must be aching and I-Sheera wasn't a swimmer by any means.

Suddenly his hand cleared the water and his knuckles scraped bare rock. They were past the air pocket before he could stop. Again, he found another pocket clear of water, but once again, they were swept past, the rush of water jerked them away. Tanden reversed his body angle so he was traveling feet first.

When he found the next air pocket, he jammed his feet upward to the roof of the tunnel and surfaced into the air. He grabbed a rock outcropping. Curling his arm to his chest, he yanked Gadon into the pocket next to him. The man came up sputtering and hacking to clear his throat and lungs. Tanden let loose of Gadon and reached for I-Sheera. She was almost swept past them before he clasped his hand around her wrist and pulled her up.

I-Sheera surfaced. She blew air and water, spraying the two men waiting in the air pocket. She wrapped her arms around Tanden's neck and held him tightly. She desperately gulped air.

The water tugged at Tanden, but he held against its insistent pull.

"Breathe quickly. I can't hold us here for long." Tanden spoke too soon. Before he took another breath of air, something slammed against his back, knocking him loose from his moorings. He rolled in the water wrapping one arm around I-Sheera. He reached to grab Gadon, but missed. Thrashing about he searched for his friend, but he and the woman were washed away from the air pocket.

Tanden felt a tug on his trousers and a weight dragging at him. He put both feet up on the rock ceiling of the tunnel, pushing downstream. He clawed with his free hand and drove with his feet in a bizarre upside-down climbing motion, propelling himself faster downstream than he could swim.

Light flooded his eyes and he shot upward. Breaking the surface of the water into the air in a large sunlight chamber, he heard I-Sheera gasping as she clung to his neck. He reached down, grabbing the hand clutching his pants. He yanked upward, pulling Gadon to the water's surface. The man was pale and shaking as he drew in a ragged breath. Each breath Gadon took in caused him to cough and gasp.

Tanden kicked at the water furiously to keep them afloat. They were not out of the tunnel yet, but the current was relentlessly tugging them toward an opening. Beyond it, Tanden could see trees and a small patch of sky. It was almost sunset. Pale light was coming from the last rays of the sun, reflecting off a small pool at the entrance.

He could not turn and look for Tuller and Seenger. Tanden held Gadon in one arm with I-Sheera wrapped around his neck. It took all of the strength in his legs to keep them afloat. The water was too deep to stand. He released his arm from I-Sheera's waist. He was sure she would not let go of him. He pulled at the water trying to reach the nearest side of the chamber.

His foot scrapped a rock. He tried to clutch at it, but missed. He hit another rock and then another. Gathering his feet under him, Tanden bodily flung himself and his charges up onto a small, barely submerged ledge. The three of them sat in water breathing heavily. Gadon hacked and coughed, doubling over to hold his sides. He shivered violently. Tanden put his arm around his friend and drew him near in a close hug. I-Sheera didn't release her grip on Tanden's neck and, in truth, he didn't want her to let go. Tanden wrapped his other arm around her and held her tight.

Tanden looked around once his eyes adjusted somewhat to the dim light. Across from them, on a dry ledge, Tuller waved back at him. The man was obviously too tired to call out to them. Seenger lay stretched out on the rocks, his chest heaving like an overworked bellows. Tanden was certain one of them had bumped him loose from the air pocket.

The entrance to the chamber was only twenty or thirty yards distant. Tanden could not see much of what lay beyond the opening aside from a few moss-covered trees hanging over the water. The sky was getting darker as the sun was dropping behind the western horizon. As tired as they were, he wanted to quit this underground crypt and reach dry land to start a fire before dark.

They were all wet, tired, and hungry. Tanden might not be able to feed them this evening, but he definitely wanted out of the water. He could feel Gadon shaking against him. The big man needed warmth to fight his chill. Tanden heard a flutter of wings above him. His eyes shot upward, scanning the ceiling.

I-Sheera screamed, burying her face in his neck. From every crevice in the rocks about them oozed flying creatures screeching and flapping their leathery wings at Tanden and his people. Releasing his hold on I-Sheera and Gadon, he slapped at the small creatures diving and swirling around them. He had never seen such foul creatures in his life. These were the incarnation of the dark demons in all of his dreams. They dove at his face and veered away at the last possible moment.

As quickly as they appeared, the creatures were gone. They swarmed out of the chamber into the evening air, swirling like smoke disappearing into a cloudy sky. Tanden shivered with revulsion. He looked across the water to see Tuller staring at Seenger.

Seenger was still lying on his back. He had caught one of the creatures and was holding it by its outstretched wings. It wiggled and snapped at the man, but he held it tight. The ogre turned the creature every which way, examining it from all sides.

Tanden called out, "What in the names of the six gods is that thing?"

Tuller replied, "Seenger says it's a cave dweller that only comes out at night. I've never seen such a thing. It looks like an angry dragonette with wings and it's covered in animal fur."

Tanden asked, "Seenger, what do you call that thing?"

Seenger answered, "It used to be called a bat." With a quick twist, the man snapped the neck of the creature. "Now, I call it supper."

Rather than dwell on the mental picture of Seenger eating a flying, furry dragonette, Tanden commanded the two men to work their way out of the chamber and find a dry place to spend the night. He told them he would follow with Gadon and I-Sheera.

It did not matter if they hurried to catch the White Wind, they could not wear themselves out getting there. They would all need their strength to retake her. I-Sheera needed rest and Tanden's concern for Gadon's health was growing by the minute. They would have to rest and then take their bearings in the morning before proceeding.

He gently pried I-Sheera's arms from his neck. He stroked her wet hair, brushing it back from her face. He tilted her head slightly and swept his lips across her forehead before smiling down at her.

"Can you make your way along these rocks? I need to help Gadon."

She nodded and gently slid her fingertips across his lips. Without saying a word, she turned and began walking slowly through the water, moving from rock to rock. Tanden watched her until she was about halfway to the entrance.

He looked down at Gadon, "Ready, my friend?"

"No, but you aren't really giving me a choice, are you?"

Tanden said, "No, I guess I'm not. I don't want to sit in this water waiting for the tide to come back in or for those bat things to come back and have us for supper. We walk out together."

Gadon nodded, "I'm sorry, Tanden."

"Sorry? For what? That you caught a chill? Don't be foolish, Gadon. You have nothing to apologize for."

"As you say. If we have to go, let's go." The two men stood up and followed I-Sheera. Gadon leaned heavily against Tanden all the way to the entrance. They stopped next to the woman at the edge of the light. Tuller and Seenger stood opposite them on the other side.

"Bad news," Tuller said. "It's a swamp as far as we can see."

CHAPTER TWENTY-SIX

Tanden stood waist deep in swamp water with Gadon strapped to his back. His feet sank in the mud and he wondered if he was in a swamp, a bayou, or a delta. He could not decide what to call it, except to call it a problem. Gadon's weight was driving him into the sandy muck on the bottom. The sunlight was fading fast and he was standing in a saltwater marsh surrounded by trees that grew on stilts directly out of the water. Reeds and tall grasses grew in tangled patches every direction they turned. Everything dripped water.

I-Sheera grasped his tunic. She pulled him forward. Her other arm was clamped wrist to wrist with Seenger. The Ogre stood on a rock outcropping, bracing his feet against the strain. Tuller pushed at Tanden's behind, trying to drive him upward out of the muck.

One of Tanden's feet slipped up and out of the sucking mud that tried to pull his boot off his foot. He curled his toes and arched his foot. Pulling his boots off would have been a good idea, but it was too late now. Swinging the free foot forward, he dropped it into the mud a step closer to their destination. Another foot, then another and Tanden stopped to twist around. He reached back and offered a hand to pull Tuller closer to him. The man sank deeper in the muck for each step he drove Tanden and Gadon forward.

Gradually, they worked their way toward the rock, the only dry spot in view. It would provide the only possible resting place for the night. It would be a cold, hard perch, but they all agreed it was better than sitting in water all night, or trying to slog their way to dry land in the dark.

Gadon burned with a fever and his cough left him breathless and gasping. The heavyset man had struggled briefly through the mud, but his strength quit. He had stopped, unable to summon more energy than it took him to breathe in the thick, dank air. He had even been too weary to complain about his weakness and made no comments when Tanden lifted him onto his back. They had only traveled a few dozen yards to where they now stood, but it took all of them to reach this point. Tanden carried Gadon the whole way while Seenger and I-Sheera pulled Tanden from the front and Tuller pushed from the rear.

Daylight had deserted them before the small troop gained the top of the dry rock. Tanden gently laid a sleeping Gadon in the middle of what space was available. There was barely room for all of them on the rock, but none begrudged Gadon the space. The sun's residual heat from the day radiated up from the rock, soothing and comforting the ill sailor, quieting his shivering.

The night was not yet fully dark as Six Finger cast its dim light over the swamp. Its annual erratic course through the heavens brought the moon low on the southern horizon, lighting more of the sea's wavetops than the air above it. I-Sheera cradled Gadon's head and shoulders in her lap, rubbing his shoulders and chest. Even in the dim moonlight, Tandon could see the look on her face was the same look of dismay and pain she displayed as she held the wounded saurus. The look said, "I want to help, but I don't know what else to do." Tanden knew the look and the feeling. There wasn't anything they could do.

Each man sat as close to Gadon as possible, sharing their body heat with the man. Seenger took the dead bat from inside his tunic to slice it with his knife. Splitting it lengthwise, he caught a handful of blood from the small creature. He leaned over Gadon, allowing the thick liquid to pour from his hands into the sleeping man's mouth. Gadon swallowed in his sleep, licking his lips.

Seenger looked to I-Sheera and said, "It isn't much, but any nourishment is better than none." He turned back to the animal and quickly dressed it, tossing the offal into the swamp. It provided only a small handful of meat. The ogre did not offer the meat to anyone. He took a bite out of it and chewed quietly.

Tanden had not wanted any of the bat. He had eaten many disgusting things in his life when he was hungry, but right now he was not hungry enough to eat something that evil looking. Still, he would have appreciated being asked if he wanted any. He certainly would have wanted to give I-Sheera the opportunity to have some small measure of a meal. He was about to confront the ogre for not offering to share when Seenger removed the chewed piece from his mouth and pushed it between Gadon's lips.

Tanden watched as Gadon, in his sleep, chewed and swallowed the meat. Tanden had seen mothers feed their young babies this way, but he had not thought to feed a sick man by the same method. He watched as Seenger ground down piece after piece of raw meat and fed it to Gadon. When he finished, Seenger wiped his bloody hands through his hair, slicking it back out of his face.

Tuller said, "In my brother's name, I thank you, Seenger."

The ogre shrugged and settled back against Gadon's bulk. His head dropped to his chest and much to everyone's amazement, he fell asleep immediately.

Tanden said to no one in particular, "Strange creature."

Tuller answered, "Yes, but a good one. Huzzuzz ogres may be ignorant, uncivilized barbarians, but I'll stand with Seenger as a friend all the rest of my days."

Tanden agreed, "Without a doubt." Long ago he had determined Seenger to be honorable and committed. Many chastised Tanden for adding an ogre to his crew. Seenger had peculiar personal habits, but Tanden would never again hear this creature criticized without taking a stand in his defense. Called many things while growing up and treated poorly by many people simply because of the circumstances of his birth, Tanden long ago decided he would treat everyone he met according to the manner of each individual's actions.

CHAPTER TWENTY-SEVEN

Dawn was near when Tanden awoke with a start to see a pair of eyes staring at him from the water. He grabbed the knife from his lap and leaped to his feet in a defensive stance. His quick movement jolted Seenger and Tuller to their feet. Even I-Sheera awoke to put her hand on the hilt of her sword.

Tanden's heart settled back into his chest as he recognized the eyes of a large bullfrog. He shook his head at his own folly and pointed for the others to see what had startled him. The three men settled back on their seats to the sound of Gadon's snores. The bullfrog raised his head out of the water to croak a rumbling response.

Tuller laughed with the others and said, "It must be true love. Maybe we should wake Gadon up before his mating call has us buried in lustful, green suitors."

Tanden said, "How is he this morning?"

I-Sheera gently placed the back of her hand on the sleeping man's forehead and then his cheek, "I think his fever broke last night. He's still warm, but he rested well for most of the night. He needs to sleep and gain his strength back."

Tanden nodded, "Yes. But, this isn't the place to rest for long. We need to be moving soon after sunrise. Let him sleep until then."

Gadon spoke, "How can a man sleep with all you little girls chattering away. Can't you see that I'm laying here on my deathbed. Oh, my aching back. Tanden, you aren't any better than a pile of maggot-covered camel spit. You profess to be my friend. Here I am, dying and you can't find me a decent place to lay my head. Look where you've dragged me! I'm stretched out on a rock in a swamp. Oh, just kill me now. Don't let Mother know how poorly I've been treated, the humiliation would be too much for her."

Gadon tried to sit up, but Tanden held him down with a hand on his chest. His attempted movement set off a coughing fit that sounded painful.

Tanden said, "Relax, you giant bag of wind. We aren't going anywhere yet."

He looked around him. Trees blocked their view on three sides. The cave behind them cut a hole through ragged rocky cliffs. He spotted a tall tree nearby. It was taller than the trees clustered around them and should give a climber a good view of the surrounding swamp.

He took an accounting of everything they carried. He only had a knife, having broken the bow in the cave. He had lost his long sword and the short sword long before they entered the cave. Tuller and Seenger each carried a long sword. Seenger also had a knife. I-Sheera had a short sword and her sling. Gadon had nothing with him. He must have left his weapons along the way in the cave network. Tanden could not blame him; fever would keep anyone from thinking clearly. They had little in the way of weapons, but still they carried more than they had at the beginning of their journey.

Tanden commanded, "Tuller." He pointed to the tall tree and gestured a finger upward.

The sailor slid off the rock and waded through the water to the tree. The group watched as he climbed. The climb was easy for a man used to scrambling up and down a ship's mast as it bobbed and weaved on ocean waves. Near the top, they saw Tuller scan in all directions.

Tuller shouted, "The sea is only a hundred yards to the south, but I can't tell where this swamp ends and the sea begins. To the east, I see swamp until more trees block my view. There's nothing behind us." Tuller pointed to the west. "That way."

He began climbing back down, speaking as he worked his way around the limbs. "It may be a trick of the morning light, but it looks like the edge of this swamp is only a few hundred yards west of us. Beyond the cave, it looks as if we may find a dryer path if we stay close to the cliffs."

Tanden said, "Good. That's the direction we'll go."

"There may be a better way. Seenger and I can mount the cliffs and see if we can find an easier path."

"I don't think so," Tanden answered. "You could make the effort and not find a better choice than we have now. Those cliffs would probably be easier to scale than some we've seen recently, but it would take two or three hours to reach the top and return. That's a long delay for unknown results."

I-Sheera spoke quietly, without raising her eyes, "Tanden?"

"Yes?"

"May I ask a question?" she queried, keeping her eyes downcast.

Tanden said, "I-Sheera, you're one of us. I believe you've done your share. You've earned the right to stand with us and speak your mind. Does anyone think otherwise?"

Tuller pulled himself up from the water, dripping wet. "I've seen her gut a man and even unseat a mounted warrior. Who am I to say anything against her! She stands in a better light with me than many others who call themselves warriors."

Seenger nodded his agreement.

Gadon coughed and said, "Woman! Speak up, let's hear what you have to say."

Tanden said, "Ask your question."

She hesitated. Looking down at the rock, she said, "I think Tuller is right. It may take longer, but Gadon needs more rest." Looking into Tanden's eyes, she quickly cut off Gadon's response. "He can't even sit up without breathing hard. The fever has affected his lungs and sapped his strength."

Tanden replied, "You're right. I'd get him out of this swamp as fast as possible. This air can't be good for him—or us. When we reach dry land, we'll find a place to rest comfortably, build a fire to get warm and find food. I don't believe this swamp will be any more comfortable during the heat of the day. We will certainly be less comfortable if Six Finger moves from the southern horizon. Its pull on the tides is considerable and its absence might allow the water to rise and cover this rock. I-Sheera, I thank you and Tuller for your suggestions, but the final decision is mine. We'll move as soon as we have clear daylight."

Gadon said, "I thank you for thinking of me, young lady, but don't start treating my like a corpse just yet. And Tuller, what are you squirming around for. Sit still, boy, you're making me dizzy."

Tuller scratched at his scalp, "You were dizzy to begin with. If you must know, the salty water on my burns is beginning to itch."

Tanden had forgotten that Bransch, the young Hummdhar warrior, had severely burned Tuller's scalp two days ago. So much had happened since then Tanden almost forgot his own wounds, scrapes, and bruises.

Tuller continued, "Last night the salt burned, but today it itches enough to drive a man crazy."

I-Sheera said, "It's healing then, just leave it alone."

Tuller said, "Tell me, I-Sheera. As a woman, do I look bad? I mean, do these burns make you want to turn away from me?"

Gadon snorted and coughing, rolled his eyes, "Oh, the pretty boy is worried about a few scars and losing some hair."

I-Sheera smiled, "Any woman who would turn away from you for such a small thing is unworthy of you."

Tanden said, "True enough. I don't think any of us are fit to dine at King Krebbem's table today. Besides Tuller, unless I miss my guess, someday you'll be a wealthy man. You'll have more women flocking to your side than you know what to do with."

Seenger said, "I should be able to give you a hand with them. Not that I'm attracted to such frail creatures, but I can keep them in line for you until a nice sturdy ogress comes along for me."

Gadon said, "While you're dreaming, little brother, pick me out a young one, so I can leave an heir for our father."

"Ha!" Tuller snorted. "Father and Mother already have a wife picked out for you and you know it."

"That thing?! She's why I keep going to sea. She's as big as a house and has an old crow for a mother. All Father can see is her father's money. Surely, Father has enough grandchildren already. He can't want my children that badly."

Tanden interrupted, "Gadon, be fair to your father. You are the eldest son. You'll take all your father's house when the time comes. And all of Marva's father's house, too—should you marry her—since she doesn't have any brothers or sisters."

Tuller laughed, "She isn't as big as you are anyway. Marva's a real sweet girl. No one in all Harkelle can match her cooking and you know it."

"Well, maybe," Gadon relented, "But I won't marry and settle down until Tanden does."

Tanden said, "Take care, Gadon. You may commit yourself to a wife before you know it."

Gadon shot back, "Ha! You'll never leave the seas. You treat your ships like your mistresses. Tell me you won't follow the White Wind to the ends of the earth to get her back."

Tanden nodded, "Yes. I'll retake the White Wind. I have to, it's my obligation. But I tell you this: I've had more pleasurable voyages than this trip. I'm not as young and spry as I used to be. And may I point out that the sun is up? Let's go. Gadon, lean on me until you regain your strength. Don't even begin to argue with me." Tanden gestured for Tuller to lead the way and for Seenger to follow.

The water was not as cold as Tanden remembered from last night, though Gadon shuddered when he slid into the water beside him. Putting his friend's arm up around his shoulders, Tanden grabbed him firmly. Without all of Gadon's additional weight, Tanden did not expect to sink as deeply into the mud as they had last night.

Tanden said privately to Gadon, "You tell me if you get tired. We'll get through this together, my friend."

Gadon nodded.

The two men moved through the murky water, fighting in unison against the quagmire sucking at their feet. They pushed through the tangled reeds. Quickly, Gadon began puffing and turned pale, but his short muscular legs pumped through the mire.

The group quickly re-crossed the stream at the cave entrance. Tuller ferried I-Sheera across and returned for Seenger. Gadon put up a halfhearted protest, but allowed Tanden to tow him across the water to the other side.

A few yards beyond the cave entrance, Tuller led them up to a rocky area along the cliff's edge. They negotiated their way over broken ground, around large boulders, and through muddy low spots, traveling much faster than in the swamp. Gadon was able to move on his own with little or no assistance, though his color had not returned and he continued to cough and fight to breathe.

The sun was now shining brightly on the swamp and the rising heat was turning the area into a morass of steam and humidity. The little group was soon struggling for air.

Tanden was helping Gadon over a mud hole full of shifting sand when I-Sheera's scream cut through the thick air. Tanden jerked Gadon up to a high spot as Seenger ran by them, bounding over the mud hole in a single leap. An angry shout from ahead of them rang through the air.

Gadon pushed at Tanden and shouted, "Go! I'll catch up."

Tanden whirled and raced after Seenger.

I-Sheera had been walking ahead of them with Tuller. Both had slipped out of sight some time ago while searching for the easiest path to follow. Tanden crested a small rise and saw Seenger leap over a boulder, disappearing from his sight. If they were running into trouble, Tanden did not want to rush headlong into the unknown. He angled away from the cliff onto a spit of land twisting away into the swamp. He should be able to flank any danger if he could move fast enough.

Vaulting a fallen tree, he circled around a small grove of young saplings, and jumped across a ribbon of water onto dry land. The ground was more solid than swamp and the area was thick with trees. Tanden ran, dodging around tree after tree, avoiding obvious bogs or sinkholes. After a short distance, he changed course, curving back to parallel the cliffs.

Struggling to fill his lungs in the heavy air, his heart pounding in his chest, he did not slow his pace until he heard shouts coming from his right. He jumped over a small, clear stream and stopped behind a jumble of vines entangling a grove. Tanden slid quietly along the stream bank. He crouched low and moved upstream using the meandering rivulet as cover.

When he heard voices shouting close to him, he hunkered down behind a deep cut in the bank. Squatting ankle deep in the stream, he strained to hear. He eased his knife from the sheath and held it at the ready. He calmed his breathing, willing his heart to slow. Reaching a cupped hand into the stream, he raised a handful of water and poured it over his head and down the back of his neck, cooling him. A few swallows wet his dry tongue. His body called for more of the refreshing liquid, but he ignored the call.

Slowly, he raised up, peeking over the bank, using small bushes as cover. Three men stood face-to-face against Tuller and Seenger. They all had their weapons drawn, ready for use in a tense standoff. Three men were hurrying out of sight away from Tanden.

One man was running like he wanted no part of any fight with an ogre coming out of a swamp. The other two were dragging I-Sheera. Her arms were bound behind her back and she was gagged, but she struggled against them.

Tanden tensed every muscle, desperately wanting to chase after I-Sheera's captors. He was certain Tuller and Seenger could hold their own, but he was not sure he could take on her kidnappers by himself.

From his current position, Tanden could blindside the men facing his two crewmen. The five were standing in a small clearing near a spring that fed the stream hiding Tanden.

Tanden darted from cover, dashing as quietly as possible toward the three men.

Tuller spotted him almost immediately and began yelling and cursing. He waved his sword menacingly at the strangers. Seenger stood frozen, eyes cold, his thick red tongue flicking out to wet his tusks. The actions of both crewmen was such a distraction that Tanden was on the kidnappers before they knew he was there.

He slammed into the right rear of the first man he came to, sending him crashing to the ground at Seenger's feet. His momentum sent him twisting into the middle man. Tanden drove the handle of his knife into the side of the man's head and shoved, driving him into the next man. The collision sent both men to the ground in a tangle of arms and legs.

Tanden veered to the side, remaining on his feet. He whirled around and quickly thrust his blade toward the top man in the tangle. He wanted to slice through the man's throat, instead, he held the cutting edge inches from the man's face.

"Hold still or die," Tanden hissed through clenched teeth. His jangled nerves spiked with energy, making his muscles twitch, causing the knifepoint to flick from eye to eye on his captive. Tuller's sword point lay inches from the other man's chest. Out the corner of his eye, Tanden saw that Seenger had cleanly decapitated his adversary.

"Who in the name of the dark demons are you?" Tanden spat at the man under his blade.

The man's clothing was leather and rough cloth like many tribes from this mountainous area, but he had light colored hair and pale bluish eyes. His companion was as dark as a Holdenite, but he sported a long red beard, braided as the Surr often did and his eyes were blue. Both men glared up at Tanden refusing to answer.

"Speak now or die," Tanden commanded. His voice was low, tense and threatening.

Seenger stepped into Tanden's line of sight where the downed men could see him. He picked up the dead man's head by the hair. Flipping his hand, he set it to spinning around and around. Seenger's face was emotionless and unreadable. He raised his bloody sword to his lips, flicking his tongue out to lick the flat of the dripping blade.

The blonde man began babbling at Tanden, his eyes pleading. Tanden did not recognize the language. He said, "Do you speak any other tongue?" He quickly asked in Geldonite, Tunstonian, Eastern, and Hummdhar, but there was no flicker of recognition on either man's face. Tanden flipped his man over onto his belly and gestured for the other man to turn face down in the dirt. Tanden put his knee in the middle of the blond man's back, pinning him to the ground.

Tanden said, "Tuller, search them and tie their hands behind their backs. We may need them alive. Seenger, backtrack and find Gadon."

From behind, Tanden heard Gadon puff, "No need. I'm here. Too late for the fun, I see."

Tanden looked at the heavyset man. He was standing with his hands on his knees. His face was pasty with flushed blotches of bright red on his cheeks. His breath wheezed in raspy gulps.

Tanden pointed at Gadon and then at a rock, "Sit," he commanded. "There's more to come. These animals have friends who took I-Sheera."

"Then why should I sit? Let's go after them." He reached for a sword laying on the ground near his feet.

"I said sit," Tanden wanted to shout, but he kept his voice low, but firm. "I don't have time to argue with you. Seenger, gather up their weapons and give them to Gadon. Hurry, Tuller, we don't want to leave the others alone with I-Sheera any longer than we have to. Gadon, you follow Seenger, Tuller, and me, bringing these two with you. I want them alive if possible, but if they give you any trouble, kill them. You catch your breath before you follow us, do you hear me?"

"I hear you, but I'm sound enough."

Tuller bound the men with their hands behind their backs, wrapping leather straps wrist to wrist, bending and immobilizing their arms. He tied a strap from their wrists to loop around their necks and tied a third strap to that strap, halfway between their wrists and necks. A quick yank on the last strap would jerk their arms at the shoulders, tightening the loop around their necks, cutting off their air supply. He handed the loose end of the straps to Gadon as if they were reins attached to the halter on a saurus.

Seenger handed a long sword with belted sheath to Tanden and a sheathed knife to Tuller. He draped the belt of another sheathed long sword around Gadon's neck, providing him with a pair of long weapons. He jammed a sheathed knife into his own belt and removed a wide copper bracelet from the dead man. With a casual flick of the wrist, he tossed the jewelry to Tuller. Reaching into the pool of blood at the dead man's neck, Seenger pulled out a delicate-looking silver amulet on a chain. Without wiping any blood or dirt from the necklace, he dropped it over his head where it lay, shining wetly in the sun.

Tuller shrugged and slipped his new bracelet onto his wrist.

Tanden pointed at the two captives and told Gadon, "What you find you can keep. But try to keep them alive. We may need them to trade for the woman. Drink from the spring quickly, then Tuller and Seenger to me." He sheathed his knife as he stepping to the spring. Watching their captives and the path where it disappeared into a small grove, he squatted and brought two quick handfuls of the cool water to his lips.

Tanden stood, spun on his heels and hurried down the path the three men had taken. It was not well trodden, but someone used it from time to time. He slowed cautiously when he reached the trees, alert for anyone coming back up the path. He did not want to stumble into the other men unprepared. He could not see anyone hiding in the trees, so he hurried on through the wooded area and halted at the other edge of the grove. The area ahead of him was not swamp, forest, or plains. There were a hundred places for a hundred men to hide. No one could cross the space unseen. There were scattered trees, rocks, and bushes, but no clusters of growth. A man would have to move stealthily from cover to cover. Tanden did not want to blunder foolishly forward, but he also did not want to spend the time slowly moving from cover to cover to remain hidden.

Tuller and Seenger stepped up next to him. Each of them held a sword at the ready. Tanden saw that the ogre had tied the severed head to his belt by its hair. Blood dripped down, coloring his leg. He had streaked his face with blood, giving him the look of a wild mountain ogre driven crazy by the dark demon and his minions.

CHAPTER TWENTY-EIGHT

Tuller said, "Tanden, this is my fault. I let I-Sheera move ahead of me. She seemed to like exploring and being out front. They had her bound and gagged before I could get to her. They would have taken me too if Seenger hadn't arrived."

"It isn't your fault, nor hers, nor mine. If you have to lay blame, it falls on the men who took her and those who command them. I intend to get her back. I'll take her from them or their leader, whether he's a man or the Dark One himself."

Holding his sword in his right hand and his knife in his left, Tanden stepped away from the trees. He quickly moved about ten paces forward following a parallel course across the open area. His new course should spoil the ambush plans of any man laying in wait for him along the path. Tuller and Seenger spread out to his right, each about five paces apart from each other. Quietly and resolutely, they pursued I-Sheera and her captives.

Tanden heard voices shouting ahead of them and began moving carefully from tree to tree, his eyes sweeping the area. Through a gap in the trees, he caught sight of a beach and the sea stretched out beyond. Quickly slipping up to a large windweathered oak, he surveyed the scene playing out on the sand.

Many old soldiers could describe the long boats the invading Surr brought when they poured out of the north, but Tanden had never seen one. Two such vessels stood anchored just off the shallow beach. They must have sailed down the DuVall River, slipping past the Holden outposts.

A dozen men were gathered on the beach, weapons ready. Another dozen herded a group of twenty-five or thirty men and women into clusters. The captors pushed and prodded until the captives huddled together, squatting in the sand. Each prisoner was tied to another, by hand and foot, with another link from neck to neck.

Many cultures used this method when transporting slaves. It allowed some measure of movement, but no one could run far or fast enough to escape.

I-Sheera was laying face down in the sand with a Surr slaver's foot holding her head down. He appeared to be unconcerned whether she could breathe or not. He gestured wildly up the path, speaking to a tall, red-haired man who had the look of someone in charge.

Tanden plainly heard their words, but did not understand the language. The slaver pointed to I-Sheera, who squirmed at his feet, and then pointed to the path leading to the spring. He leaned down, reached under I-Sheera, grabbed her breast and jiggled it. He stood up to the laughter of the men gathered around him.

The red-haired man answered him with a laugh and a nod, then gestured to those around him and pointed at the path. The command was obvious. Tanden concluded that as wild as Seenger was, as smart as Tuller was, and as determined as he was, the three of them could not overcome twelve armed men. He was also convinced he would not give up I-Sheera without a fight.

Tanden sheathed his weapons. Leaving the safety of the oak tree, he stepped into the open at the edge of the sand, shouting in Geldonite, "Surrender or die where you stand." The Surr slavers stopped in their tracks. Geldonite was the most commonly used language among the civilized, trading nations of the world, but Tanden doubted they understood his command. His presence and boldness caused them to hesitate. He decided if he could keep them hesitating, he could turn the situation to his benefit.

He shouted in Geldonite again. "I'm the high and mighty governor of this region and the military commander of the third and fifth armies under the leadership of His Mighty Emperor Garterious, the Magnificent. Who here speaks a civilized tongue? Come now! Speak, for you delay me and my troops on our march toward Stantinstadt."

The red-haired man stood forward, with a small dark man beside him. Both men looked skeptical, but neither looked willing to attack Tanden without knowing the size of the force that might be with him.

The dark man pointed to the red-haired man and spoke in halting Geldonite. "This is Orrick. He commands here. I am Narol of Garrold. I understand you well enough, but I know not of this ruler you speak of or of your armies."

Tanden bellowed, "Fool. I don't care what you know. Orrick commands nothing of importance here. Does this Orrick understand my language?"

Narol said, "Of course, he is an educated man."

Tanden dismissed the little man with a wave of his hand. "I don't speak to underlings. You!" He walked straight up to Orrick and jabbed a finger at the man's chest. "You hold my property. I want it back." Tanden gestured with a casual hand toward I-Sheera.

Every Surr on the beach turned to look at I-Sheera and then back to Tanden.

Orrick laughed, "You plan to take this one by yourself? I see no others with you."

Tanden shook his head as if he was speaking to a small child or a fool and said in a patronizing tone, "Nor will you until it's too late."

A shadow passed over Tanden causing him to glance upward. The severed head Seenger had carried, spun through the air. It landed with a dull thud in the midst of the Surr slavers. Several backed away, awkwardly stumbling over each other. A babble of arguing voices broke out among them.

Orrick shouted at them and they quieted. Most of the slavers appeared ready to run for their boats. Only three or four gripped their weapons tightly. Tanden saw their knuckles turning white across their sword hilts. These men were true warriors, men who held their fighting spirit in check by the tightest of reins. If they rushed Tanden, the others would follow.

The Surr slaver shouted again and the men guarding the slaves on the beach began hustling their charges toward the ships.

Tanden said, "There are one or two in that bunch that I might be willing to purchase from you for the right price." Then he roared, "After you give me back what is rightfully mine."

Tanden noticed Orrick and Narol eyeing the area behind him where Tuller and Seenger were hiding. Soon all of the Surr were looking behind him. Tanden turned his back on the Surr as if unconcerned. Kneeling next to the oak tree, bound and gagged, were the two Surr captured by the spring. Gadon was out of sight, but the flat of a sword reached from behind a tree to rest on the head of one of the captives.

Tanden turned completely around, slowly showing the Surr he had no fear of them. He used that time to look for Seenger and Tuller. Neither was in sight.

"You!" Tanden said, jabbing a finger at Orrick's chest, "Orrick is it? Yes, I'm sure it is, but no matter. These two are yours, I think. I'm feeling generous today. You may have them back, but release that,"—he jiggled his finger in I-Sheera's direction and continued—"now, or I'll command my archers to fire and I'll take everything."

Orrick started to speak, but Tanden shouted, "Count yourself blessed by the great six gods this day that I don't exact a toll from you for trespassing on the emperor's realm."

Tanden watched Seenger step onto the beach. The Surr were focused on Tanden, so to them it looked like Seenger appeared out of thin air. A few of them broke and ran at the sight of the ogre. Tanden was accustomed to the creature's looks, but had he not known Seenger, he might have run as well.

Seenger's leather clothing barely covered his massive size. The garments were torn and filthy, remnants stolen from dead Hummdhar warriors. A sword casually propped across one shoulder, he had two knives stuck prominently in his ill-fitting trousers. His hair was a wild tangled mass, matted with bat blood and mud from the swamps. Red blood streaked his face. His bone white tusks and fangs were shining in the bright sunlight. One leg was painted with blood from mid-thigh to the tip of his boot. Every exposed area of his thick pebble-like hide was scratched, bruised, and mottled.

Seenger walked by Tanden. The Surr milling about parted as Seenger walked directly toward where I-Sheera lay in the sand. Her captor still had his foot on her neck. He leaned backward at the ogre's approach, but held his position until Seenger placed his hand flat on the middle of the man's chest and gave him a mighty shove. The slaver flew backward, scattering sand as he landed on his back, sprawled on the beach.

During the commotion, Tanden glanced toward the trees to see Gadon slipping from tree to tree, quickly making his way toward the west. Tuller was not in sight. He turned back, relieved to note that all of the slavers were watching the ogre.

Seenger reached down to I-Sheera. He clutched a fistful of tangled black hair and lifted her bodily into the air. The woman screeched in pain through the gag covering her mouth. He set her down on her feet and slapped her backhanded across the face, forcefully sending her crashing to the sand. He stepped to her and bent to pick her up, but she scrambled out of his way, able to get to her feet.

Seenger swung at her again and missed.

Nimbly, she darted out of his way, raced through the Surr slavers and ducked behind Tanden. Grabbing her shoulder, Tanden spun her around to face where he thought Tuller might be hiding, and he pushed hard. The shove sent her careening off the beach. He aimed a well-timed kick, barely missing her as she ran from them.

Tuller stepped from behind a tree in time to catch I-Sheera in his arms. Tanden noticed the man looked almost as wild as Seenger. His hair was a mass of scabs and burns, with tufts of hair pointing in all directions. Dried mud covered him from the waist down. He was matted with leaves and bits of weeds. Seenger looked more animal than ogre, but Tuller looked more like a thorny plant than a man.

Seenger casually strolled past Tanden, following the woman without looking back.

Tanden faced Orrick and said, "Some of them are almost more of a problem than they're worth, don't you agree?" Without waiting for a response he shouted, "Orrick. Get out of my sight. Take what's yours. I don't care about them. No! Wait."

Tanden needed to stall and delay the Surr until his friends could put some distance between them and the group on the beach.

He stood eye-to-eye with the red-haired Surr. "I don't care if you trade in Hummdhars, Coodhars, or even those damnable Holdenite bastards, but have you stolen my lord's subjects? Maybe I should have my men board your ships to inspect your stock, what do you say to that, Orrick?"

Without waiting for a response, Tanden spun on his heels to walk eastward, the opposite way Gadon had gone. Over his shoulder, he shouted, "I'll leave a detail here to watch your departure. You have one hour to be gone from my sight or I will come back, kill you all, and burn your puny ships."

He walked casually up the path toward the spring without turning around. Sweat trickled down his back, tickling him between his shoulder blades. He wanted to turn and run after his friends, but he looked neither to the left nor to the right, keeping his eyes fastened on the path. He willed the Surr to watch his departing back. The longer they watched him, the more distance the others could gain.

Tanden did not know how he had bluffed the Surr into inaction. An old saying rumbled through his head, "The man who wavers eats the loser's sparse meal, but the man of bold action gains his own kingdom." Usually Tanden did not have much use for old sayings, but today he greatly hoped this one might hold some small measure of truth.

Once he was out of sight of the beach, Tanden glanced back over his shoulder. No one was following him. He turned abruptly and ran as fast as his legs could carry him, angling away from the beach, but heading in the approximate direction of his crew. He watched the area in the direction of the beach for any sign the Surr slavers were following him. He scanned the area ahead of him looking for any of his crew.

There was nothing in the clear open area to slow him down. He was well away from the swamps and on solid dry land. However, Tanden tired quickly, even with a full night's sleep behind him. The air was thick and humid increasing the effort he was forced to take to breathe while running. Still, he ran. Gadon, in his weakened condition could not have traveled far or fast. He should meet up with the others sooner than he would like.

Tanden was beginning to think he had passed them when a rock sailed over his head and thudded into the ground. He spun about, dropping to the dirt. Looking back he saw the sun reflecting off metal in the grass. Attached to the metal was Tuller's hand waggling at him to stay down and crawl to him.

Lying in the dirt, surrounded by tall clumps of weeds, Tanden could not see beyond a dozen yards in each direction. Slowly, he slid on his belly from one patch of weeds to the next.

A clank of metal on metal and a shout froze Tanden in place. The Surr must have shaken themselves into action and were searching the area. Tanden had not been seen. He would not be alive if he had. The weeds afforded him only minor protection, so he needed to find solid cover soon. Tuller must have found some hiding place, because Tanden had almost run him over without seeing him.

Tanden slithered silently a few feet toward Tuller and dropped into a depression next to the sailor. The depression was no more than a low spot in a field. It probably filled with rainwater at times. Even now the bottom oozed mud. Its value as a hiding spot lay in the fact that it was ringed by bushes and weeds and enabled them to stay below the visual plane of the field. His entire crew was hunkered down in the mud. Gadon lay on his side curled up. Tanden fought to control his ragged breathing. Their hiding place was precarious enough without making noise to easily give their position away.

Tuller held up seven fingers and pointed toward the beach, indicating seven slavers were searching for them in that direction. Tanden saw a flash of sunlight reflecting against metal again. The rays of the mid-morning sun were shining off the brass bracelet Seenger had given Tuller back at the spring.

Tanden pointed at his own wrist, wiggled his flat hand, then drew a finger across his throat, frowning deeply. Tuller looked down at the bracelet. He scooped a handful of mud from the bottom of the hole to smear the brass, successfully hiding the shine.

Tanden looked over at Seenger who was cautiously watching the opposite direction from Tuller. Tanden caught the ogre's attention and signaled a question.

Seenger shook his head and held out a clenched fist. No one was coming from his direction.

Tuller continued watching the slavers moving between them and the sea.

Tanden glanced at I-Sheera. He smiled at her, but she did not meet his eyes. Someone had untied her hands and released her gag. She was visibly upset. She sat shaking, huddled in the mud with her arms wrapped around her sides.

Tuller silently signaled, "All clear."

Seenger whispered, "I don't see anyone."

Tanden softly asked Tuller, "Which way did they go? Toward their ships or away from them?"

"Seven walked away and six came back," Tuller answered.

"Surr slavers?"

Tanden nodded and said, "First, we find both Hummdhars and Coodhars coming out of the mountains and moving to the coasts of the Black Sea. Then we find Surr slavers as open as you please. When Warwall pulled his red troops out of Stantinstadt, he left this area wide open to all. I told Father, King Krebbem was making a mistake not to retake Stantinstadt. That town is the key to controlling the Oggy Strait and all of the Black Sea. Something will have to be done or the Holden Empire will be fighting more than one war at a time, and fighting for our very survival."

Tuller said, "I agree. Something will have to be done, but not by us. I think we have enough problems of our own."

Tanden snapped, "Damn politicians! We wouldn't be having problems if it weren't for politicians."

Gadon looked up and wheezed, "Careful. That almost sounds like treason against King Krebbem. Men have been hanged for less. Not that I'd mind if you get hanged, but everyone knows that I'm your friend. They would hang me just for good measure. Now, I enjoy a good hanging every now and again, but by my very breath, I don't think I'd enjoy any personal participation in that activity."

Tuller smiled and said, "Don't worry, big brother. We may not live long enough to die from a comfortable hanging."

Gadon smiled weakly, "True, all too true."

Tanden shook his head. "Tuller, any sign of the slavers?"

Tuller replied, "No."

"Good. Then we move west, away from their ships. Stay together. Try to stay out of sight as much as possible."

Each man stood, trying to watch every direction at once. Tuller pulled Gadon up and out of the mud hole. Tanden stepped out and signaled for them to move west. Seenger stepped up next to him, continuing to watch the area to the east near the beach.

I-Sheera was the last to stand. She was still shaking and holding herself. Tanden reached out a hand to pull her up next to him. Slowly, she accepted his hand and joined him and Seenger. Facing the two, she suddenly doubled up her fist, swiveled her hips and punched Seenger dead center in the middle of his chest. The punch was well delivered and sharp, but the ogre didn't even flinch.

She hissed, "You hit me!"

Tanden would have laughed, but she spun on him and said, "And you tried to kick me." She swung her fist at him, but Tanden backed away from her in time.

He said, "But I missed. And I meant to miss. Great glory, girl! We were trying to rescue you from slavers."

She spat at him, "And I missed you just now. I won't miss next time." She turned and stalked off after Gadon and Tuller.

Seenger looked at Tanden, rubbing the spot on his chest, "She carries a mighty fist for one so little. I assume that among human women such a strike is not an invitation to bed?"

Tanden laughed and shook his head. Speaking so softly that I-Sheera couldn't hear, "She is odd, even for a human woman, Seenger. One moment she's as playful as a kitten, or as shy and quiet as a kitchen mouse, and the next moment you'd swear she's a lioness looking for lunch. A hellcat, for sure."

CHAPTER TWENTY-NINE

I-Sheera stormed away. Anger flared in her eyes.

Suddenly, she turned and walked back. She stood there quietly with her head down for a moment. She put the palm of her hand flat against Tanden's chest. "I'm sorry, my Lord. Thank you for coming to save me." Turning to Seenger, she stood on tiptoes and stretched up to kiss his cheek. "Forgive me, Seenger, I struck in anger, but I wasn't angry with you."

Seenger wiped his cheek with the back of his hand. He looked to Tanden and said, "Captain, I would send this one back where she came from. I think her mind isn't right."

Tanden said, "Follow Gadon and Tuller. We need to put some distance between us and the Surr." He gestured for Seenger to move on ahead. He took I-Sheera by the elbow and turned her, propelling her after Seenger.

After a time, she asked, "Tanden?"

When he said nothing she continued, "I want to tell you why I hit Seenger." Still, Tanden did not speak. "I know you're ashamed of me. I'm sorry."

"Woman, you said you were sorry once. I believed you then, you don't need to repeat yourself. I'm not ashamed of you. It's true, I don't think you are like other women at all. Of course, that's not entirely a bad thing."

Her voice quivered as she said, "I've been thinking and I don't know why I hit Seenger. I was running ahead of Tuller and I felt free. I think for the first time in my life I felt free to make my own choices. And then, suddenly, it was all gone again. I didn't understand what you said to those men, but you acted like I was unimportant and I felt that way all over again."

Tanden took her hand as they walked along side by side. "We were trying to make the Surr think you are unimportant to us. We might not have gotten you away from them if they thought otherwise. You are a free woman to make your own choices. You made the choice to run ahead of us. That choice got you captured by the Surr. Freedom isn't always easy, I-Sheera. Every action or decision you make has results, some good and some bad. We're where we are today, because of the decisions I've made. You'll be where you'll be tomorrow because of the decisions you make for yourself."

They had moved four or five miles along the coast away from the slavers when Tuller waved to catch their attention. He was urging them to hurry. Seenger joined the brothers crouching behind a cluster of bushes. Each of them drew a weapon. Gadon held his sword point down as if it was too heavy to hold upright, but his hand tightly gripped its hilt. Tuller and Seenger flanked him.

Tanden and I-Sheera joined them. He looked at Tuller, gesturing a silent question in Gadon's direction. Tuller shook his head slightly, a look of deep concern on his face.

I-Sheera stooped next to Gadon. She brushed her hand against his forehead. He weakly pushed it away, but she persisted, touching the back of her hand to his cheek and forehead. She took the sword from his hand and laid it against her own knees. She cradled the man in her arms and he seemed to melt against her.

She said, "His fever has returned. It's burning the strength from his body."

Gadon mumbled, "Leave me alone, girl. I'm not a baby to be pampered." However, he made no effort to move away from her.

Tanden put a hand on his shoulder and squeezed it gently. Turning to Tuller and Seenger, he asked, "What's ahead?"

Tuller answered, "It looks like a small fishing village. There are a handful of small huts and one big building. I don't see any people around. There's one small fishing boat pulled up to the dock."

Seenger asked, "Why didn't the Surr anchor off this shore if they took the people from this village captive? Instead, they pulled to shore down the coast. There's good water, look." He pointed toward the buildings.

Tanden's eyes followed Seenger's fingers. He saw a diverted stream flowing into a cistern before overflowing and running out to the sea. A small fishing boat was tethered to a little dock with its nets drying on racks nearby. The morning's catch was gutted and strung up to dry in the sun. A mid-morning cook fire burned in front of one of the huts.

The village did not look prosperous, but it also did not look like it had just been ransacked and looted by invaders. The Surr were only a few miles to the east. This village was in grave danger if the slavers were sweeping along the coast, plying their trade.

Tanden said, "Seenger, come with me. Tuller, stay here and watch our backs. Gadon, you stay, too and watch I-Sheera. Make sure she doesn't get into any more trouble."

Gadon croaked hoarsely, "You can count on it."

I-Sheera's glared at Tanden, but before she could respond, he winked at her. She nodded and smiled. Turning back to Gadon, she drew the man's head into her lap.

Seenger looked ready to move into the village, but Tanden stopped him, gesturing for him to follow. Tanden led the ogre in a sweeping circle around the backside of the village. They entered the village from the west, opposite of where the other three were hiding. Both held their weapons at the ready as Tanden called in Geldonite, "Hello the village!" There was no response.

"Seenger, stay close and watch our backs."

The two looked into two huts. Possessions were scattered about, but there were no people. They walked to the hut with a cooking fire burning slowly in a pit.

Seenger pointed at the fire and said in a whisper, "That top log was just added. See, it's hardly burned."

Tanden nodded. He was reaching for the curtain covering the doorway when a wild-eyed man burst through waving a rusty sword. The small toothless man had the rough hands of a fisherman. Seenger backtracked out of the way as Tanden used his own sword to turn away stroke after stroke. The man was not a swordsman. He hacked and cut at Tanden like he was chopping wood.

Tanden shouted, "Stop this. Stop before you hurt yourself."

Tanden noticed Seenger shift to a defensive position as a younger version of the fisherman rushed from the hut. Using both hands, the youth held a long sword over his head. He was no more than thirteen or fourteen. Running past Tanden, the youth moved to attack Seenger.

Tanden parried a wild cut from the older man. Throwing his weight into his shoulder, he pushed the old man backward. Shifting his stance, he reached out to grab the running youth by the back of his shirt. Tanden threw the boy to the dirt at his feet. The boy's sword flew out of his grasp. Tanden placed his foot firmly on the youth's chest to pin him to the ground. He was certain Seenger would have killed the boy without a thought if Tanden had not intervened.

Something had driven the boy to attack a full-grown ogre with just a sword. Seenger was exceptionally strong, but not a great swordfighter, yet it would not take a skilled fighter to kill a youngster.

Tanden shouted in Holdenish, "Stop this, damn it, before I have to hurt both of you!" The old man froze in mid-stroke, backing away. "Better. Drop your sword."

"You're Holdenite?"

Tanden nodded, "Drop your sword, please."

When the rusty blade clattered to the ground, Tanden took his foot off the youth. The boy scampered up and darted behind the older man. Defiance blazed in the youth's eyes. The older man looked more scared than angry, not quite meeting Tanden's gaze.

"I'm Tanden from Harkelle. This is Seenger. Who are you and where is everyone else?"

The man looked wildly about and asked, "Are you alone?"

Tanden answered, "No. Do you know of the slavers up the coast?"

The two fishermen looked at each other. The old man eyed Tanden, then his look seemed to slide away again. He asked Tanden, "Have you seen the Surr?"

"We had a brief meeting."

The old man bobbed his head and squatted by the fire, indicating Tanden should join him. As Tanden dropped to eye level, the old man said, "My son and I saw their ships this morning as we returned from fishing. We told the others they were coming. They all ran to the hills to hide. The boy and I wanted to get our catch dried and get back on our boat. Once aboard her, the slavers can't catch us. She's a fast ship." The man cackled, "A pretty ship, isn't she?"

"Yes, she's a fine looking vessel. But you risked your life and freedom from slavers for a few fish?" Tanden looked into the man's eyes and realized he was most likely no older than Tanden, but the hard life of a poor fisherman had aged him well beyond his years.

The man looked back at Tanden and said, "A few fish to you, but to the people in this village, those few fish are the difference between eating and starving. The Black Sea is stingy and only the freshening waters of the DuVAll allow any of us to live here at all."

Clasping a hand on the man's shoulder, Tanden said, "You're right. I didn't mean to question your judgment. I meant only to comment on the bravery of you and your son. You have my deepest apologies if I failed to speak clearly."

"Nothing to it, nothing at all. Besides, the slave ships may not come this far."

"Seenger, call the others in. You best keep a sharp look out eastward for the Surr."

The fisherman's eyes grew wide like he was seeing Seenger for the first time. The boy backed away but watched with curiosity on his face.

The man asked, "An ogre?" Without waiting for an answer, "How many are you?"

Tanden said, "Five. Is it just you and your boy remaining in the village?"

The man said, "Yes. Oh, forgive my rudeness, I'm Mark. This is my son, Little Mark."

Tanden smiled at the boy, but spoke to the father, "Little? I do not think so. He has the look of a full-grown man to me and courageous to attack an ogre single-handed."

Little Mark's chest puffed out at the flattery.

"I'm looking for my ship. I believe she's sailing the coast toward Stantinstadt. Have you seen her?"

Mark's eyes lit up, "Aye. Aye, I think I have. A Holdenite merchant ship riding low and slow, full of cargo? From Harkelle?"

Tanden nodded, "Then the White Wind has passed by here?"

Mark's head bobbed as if yanked by a string. He turned to watch Gadon and I Sheera sink down next to the fire. Tuller stood over them.

"The ship?" Tanden prompted.

"Huh?" Mark did not take his eyes off Gadon, "Oh, yes. Your ship. Little Mark and I saw her pass by yesterday at about this time. We signaled for them to come to anchor. Thought to trade a bit, you know? She sailed right on past. Going to Stantinstadt? That's south by southeast of here. Why would your ship be sailing west along the coast?" Before Tanden could answer, the man rambled on, "Looking for you, I'll wager. Yes, I understand. Makes sense. Do you think she'll sail back this way if they find they missed you?" Almost without a breath, Mark continued, "Your man is sick."

"Yes. I believe he has a fever."

The fishermen scooted back a few feet and eyed Gadon carefully. Tanden understood their fear. Unknown illnesses had been known to decimate whole villages. Unhealthy strangers were not normally welcome.

Tanden said, "It's a fever from a chill. He was caught out in a cold rain."

Mark said, "Okay." Not moving any closer, mark kept his eye on Gadon. "When did you say your ship would sail back this way?"

"I didn't say. Since she has sailed past, we'll catch up with her in Stantinstadt. Mark, may we call upon your hospitality for a meal?"

The fisherman's head bobbed again, "Of course. Of course, without a doubt. Yes, yes, yes. I can offer you fish aplenty. What's mine is yours! Please help yourself." The man shuffled over to his son. He put his arm around his boy and said to Tanden, "And we have an old woman of the village who's a healer, for your sick friend. I'll send Little Mark after her."

Mark turned the boy around and spoke quietly to him for a moment. Little Mark started to run, but Mark grabbed him, hissed quietly in the boy's ear and pointed at the cliffs. Giving the boy a slap on the rump, he sent him rushing off toward the hills.

Tanden asked, "Won't your healer be afraid to come back with the slaver's so close?"

Mark's eyes rolled around, looking every which way but at Tanden, "Oh, huh, no. If they come by ship, we can get away into the hills before they reach shore. And…and if they come by the beach, then your ogre can give us warning enough we can get away on my ship before they get here. Once aboard the Wave

Master, their ships won't be able to catch us." The old man cackled happily at his logic. Mark quickly grew sober again, "Ungh, besides, uh, I don't think your man is fit to travel much anyway."

Tanden looked down at Gadon, who had fallen asleep by the fire. The big man's breathing was labored. However, he appeared to be sleeping soundly.

Tanden pointed out to I-Sheera a Eucalyptus tree shading the small hut, "Gather some leaves from that tree and find a pot to make a tea for Gadon. It should soothe his cough."

Mark said, "Aye. It's a good tree for that. Don't know why I didn't think of it myself. There are pots in my hut, young lady. Bring the big one as well and we can cook up some of these fish."

Tanden said, "Mark, as you see we're in need of a boat to sail to Stantinstadt. Are you willing to sail us?"

"No. No. No. I need my boat to fish. If I don't fish, we don't eat."

Tanden nodded his understanding, "What would you trade for the use of your ship? I have many goods aboard the White Wind. I'll pay your price when I reach my ship."

"Trade now. Pay me now, not later."

"Mark, we're all honorable men here. As you can see, I have very little to trade."

"No. No trade, no ship."

Tanden sighed, "I thank you for what hospitality you're giving us now. Let me know if you change your mind. I'd pay you well for a few days sail."

Mark shook his head violently from side to side and exclaimed, "Two days there, with the wind and three days back against the wind. Five days without fishing. No. No ship unless I get trade goods first. But, you rest here. Relax. Your man needs rest. Sit here for awhile. The sun will be hot today and your pet ogre watches."

Tanden said, "Tuller, see what you can do to give I-Sheera a hand. When you get some food together, take something out to Seenger. I'm going to walk around a bit. Stay alert and ready to move. Wake Gadon up to eat. Force him to drink as much tea as you can, otherwise let him sleep."

Tanden turned on his heels. He retraced his steps to the west, walking out of the village. He was not comfortable in the village. He found the little fisherman and his son repulsive. He was unsure if his feelings were infecting his judgment about their safety. The Surr were close, only five or six miles eastward along the coast. Tanden was not as ready as the fisherman to discount the danger they presented. But, they did have to eat and rest for Gadon's sake, but they would not stay long.

CHAPTER THIRTY

Tanden walked in a slow circle around the small fishing village watching the surrounding area, looking for clues to his uneasiness.

"*What is the matter with you, Tanden? Have you become a man that dislikes another just because he's poor and a little dimwitted? That's no reason to distrust him. It's his home and hospitality, after all.*

"*No. The man doesn't look me in the eyes when he talks to me. I don't like that. But that isn't it. I know something isn't right. Damn it! I feel something is wrong and I'm just not smart enough to figure it out. Well, there's the whole package. I deserve to be with Mark and his son if I'm no smarter than them.*"

He shook his head as he thought of the White Wind, "*Missed her! What in the name of all six gods could I have done to reach this coast faster? No. It's not good to dwell on the past. There's nothing to be done about what has already happened. Forget it. Think forward, Tanden. How do we get to Stantinstadt before the White Wind sails for Tunston? We could take the fishing boat by force.*

"*No. That's theft, no matter what my reasons. I don't think it's a good idea. We could attack the Surr and take one their boats. No, I'm sure that isn't a good idea. I have no answers.*"

Tanden stopped and stared at the ground beneath his feet. Footprints in the dirt led away from the village toward the hills. He recognized them as Little Mark's footprints because the boy was shoeless. "*The boy runs carelessly and doesn't try covering his tracks. But, why should he?*"

Tanden spun about and began searching the ground around him. It was easy to read the boy's tracks and his own bootprints, but he did not see any other fresh prints. There should be more tracks in the dirt if the whole village left in haste. Yesterday morning's storm would have washed out any earlier tracks. Dimwitted or not the boy should have taken care not to leave tracks for slavers to follow to the villagers hiding in the hills.

He picked out Little Mark's trail and began following it toward the hills. Once he was out of sight of the village the boy's tracks turned eastward toward the Surr anchorage. Tanden continued following the boy's footprints until he was positive the boy was heading straight to the slavers.

Tanden stopped in frustration. "*The mouth of the DuVall River is to the west. The slavers would have to pass by this village to beach their boats east of here. Passing by such an easy target isn't the Surr way Even if the people managed to escape, the village would have been ransacked and burned to the ground.*"

Turning toward the sea, he found Tuller and Seenger standing under a few trees east of the village, eating fish stew from crude wooden bowls. They must have seen him coming long before he spotted them. Though they were eating and appeared to be relaxing, they remained alert and watchful.

Before Tanden could speak, Tuller said, "We have the fisherman's ship. The Wave Master! Silly name for a slow-looking fishing tub, but he agreed to sail us to Stantinstadt."

"How?" Tanden asked, "When I talked to him, he was firmly set against sailing us."

Tuller said, "I-Sheera did it. She's a good bargainer. With a few tips from an expert, she could be almost as good as I am."

Seenger interrupted, "Food is on the fire, Captain. Shouldn't you eat?"

Tanden nodded, "Time enough, I think. We should have about half an hour before unwanted visitors show up."

"Half an hour? How? Where?" Tuller stared back at Tanden.

"Trouble is coming, but first, I want to hear about this trade. How did we get the boat?" Tanden asked.

Tuller replied, "She offered to trade the jewel. The little man's eyes lit with fire when he saw it glittering in the sun. She drove a hard trade with what little she had to trade."

"Little!" Tanden exclaimed. "That little represented her freedom."

"I don't mean little in value, but in making a good bargain, there has to be give and take. Give a little here, take a little there. With one piece of jewelry to trade, it's all or nothing. He almost didn't make the bargain." Tuller held up his naked wrist, "She even gave him my new bracelet, but she made him promise to sell it back to me when we reach the White Wind."

"He holds the jewelry?" Tanden asked.

"Yes. He was very insistent he held the trade before we sailed."

Tanden nodded, "Like before; he was insistent with me. I don't believe he expects to sail us anywhere. I believe he's made an alliance with the Surr." He told them about the boy's tracks heading straight for the slavers.

Tanden said, "I believe it'll take the boy at least half an hour to reach the Surr and another half hour for them to reach us. I don't believe we have to run, but I'd prefer to be gone before they get here." He gestured with his head for them to move back to the village.

Tuller's eyes became slits. As they walked, his temper flared, "I'd be willing to wager the boy was in the group of slavers on the beach. Remember there were seven Surr who went by us, but only six returned? The old man and the boy pegged us from the moment we walked into the village."

Tanden agreed, "And the father is trying to delay us until the son brings enough slavers back to capture us."

The three walked up to the little fisherman sitting by the fire. He looked fitful and worried, but Tanden knelt beside him and put an arm around his thin shoulders. Tanden smiled and patted the man gently. The man looked beyond Tanden to Tuller and Seenger.

Tanden could imagine what the little man saw. Tuller must be seething with anger. He had been through a lot in the last few days and was on the edge of unreasonable violence. However, his ability as a negotiator allowed him to conceal his anger from strangers. Seenger would appear calm and relaxed, but Tanden knew he was the more dangerous of the two.

Ogres were never to be taken lightly. Seenger would strike and kill the fisherman without remorse or hesitation. The fisherman only saw their calm faces and Tanden felt him relax slightly.

Tanden said, "I understand you have generously relented after successful bargaining to sail us to Stantinstadt?" Tanden took a bowl offered by I-Sheera and began eating as he talked. The fish stew was bland and pasty, but it was hot and filling.

Mark nodded and reflexively put a hand to his chest, patting a small bulge that had not been there earlier. "Good trade."

"Yes. I'm told you bargain well. And may I say you have a nice village? While we eat, my men can put provisions in the boat for the sail to Stantinstadt."

"Provisions?" Mark asked.

"Surely we can't sail for two days without food and water? Don't worry, I'll pay you well for your goods."

"But...but my boy can stow supplies when he returns. Your men should rest. It'll be a long sail."

"True. Very true, Mark. You're a man of good judgment, but these are hardworking men. They can work now and rest on the voyage, besides, wouldn't it be best to be fully provisioned in case we have to get to the boat quickly to escape the Surr?"

Mark said, "You eat and take your rest, I'll watch for the Surr. I'll give you plenty of warning."

Tanden tossed his bowl to the ground and he stood over the man. "You are a generous man, but, if you please, show my men where you keep your water skins. I'll rest much better once we're prepared."

Mark glanced around him and said, "I don't know if we have enough skins for everyone."

Tanden grabbed the man by the front of his tunic and lifted him bodily to face him eye-to-eye. He hissed, "I've had enough of your lies. If you speak any word other than the truth, I'll cut out your tongue and use it to flavor this stew."

The little fisherman was shaking as Tanden set him on his feet. He did not resist when Tanden reached into his shirt to retrieve the jewel and bracelet. Tanden continued holding the man in place with a firm grip on his tunic. He tossed the bracelet back to Tuller and dropped the jewel into I-Sheera's hands.

She said, "I don't understand. I made an honest trade. The jewel is mine to do with as I wish. Didn't you tell me that?"

Tanden answered, "Yes I did, but our friend Mark wasn't bargaining in good faith. Were you, Mark?" Tanden shook the little fisherman until his eyes rattled.

The man struck at Tanden, but when Tanden refused to flinch, the man put both hands on Tanden's wrist and hung limp in his grip.

Tuller said, "He's in league with the slavers. He took your treasure and planned to sell us all to the Surr."

Looking at Tuller and Seenger, Tanden commanded, "Find all the supplies you can to stock the boat. Take whatever you find that we might need. I-Sheera, get Gadon on the boat. Make him as comfortable as you can, then help the others gather what food and water you can find."

He stared into Mark's face, "And you little man." Tanden left the sentence unfinished. He dragged the man to the drying racks where the fish had been gutted and strung up to dry. He tied the man hand and foot to a post among the fish. "Did you sell the other villagers to the Surr?"

Mark shook his head, "No. No. I wouldn't do that. They're my family. They hide in the hills whenever the slavers come."

"Why?"

Mark shrugged, "Who can trust the Surr? They hid so the Surr wouldn't take them, too."

Tanden said, "Too? Who did the slavers take?"

The little fisherman shrugged, refusing to answer the question.

"Speak. I'll gut you and leave you to dry with your catch if you so much as look like you're not going to do as I command."

"We trapped other travelers and people from other villages and held them for the Surr. We didn't have any choice. It's not our fault. If we hadn't done it they would have made slaves of the whole village."

Tanden nodded, "Yes. I can see you've been poorly treated. How many times have the Surr visited here? And why do they set anchor to the east instead of at your dock?"

"Three," Mark gulped. "Yes. Yes. Yes. Three. See. They built the big building for us to hold their slaves for them. They don't sail up to our village. That way no one passing by becomes suspicious of us. It was their plan. They made us do it. We didn't have any choice."

Tanden walked away from the man, ignoring his whining pleas for mercy.

Tanden checked on his crew. I-Sheera was helping Gadon into the stern of the boat. Tuller and Seenger had found skins and clay jugs and were filling them from the cistern. Tanden walked back to the fisherman's hut to search for anything of use. He found a bag of tubers and a basket of berries and wild fruits. He stepped outside in time to hand the food to I-Sheera. She took them from his hand and rushed back toward the boat.

Tanden looked into other huts. The occupants either left in a hurry or were poor housekeepers. He doubted there was anything worth retrieving from any hut. The villagers would have taken anything of value into the hills or the Surr would have taken it. He stepped into another hut. Everything inside was stacked neatly and stored away. The only thing of value Tanden found was a warm, woolen blanket.

He walked over to the big building that served as the holding pen for the slaves awaiting delivery to the Surr. He stopped at the doorway. It was empty, except for poles sunk into the ground, spaced evenly around the interior. Each pole had rings set into it to secure slaves. Even in the shadows, Tanden could see that the villagers let the slaves lie in their own filth and garbage.

He turned again to check on the progress of the crew. I-Sheera sat in the boat fussing about Gadon. Tuller had stowed the provisions and was making ready to sail. Seenger stood next to Mark with his knife in his hand, its blade glinting in the sun. Tanden was about to call to Seenger, when the ogre sliced through a line holding fish to the drying rack. The ogre bundled the fish in his arms, moved to the other pole and cut loose the other end.

Tanden nodded his satisfaction. He did not want to kill the little fisherman. Once the Surr found them gone and their trap spoiled, they would most likely enslave the man and his son. It would give them a taste of their own treachery. Their preparations for departure were proceeding at a good pace. They should be well away before the Surr could respond to the boy's call.

Still holding the blanket and before heading to the boat, he had one more task to perform. He walked to the fire and picked up a flaming brand. He walked to the far end of the village and, one by one, set each hut on fire. At each hut, he stood patiently to ensure the flames caught. Slowly, he walked back to where Mark stood, shaking against his bonds.

Standing quietly in front of the little fisherman, Tanden looked at his crew. Tuller had the small craft loaded and ready for a fast exit. The boat's sails were up, but luffing without catching the wind. A good strong wind blew steadily from the west. A quick twist of the tiller would bring the sails into the wind.

Tanden doubted the little man's claim that his fishing tub could outrun the Surr boats. It was the best ship to get them to Stantinstadt because it was the only available ship. It certainly would be better than walking.

I-Sheera and Seenger ran to Tanden.

He handed the woman the blanket, "For Gadon. Wrap him up tightly against the sea breezes. Get him to drink as much water as you can, then let him sleep. Go, I-Sheera." He pushed her, not unkindly, toward the ship.

Seenger pointed his knife at the little fisherman. He asked Tanden, "What do we do with this thing?"

"Well," Tanden said, "I haven't had good liver in a long time, but we don't have time. Leave him here. I doubt the Surr will be happy with him for letting us to get away."

At Tuller's shout, they spun around. The man stood on the rail of the ship, pointing out to sea. Tanden could see both Surr boats slicing through the waves. With their sails down, they must have put men to the oars to make headway against the wind coming straight out of the west.

Tanden and Seenger started to sprint toward the boat.

Tuller called, "Come on, hurry."

Tanden caught sight of Surr coming through the trees and bushes at the edge of the village. They would cut him off before he could reach the little dock. He grabbed Seenger's arm and spun him about to face the invaders.

Tanden shouted to Tuller, "Stay with the boat."

Tanden must have underestimated the speed of the boy or the reaction of the slavers. The four Surr bearing down on them must be the fastest of the slavers. Others would surely follow. The men did not look tired for having run five or six miles. They bellowed war cries and ran straight at Tanden and Seenger. Only the craziest Surr berserker warriors attacked an armed ogre.

Tanden and Seenger roared their response and charged directly at the oncoming warriors. Tanden focused his attention on the two men on the left. A large blond warrior stood foremost in his sight. The man carried a huge wood hammer, carved and banded in black iron. The muscles of his bare arms rippled as he raised the hammer over his head, ready to crush Tanden's skull when he was in range. A second, darker man, followed close on the heels of the blond. The dark man carried a short sword in each hand.

Tanden raced at the blond man, watching his eyes. Then, two steps before they collided, Tanden dived into the dirt, rolling into a somersault. Completing the roll, he came to his feet, crouching inside the man's swing. The blow that would have crushed Tanden's head, whistled harmlessly over his back.

Tanden buried his shoulder into the man's midsection. He reached behind the warrior, thrusting his sword at the second man. Pushing up with his legs and flexing his knees, Tanden flipped the blond man over his back and with the same motion, drove the point of his sword into the stomach of the dark Surr.

The blond man had his back to Tanden as he struggled to his feet. Jerking his sword free, Tanden spun around in an arc. Using his momentum, he slashed deeply into the side of the big man. He released the sword and whirled around to face the dark man who was still standing but seemed stunned.

Blood ran freely from his stomach wound. Tanden whipped out his knife, stepped inside the man's weak thrusts and drove the point of the blade under the Surr's chin and up into his skull.

As the dark man fell, Tanden ripped a short sword out of his hand. Turning about, he shoved the sword through the back of the blond man until the point protruded from his chest. As the warrior fell to the dirt, Tanden grabbed the hilt of his long sword, jerking to free it from the man's side. It came free suddenly with a sucking noise causing Tanden to stumble backwards over the dark Surr, lying dead behind him. Dust puffed up as his butt hit the dirt.

Tanden looked around for Seenger. He was slashing and backing away from his two attackers. Seenger bellowed his rage and hacked at the men with all his might as they continued pressing him slowly toward a burning hut. Seenger had a light cut on his sword arm and a deep gash on his thigh, but he was not allowing either man to circle behind him.

Two skilled swordsmen against one ogre was not even close to a fair match, no matter how overpowering the ogre was. This was a match of skill, not strength. The larger Surr would slash mighty strokes at Seenger, engaging the ogre's sword, while the smaller, much faster Surr danced forward inside the ogre's reach, trying to slice unprotected flesh.

Still on the ground, Tanden reached between his legs and pulled the knife free of the dead man's skull. Blood spurted across Tanden's torso and legs, but he flipped the knife to hold it blade first and let fly at the back of the nearest slaver. The blade bit deep into the middle of the man's back. The man shouted apparently more from rage than pain. He spun about and leaped at Tanden.

Tanden rolled to his feet, slicing his sword upward at the slaver. Blade up, it sliced between the man's wide-spread legs. Tanden straightened his back, pulled up on the sword, cutting into the man's midsection. The Surr fell forward against him, grasping weakly at Tanden's throat. He reached behind the Surr and gripped the hilt of his knife stuck in the man's back, then twisted, and pulled it free. Though pale and weak, the Surr still stood with his hands clutching at Tanden's neck. Tanden's knife blade flashed across the slaver's throat, finishing the kill. As the man fell to the ground, Tanden let the dead man's weight pull away from his sword.

The remaining Surr swordsman was pushing Seenger backward driving him closer to the fire. The ogre was desperately slashing at the slaver. Tanden drove his shoulder into the slaver's lower back catching the man unawares and he picked him up off his feet. The Surr flailed about, kicking Seenger in the middle of the chest, knocking the ogre off balance.

Tanden hurled the slaver into the flaming hut. With a quick flick of his wrist, Tanden dropped his knife. He stabbed a hand at Seenger, grabbing the ogre before he fell backward into the flames.

A war-whoop split the air. Tanden whirled about to see three additional Surr pounding toward them. Still clutching Seenger's tunic, he yanked the ogre toward the dock. He bent down, grabbed his knife, straightened, and threw it backhanded at the three men running at him. Without waiting to see if the knife made contact, Tanden turned and sprinted after Seenger.

Running is never an ogre's strong suit. Catching Seenger halfway to the dock, Tanden put an arm around the ogre's waist and pushed, his legs churning to propel them both toward the waiting boat.

Tanden's heart was pounding as they reached it. He leaped over the rail, dragging Seenger with him. The ogre crashed to the deck, tangling up in the ropes and nets scattered around the small deck. Tanden whirled about with his sword ready.

Tuller's sword slashed down across the line tying the bow to the dock. He shouted a command to I-Sheera and she yanked the tiller, pulling hard as if by the force of her strength alone she could bring the boat around to the wind. Sluggishly, the fishing boat turned and the sails began to fill with the wind coming from the west.

Tuller had set both sails possible on the little boat, the main and the jib. The little boat faced the west, into the wind. Turning slowly to sail eastward and catch the wind, they crept away from the dock inches at a time.

Tanden calculated they would not be far enough away from shore before the first of the three Surr warriors reached them. As the boat rotated on its centerboard, he moved toward the port side near the bow of the ship.

A quick check of the filling sails told him any further turn on the rudder would cause the ship to circle and spill what wind they had gathered. He called over his shoulder to I-Sheera, telling her to center the tiller. He quickly turned back to face the slavers.

Seenger had untangled himself. Bleeding from several cuts, the beast stood ready to repel boarders. Tuller stood next to him. Both sailors shouted challenges at the Surr.

Tanden dropped his weapons to the deck and grabbed a long boarding pike. The pike was a primitive, but incredibly effective weapon used to repel boarders. This one had a foot-long blade fixed on the end of its eight-foot wooden shaft and an additional hook welded at the base of the blade, creating a multipurpose tool for docking and hauling in nets. Placing the flat end against the dock, he leaned his weight against the opposite end of the pike, willing the boat to move faster. The first man outdistanced the other two Surr. His feet pounded two steps across the little dock. He looked unconcerned about facing two armed men and an ogre. Shouting his defiance, he jumped from the dock toward the slow-moving boat with his sword held high, ready to slash downward.

The man was in mid-leap when Tanden whipped his pole into the air, driving the flat end against the man's chest. With an audible whoof of air, the man halted in midair hanging on the end

233

of the pike. He fell into the water between the boat and the dock. Leaning hard against the pole, driving the Surr under water into the mud along the shore, Tanden pushed the boat away from the dock, walking the pole down the side of the ship to the stern.

The sails filled and they began to pick up speed. They were four feet from the dock, ten, then fifteen. Tanden released the pressure on the pole. He saw the slaver bob to the surface, spitting water and dripping mud. The two remaining men stopped at the end of the dock, watching the boat move out of range.

Seenger shouted a challenge and a curse at the two in his native tongue. Tanden doubted either man understood ogre. Still, the hand gestures from both sides were easily understood, if not universal.

The boat was moving quickly. I-Sheera held the tiller with the wind directly at their backs. Tanden looked at the sails. The mainsail was full, robbing the jib of its full share of wind. They would soon be at their top speed on this course. With a practiced sailor's eye, he concluded there was no course available that would enable them to outrun the slavers. The slaver's boats were slicing through the waves, oars flashing as they furiously rowed westward. Tanden's newly acquired boat, pushed forward by the west wind, raced east, directly at the Surr boats. Armed slavers stood at the bows shouting at them, but they were still too distant to catch any words.

Tanden jumped to the tiller and shouted, "Hard to starboard. Come about, now. Set for beam reach." Beam reach was a speed building position with the wind blowing straight sideways across the ship filling both sails, slanting the deck. Without waiting for Tuller and Seenger to set the sails, he pushed the tiller hard to the left. The mast groaned as the boom jibbed, snapping around to the other side. The deck tilted.

The sailors danced over the jumble of items sliding about the deck as they ran to reach the sails. Each ducked expertly to avoid the swinging boom, the ogre bending lower. Tanden hoped the little boat would stand the strain of such a rapid maneuver, but it came around smoother and faster than any large ship could. Tanden centered the rudder as the ship shook and seemed surge forward. He felt the fishing boat settle back down, its deck and masts tilted precariously toward the sea.

I-Sheera lost her grip and began sliding across the deck. Tanden braced his feet against the side of the boat and grabbed her by the back of her collar. He lifted her onto the helmsman's seat next to him. Tanden set one of her feet firmly against a brace. Her other foot he set against a nearby cleat. She was pale and her knuckles turned white as she clamped her hands onto the bench.

"Don't tighten up," Tanden said. "Keep your knees flexed and feel the movement of the ship." He pried one hand loose from the bench and set it on the tiller. She tried to pull back, but he placed his hand over hers. "Hold the tiller here until I say otherwise. Understand?"

She nodded, "I'll try."

"Do more than try! Do it! Tell me you'll do it."

I-Sheera clamped her jaw shut. Her eyes took on a determined look. Through clenched teeth, she said, "I'll do it. I'll hold here until you say otherwise."

Tanden patted her quickly on the leg, "Good girl. We aren't done yet." He released the tiller to her keeping. He spared a glance at Gadon lying in the bottom of a fish hold at their feet. I-Sheera had bundled him in the blanket and wedged him securely between two ribs of the hull. The angle of the deck made him look like he was standing on his head, but Tanden could see he was sleeping soundly.

Tanden checked the wind and the sails. His two crewmen were lashing the last sheet on the jib. He laid a weathered eye toward the Surr boats. They had changed course to intercept them farther along their tack. Tanden was sure they knew as well as he did that this little fishing boat could not outrun either of their boats unless the Wave Master could gain the downwind tack. Tanden could not see how that was possible against two boats unpowered by the wind.

Tuller and Seenger worked furiously to reset the sheets to their new course. Each used their knowledge of sails and the wind to eke out the last bit of speed. However, the tack they were on would only delay their inevitable capture at the hands of the Surr slavers.

CHAPTER THIRTY-ONE

Both crewmen worked their way astern toward Tanden. The fisherman and his son had not kept their ship any better than they had kept their hut. Lines, sheets, and nets lay tangled about the deck, sliding every which way, forcing his crewmen to move carefully to avoid becoming entangled. Noticing that Seenger was slowing down, Tanden saw the blood seeping down his leg.

"Tuller," Tanden called, pointing at Seenger, "sit him down and bind that wound. We have enough garbage on this pigsty without having to slip around on his blood."

Without a word, both sat down and Seenger leaned back allowing Tuller full access to his leg. Tanden knew they would respond without comment, shipboard discipline required no less.

Tanden began scooping up and shoving loose nets, ropes, and floats into jumbled piles on either side of the deck. He quickly secured loose running lines or sheets, tying them up out of the way. They did not have the time to be tripping around the deck. While placing the long boarding pike in beckets near the port rail, he spotted another and set it in the starboard rail beckets.

As was his sailor's nature, he was loath to throw anything overboard he might be able to find a use for later. Anything else he found, he tossed into an open fish hatch. He could hear it clattering around in the narrow area below decks.

Tanden worked his way back to I-Sheera at the helm. He said, "You must do exactly as I say and do it exactly when I say. No questions. No hesitation. I know you can do this. I wouldn't ask you to do something that you couldn't do. Trust me in this."

She looked back at him, pale, but smiling, "Yes. I can. If you tell me I can do it, then I can."

As Tanden explained his plan, she looked ahead and nodded, grimly determined to stay the course and follow his commands, come what may. He leaned down and kissed her quickly on the forehead startling her. She smiled up at him and then re-set herself to her course.

"Captain," Tuller called, waving him over to his position. Tuller's hands were bloody, but he had managed to bind

Seenger's wound. Seenger stamped his bad leg on the deck, testing the bandage.

Seenger said, "It looks like it'll hold."

Tuller agreed, "It'll hold for a while, but it's a deep gash. It probably hurts like a scalded pig, but this stubborn fool will never admit it. He should stay off his leg until we can get a needle and thread."

Seenger snorted, "It doesn't look like it'll matter whether it gets sewn up or not." He gestured in the direction of the slaver boats. For each boat length the fishing boat gained, the Surr boats gained two. They would catch up to them shortly.

Tanden could clearly hear the slavers shouting in their native tongue. He outlined his plan quickly and sent Tuller to the starboard rail on the upside of the deck, positioning Seenger downside on the port rail. Each man stood near the lines and sheets for the main sail. Tanden carried a pike to the bow. Balancing upright against the slanted deck, near the cleats for the lines to the jib, he placed the pike on the deck near his feet.

Watching the Surr draw closer, it suddenly occurred to him there might be some of his kin among them. He had never before considered himself of Surr blood, but it was not a secret his mother had been raped by a Surr invader. He thought about the Surr he had fought and killed already.

He asked himself, *"Have I killed a cousin, a brother, and do I now stand ready to kill my own father? Ha! Kill a man who brutally raped my mother? Kill a man who left her with half a mind to die an early death? So be it, I'll gladly do it."*

Tanden shouted in Holdenish, "Come on you sons-of-bitches."

Tanden saw Orrick standing in the bow of one of the boats. He bellowed in Geldonite, "Come to me you red-haired, foul-smelling dog. There are no children here for you to lie with. Come face a man if you have the courage, or run home to your goats, they miss your bleating. I'll wager there are herds of sheep in the north with red wool."

Orrick's face turned as red as his hair. He shouted back at Tanden in Surr, shaking his sword in the air, cursing the rowers to drive their oars faster. His boats were slicing through the water, racing side by side, an oar's length apart. They were almost a matched pair, with the oars plowing stroke for stroke through the water, each pull causing the boats to lurch forward. They were close enough Tanden could see the Surr had pressed slaves to the oars. Tanden had a moment of regret that what he was about to try would injure and possibly kill innocent men. He dismissed the thought, as his plan would most likely kill him and his crew as well.

The slaver boats were close when Tanden turned to I-Sheera and shouted, "Now!"

I-Sheera leaned against the tiller with all her weight. Tanden, Tuller, and Seenger leaped to reset the lines and sheets as the rudder spun the little boat about to face the on-coming Surr boats. Their speed and momentum from the long run across the wind on a beam reach continued to push them swiftly through the sea. The woman centered the rudder on a heading to slice between the slavers. The Wave Master's deck leveled as horizontal as the sea itself. Tanden quickly re-set the jib sail and picked up his pike.

He saw the comprehension in Orrick's eyes at the last moment. The man turned to shout at his crew to pull in their oars. Tanden braced his feet against the deck. Raising the long pike, he caught Orrick in the ribs with the spear point. The opposing speed of the boats sent the Surr slaver flying backward into the sea before he could utter a sound.

Tanden whipped the pike around to the other boat. The man standing on the bow was more prepared than Orrick. However, he misjudged the oncoming boat's speed in relation to the speed of his own craft. The pike's hook caught the man in the upper thigh, sending him sprawling backward over the first set of oarsmen. The jolt of contact tore the pike out of Tanden's hands.

He retrieved his long sword from the deck, bracing himself against the jib mast. The sturdy little fishing boat knifed between the two Surr slaver boats. As Tanden had calculated, the Surr boats were barely far enough apart to allow the Wave Master to slide between them. The fishing boat crashed through the oars extending into the water from both boats.

Oars disintegrated, sending shattered pieces spinning through the air in all directions. Men were thrown to the decks, sprayed with shards of wood, or hammered by displaced oars. The force of impact brought all three boats crashing together, their sides slapped with a jarring crunch taking the feet out from under every unprepared man. Wood screeched and moaned louder than the screams of injured and dying men as the boats grated past each other.

The sturdy little fishing boat ground its way between the slaver vessels, pushed by the wind and her gathered momentum. Tuller and Seenger swept up armfuls of ropes and nets, throwing them onto the struggling men on the other boats. Tuller, standing along the port side, quickly grabbed the pike. He stood ready to spear any man who cleared himself from the melee of ropes, nets, and wounded men.

Tanden and Seenger moved along the starboard rail sliding toward the stern as the boats passed. Each man held his sword tightly, ready to repel boarders. Only one Surr cleared himself from the tangle of nets, ropes, and bleeding men. One of his captives dragged him down from behind before the slaver could regain his bearings.

The little fishing boat broke free and a fresh blast of wind captured them, snapping the sails full. The wind was sudden, as if it came out of nowhere with perfect timing. They shot forward like a giant hand was pushing them. Clear of the slavers, the Wave Master picked up speed. Tanden shouted to his crew, "Turn to starboard. Set the helm for due south. Re-set the sails to beam reach." He planned to put as much distance between the disabled boats as he possibly could. The course he chose would provide the best speed for their newly acquired boat.

By the time the Surr regained control of their boats—if they ever did—the Wave Master would be long gone. Once out of the slaver's sight, he would change direction, setting a course for Stantinstadt.

CHAPTER THIRTY-TWO

Tanden ducked under the guard's club on the Stantinstad docks. It whistled past his head. He lashed out with a foot at the man behind him and was gratified to hear a whoof of air. Grabbing the man in front of him with both hands, he threw all of his weight forward, pushing the man off-balance and off his feet. The two men slammed onto the hard, wood plank of the wharf. Driving his weight into the man's midsection, he rolled and whirled around to face the man with the club. He blocked a blow with his left arm, the jolt sending pain shooting all the way to his shoulder. He stiff-armed a punch to the man's nose, causing him to drop his club and grab his face.

Tanden took the opportunity to shoulder past, sending him spinning to the dock. Sprinting to a low wall, he dived over it, blending into the shadows. He crab-walked beside the wall until he came to the side of a shipping warehouse. In the night's shadows, he climbed the rough rock exterior and rolled onto the flat roof. The night was dark. The pale light of the Potato, the only moon in the sky, barely produced shadows.

His heart was pounding and he fought to control his breathing. He flexed his left hand and fingers to bring feeling back into his arm. It tingled painfully, but nothing felt broken. It had been a long night, climaxing in the dockside brawl with two guards on the wharf, but was all worthwhile. He had found the White Wind in Stantinstadt's port.

It had only taken a day and a half to sail into port with Tanden and Tuller taking turns at the helm. They barely had to trim their sails against a constantly favorable wind, seeking only to harvest the last measure of speed from the little boat. The trip was uneventful and restful, except when Tuller found a needle and thread used for patching torn sails under the helmsman's perch. Tanden sat on Seenger's chest while Tuller sewed the ogre's thigh wound closed.

Gadon slept the whole voyage. The heavyset sailor still rested, despite his complaints, on the deck of the Wave Master. His fever was subsiding, but he remained terribly weak, his breath coming in short gasps. Throughout the trip, I-Sheera quietly cared for the ill man.

They sailed into Stantinstadt at dusk, slipping into port near the ragged fleet that fished the waters of the straits and the northern reaches of the Almodovar Ocean. Their commandeered ship was almost indistinguishable from similar ships anchored in the poor, rundown side of the harbor.

Seenger was watching I-Sheera, Gadon and the fishing boat while Tuller and Tanden searched separate sections of the port. Each man slipped quietly through the shadows searching the dark silhouettes of each ship looking for the White Wind.

Travelers the world over agreed that Stantinstadt was a wide-open port. Any diversion and any kind of trouble was available for any man who went searching for such things. Travelers would also agree that in the last few years the port took on a more malignant air. Warwall, the Red Wizard of Drohnbad, had seized the port at the end of the last war. When he suddenly withdrew all red troops, the city and port were left void of any capable controlling authority, beyond the contentious merchant council, barely more than a loose pirate confederation. This was why Tanden had decided to sail past the city on their voyage north to Harkelle. Even with a full crew, he deemed the city too unsafe to lay over, especially with a full, tempting cargo.

At any given time, half of the men on the docks were thieves seeking an easy opportunity to steal. The other half were sailors on watch and guards hired to protect ships in port. Both guards and thieves were wont to bash heads at night. Any person with a legitimate reason to be on the wharf conducted their business during the day. Tanden and his crew no longer looked like they were conducting legitimate business. Their blood stained leather garments taken from the Hummdhar warriors caused many to turn their heads, even in this city.

Tanden was also concerned about any assistance Gregin and Heraclius may have secured while in port. Being an open city, Stantinstadt had red order schools, green order meeting rooms, and blue order businesses operating side-by-side. Gregin, as a blue priest could easily seek the aid of the city's blue wizard with a sizable force of magicians, priests, acolytes, and blue soldiers at his disposal.

Tanden and Tuller spent most of the night slipping from shadow to shadow, following the curve of the harbor, looking for their ship. Finally, Tanden was rewarded for his labor, catching sight of the White Wind in a walled off section of the port reserved for the wealthiest families and largest trading companies. She was tied along a small walkway across from another ship. Both vessels were docked bow forward. Their gangplanks lay open to the landing pier between them. He was trying to get close to her berth when he had bumped head-on into a pair of night watchmen.

Now, he was resting on the roof of a warehouse, waiting to catch his breath. Rolling over, he inched toward the edge of the roof, careful not to show a silhouette against the sky. He re-scanned the area until he fixed the White Wind's location in his mind.

She was masked by other ships set at near anchor and was all but hidden from the casual observer. A burning torch lit the dock area near the ship where a man stood watch, but he was too far away for Tanden to recognize.

Two others had run to help the men Tanden had fought. All four milled about, poking at shadows and looking over the wall. Tanden did not expect the small skirmish to result in a broad hue and cry. Brushes with petty thieves were common.

The White Wind sat low in the water indicating her holds were still full of goods from Drohnbad and the East. Merchants in Stantinstadt would give Gregin and Heraclius a considerable price for the cargo, stolen or not, but they could collect twice the price in Tunston. Although, from the rumors Tanden heard, Tunston's Blue Wizard collected a stiff tax or *donation* as his magicians and priests called it.

Tanden doubted Gregin would mention any tax to a greedy Heraclius. Still, with Gregin eager to reach Tunston, he might sell the cargo and hire a more competent captain for a faster voyage.

He was positive Gregin would take the White Wind to Tunston, trying to keep the theft and kidnapping secret to protect the Blue Wizard's reputation. Leaving the ship behind in Stantinstadt was far too dangerous, as too many traders from Harkelle sailed these waters. Any number of Holdenites could identify the White Wind and would conclude she was stolen.

People might consider her lost at sea if the ship and her crew disappeared without a trace. Plus, Gregin would be hard pressed to find a faster ship. Stripped of her cargo, the White Wind could make the trip to Tunston faster than a harlot lies about her age.

Tanden felt sure the White Wind could not have anchored earlier than the same day the Wave Master reached port. He did not believe Gregin could finalize a sale of the cargo quickly. Any respectable merchant needed time to catalog the cargo and would spend an inordinate amount of time haggling over the price. Incompetent merchants did not survive long enough in Stantinstadt to complete their second bargain. If Gregin intended to sell the cargo, Tanden guessed he had another full day before the dockworkers would begin unloading his goods from his ship.

Tanden thought about Lady Yasthera il-Aldigg, Warwall's neice. She had been given to his keeping. He needed to find her and deliver her to Harkelle, safe and sound. It would ruin his adopted father to do otherwise. She must be his first consideration. If she still lived, he must rescue her, even if it cost him the cargo.

He needed to get off the warehouse roof before sunrise trapped him there, so he scrambled to the rear of the building and climbed down to an alley. It was still dark, but dawn was approaching closer by the minute. He wound his way through the alleys and back streets into the section of town known for inns, taverns, and brothels servicing sailors from the harbor.

Standing in the dark, he watched the street from a passageway between two buildings. Many businesses remained open into the early morning hours. He saw a rowdy group of men leave a small tavern across the street. They staggered to a well-lit, walled building a few doors down the street. There was a small blue light and a painted blue circle on the gate. The men sang and laughed as one of them rang the small bell, waiting for admittance. No one was singing the same song or able to stand without leaning against another. The building had the look of a blue order school. He doubted they were planning to attend a training session at this time of the night and none was wearing an acolyte robe.

Such scenes played and replayed throughout the known history of men and ships. After weeks or months between ports, too many common sailors drank until they could drink no more, sang until they could sing no more, and whored until they ran out of money. Day or night, it made no difference, these men knew no time constraints aside from getting back to their ships before they sailed. Fishermen, dock workers, guards, and soldiers mixed with sailors in a simmering stew held together by cheap wine and bad women, or bad wine and cheap women. Stantinstadt businesses catering to sailors never seemed to close.

"*What next?*" He shook his head. "*Do something. Do anything!*" He commanded himself, but he did not move. He stood still, watching the street.

"*Either go back to the Wave Master or go to a tavern looking for news. How cowardly are you to get this close to your goal and simply hide in the dark? You fool, don't you know what to do? Are you going to stand frozen in your tracks, afraid to go forward or to go back, like a lost, newborn sheep? No. Logic demands I act, but my heart says wait and watch. Am I such a fool to not know my own thoughts?*"

He took a deep breath, trying to relax the turmoil in the pit of his stomach.

"*I'm at an impasse. Maybe I should check with Gadon and the others. Yes, maybe that's a good idea. There's safety in a multitude of councilors. They're smart, they'll give me good advice.*"

Tanden stood still and watched, like his boots were stuck in a rock.

The eastern sky was dark. He needed to be back aboard the fishing boat before dawn. Shaking his head, he was about to begin making his way back to the harbor, when he saw a familiar man stagger from the tavern. The man stumbled and caught himself, banging a bandaged hand against the wall. He stood upright, moaning and cradling his hand.

Tanden plainly heard Obert's whiny voice, "Slut. Got what she deserved. Cut me, the witch. Should have buggered her and tossed her overboard." The man giggled. "Would have been cheaper than what we got tonight. That son of a bitch, Tuba! He took her twice. Oughta go back and get what's mine."

At the corner of the tavern, Obert stepped to the edge of an alley. Weaving about, the drunken man dropped his trousers to his knees and with a loud sigh, began urinating against the building wall. He started to sing a tune only he could recognize.

Tanden took one step toward the man and froze. A soldier that Tanden had not seen, stepped from a doorway. The small, blue circle sewn over his heart stood out starkly against the gloss of his black leather tunic. A second soldier walked casually down the street. They converged on Obert from opposite directions. A pair of hands reached out from the darkness behind Obert jerking the drunken man backward into the shadows. Tanden heard a muffled cry and then silence.

A few thumps and the squeak of a dry axle preceded two men in uniform casually pushing a cart out of the alley. The contents of the cart were covered by a tarp. The size of the lump under the tarp was an approximate match for Obert's body. The soldiers pushed the cart toward the wharf.

Tanden agreed that the harbor was as good a place to dump the body as any. One more dead sailor would not cause Stantinstadt's citizens to raise their voices in concern. Tanden agreed with the citizens. The soldiers saved Tanden time and effort.

Two more blue order soldiers stepped from the alley shadows. One pointed directly at the narrow passageway hiding Tanden before stepping back into the dark. The second man nodded and leisurely started walking toward Tanden. The outline of a plan raced through Tanden's thoughts. When the soldier reached the middle of the street, Tanden staggered into the dim light, turning to search behind him like he was looking for the offending rock that caused his stumble. Turning back around, he bumped into the soldier.

"Drunken fool." The man pushed Tanden sending him reeling across the street.

Tanden slurred his words drunkenly and said, "'Scuse me, frien'."

He steered an unsteady course to the tavern door the late Obert had recently exited. Stepping through the door, he quickly closed it behind him as he moved to the right.

The tavern was dimly lit and the air was dank, but the light was better inside than on the dark streets. Tanden spotted another member of his mutinous crew. The man sat with his head propped in his hands, elbows on the table, and his back to the door. He was mumbling into a mug set before him, talking to himself. A mug lay on its side in front of an empty chair across the table. A bowl of hard bread and cheese sat in the center.

The only other customer was snoring with his head on the table. The tavern keeper, a large balding man with a huge belly had his hand deep in the pocket of the sleeper. He glared at Tanden, while patting a small wooden club stuck prominently in a pocket with his free hand. The drunk would most likely wake up in an alley with no money and a headache as a reward for drinking alone. Any man foolish enough to drink alone in a strange city was headed for trouble, whether he was robbed by a tavern keeper or roving gangs of children.

Tanden shrugged, brought his hand to his lips in a drinking motion and pointed to the seat across from his ex-crewman. He sat down on the seat Obert had probably vacated. He quietly watched the other man whose eyes never left the rim of his mug.

The tavern keeper delivered a pitcher to the table, silently rubbing his thumb and forefinger together in the universal gesture for payment. Tanden pointed to the coins scattered on the table near the other man.

The tavern keeper nodded, set the pitcher down on the table, and scooped up all the coins. Tanden had not counted the money, but he was sure the man had just collected the price of many full pitchers. The tavern keeper picked up the empty mug, filled it with dark red liquid, and set it firmly in front of Tanden. He splashed half a mug of wine into the other man's mug. The tavern keeper's eyes challenged Tanden. When Tanden refused to react, the man left, taking the pitcher with him.

Tanden took a sip of the wine. The drink was little better than vinegar, but actually better than he expected to find in such a dump. He selected a small hunk of hard bread from the bowl in the middle of the table. Dipping the bread in the wine, he chewed slowly, watching the man across the table.

The man continued staring at his mug oblivious to his surroundings, mumbling to himself, chuckling occasionally, and weaving unsteadily in his chair. Suddenly he reared his head back to laugh and saw Tanden sitting across from him. He choked back the laugh as the color drained from his face.

Tanden smiled sweetly, raising his glass to the man. "To your health, Tuba."

Tuba stared at Tanden, his head wobbling slightly.
"Well, Tuba. Don't you have anything to say to your former captain?"

CHAPTER THIRTY-THREE

Tuba said, "Spirits an' ghosts! I may have helped tossin' Tanden into the sea to drown, but good spirit, I haven' done nothin' to you."

Tanden nodded. "Are you sure?"

Tuba slammed his hand flat on the table, "Spirit, I'm as sure as I'm drunk. You're the firs' spirit I've ever drunk drink wit'. To your health, Spirit." Tuba lifted his mug to his lips, spilling more down the front of his tunic than he swallowed. He belched loudly and set his mug down, missing the table entirely.

"Well?" said Tuba.

"Well, what?"

Tuba giggled, "Well what're you gone do to me? Are you here to kill me because…" His voice grew to a whisper, "Because I mutinied against Tanden and helped to kill him?"

Tanden whispered back, "It's a secret. The six gods liked that part. They laughed when you tossed him and that woman into the sea."

Tuba roared, "Ha! I knew it, even the gods didna like that arrogan' bastard or the easterly bitch."

Tanden put his finger to his lips, shushing the man, "Tuba, I've been sent by the gods to rescue you, but first you must tell me about the others and Lady Yasthera il-Aldigg."

"Rescue me? Why would anyone wan' to hurt me?"

Tanden leaned close to him and said, "Gregin works for other gods. My gods are jealous gods. Gregin wants to keep what you did a secret. He'll kill you to keep you silent."

Tuba said, "Slimy bastard. Paid me only 'nough to get a few drinks and to toss off a whore. Hadda whole ship full of money but wouldn' give me enough to even get home. Heraclius and Greeta decided to go to Tunston. They got to stay on the ship, but that cheap pile of dog dung threw me and Obert off the White Wind. Didn' I help take her? Don't I deserve a full share of cargo?"

Tanden nodded in sympathy, "Yes, the gods aren't happy with Gregin. They want you to be rich and happy. But first, you must tell me about the woman."

Tuba looked suspicious and said, "Why? Wait. Are you sure you're really here?"

Tanden smiled, "Of course, I'm here. Where else would I be? Tuba, the gods want you to have all of Gregin's money because they like a good story. Tell them about the woman."

Tuba chuckled, "We fixed 'em good, Obert and me. Gregin had his soldiers haul her off for safe keeping at one of his blue wizard's convents." Tuba pointed a thumb over his shoulder, indicating the brothel a few doors down the street.

Tanden nodded his understanding. Many of the blue convents and schools were nothing more than ill-disguised brothels collecting money for the blue order in Tunston. "Keep talking," he prodded.

Tuba said, "Gregin wouldna let us touch her on the ship. So, I wanted to give her what for. Teach her what it was like to be with a real man." He grabbed his crotch and pumped his hand up and down. "Best thing she ever had. Well, me an' Obert followed 'em. The snooty priest running the place said she was for a rich man. Too good for the likes of us. Said we didn't have the money for both of us to have her."

Tuba stopped talking and sat quietly smiling.

Tanden prompted, "And?"

Tuba said, "An' Obert gave me his money. The priest let me in. The man was a fool, 'cuz I went in an opened a window for Obert to crawl in. I had her good. She liked it 'cuz she didn' scream or nothin'. Just lay there and took us both. I was so good it brought tears to her eyes, but I tell you, Spirit, that Obert ain't much of a man. He couldn' get it up a second time. Stupid priest, we had her three times for the price of once."

Tuba hesitated and said, "Ho here! Where's Obert?"

Tanden said, "I'm the messenger of the six gods and Obert wouldn't listen to me. Gregin's soldiers have already killed him, probably on Gregin's orders."

Tuba's eyes grew wild and he made to stand. Tanden put a hand on his shoulder, pushing him back down in his chair. The man reached for his mug. He found it laying on the floor with the remains of the wine soaking into the dirt between the flagstones.

Tuba said sadly, "Another vessel sunk to the bottom."

Tanden took a small swallow from his mug and handed it to the sailor. "Drink up." As Tuba tilted the mug back, Tanden leaned in closer. "Listen, Tuba. I'm a spirit from the gods. No one can see me, but you, and when you're with me, no one can see you, but me. Gregin's soldiers are waiting for you in the street, but we can walk past them arm-in-arm and they won't be able to touch you, if you stay with me. Do you understand?"

Tuba nodded, "Le's go. I need ta sleep." He deliberately dropped the mug next to the one on the floor and chuckled as they clattered together.

Tanden stood and wrapped an arm around the drunken sailor, navigating him through the door and into the street. Knowing where to look, Tanden easily spotted the two soldiers hiding in the shadows.

Tuba began chanting, "Can' see me. Can' see me."

The two men staggered and stumbled into the middle of the street, Tanden chanting and stumbling along with Tuba. Tanden kept steering the drunken sailor to the middle of the street, even when one of the soldiers stepped into the light.

Tuba stuck his tongue out at the soldier and said, "Can' see me."

Tanden watched the soldiers out of the corner of one eye. Two soldiers conferred for a moment, then followed Tanden and Tuba at a distance. Tanden smiled, knowing that if these soldiers were like others he had met, they would be inclined to wait for a dark alley before attacking, so they simply followed what appeared to be two drunken sailors heading in the direction they would have to haul the body anyway.

Tanden would have help dealing with the soldiers if he could reach the Wave Master before they attacked. For his newly formed plan to work, he needed both soldiers to continue following them.

Dawn was coming and the eastern sky was turning light as Tanden and Tuba approached the wharf. Tanden estimated this part of the docks would soon come alive with men returning to their fishing boats to ride the morning tides out to their fishing spots. The soldiers would not want an audience. Tuba grew quiet. Tanden was almost dragging him as they hurried along trying to stay ahead of the soldiers.

Tanden realized they probably would not reach the Wave Master before the soldiers attacked. He could hear the soldiers behind him, rushing forward to take them. Suddenly, a figure stepped from the shadows to block his path. Tanden pushed Tuba into the man and spun around to face the soldiers to his rear. He saw no one. He crouched defensively and whipped a knife from the sheath in his boot.

Tanden stood at the sound of Gadon's voice from behind him, "And what do you want me to do with this flaccid piece of pig dick?"

Tanden interrupted, "Soldiers coming. Quick."

Gadon snorted, "Easy. You'd think no one has any brains, but you."

Tanden looked again and saw no soldiers on the dock, just a couple of fishermen coming down the wharf.

Gadon complained, "Here I come to greet you and welcome you back to the boat after a hard night of work and what do I get? You toss this vomitous mass of putrid bile at me. That's gratitude for you. Or did you bring this to me so I get the pleasure of cutting his throat?"

Tanden said, "Alive. I need him alive—for now."

Gadon dropped Tuba to the dock and smiled as the man's head made a satisfactory thump on the wood planks. He looked at Tanden and shook his head, "Of course, you need him alive. Do I look like a newborn babe? Am I a white-haired, doddering, old idiot? You wouldn't have dragged him this far if you meant to kill him. Oh, will I never be appreciated in this life?" He rolled his eyes upward as if imploring understanding from the heavens.

Tanden rescanned the docks and turned back to Gadon. "I thank you for coming to greet me. As always, my friend, you are a welcome sight."

Tuller spoke from behind Tanden, "And what of Seenger and me? We do all the hard work and old round bottom gets all of the praise?"

Gadon said, "Old! Who are you calling old, you young pup?"

Tanden said, "I'm glad to see all of you." He gave a few brief instructions to Tuller and Seenger, then turned to Gadon and said, "Let's get Tuba out of sight. I have some questions to ask him."

CHAPTER THIRTY-FOUR

Tanden gripped Tuba's hair, pushing his head into a cold bucket of seawater. He could feel the man awaken and pulled his head out of the bucket—holding his face away from him as Tuba sputtered, gasping in the air. Pushing the man's head underwater again, he held it there for a moment before yanking him up for air.

Most of the fishing vessels had departed with the morning sun. A few boats remained, floating lazily about in the water with a man or two repairing sails or nets. Tanden had ordered the mainsail removed from the mast and spread out over the deck. He set Tuller to pretending to sew. Gadon, Seenger, and I-Sheera sat out of sight in the shade beneath the sail. It would not fool any close inspection, but too many people sitting around would generate suspicion.

The fishing boat docked next to the Wave Master had not sailed this morning. Four men had started to re-string and mend their nets. Their work masked much of the activity on the Wave Master from view along this section of the port. All four men stopped working to watch Tanden with curiosity. By their dress and speech, Tanden knew them to be eastern followers of the red order with no desire for drink and little tolerance for men who did.

Tanden spoke to the men in Eastern, "Drunkard."

The men nodded. That one word spoke volumes to them. The eldest man smiled at Tanden and said in Geldonite, "He's a fool then. Is he worth the effort to revive? Throw him to the fishes and be done with him."

Tanden pushed Tuba's head underwater again and spoke to the old fisherman in Eastern. "He's also a thief. I would like know what he has done with what he stole."

The old man answered, "You speak the true language well, for one not born in our country."

Tanden said, "Thank you, good sir. It is a beautiful tongue and one worthy of the many wise men your people have produced."

The old man pointed at Tuba and the bucket.

Tanden said, "Yes, I thank you." He yanked the man up for air again.

Tuba gasped and coughed trying to clear his throat of seawater.

Tanden flopped the man over the rail and held him head down as the man vomited into the sea.

One of the young eastern fishermen plucked at his father's tunic sleeve, "Father." The youth nodded up the wharf. A half dozen uniformed blue soldiers marched along the dock.

The old man hissed an order.

The young man vaulted the space between the two ships and quickly sat down on the edge of the sail aboard the Wave Master. He spread a small net around his lap, his fingers flying, twisting, and tying knots. His action pushed the cloth sail to the deck, holding it down. He blocked all view of Gadon, Seenger, and I-Sherra sitting in its shade.

The man in charge of the soldiers called out in Tunstonian to the two ships.

Tanden turned to the old fisherman, asking in Eastern, "What does he say, good father?"

Another soldier shouted out in Eastern, "You ignorant buffoon. He asks if you have seen two of our men."

The old fisherman replied in Eastern, "As you can see, unmagic one, my sons and I are mending our nets. Praise be to the Red Wizard, we mind our own business. We're not blind men. I can truly say your kind stands out among hardworking men."

The soldier translated this into Tunstonian for the leader of the group. Even if Tanden didn't speak Tunstonian, he would have easily seen both men misunderstood the easterner's comment, mistaking his insult for a compliment. The leader nodded and waved for the old man to continue speaking, using a gesture normally reserved for royalty acknowledging a minor servant.

The old man smiled and continued, "Praise be to the flame and fire, I haven't seen such as you on these docks for many days. My sons?" One by one, he looked at his children who responded in Eastern. Each repeated that he had not seen any soldiers. They directed their answers to the old man, not the soldiers.

The old man looked at Tanden and said in Eastern, "And you, my cousin? Have you seen any soldiers this morning?"

Tanden answered the old man, "Good father. I haven't seen any uniformed soldier on this dock this morning except for these who stand here now."

Tuller called out in Eastern, "I haven't seen any living creature dressed like these since the sun rose this morning."

The old man nodded at Tanden and Tuller. Followers of the red way did not approve of lies. Tanden wondered how the old man would respond to his answers. Calling the old man "good father" and being called "my cousin" were not lies. They were terms of honor and respect among the people of many eastern cultures and not always indicative of a true blood relationship. Tanden believed the soldier who spoke Eastern was not as well versed in the language as he pretended.

The fisherman turned to the soldiers, "As you heard, no one says they have seen your men. We must get back to our nets. How else can we help you?"

The soldier pointed at Tuba, who was hanging from the rail of the Wave Master, "What's this?"

Tanden answered, "He woke up this morning feeling very ill, as you can see. Have you heard any news about a sickness with head pains, aching joints, and a stomach that can't hold breakfast? This man is weak and his head whirls about with dizziness. Do you know a cure for this disease?"

When the soldier translated the symptoms to his leader, the man frowned and unconsciously stepped back. Without further words, the soldiers turned and continued along the wharf, leaving the group to breathe a sigh of relief.

Tanden heard whispers of metal on leather. He looked around and saw men from both boats sliding knives back into their sheaths. Each of the easterner's sons had slipped their knives free, yet kept the action hidden. Tuller raised his eyebrows and withdrew a short sword from where he held it out of sight, under the sail.

The old man looked at Tanden and said, "I'm Bramme."

"I'm Tanden from Harkelle on the Uube River. You're named for the first wizard of the red?"

Bramme smiled, "You know the history and truth of the red order as well as our language. Indeed, we're well met. I wish I was named after the great wizard, Bramme. It's my misfortune to be named after my mother's brother, a foolish man. Trust me, Tanden. I'm not as foolish as my uncle. We saw your men kill the soldiers just before they stepped onto the dock. But," he smiled slyly, "no one can say we saw them on *this* dock. And no one can say your men saw them after the sun came up. You carefully avoided lying, my friend. Take care your tongue doesn't slip away with you."

"I thank you, Bramme. You and your sons are brave men. You'd have fought the soldiers with us?"

"Followers of the filthy blue order." Bramme shrugged as if those words were sufficient to answer Tanden's question. Then in rapid fire Eastern, he ordered his sons back to their nets.

Tanden jerked Tuba back to the deck and sat next to him.

Tuba moaned and rolled his eyes to look up at Tanden. He wiped his face clean of bile with the back of his hand. He turned his head to look at Tuller, then at Gadon and I-Sheera who watched him from the shade of the sail. He grimaced and looked as if he was going to retch again when he saw the look on Seenger's face.

Tuba said to Tanden, "Are you going to kill me now?"

Tanden shook his head, "Not yet. I may let Seenger have you to play with later, or I may give you to Gadon, or I may let you live. What happens to you will depend on you. Do you understand?"

Tuba said, "I understand you should be dead. All of you."

Tanden replied, "We aren't dead. Some have died because of you. You may yet join them."

Tuba said, "I won't beg, but I don't want to die. I can't deny what I did, you know it full well. Tell me what you want? I'll do it if I can."

Tanden said, "Answer my questions. That's all. If I believe you're lying to me, I'll give you to Seenger, Gadon, and Tuller. If you answer me honestly, I'll let you live, unharmed by any of us on this boat."

Seenger growled and Gadon started to protest, but Tanden waved them quiet.

Tuba said, "Do you promise, Captain? I'll tell you the truth if you give me your promise no one on this boat will hurt me."

Tanden nodded, "Everyone on this boat will leave you whole and healthy, we won't touch you except to restrain you from escaping until we leave this city. You have my word."

Tuba struggled to sit upright, putting his back against the deck rail. Placing his head in his hands, he moaned, "I accept your promise, Captain. But, right now I almost wish I could die. Oh, my head."

Tanden was unsympathetic to the man and said, "Any one of us is more than willing to fulfill your wish to die. Make no mistake, Tuba. Even this woman will slit your throat at the slightest cause. I only have a few questions. Is Heraclius still the captain of the White Wind?"

Tuba shook his head slowly, "No, Captain. Gregin paced the deck the whole way back to Stantinstadt. He was unhappy with the course and speed set by Heraclius."

"Who is the captain now?"

Tuba said, "I don't know." His already pale face blanched, "Honest, I don't. I heard the city's blue wizard was giving him a captain who recently sailed from Tunston and a crew of the new captain's choosing. Captain? Where's Obert? I know he isn't much, but he is my friend."

Tanden replied, "I ask the questions, Tuba. I saw blue soldiers kill Obert last night. They took his body away in a cart. Gregin will do the same to you if I send you back to him. He won't leave witnesses alive to testify to his theft and kidnapping. Now, Tuba, are the new captain and crew aboard the White Wind?"

Tuba shook his head. "I think only Greeta and Heraclius stayed on the ship. They wanted to sail on to Tunston. Gregin let them stay aboard to watch the cargo. Gregin stays at the blue wizard's palace. Last I knew, the new captain and crew wouldn't board until later, today or tomorrow maybe. No. I really don't know."

Tanden said, "One last question for now, does Gregin plan to sell the cargo here or take it to Tunston?" Tuba shook his head and shrugged. Tanden turned to Gadon, "Tie him up and put him in the fish hold in the stern. And Gadon, remember my promise not to hurt him."

Tuba said, "Thank you, Captain. You have every right to cut my throat. I'm thankful you've given me a second chance. I won't fail you again."

Tanden leaned forward, Tuba's his face inches from his nose, "Make no mistake, you mutinous son of a diseased harlot. I'll never trust you again. You're alive by the barest mercy of the six gods."

The six gods were rocky, lifeless moons without merciful hearts. Calling on their mercy was a warning to Tuba of how little leeway he had in the walk between this life and the next. Even Tuba understood he was living on a razor's edge.

"Gadon, gag this pus bag if he so much as belches without permission."

Tanden sat deep in thought until Gadon returned. Then, he explained his plan, setting each person's role, and admonishing them to take extreme care.

CHAPTER THIRTY-FIVE

The sun was two hours into the sky when the two blue magic soldiers rang the bell over the gate at the convent. Due to the time of day, they had to wait until a blue priest came to open the gate. It was the same priest who had worked through the night. He looked more than a bit blurry eyed and rushed like he was iching to go to bed with no further delays.

The blue priest waved the soldiers through the gate, across an open courtyard, and along an open air corridor without much more than a passing glance at their uniforms. The bright blue circle prominently displayed their allegiance. He shuffled past the two soldiers, leading them deeper into the convent. The tall soldier noticed his startled expression at seeing the fire in the eyes of his smaller comrade. The priest looked away and quickly swirled his hands gathering a bit of magic through the movement of the clouds above.

The priest cleared his throat and spoke in a low voice to the tall soldier. "I've been assigned to this convent long enough to see many a man with hate in his eyes." Flicking his eyes in the direction of the smaller man, he continued. "It always means a rough time for someone. I don't understand it, but for some reason some men take that anger out on women. I've cast a small protection spell for the girl servicing your friend."

The tall man smiled at the priest's concern, knowing the priest would not be entrusted with the gatekeeper position at the convent if his magic was not strong enough to repair any damage short of death that might be inflicted upon those in his charge. Even the blue magicians and wizards did not have the power to repair death. He patted the priest on the shoulder as he passed. The priest looked up to see the man smiling down at him. The tall soldier said, "Been a long night, priest?"

The priest nodded, "Very long, indeed. Offerings to the Tunston blue order were slow. That always makes the night drag on too long."

The soldier chuckled, "True, very true. It was a slow night on the town. We had night watch and thought we would drop by to relieve our boredom before going to sleep."

The little priest said, "Don't forget, it's Saturday."

"Saturday? Already?"

"Yes, Saturday. You boys don't forget to go to your cleansing before this week's ending gathering tomorrow morning."

"Of course, good priest. How could we forget? Going to a gathering tainted with red or green magic residue is unthinkable."

The priest shied away from the little soldier and said to the tall man, "I don't think I've seen you two boys here before, have I?"

"No, priest. We haven't been in Stantinstadt long and the officers have kept us pretty busy until now. You know how that is."

The priest nodded.

The tall soldier said, "Say, priest. My friend and I were wondering if you had something a little different for us? Perhaps a dark woman or maybe an eastern woman?"

The priest nodded, "We have the best in town. We have two black women from Thopie in the southern continent. We have a yellowish woman with thin slanted eyes. They say she's all the way from east of the East. We do have one eastern woman, but I think you boys might be happier with a couple of Geldonite girls we have. Why don't I have some of the girls line up so you could take your pick?"

The soldier put his arm around the priest and said, "I like you. You're just about the nicest man we've met since we came to Stantinstadt. We came here from duty in Rath, in Geldon, and well, you know how it is with us poor soldiers. We're looking for something a little different. Do you suppose you could point out your eastern woman to us?"

"But," the priest hesitated, "both of you? I mean…"

The small soldier turned his back on the priest to stare at a crude painting of a naked woman on the wall.

"The blue grant you magic, priest," the tall soldier chuckled. "We don't mind sharing a bit if we can save a coin or two."

The priest leaned close to the soldier and said, "Is your friend all right? I mean, he won't hurt the girl or anything will he?

The city's wizard doesn't like that kind of thing. It's bad for donations, you know?"

The soldier nodded and whispered so only the priest would hear, "He does get a bit rough every now and then. If we share a woman, I can keep an eye on him. You know, priest, you look sleepy."

The priest led them down a hallway and said, "Well, my son, I am tired. I'll be able to go to bed after you two boys finish up."

"If you'll pardon my saying so, I hate to rush a thing like this. Why don't you go off to bed now. We can let ourselves out when we're done."

"You wouldn't mind if I went off to bed? Priest Arcton will be here in a little while. He can show you out."

"We're all in the service of the same blue order, right?" The soldier pulled a jumble of coins from his pocket and pressed them into the hands of the blue priest.

"Oh, this is too much. The wizard grants a lower dispensation for his soldiers."

Rolling his eyes to heaven, the soldier said, "Blue grant the good wizard power. Priest, you're welcome to the extra for your trouble and for having to stay up late for us." He reached over and jiggled the priest's hands. A brief flash of light glinted off the coins, distracting the tired gatekeeper. He voiced no further objections to leaving the soldiers unsupervised in the convent.

The trio stopped at a large door with a heavy lock. The priest took a key ring from a little table and unlocked the door. After the two soldiers stepped into the room, the priest shut the door firmly behind them. The soldiers heard him toss the key ring onto the table. They listened to him walk down the hallway.

Looking around the room, they saw nothing more than a bed and one shuttered window. Chained to the bed was a woman laying with her back to the door.

Tanden knew he was Lady Yasthera il-Aldigg. He looked at I-Sheera and gestured for her to go to the woman. I-Sheera took off her hat and shook loose her long black hair. She quickly ran to the bed and reached out to touch the woman's shoulder. Yasthera shrank from the touch, but nothing more.

I-Sheera moved to the other side of the bed, sat down and looked into the captive's face. She gently put her hand under the woman's chin and lifted her face up to see her.

Recognition dawned immediately. She sobbed and she reached out to hug I-Sheera.

I-Sheera patted her, making small comforting shushing noises. She looked over the woman's head at Tanden, pointing to the chain on Yasthera's wrist.

Tanden nodded. He saw no keys in the room, but he doubted the blue priests would have taken them very far. Quietly opening the door a crack, he peeked down the hallway. Verifying it was empty, he grabbing the keys off the table, retreated back into the room and shut the door behind him.

He was correct, there were two keys on the ring. He slipped around the bed behind I-Sheera. When Yasthera saw the uniform, she stiffened up, clinging to her former maid.

I-Sheera said, "It's all right. It's Captain Tanden. Shush now. It's all right. We've come to take you out of this place."

Tanden reached over I-Sheera and tried the small key in the lock on Yasthera's wrist. It popped open with a well-used click. I-Sheera took the woman's wrist in her hands and rubbed gently, talking quietly to soothe her. This verified to Tanden that he had made the correct decision to bring I-Sheera into this danger. She was the best and only person to get a calm response from Yasthera.

Swiftly placing the keys back on the hallway table, Tanden re-entered the room. Picking through a small bundle of clothes in the corner, he found a long flowing robe with a hood attached. He handed it to I-Sheera, who looked helplessly to Tanden. Yasthera was crying uncontrollably in I-Sheera's lap.

Tanden said, "I know she's had a bad time, but so have we, with more to come. There'll be time to cry later."

I-Sheera said, "Tanden, please. I don't know what to do."

Tanden sat down next to I-Sheera and grabbed a handful of Yasthera's hair. He slowly raised her head until they were staring at each other's face. The woman's face was streaked with tears. His heart went out to her, but they did not have much time to delay. Jerking her hair caused her to gasp.

"Look at me," he commanded. "Look at me. Who am I?"

Yasthera sobbed. "I thought you were dead."

"Who am I?" he hissed.

"Captain Tanden of the White Wind," she said, choking back a sob.

"That's correct. You're Lady Yasthera il-Aldigg. The niece of Warwall, the Red Wizard of Drohnbad and Conqueror of Stantinstadt." She looked toward I-Sheera.

"Look at me. Who are you?"

Yasthera closed her eyes. I-Sheera leaned close to the woman's ear and said, "It'll be all right. You must do as Captain Tanden says. Please, Lady. Answer him for all our sakes."

Tanden pointed at the robe and said, "I-Sheera, get her dressed. Now."

Tanden yanked Yasthera to her feet so I-Sheera could wrap the robe around her. He repeated, "You are Lady Yasthera il-Aldigg, the niece to Warwall, the Red Wizard of Drohnbad and Conqueror of Stantinstadt. Now, who are you?"

Yasthera looked into Tanden's eyes and said, "I am Yasthera il-Aldigg."

Tanden said, "That's correct. You're of a royal household, act like it."

Yasthera sobbed, "But, you don't know—"

Tanden interrupted, speaking slowly and distinctly, emphasizing each word, "I don't know everything, but I know enough and I don't care. At this moment, you're Yasthera, a common whore for common sailors. Nothing more. If you want to regain your life, control yourself or you'll die here."

He jerked her hair again for added emphasis.

"Now!" Tanden hissed, "Who are you?"

Yasthera spit back at him, finally roused to anger, "I'm Lady Yasthera il-Aldigg, the niece of Warwall, the Red Wizard of Drohnbad, betrothed to Tarran, the youngest son of King Krebbem of the Holden Empire. They'll kill the pigs who did this to me."

Tanden nodded, "Good. However, Lady il-Aldigg, I believe it would not be in your best interests to ever tell your uncle or your new husband about any of this."

Yasthera looked at I-Sheera as she tied the final bows on the robe and pulled the hood up over her head. I-Sheera nodded in agreement. She tied the hood tight around Yasthera's head and said, "They may not understand, Lady."

Yasthera said, "But how? Certainly they'll find out."

Tanden said, "They won't find out from me or my crew. They'll only know if you tell them. Treat Tarran as any good, loving wife should and he'll believe everything you say. Trust me. Now we must go."

Yasthera nodded, "Yes, Captain Tanden. I thank you. But one thing—"

I-Sheera implored, "Please, Lady. Quickly?"

Yasthera said, "The men who did this to me…?"

I-Sheera grabbed Yasthera by the hood on the robe, grabbing her hair as Tanden had. Jerking her head around, she hissed into the woman's ear. "To you? Listen carefully, you spoiled little brat. These men mutinied against Tanden. They stole his ship and cargo. They tossed us into the sea to drown. They killed and caused good men to die. You wail because you had to take a man between your legs. Woman, you were made for that."

Yasthera looked shocked. She yanked her head away from I-Sheera's hand and looked from I-Sheera to Tanden and back again. No one spoke for a moment. Then, Yasthera dropped her eyes to the floor. She leaned across and kissed I-Sheera on both cheeks.

It was I-Sheera's turn to look shocked.

Yasthera said, "You're right. You've always been kind to me, I-Sheera. I'm sorry, but I don't want the men who took me to go unpunished. Captain, two of those pigs violated me here."

Tanden replied, "I know. One of them is already dead. I captured the other. He'll pay for what he did."

Yasthera said, "Good. I trust you, Captain Tanden, to be the agent of revenge for us all."

Tanden nodded and led the women to the window. The shutters were not locked from the outside. He peered through the slats. The window faced a sun-filled courtyard. Seeing no one around, he opened the shutters. The ground was only a short drop.

Tanden said, "I-Sheera, put your hat back on, fast. This took too much time."

I-Sheera rushed across the room and dashed back with her uniform hat. Knotting her hair, she jammed it under the hat, stuffing loose stands out of the way. She was obviously surprised when Yasthera poked at a few wayward wisps of hair, giving I-Sheera a weak smile.

Tanden gestured for I-Sheera to sit on the window ledge and swing her legs over the edge. He grabbed her hands and gently lowered her to the ground. He quickly set Yasthera on the ground next to her. He vaulted through the window landing easily in the courtyard. The area surrounding the convent, inside the walls, was a carefully tended garden. Flowerbeds and fruit trees lined flagstone walkways. A pool glistened smoothly in the morning sun.

He breathed in deeply the fragrant air and winked at I-Sheera when he saw her looking at him. He vowed if he lived and succeeded that he would have a garden like this to enjoy every day.

Tanden led the way through the little gate, into the street. Merchants were busy and the streets were crowded with people of all types. A robed, hooded woman escorted by two uniformed blue soldiers did not warrant more than a passing glimpse. The trio reached the Wave Master unchallenged.

CHAPTER THIRTY-SIX

Tanden and I-Sheera stood on the wharf watching for activity around the White Wind.

They still wore the same blue order soldier uniforms. I-Sheera rolled up the sleeves and trouser legs looked far worse in the daylight than in the dark. The pants had to be held up by a rope tied around her waist. However, it fit well enough to avoid suspicion, assuming no one bothered to look at her. Gadon and Seenger lay hidden behind a long rock wall between warehouses. Neither could have squeezed into the uniform I-Sheera wore, not that Gadon was well enough to do more than trudge from one place to the next and Seenger was easy to spot as an ogre even in a perfectly tailored uniform.

The soldiers appeared to be relaxing out of the bright mid-morning sun along the rock wall near an unused warehouse. Tanden felt anything but relaxed. He preferred to approach the White Wind at dusk, but he could not afford to wait, not knowing when she would sail to Tunston. The incoming noon tides would make sailing out of the harbor difficult. The fishing fleet would be returning on the selfsame tides, choking the harbor mouth. An experienced captain with a full crew could fight the tides and make the smaller fishing boats give way.

His plan was to retake his ship quietly at the earliest possible moment. The uniforms Tanden and I-Sheera wore made gaining an entrance to the segregated wharf a simple matter. Escorting an ill man and an ogre had not caused more than a few sideway glances. Still, they needed to get aboard the ship, capture everyone, secure the cargo, and sail her out of the harbor—all without raising anyone's suspicions.

I-Sheera tapped Tanden on the forearm and gestured with her eyes for Tanden to look up the wharf. She was under orders not so speak. Her voice and accent were not those of a soldier, not to mention she was a woman. A woman in a blue order soldier's uniform would bring a flood of attention Tanden desperately wanted to avoid. A woman in any uniform would cause a flood of unwanted attention.

Tanden followed I-Sheera's eyes. Coming along the wharf was a detachment of soldiers led by Gregin. The blue priest had dropped all pretenses. He was wearing his blue order robes. He walked ahead of two soldiers, who preceded a soldier pushing a cart, who was followed by two soldiers. The four soldiers on guard were alert with their swords drawn and at the ready.

Tanden could not hope to go unnoticed by other soldiers. The city's blue garrison was small enough that each man probably knew every other. He pulled I-Sheera with him as he jumped over the wall. Crouched down to hide behind it with Gadon and Seenger, he hoped they had not been seen. Listening to the creak of the cart until it was well past, he risked a peek over the wall. Gregin and his small force went directly to the White Wind. From where Tanden hid, he was unable to see much of what was happening on the pier. The longshoremen milling on the narrow wharf between the White Wind and the next ship were pushed aside by the armed soldiers. He gestured for I-Sheera to remain hidden. He crept along the wall until it intersected against a higher wall.

This section of the dock was a jumble of private warehouses surrounded by gated storage yards. In the warehouse yard beyond the taller wall, Tanden heard men working. Peering over the shorter wall, he looked toward the harbor. A constant stream of men carried, rolled, and carted goods from a ship next to the White Wind, into the yard just behind the high wall. The ship was a squat, squarish vessel of Allexian design. The longshoremen shouted and called insults to each other as dockworkers normally do. The swirl of workers would help to conceal any approach to his ship.

Tanden could see much of the White Wind's top deck. Heraclius and Greeta were struggling to carry a large chest across the deck. They followed Gregin down the hatchway to the cabins under the foredeck. The five soldiers were returning with the empty cart. They jostled and collided their way through the stream of men crossing the dock.

As they passed by, Tanden turned. Still hidden by the wall, he paced the soldiers until he reached the wall of the empty warehouse where his crew waited. Tanden could not hear the solider's passage over all the noise on the dock. He counted to ten and glanced over the wall. The soldiers were turning up a street, moving away from the docks.

He waved for everyone to follow him. I-Sheera and Seeger leaped over the wall while Gadon slumped and rolled over the top. Tanden straightened his uniform and reset his hat squarely on his head before turning to I-Sheera and tugging her uniform into a reasonable semblance of order. Without further hesitation, they stepped out of the shade into the heat of the late, morning sun. Walking to the water's edge, they turned purposefully toward the White Wind's berth.

Tanden barged through the stream of men carrying goods from the Allexian ship to the warehouse. At the foot of the White Wind's gangplank, they encountered three armed men standing guard watching the activity of the workers. Glancing at the uniforms Tanden and I-Sheera wore, the guards stepped aside to let them pass. Most common laborers or dock guards would not question anyone or anything in a uniform. Their sideways glances at an ogre distracted them from noticing I-Sheera.

No one was on the deck of the ship. Tanden knew there were at least three men aboard—Gregin, Heraclius, and Greeta. Gregin must have trusted the watch on the dock to keep intruders off the ship. If the new captain and any of the new crew was aboard, Tanden may have grabbed a larger snake than he could skin.

Gesturing for I-Sheera to stay with Gadon, he motioned Seenger to follow him forward.

Tanden had his hand on the passageway hatch when he heard someone coming up the ladder. He waved Seenger away from the door and stepped two paces back. He turned quickly to check the dock and the deck of the Allexian ship. He could not see the longshoremen on the pier from his angle. If he could not see them, they could not see him. Men going up the gangplank to the Allexian ship had their back to the White Wind. Men coming down were more concerned with the bundles they carried and their footing on the narrow gangplank. No one standing on the deck of the other ship appeared to be watching anything other than the cargo off-loading.

Tanden nearly tripped over a tarp laying at his feet. He silently cursed the lazy man who left it on the deck. As captain, he never allowed a sloppy ship. He waved Seenger further back.

Greeta stepped through the hatch. He was grumbling about being sent topside as he squinted into the sun. A bright white light from the sun glinting off the wave tips in the harbor seemed to funnel directly into the hatchway, temporarily blinding him. Three steps onto the deck, his eyes re-focused and widened when he saw Tanden standing in front of him.

He turned and opened his mouth to shout.

Tanden knotted his fist and knocked Greeta backward with a blow to the middle of his face. Greeta fell backward into the arms of the waiting ogre. Seenger spun the man face down onto the deck and drew a small blade from his waistband. Sliding the knife under Greeta, Seenger slit the mutinous sailor's throat with a swift, smooth motion. Greeta jerked and twisted, but Seenger sat on his shoulders holding the dying man flat until he stopped moving. Deep, red blood pooled on the deck. Seenger looked up at Tanden as if expecting a challenge to his right to kill the thief.

Tanden nodded his approval. Seenger had performed swiftly, silently, and with justification. Grabbing the tarp, he tossed it to Seenger for a covering. He looked back to the deck of the Allexian ship. No one appeared to have noticed any activity on the White Wind. They would dispose of Greeta's body once they completely regained control of the ship and reached the open sea.

Tanden stepped through the open hatchway and noiselessly slid down the ladder to the passageway. The doors to all three cabins were closed. Tanden dismissed the door to the cabin to the left. It was normally shared by Gadon and Tuller, but was now packed floor to ceiling with trade goods. The door on the right was the cabin shared by I-Sheera and Yasthera.

Forward was the door to his cabin. The captain's cabin had little room to spare as it also had cargo stuffed into every available nook. The women's cabin had more room, but was filled with all the assorted baggage of a woman traveling to meet her new husband. Gregin and Heraclius could be using either or both cabins.

Bypassing the woman's cabin, he listened at the captain's door. He heard no movement or voices behind the door. He looked behind him at Seenger. The ogre stood at the foot of the ladder, waiting for direction. Tanden pointed at both doors and shrugged. The ogre shrugged in response and reached out to rap his knuckles on the door of the women's cabin.

Heraclius shouted from inside, "Greeta, are you such a fool—" The door flew open. Heraclius stepped into the passageway. Turning toward the deck ladder, he raised his hand to strike at Greeta. He froze when he saw Seenger standing there.

Tanden slammed the butt of his knife handle into the back of Heraclius's head.

The man collapsed to the deck where he lay unmoving. Tanden stepped over the unconscious man to enter the women's cabin. Yasthera's baggage was open with the contents scattered about, but otherwise the room was empty. He grabbed a handful of silk strips. Tanden could not begin to fathom what their original purpose was, but he was sure they would secure Heraclius. With the practiced hands of experienced sailors, Tanden and Seenger quickly tied the unmoving man hand and foot.

The two stood at the captain's cabin door. There were still no sounds coming from inside the cabin. Without delay, Tanden eased the latch open and stepped into the little cabin, Seenger following quickly behind him.

Gregin sat alone at the small writing desk. He looked at the men when he heard sounds of the intrusion. No expression passed his face, even when he recognized Tanden and Seenger. He slowly closed the book on the desk and turned to face the door. He leaned back in the chair and put his feet up on a chest.

Tanden put an arm out to stop Seenger from rushing forward.

Gregin said, "Well, Captain. I can see that you and your pet ogre don't take to death easily."

Tanden said, "Do you?"

Gregin laughed, "Oh you poor fool. I've already beaten you. You're dead, just too stupid to lie down."

Tanden said, "Don't bother calling for Heraclius and Greeta to come save you. Greeta is dead and Heraclius is tightly bound."

Gregin shook his head as if talking to a small child, "By killing Greeta and Heraclius—you will kill him soon, I guess?—anyway, you've done nothing more than save me from having them killed and thrown into the sea. You killed them sooner than I planned, but they're where they would eventually end up."

The blue priest raised his hands parallel to each other spaced apart about the width of his head. Before Tanden or Seenger could react a blue wall slammed into them. The ogre was tossed back into the hallway, crashing to the deck on top of Heraclius with a grunt. The force plastered Tanden against the wall, holding him there as if he was crucified, nailed in place. With one hand Gregin held Tanden, with the other, he picked up a dagger from the desk. Twirling it lightly, a blue sheen spread across the blade.

Just as Gregin was about to hurl the knife, I-Sheera stepped past Seenger through the doorway and into the cabin. Without anyone blocking the light reflecting off the waves in the bay, a blistering white beam bathed Gregin causing him to drop the dagger. As he bent to pick it up, I-Sheera hit him in the head with a chamber pot from her cabin.

Blinking furiously, Gregin shook his head in a daze. His hand came away from his head bloody. Still, he smiled. The man thrust his hands out, but nothing happened. The magic he had stored had either dissipated, already been used, or his head injury would not allow him to focus his mind well enough to bring his magic into action. He held his wrists together offering bondage.

With a shrug, Gregin said, "It doesn't matter. Tie me up and together we can wait for what's sure to follow."

Tanden and Seenger quickly recovered from the blue priest's magic onslaught. The ogre was seething. He was probably not used to being tossed around like a ragdoll.

"Tie him tight, Seenger. Lash him to the chair."

Gregin offered no resistance. He smiled and said, "Your Holdenite alliance with the red order's empire is broken. That eastern cow is where she'll never be found. The Red Wizard will blame Holden and the green order for losing his niece. Furthermore, Tuba and Obert have been dealt with by now. Once you three are captured, there'll be no one left to tell the story of what happened here. You know as well as I do, you can't sail this ship with just two men and a scrawny woman."

Tanden said, "You seem to be very confident you'll live through this."

Gregin laughed, "Oh no, not at all. I've already done what I was asked to do. If I die now, it makes no difference. I will be martyred for the glory of the blue order. His majesty, the Blue

Wizard will know what I've done. He'll raise me to the afterlife with more power than I have in this life. If I live, I win. If I die, I still win. You'll be captured and hung as thieves and murderers."

Tanden asked, "And Gregin, how are you going to capture us?"

"Me? No me. This city's blue wizard is sending a captain and crew who will be arriving here soon. Where can you go until then?"

Tanden said, "Perhaps you're right, Gregin. But, I think we'll follow our own course, just to see what happens—if you don't mind? No? I thought not."

Tanden looked to the ogre, "Seenger, gag him. I've had enough of his talk. Make sure his hands are tied and wrapped so he can't collect magic. If he complains that his bonds are too tight, cut his hands off for all I care, he can try his magic in the next life without them." He jabbed a thumb over his shoulder at Heraclius, "And gag him, too. Then, meet me on the deck."

Followed by I-Sheera, he stepped over the still unconscious man and made his way topside.

Gadon grunted a greeting. "Leave me to sit in the hot sun with nothing but a stinking corpse for company? What kind of friends are you? From the sounds of it, I thought you were having bit of trouble down there and I might have to come rescue you."

Tanden replied, "I-Sheera, take him down to my cabin. He can rest his fat bottom while he keeps an eye on our guests. Then, if you would please, come back up on deck."

The sun had risen to straight overhead. The longshoremen were no longer in sight, but cargo still littered the deck of the Allexian ship. Two of the guards at the foot of the gangplank sat on the pier. The third was leaning against one of the pylons. The heat of the day and the inactivity was wearing down on the men.

The standing guard noticed that Tanden, a soldier, was watching. He tapped his foot against the other man and stood away from the pylon. The second man tapped the third and soon all three men had struggled to their feet in a pretense of being alert.

Tanden called down to the men, "Where did the workers go?"

The guard, who had been standing, shaded his eyes to look up at Tanden. I-Sheera joined him at the rail, both standing silhouetted against the bright sky. "Midday meal, I guess."

Tanden gestured towards the ship's cabins and said, "Blue priest Gregin wants to know if you'll be getting a relief soon as well?"

The guard snorted, "Not this side of the next life."

Tanden laughed, "A truer word was never spoken. We're to stand guard on deck, even in this heat with nothing to guard against."

Turning, he saw I-Sheera by him and Seenger nearby. In a low voice, he said, "I-Sheera, move to the bow. Stay along the rail. Let these three see you at all times, but try not to be seen from the docks. Don't let anyone come aboard the ship. And remember, don't speak or they'll know we aren't who we pretend to be. Seenger, try to stay out from sight of the docks as much as possible, but find some suitable weapons. We may need them soon."

Tanden crossed the deck and looked along the other side. There was too much activity to toss Greeta's body overboard. Two empty berths sat next to them. The gap made the side of the ship open to easy view. However, without a ship crowding their port side, sailing out of the berth would be much simpler.

"*That is, if we ever get to sail out.*" Tanden turned to pace toward the stern. "*Gregin is right in a lot of respects. If his new captain and his crew show up before Tuller gets here, we hang. If Tuller does get here, can he get past the guards on the pier? There are too many ifs and what ifs. Why can't I steer a course I have set without having to guess and re-guess every step of the way?*"

Tanden shook his head to chase away the worries. Worry was nothing more than paying interest on a loan that a man may never borrow. Stopping a worry was easier said than done.

He cautiously peered into each hold on the ship, but there was no one else aboard. Lastly, he found himself at the hatchway to the ship's stores. Opening the door, he found it in a state of utter disarray. Items were thrown every which way. Empty wine bottles were scattered and broken around the floor. The mutinous crew had gone through most of the alcohol onboard. Poor

Durrban would have taken a club to any man who dared defile the part of the ship he considered his domain.

Tanden never allowed any part of his ship to fall into disorder. On a fully equipped sailing vessel, everything must be kept properly in its place. To do otherwise courted disaster. Any loose item in a cabin or on the deck was free to fly about with any sudden tilt or turn of the ship. Loose rope could easily tangle a man's feet or be so knotted as to be useless in an emergency.

Tanden flipped the lid off a water barrel finding it almost full. Finding a cup, he drank his fill as he completed a quick visual inspection. He could see the new captain would not be sailing to Tunston without restocking. He estimated he should be able to reach Kalos or Fortin across the Black Sea with the stores already aboard. Grabbing a bucket, he collected a couple of loaves of hard bread, salted fish, and two bottles of wine. Refilling his water cup, he stepped back into the sun. He gestured with a nod of his head, directing Seenger into the ship's stores.

He walked directly to I-Sheera and handed her the cup of water. She drained the cup without taking a breath, raising her eyes at the food and the two bottles of wine.

Tanden said, "They aren't for us, but we should eat soon. As for the wine, we'll celebrate long and hard in Harkelle." He added to himself, "*If we live that long.*" He would never express his doubts to a woman or a crewman.

He walked slowly down the gangplank, looking like he was melting in the heat. The three guards turned to look at him with suspicion in their eyes. Soldiers in the employ of any of the magic orders were not known for being overly friendly. He said, "Priest Gregin sent you these." He held out the bucket of wine, fish, and bread.

The men looked at Tanden.

He answered their look, "What? It isn't my idea. You know how some of these priests are, always passing out bread and wine. I'm not going to beg. If you don't want it, I'll take it back to the priest. What do I care?"

"Wait." One of the guards reached out and took the bucket. He said, "If he sent it, I'm not one to offend a priest." He looked at the other guards and said, "Who's to know?"

Tanden said, "We have to stand watch up on deck and have a good view of the docks. Sit while you eat. We'll call you if we see someone coming."

"Thank you, soldier. That's goodly kind of you."

Tanden agreed, "Yes it is, but you'd do the same for us if our roles were reversed."

The guard nodded vigorously, but Tanden could read the denial in his eyes. Turning to go, he stopped and said almost as an afterthought, "Oh, Priest Gregin says no one, and he means no one, comes aboard without his or my say so. Understand?"

The guard nodded with his mouth full of fish.

Back on deck, Tanden told I-Sheera, "That was a two-edged bribe. Not only are they now in our debt, but the dry bread and salty fish will make them drink the wine. With wine inside and this heat outside, they should be as useless as a saurus without legs in no time. Stay alert and keep moving around. Let your uniform be seen, but don't let anyone get a close look. I'm going to check on our guests. I'll be back shortly."

Heraclius was awake. He glared with hatred at Tanden as he walked past. For his part, he completely ignored him. Back in his cabin, Gadon was snoring softly in Tanden's bunk. Tanden walked over to Gregin. Gagged and tied tightly in his chair, the man could only watch Tanden.

Capturing a blue priest was not as difficult as he thought it would be. In the heat of the day, under a bright noon sun, there was no wind and no moons moving about the sky for Gregin to collect and condense his magic. A man with enough skill to become a priest should have the ability to store magic, but Gregin appeared to be powerless. Maybe he was so confident about being protected by the blue order he had failed to build up a power reserve. Without magic, the blue priest was no more dangerous than any other man.

Tanden glanced at the chamber pot I-Sheera had brought into the room. The side was dented. That bright flash of white light had distracted the blue priest enough that the woman had not gotten hurt. He would be exceedingly sorry if she had. He glanced at the doorway curiously. The sun had not shifted much, but no light flooded the room.

I-Sheera lit his heart. Had she lit the room? Shaking his head, he knew that was not possible. Women could not operate magic. Or could they?

He would have followed that thought, but Tanden remembered the chest Gregin and the soldiers had carried aboard and his curiosity chased away other thoughts. The chest was obviously heavy from the way Heraclius and Greeta had struggled to carry it. A heavy lock held the chest's hasp closed. Tanden tugged lightly at the lock, testing its weight and strength.

A grunt caused him to look up at Gregin. The priest's face had turned red at Tanden's touch on the lock. The man was shouting at Tanden, but his voice was completely muffled by the gag.

Tanden said, "What? This isn't mine to play with? So hang me for it." He slipped his knife from his belt and slid it under the hasp, jerking the blade upward. The lock remained intact, but the hasp pulled away from the wooden chest. "Good lock, Gregin. It held up quite nicely. Your choice of chest wasn't the best, but then I give my word not to inform your city wizard. Wait. I believe this is the Blue Wizard's chest. Correct?"

Tanden saw the rage in Gregin's eyes. He smiled at the bound man. "I see I'm right. I believe it's within my rights as captain of the White Wind to inspect all cargo brought aboard my vessel." Tanden flipped the lid up and stood back in surprise.

The chest was filled almost to overflowing with jewels, silver, and gold pieces. Much of the silver and gold was partially melted and hammered into almost shapeless hunks of metal. Tanden could barely recognize some lumps as cups and plates. A large number of items must have been pagan idols and icons. Other pieces were stamped with marks from the red and green magic orders.

Tanden shook his head in amazement. The value of the chest had to equal the cost of the White Wind and all her cargo.

Tanden looked into the priest's eyes seeing only hatred and evil. He said, "And what's this, Gregin? A gift from the city's blue wizard to the Blue Wizard in Tunston? Spoils from the poor of Stantinstadt? It doesn't matter. I thank you for your gift."

Tanden thought to himself, "*If I live to spend it.*"

He stepped around Gregin, checking the knots and bindings. The priest rocked the chair at Tanden, in a futile attempting to fight. Seenger had wrapped the priest's hands in thick burlap, blocking any possibility of magic.

Gadon grunted. "Can't a man take a quiet nap without you jumping around like you got hot coals down your pants? Leave poor Gregin alone. I'm sure I can gather up enough strength to open him from gullet to gobbler if he causes any problems."

"You nap, old man." Tanden laughed. "I'll need your strength soon enough." He took a long leather strap from a locker under his bunk. He tied it over a cross beam in the ceiling and looped the other end around Gregin's neck. The priest could not move more than an inch or two without hanging himself.

Tanden said, "Behave yourself like a good little boy or I'll let Gadon kick your chair out from under you." He took another leather strap with him to the passageway and without comment, jerked Heraclius's ankles up and tied them to his wrist bindings. He looped the leather from the man's ankles around his neck. Heraclius would choke himself if he struggled against his bonds. Tanden patted the man softly on the shoulder.

Back on deck, Tanden paced along the rail. To anyone watching, it appeared as if he was marching on a watch, when in truth, he paced to burn off nervous energy. He sent I-Sheera and Seenger to eat, drink and rest in the shade. Two of the three guards dozed. The third man sat quietly swatting at flies.

Tanden noticed the dockworkers returning to finish unloading the Allexian ship. He rushed down the gangplank to the guards. He shouted, "Get on your feet. Someone is coming. Quickly."

The guards shot to their feet just as the first longshoreman came into view along the pier. The guards shook themselves awake as they set themselves in order around the gangplank, clubs in hand. Tanden had to admit they looked the part of alert guards.

The guard who had spoke earlier said, "Thanks for the warning, soldier. When this day is over, meet us at the Fat Pig Tavern. We'll buy you and your friends a drink, um...the ogre may have to drink it out back in the alley since they don't allow, you know, his kind inside the tavern, but you and the little soldier are more than welcome."

Tanden said, "Thanks, friend. We accept your offer."
Tanden said to himself with mock offense, *"Why you cheap son*

of a diseased whore, I give you two full bottles of wine, plus a meal, and you offer me one little drink."

He walked back to the deck and continued his pacing along the rail. I-Sheera stood at the bow of the ship. Standing in the shade of the main mast, Seenger watched the dock area in both directions.

As the day wore on, the heat became oppressive. The sea air was humid and felt thick. Tanden was sweating under the heavy leather tunic. The working pace of the longshoremen slowed to a dreary crawl and their banter all but ceased. A water barrel was set in the shade of the warehouse wall. The workers stopped frequently to drink and pour a cupful of cool fluid over their heads. Unloading the ship would take the rest of the day at this slowed pace.

During the mid afternoon, Tanden carried a bucket of water to his two captives. He admonished them both not to speak when he removed the gag or they would not get to drink. With that exception, Tanden remained on the deck, watching the men unload the Allexian ship.

To keep his thoughts off their predicament, he worked out ways to improve loading and unloading ships. He had never given the process much thought in the past. Any captain in a great hurry to unload simply hired a magician or wizard to shift cargo from the ship to a warehouse. Paying a priest's hefty stipend greatly sped up the process, but magic cost more than gangs of laborers. Tandon surprised himself by devising several new methods, some foolish and some not. He quickly ruled out lowering the ship to match the level of the dock and thereby avoiding going up or down a gangplank. He also realized raising the dock to the level of the ship's deck was just as unworkable, as most ships sat at different heights from the water by design or the amount of cargo they carried. Even the deck of the White Wind would rise considerably when off-loading of her cargo.

Still, he reasoned, since they were berthed parallel to the wharf, why not use multiple gangplanks? Some planks could be designated for foot traffic to the ship and some could be designated for carrying cargo off the ship. He devised a mental plan for a trough to slide cargo from the deck of a ship to the docks. He was working on a design for a hoist based on the principles of a lever that could transfer cargo to a ship and remove it without men carrying it on their backs, when he noticed I-Sheera running toward him.

She pulled at his arm and pointed up the wharf. A group of eight or nine men were heading directly toward their berth. They could be heading to the Allexian ship or to the White Wind. Even if Seenger had not been wounded in the fight with the Surr slavers, Tanden knew the two of them alone could not defend the White Wind against that many, even with I-Sheera's capable help. He believed the three men guarding the gangplank would crumble at the sight so many men. Tanden decided his best option was to put on a bold face and confront the group.

Tanden called down to the guards, "Someone is coming. Stand ready. Remember, no one comes aboard the White Wind until I say so. I'll be there shortly." The three men nodded and shifted their clubs from hand to hand, looking the part of men ready to fight.

He told I-Sheera, "Draw your sword and hold it like you're more than ready to use it. Stand at the top of the gangplank." He did not bother giving instructions to Seenger, he knew what to do.

Tanden marched resolutely down the gangplank, stopping near the bottom. Spreading his legs wide and holding his sword blade ready across his chest, he watched the end of the pier, until the first man came into view. It was a common sailor carrying his few belongings in a crude, cloth sack. The man walked in and around the slow moving longshoremen, but his eyes raked across the White Wind with practiced appraisal.

Tanden said to the guards, "Do your work, men. Hold them away from the ship's gangplank until we find out whether they can come on board or not."

The three guards called to the man, halting his progress, and began shouting at the same time. Tanden recognized the phrases the men used as universal to guards and soldiers the world over.

"Hold up, there."
"Wait just a minute."
And even, "Where do you think you're going, pal?"

Two more sailors stopped behind the first as he faced the three guards. Longshoremen coming from both directions began milling about on the narrow pier. An impasse quickly developed with three guards blocking the width of the walkway from one direction and the three sailors blocking the other way.

Dockworkers gratefully placed their cargo bundles on the dock and sat down. The other sailors pushed forward to see what was holding up their progress, each man shouting instructions to someone else. The dock foreman shouted from the back of the knot of workers. Officers from the Allexian ship shouted orders to clear the pier.

Tanden saw Tuller in the midst of the sailors, waving to get his attention.

Tanden called to I-Sheera and Seenger, "We are letting this bunch up. Hold them on the mid-deck."

Without waiting for a reply, Tanden drove into the mass of men. He shook his sword in the air and shouted for quiet. He tapped the tallest guard on the shoulder and told the man to let the sailors pass one at a time.

The man nodded and began bullying men, pushing them in one direction or the other. His two companions joined in and under Tanden's direction, they quickly had everyone standing in two columns. One line of men was for incoming traffic and one line of men was for outgoing traffic.

In single file, the guards let the sailors pass up the gangplank under Tanden's watchful eye. Tuller passed him without comment or a second glance. Tanden recognized a couple other faces from the docks in Harkelle. One of the men stared at the soldier's uniform and started to speak.

Tanden interrupted him, "You're holding up the line, sailor. Get aboard." Although Tanden had seen the man before, he could not remember his name. Before following the men up the gangplank, Tanden turned to the three guards and said, "You men do excellent work. Have you ever thought about joining the wizard's garrison?" He could see the men puffing their chests. He continued, "I'll buy the second round at the Fat Pig Tavern tonight."

Tuller had found seven sailors, in addition to himself.

Tanden followed the men up the gangplank. He was more optimistic about their chances for success, but cautioned himself not to get ahead of the plan. They were not out of port yet.

Tanden motioned I-Sheera to move to the bow once again and continue to watch for activity on the wharf. Tanden walked over to the small knot of men standing at the far rail. He placed his hand on Tuller's shoulder, giving him a gentle squeeze.

Before he could speak, one of the sailors said, "Tuller, I know you and you know me. I didn't sign on to be pushed around by any man's soldiers." He pointed at Tanden's uniform. "And no one said anything about working with an ogre."

Tuller said, "Shut your mouth and listen. This is Tanden. He's the captain of the White Wind. You gave me your word to sign on for a quick sail to Harkelle. No questions asked. Teil, I didn't ask you why you were stuck in port at Stantinstadt without a ship and no way to get home, did I?"

Teil said, "I don't care what I said. This don't look right."

Tuller answered, "You're correct, Teil. This isn't right, but we're here to make things right. I promised you work on a boat sailing to Harkelle. And I gave the captain's promise to all of you that you'll earn double the wages. You can listen now or go back to whatever hole you crawled out of."

The man who had recognized Tanden from the gangplank spoke up, "I'm Kerrel. Most of you know me. I got into a bit of trouble on my last ship and couldn't get another. I know Tanden and his reputation as a captain. I know the ogre is part of this ship's crew. I'll sail with Tanden even if he's wearing the royal robes of King Krebbem himself if he's willing to give me a chance to get home."

Tanden said, "Good to see you again, Kerrel. If you're that happy to sail with me, then you must be willing to sail without wages?" Tanden laughed as the sailor tried to take back his words. He reassured the man, "I stand by the promise Tuller gave you of double wages. We don't have much time to delay. I will tell you this, Teil is correct. Things aren't right. This ship is mine to captain. It was stolen from me and I'm here to take it back. There may be trouble before we get out of port, but all I ask of you is a crew to sail my ship home."

There were nods of agreement all around, except for Teil. Tanden looked at the man and said, "Do you want off my ship?"

Teil said, "You said trouble. I don't mind a good fight—"

One of the other sailors grunted and said, "That's what you said just before the fight that got you thrown out of the Dog and Rooster last night."

Teil said, "Shut your bung-hole, Bone. It was them soldiers," he pointed at Tanden's clothing "in that uniform, what done started it. Called King Krebbem a fool for turning to the green order. I'm no convert myself, but I don't take to listening to insults to Krebbem. Captain, I wants to know where this trouble comes from. Like I said afore, I don't mind a good fight, but I don't fight against my own kind."

Bone snorted and laughed, but held his peace under Teil's glare.

Tanden said sharply, "All of you. Trouble can come at us from a hundred different directions. From bad weather to this city's blue garrison. Teil, you stand with me or you don't. I don't have time to tell you my life's history."

Teil said, "Captain. I didn't say I wouldn't stand with you. I just wanted to know what we might expect."

"That's right and reasonable. But, I don't have time to be right and reasonable. When trouble comes, it comes, whatever its uniform or disguise. Stand with this ship or get off." Tanden glared at Teil until the man nodded.

Tanden turned to Tuller and said, "Get their gear put away in ship's stores. Prepare to make sail as fast as you can. Everyone. No delays!"

The men followed Tuller to ship's stores, tossed their belongings in a heap and began scurrying around the deck, performing tasks to make the ship ready to sail. At Tanden's command, they coiled lines and untangled sheets. He sent two groups of men to prepare the main and jib sails, ensuring they were not tangled.

Tanden wanted to give as little indication of departure as possible. He also needed to be positive that when they broke away from the docks, the White Wind would be able to raise her sails and pull away smoothly. Tangles in any of the running gear would cause her to wallow enabling them to be trapped.

Tanden called Tuller and Seenger to him, "When we sail, we sail out as fast as we can. Tuller, when the time comes I want you at the helm. We face the wind, so back us until we're free of the dock, bringing her around to catch the wind. Seenger, this is no time for niceties. Be prepared to cut the mooring lines. We should be ready to raise sail in another quarter of an hour or so."

Tuller pointed back up the dock, "We may not have a quarter of an hour."

Walking along the wharf was a small group of three men. One of them, a robed blue priest, was pointing out the White

Wind to the other two. Following a short distance behind them was another group of fifteen common sailors, shoving each other and laughing, each carrying a bundle of belongings.

CHAPTER THIRTY-SEVEN

"Tuller," Tanden commanded, "Get us ready to sail. Now! Seenger, we have to keep those men off the White Wind."

Tanden and Seenger strode to the gangplank.

Seenger halted at the top with his sword drawn.

Tanden stepped down to stand by the three guards. He shook his head sadly. "Men, the blue priest was right. There are men coming to steal this ship and all her cargo. They're coming now, as bold as you please, in the pure light of day."

One of the guards said, "Don't you worry. We'll stop them."

Tanden said, "Good. The Blue Wizard is counting on us to do the best we can and he can be a most generous man to those who serve him well. These men will pretend this is their ship, so don't let them trick you. One of them is even pretending to be a blue priest, but he's just another man in the gang of thieves, wearing stolen robes."

The priest and the two men came into view along the pier as Tanden raced back up the gangplank to stand next to Seenger. They watched as the guards moved along the pier. Standing shoulder to shoulder the guards completely blocked the pier.

Longshoremen coming from the Allexian ship put their bundles on the ground and sat down again. The dockworkers going to the Allexian ship began to knot up behind the priest and the two men, unable to pass. The dock foremen at the end of the pier, threw up his hands, plowed into the gathering crowd and began shouting at his crew to clear the way.

A man on the Allexian ship shouted curses about not being able to get his cargo unloaded before dark and shouted at his crew to clear the pier. The larger group of sailors, still laughing and shoving each other good-naturedly, collided into the back of a group of hot sweaty tired dockworkers who had long ago lost their sense of humor. A few heartbeats later, tempers flared. Pushing and shoving began in earnest. Fists flew in each direction; punches connected and, faster than a grass fire on a dry summer day, a melee spread across the dock area around both ships.

The two men with the blue priest had the look of the captain and his first mate. Tanden could not hear what they were saying over the shouting, but the captain and the priest gestured wildly at the White Wind.

The guards stood firm and unmoving, but Tanden doubted they could move more than a smidgeon with the press of bodies pushing at them from opposite directions. The priest tried to push his way between two guards. Raising his arms, a swirl of blue magic collected around the man's hands. One of the dock guards raised his club out of the tangle of bodies and brought it smashing down across the shoulder of the priest. The robed man crumpled to the dock, his blue magic withering way in the bright daylight.

The first mate grabbed the club, twisting it out of the guard's hand. Holding it by the fat end, he jabbed the club into the stomach of the front guard. The guard folded in half, bent at the waist. The first mate brought his knee up into the guard's face, sending him crashing backward into the press of dockworkers behind the guards.

The first mate quickly reversed his hold on the club and sent it crashing into the head of another guard, sending him sideways. The guard slammed into the side of the White Wind and slid down, splashing into the harbor.

The captain slid a knife from its sheath on his waistband. The remaining guard tried to back up but was unable to move as the captain shoved the blade at the guard's midsection. The guard lifted his hands defensively and the blade sliced across his forearm. He crumpled to the pier, covering his head with his bleeding arm, pleading for mercy.

The captain and his first mate shoved men out of their way and made for the gangplank. The captain stood on the bottom, raising his head over the crowd, shouting in a booming voice, "My crew. Hear this, my crew. Board this ship, up the sides. All others clear this pier now!"

The first mate charged up the ramp. Seenger bellowed and threw him bodily back down the ramp.

Tanden heard Tuller shout behind him. "Teil. Bone. To the rail. Prepare to repel boarders. All others set sail."

Tanden kept his eyes on the action along the side of the White Wind, though he wanted to turn and watch the progress of this new crew.

A sailor had almost reached the rail by climbing along the bow mooring lines. Tanden pointed at the man and sent Seenger running forward, but before the ogre could reach the spot, Teil bashed the man in the side with a pike.

Tanden felt the White Wind give a familiar jerk backward. The mainsail had set.

"You," the captain at the foot of the gangplank shouted at Tanden. "Clear the way. We're on orders from Standtinstadt's blue wizard. Help that priest or face the wrath of the Blue Wizard of Tunston."

"You speak for the Blue Wizard? I don't think so. I assume he speaks for himself." Tanden shouted, "Seenger, cut the bow lines." He heard shouting from the bow and the clank of swords, but he kept his eyes focused on the scene before him.

The man at the bottom of the gangplank stared at Tanden. "Are you a fool, soldier? This ship belongs to the Blue Wizard in Tunston. I'm Captain Yarro Herd. I command this ship in the name of the blue wizard of Stantinstadt. Stand aside or I'll gut you myself."

Tanden laughed, "I work for Gregin, formerly of Tunston. This is now his ship. He's decided the Blue Wizard and his city wizard are rich enough. We take this ship and her full cargo as our own. Gregin says the Blue Wizard can go straight to hell and you'll precede him if you try to gut me."

The ship slid backward moving away from the dock. It moved only inches, but it was enough to jerk the gangplank. Tanden felt the White Wind slipping free from the dock at the bow. The lines at the gangplank and the aft mooring lines were still attached.

The first mate regained his feet and rushed Tanden. He swung his club at Tanden's head but Tanden ducked under the blow. It missed his head, but sent the uniform hat flying through the air. From a crouch, Tanden kicked at the first mate. The flat sole of his boot connected with the mate's chest, but the man braced himself and held his place. The first mate raised the club over his head and swung at Tanden with both hands.

Tanden leaned back allowing the club to swish past his head. The man calling himself Captain Yarro Herd charged up the ramp, pushing his weight against his first mate, driving the man into Tanden. Two other men from the docks bounded up the gangplank, each man vaulting to the rail of the ship. One man jumped to the left and the other man jumped to the right. Tanden was unable to stop them. He had his hands full with the first mate and the captain.

To his left Tanden saw I-Sheera drive a knife through a hand grasping the rail. When she jerked it loose, the man fell backward. The sailor hit the edge of the pier with a dull thud and dropped into the water.

Tanden swung his sword at the first mate in a wild cut. He missed, but it was close enough to make him hesitate. He slashed at a man lifting himself over the rail and missed as the man threw himself onto the ship, rolling out of range of Tanden's sword.

Tanden roared and swung his sword in wild cuts at the first mate, forcing him and Yarro Herd back down the gangplank. Tanden leaped up and landed on the gangplank with his full weight. Jumping again, he brought both feet down on the ramp. His action and the movement of the ship caused the gangplank to jerk from side to side. The taut lines holding the gangplank in place strained against the ship. Her sails were catching the wind, pulling the lines tight against the dock. The ramp jiggled, but experienced sailors should have been able to keep their feet. Tanden currently faced experienced sailors. Landing hard the second time caused Tanden to bounce rearward into the air, landing on the deck of the ship.

The first mate rushed up the gangplank again. Tanden thrust his sword point forward, but the man's club deflected it. Tanden grabbed the man by his tunic, slammed the butt of his sword hilt against his head, and threw him to the side.

Yarro Herd used the diversion to reach the deck of the ship. Holding only his knife, he danced in a circle out of Tanden's sword range. Tanden turned to keep facing the captain. The gangplank was now wide open and he heard feet pounding up the ramp.

Tanden spun around and severed the lines to the gangplank with one clean swipe of his blade. Continuing to spin from momentum, Tanden faced the captain's knife. He felt the White

Wind lurch away from the dock. The stern hawser held the ship. He heard the ramp and men on it crash to the dock and splash into the harbor.

At the edge of his vision, Tanden saw Bone pushing against a pier pylon with a pike, driving the ship back, widening the gap between its bow and the dock. Teil was wildly swinging a pike at the men on the pier.

Tanden heard Tuller shout, "Bring the mainsail about. Set the Jib."

Tanden smiled at Captain Yarro Herd, "I graciously give you approval to get off this ship. You can't stop us from making sail, nor can you catch us once we're underway. Gregin has decided to sail us to Allexia. We'll all be rich and there's nothing that you can do to stop us."

Yarro Herd's eyes flicked to the side.

Tanden dropped to the deck and rolled sideways. Completing the somersault, he rolled to his feet, sidestepping around the first mate. The man had regained his feet and retrieved his club. He charged at Tanden swinging the club, driving him away from Yarro Herd.

Tanden flicked the point of the sword at the man to keep him away, but the first mate continued to swing wildly. He moved backward slowly, keeping the first mate between him and Yarro Herd. Tanden slipped a knife free from his waistband and threw it at the first mate. The throw was bad. He had not aimed and had released it too quickly. The flat of the knife struck the first mate in the stomach. The man flinched, taking his eyes off Tanden to glance down.

Tanden drove his sword forward catching the man in the throat. The cut went deep. Tanden easily pulled the sword free and slashed the man across the face, driving him backward. From the side, Teil and Bone rushed at Yarro Herd. Teil grabbed the wrist holding the knife and in one swift motion, lifted him clear off his feet. They propelled him over the rail, into the water.

Tanden stepped over to the first mate and drove the point of his sword through the man's midsection. He felt it scrape bone as the point exited the man's back. He dropped to the deck, dead before his knees touched wood. Tanden let the sword fall to the deck with him.

The White Wind was straining to slip away from the dock. She was pushing herself sideways through the water. The wind and sails were struggling to drive her backward, but the aft mooring hawser held her to the pier. Tanden needed to cut the thick dock lines. He grabbed the handle of his sword and jerked, but the dead man's body refused to release it.

Tanden shouted, "Someone cut the aft hawser."

I-Sheera and Seenger raced past Tanden. The woman appeared to be uninjured though her short sword dripped red. The ogre was covered in blood and weaponless.

Tanden yanked at his sword again, but the dead body held it tight. He saw Seenger grab I-Sheera's sword and hack at the aft hawser, but the sword slid away from the thick rope, well seasoned by salt, sea, and hot sun.

I-Sheera glanced seaward across the bay. The wind and tides were causing waves to skitter about in long evenly spaced rows. She shouted at Seenger. "Get us free!"

Tanden was not sure if his eyes were tricking him, but he saw a pure white ball of light bathe the woman. She glowed, her eyes flashing determination as she glared at the offending line. He watched the pylon at the corner of the pier give way to the pull of the ship. The wood must have rotted below the water line. With a snap and a moan, the dock boards gave way, dropping men and cargo into the water.

The pylon slowed the White Wind, acting like a sea anchor, until Seenger's cut finally sliced through the mooring hawser. Tanden expected the White Wind to leap forward, but instead, little by little, she began picking up speed.

Tanden shouted, "Loose the full jib. Re-set the main." He turned to Tuller at the helm and commanded, "Set course east by north east. Get us out of this harbor."

Teil, Bone, and Kerrel raced past Tanden to respond to his commands. He grabbed Kerrel by the shoulder and pointed him toward the helm.

"Take the helm. Hold the course Tuller sets."

Seenger was leaning against the rail at the stern of the ship, his chest heaving. Tanden shouted at Tuller and pointed to the ogre. Tanden's eyes swept over the ship and her crew. He had lost track of the man who vaulted the rail to his right, but he was nowhere to be seen. He could not see any wounded among his sailors. One dead body lay at his feet and Greeta's body still lay covered by the tarp.

Tanden shouted commands to his new crew, telling this man to tighten a slack sheet and that man to coil the line tangled at his feet. The crew was rough, but for the most part the men looked as if they knew bow from stern and port from starboard. Under his constant attention, the White Wind was moving faster and faster through the water of the harbor, dancing through the waves.

I-Sheera stood at the bow rail. Glancing from the sky to the sails and back again, she waved her hands like any little movement would help fill the sails. A smile escaped her lips as the sails puffed to their fullest with a suddenly gusting, fair wind.

Tanden stared at I-Sheera. His heart swelled, knowing this woman was special, not just because she was his and he was hers. He could not explain it. Tested time and again, he knew he had no magic. I-Sheera could not hold magic, she was a woman, and everyone knew that magic was denied to women.

Standing in the sunlight, the wind whipping around her, I-Sheera stood with her arms outstretched. A tingle of white light shimmered from her fingertips as the sun lit the wave tops behind her. The wind whipped her wild black mane about alternately covering and uncovering her flashing eyes.

It was late afternoon and all the fishing boats should be at anchor, well out of the main channel. With the new wind at their backs, the White Wind could easily pass by any incoming trade ships. Tanden did not expect anyone to lay chase. No ship could get underway fast enough to catch them. Even though the White Wind was fully loaded with cargo, she could slip the harbor and gain the horizon to drop out of sight before any other vessel could get under sail.

Satisfied, he looked to Seenger. Tuller had the man stretched out on the deck, blood was running from his large, open, thigh wound. Tanden walked to the helm.

He turned to Kerrel and said, "Two points to starboard." Tanden was about to help Tuller with Seenger when he realized Kerrel had not obeyed the command. Tanden saw the confusion in the man's eyes. "Easy does it, sailor. Is this your first time at the helm?"

Kerrel gulped and nodded.

Tanden continued, "It's good to learn new things. Just turn the helm to starboard until I tell you to stop."

The sailor said, "Captain. That's why I was thrown off my last ship. I can't seem to learn which way is starboard and what way is port. I'm a good sailor otherwise. Honest, Captain. I ain't gonna lie to you."

Tanden removed the knife from Kerrel's waistband to slice a short length of leather from his soldier's tunic. He slipped the knife back into its sheath and knotted the leather strap around Kerrel's left wrist.

"As you face the bow of the ship, that side is port. The side without this bracelet is starboard. Understood? Good." Tanden jerked and spun the wheel two points to starboard. "And that is two points. Hold this course for now."

"Captain?" Kerrel asked, "Maybe you should get someone else to stand the helm?"

Tanden answered, "No. You do as I command. Kerrel, I won't ask you to do a task you aren't able to do. Don't worry, I'll be nearby to guide you." With that, Tanden turned to Tuller and Seenger who were close enough to overhear his training session with Kerrel.

Tuller shrugged as if to say, "I got the best I could find."

Tanden said, "Seenger, your leg is bleeding on my nice clean deck. I don't know how things work in your country, but on a Holdenite ship, we don't do such things."

Seenger replied, "I told Tuller to wrap it up. I'll be all right."

Tuller snorted, "No. You will not. Captain, he pulled the stitches out of his wound. It won't heal just wrapped up. Hold still, Seenger. You're going to bleed to death if you keep wiggling around like a little boy with bugs in his pants."

Seenger said, "I would rather bleed to death than have you keep fussing over me."

"Quiet, you two," Tanden shouted, "Kerrel, two more points to starboard. Excellent. Hold it there. Now, you two old ladies go bicker somewhere else. Tuller, take him to ship's stores. Re-sew that leg. Then take him to the captain's quarters to rest. He can help Gaden watch Gregin and Heraclius. No arguments from either of you. Move!"

Tanden stepped back to the helm next to Kerrel. He said, "Again. Two more points to starboard, sailor. Very good, Kerrel. Just relax, the helm isn't as hard a task as you think it is."

He looked out over the deck of the White Wind. Six crewmen stood anxiously around waiting for the next command. Tanden shouted, "Bone, take three men and reset the main to the wind. This breeze is stiffening and she's luffing badly. I shouldn't have to tell you everything. We're short handed on this voyage, so use your head. Teil, bring another man with you and come here." Tanden stepped forward to meet the men as Teil quickly dragged another man to stand with him before their new captain.

Tanden said, "Teil, there are two dead men on the deck of my ship. That one," he pointed at the dead first mate, "and one under this tarp. I want them off the White Wind before we clear the port, is that understood?"

Teil answered with a grin, "Yes, Captain. As easy as taking a pee downwind."

Tanden smiled and added, "And Teil. We aren't wasteful on this ship. Strip those bodies of anything of value and put it in ship's stores. I've already watched you and Bone toss one man overboard and that man was probably the only one of the whole gang with coin in his pockets."

They were approaching the entrance of the harbor quickly. Watching Teil strip the dead bodies, Tanden was sure the man would make his deadline. Teil worked with the quickness of a man who had put his hands in other men's pockets many times before.

The White Wind would be hidden from the view of the city once they entered the strait.

He shouted, "Prepare to come about."

The crewmen sorted themselves out and prepared for the course change. Without looking behind him, Tanden called to Kerrel, "Hard to port." The ship's deck shifted under his feet and the crew rushed to keep the main mast from jibbing across the centerboard. Tanden noted some missteps and shoving about with the new crew, but he was unconcerned. Even on such a short voyage, this crew should be working as a team before they reached Harkelle.

He smiled, looking back at I-Sheera. Her eyes were closed and she was smiling, her face beaming in the sun.
The wind shifted, following their course.

CHAPTER THIRTY-EIGHT

Dusk was coming on them quickly by the time the White Wind entered into the area where the Oggy Strait took its water from the Black Sea. The White Wind had sailed a direct course from Stantinstadt to this point.

Gregin and Heraclius, still bound and gagged, were brought up on deck and secured to the stern rail. Gregin's hands were still bundled in thick burlap. Seenger and Gadon sat near them, loudly contesting which of them could think up the most gruesome punishment they could inflict on the pair of mutineers.

Tuller and the rest of the crew organized and inventoried the ship's stores. They also straightened lines and sheets. No sail was allowed to luff without a team of men going aloft to set it right.

Tanden was as relaxed as he had been for days, but he was not yet ready to sail home. He shouted, "All eyes to sea. Watch for sail."

Before long, a man at the bow rail spotted a sail near the coastline.

Tanden shouted, "Hove to." Kerrel spun the helm to starboard dumping the air from the sails, and then back to port, facing the sails directly into the wind. Tanden nodded to the helmsman. The maneuver, smartly done, brought the ship from racing downwind, to standing dead in the water within her own length.

Tuller's crew raced to stations to drop the sails. Tanden waited patiently as the Wave Master plied the winds to join the larger ship. The little ship was faster with a shorter keel and made the approach without incident.

Without orders, Tuller rallied the crew to the rail with ladders and pikes to assist the little boat in coming along side. In short order Lady Yasthera il-Aldigg stood on the deck. Beside her was Tuba. I-Sheera skipped up to take Yasthera in her arms, kissing her.

Tanden said, "You and the Lady should retire to your cabin. You'll find it in quite a state of disarray. It'll take some doing to put your possessions right. I'll come see you later if that's acceptable to you?"

I-Sheera grabbed him by the collar of his tunic and pulled his face down to her height, "You'd better come see me or I'll come looking for you."

She kissed him. He kissed her back, his passion surprising both of them.

Finally backing away, she took Yasthera by the hand and led her to the passageway door. She stopped and looked back, "And Gadon, I've decided you should buy me a black saurus with a white face."

The heavyset man sputtered, "Buy you a black saurus? Why in the name of my father's old hunting dog would I want to buy you a saurus of any color?"

I-Sheera smiled, "Didn't we wager on whether Captain Tanden could swim while towing us both? As a man of honor, Gadon, I'm sure you pay an honest debt when you lose a wager, don't you?"

Gadon coughed and said, "Wager? No. Wagers made in caves to women aren't valid."

Tuller laughed, "Buy the lady a saurus, you fat, old goat."

Laughing, Tanden said, "Gadon. You argue like a doddering old man. You wagered and lost."

Gadon jerked a thumb over his shoulder at the Wave Master. He asked, "What about this boat? I wouldn't send it back to the man who tried to sell us into slavery."

Tanden said, "I sold the boat to our good friend Bramme. Got a good deal, too. I got passage for Yasthera to here and enough fresh vegetables and salted beef to get us home. I even got a bottle of wine to ease your cough."

Bramme and his sons were swarming over the sides of the White Wind, carrying baskets of goods that immediately went into ship's stores.

Gadeon said, "You must be sick if that's the best trade you could make. A whole ship for a few bundles of vegetables that I don't want to eat anyway? Shame on you."

Tanden said, "Bramme, my friend, haggles with the wisdom of the ancients."

Bramme nodded, "It is true, but you pushed for a hard bargain. However, I offered you valuable nourishment for your crew and wine to lighten your spirits. All you had to trade was this puny fishing boat. To make a profit from this ship, my sons and I will have to work."

"Bramme, until next time, go with the red order, my friend."

Bramme smiled, "And you go with yours."

Tanden turned back to the men waiting on deck, shouting, "Someone tie Tuba to the stern rail with his friends. Prepare to make sail."

CHAPTER THIRTY-NINE

Tanden stood on the mid-deck on the White Wind with his arm around I-Sheera, holding her close. Her clean white dress was dazzling in the morning sun. Tearing his eyes away from her, he stared at the high rock walls on all three sides of the little bay. The ship was anchored deep in the bay only a few ship-lengths from shore. Gadon, Seenger, and Tuller stood near them with the rest of the crew standing around the deck watching.

Tanden asked I-Sheera, "What of Lady il-Aldigg?"

She said, "We've talked a lot, I think she'll be all right. She's sleeping now. The rest is good for her. She asked me to be her friend. I never had a friend before."

Tanden smiled and said, "Girl, look around you. You have more friends here than you know."

With a sad smile, I-Sheera said, "I know we have to do this, but I won't watch." Turning, she walked away.

Gregin shouted, "Enough of this. Kill us and be done with it." He was still tied to the stern rail. The Potato and Lumpy were both in the sky and the offshore wind was freshening. The blue priest's hands were bound and bundled in thick burlap, preventing him from collecting any magic. Heraclius lay in a heap beside him, weeping and crying for mercy. Tuba sat quietly.

Tanden said, "Kill you? Is that your wish? You're well and truly guilty of mutiny, theft, and murder. I won't give you a choice, Gregin. You deserve death, but you'll take your chances in the sea and on land. Nothing more than you did for us."

He stepped toward the men and cut Tuba's bonds. Tanden said, "No one of this ship will hurt you as I promised, but you're not welcome aboard the White Wind. Never cross my eyes again or I'll unsheath my sword."

He cut Heraclius lose and continued, "Over the side or I'll throw you over like you did me. Alton didn't survive the sea. Durrban didn't survive the land beyond. Those of us standing before you did survive." Both men went over the side, although Heraclius sobbed and required a shove to his chest to get him over the rail.

Tanden looked at Gregin. "You might live as well. Your magic should stand you in good stead. However, if you are fortunate enough to live, remember this, the Blue Wizard believes you're responsible for the theft of the White Wind and her cargo. I doubt you'll ever again be received with open arms by your order."

Gregin held his hands out to be cut free. Tanden sliced the bonds. If the priest tried anything, he could not collect enough magic to protect himself from all of the crew. Still, the priest chuckled, raising his hands skyward as a strong wind began blowing offshore. A blue wall of light began building around him. It fizzled as quickly as it started. His magic failed. His face betrayed his shock as he stared at his hands.

Tanden glanced behind him and looked up. I-Sheera had climbed the mainmast. She was standing on the topmast tresstletree with one hand braced against the mast. A smile lit her face as the sun reflected off her white dress, the light basked the whole ship in its glow. Wind blowing offshore pushed the White Wind. Even without sails, the ship strained at its sea anchors, like it was anxious to be free on the open seas.

Seenger took one step toward Gregin, flicking his red tongue across his tusks. Rather than wait to see what the ogre had in mind, the priest turned and jumped into the sea.

Tanden shouted, "Prepare to make sail before this kind wind pushes us there without our help. Tuller, help Kerrel set a course to Harkelle. We're going home."

The End

About the author
www.alanblackauthor.com

Alan Black has been writing novels since 1996 when he started *Eye on The Prize*. He is an Amazon #1 bestselling science fiction author for *Metal Boxes*, *Larry Goes To Space*, and *Metal Boxes Rusty Hinges*. His novel *Metal Boxes - Trapped Outside* was awarded "Book of the Conference" at the Cirque du Livre Writer's conference in Mesa, Arizona in 2016 where the judges specifically noted the novel did not read like a sequel even though it was the second book in a series. He's a multi-genre writer who has never met a good story he didn't want to tell.

Alan spent much of his adult life in the Kansas City area. The exception came at the orders from the U.S. Air Force when he was stationed in Texas, California, Maryland, and Japan. He and his wife were married in the late 70s and lived in Independence, Missouri, but now live in sunny Arizona.

Alan Black's vision statement: "I want my readers amazed they missed sleep because they could not put down one of my books. I want my readers amazed I made them laugh on one page and cry on the next. I want to give my readers a pleasurable respite from the cares of the world for a few hours. I want to offer stories I would want to read."

Praise for Alan Black's books

Chewing Rocks
Chastity Snowden Whyte only has a small chip on her shoulder. No problem. She's an asteroid miner and works alone. But author Alan Black knows that comfortable characters don't make for good reading. From page one, he piles problem after problem on Sno, keeping the reader turning pages to find out what happens next. Chewing Rocks is engaging science fiction and a fun read.
Goodreads review by Paul Bussard on July 06, 2014

Empty Space
Funny, disturbing, and poignant.
Funny, disturbing, and poignant...not how I would usually describe a SF space novel. This book, while well written SF has a lot to say about social class, society, humanity, and the human condition. Our protagonist is almost an anti-hero as he's someone you root for throughout the novel, even though he's a serial killer at heart.

This is a great book, and I didn't want to put it down but it has thought provoking components throughout the novel and intertwined with action, adventure, and technology.
Amazon review by Fred on March 20, 2015

Larry Goes To Space
Easy read with some surprising depth
This is a fun book full of wry humor. It's an easy read with what seems to be a fairly straight-forward plot. But, there is an underlying genius in the narrative. I think a lot of different types of readers can get something out of this. Definitely recommended.
Amazon review by Greg Trickey on January 23, 2016

Metal Boxes
WOW!
What a great rip-roaring adventure, I loved it from page one to the end. A grand space opera with a very likeable main character of Midshipman Stone.
I am reminded of Heinlein's writing with the humor, drama and palpable love the characters show for each other, I felt like I was reading a Lazarus Long story. Which is very high praise! This is the first novel I've read by author Alan Black, but it won't be my last. I don't give very many five-star ratings but this one is well deserved, I'm sure it will come to be considered a classic of the sci-fi genre, it's that good.
Amazon review by last spartan on April 28, 2015

Metal Boxes - Trapped Outside
Page Turner...who needs sleep?
Shades of Heinlein and Ringo. I am hooked and can only pray that Alan Black continues to bless us with his yarns. So fresh in theme and direction reading his stories reminds me of so many firsts as a teenager. I've read each of his Boxes stories twice to glean any facet I may have missed the first time. Sad to have come to an end...now I wait for sequels.
Amazon review by Reg Tyson on September 12, 2015

Metal Boxes - Rusty Hinges
Very good sequel in the Metal Boxes series
Funny, thought provoking and action packed. Stone seems to grow up and take responsibility for his life instead of letting life be responsible for him. His relationship with Allie progress well and hopefully will become more permanent. I found it quite humorous when the author references the prior books and how he has one of the characters ask Stone to autograph his copy. There continues to be a mention of the 'Emperor's College' which make me wonder is Stone is a candidate. The ending of the book seems to move the Dracos out of further equals but i don't know for sure.

Lloved it, want more.
Amazon review by James R. Norton Sr on April 30, 2016

Steel Walls and Dirt Drops
Military sci-fi ground pounder action in space–so cool!
A long time reader of military science fiction, I found this book to stand with the best like David Drake's Hammer's Slammers and Redline and anything by Dietmar Wehr. I hate spoilers in reviews so am in a turmoil because I very much want to shout out the so cool surprise ending – but I won't.

I thoroughly enjoyed how the author builds the story putting the hero in situation after situation that challenges her abilities causing her to grow and develop. Even more, she is a commander we can all like. She is smart, savvy, honest with herself, deals well with her people, has self-doubt where it makes sense to, and not automatically so beautiful she would be completely unbelievable. I even like her better than David Webber's Honor Harrington because she feels more real.

The author does not take the easy, predictable route to the good guys always doing the exact right thing. There are plenty of good guys doing the wrong things–sometimes for the right reasons, but still wrong. There are other good guys mostly doing the right things, but then have lapses of judgment. Sound like what a real commander might face in a tight situation? It all rang true to me. So not only are there good human insights (in outer space–people are still people after all) there is also a lot of quick well-paced exciting action with a great military elite.

The science is believable and just the right amount to support the deep space situation and keep the story moving without being overwhelming. There a few twists I absolutely didn't see coming–I love that in a book.
Amazon Review by Sandy on September 28, 2014

Titanium Texicans
Alan Black's work will suck you in!
I am not good at reviews, but this is the third work of Mr. Black's that I have read in three weeks because his writing captures my imagination. I like good space operas because they last longer, but Black's stand alone works are great because they leave me satisfied at the end and not disappointed that there isn't more to come.

Titanium Texicans is a page turner full of authentic dialogue with concepts greater than the satisfying amount of sci-fi technology woven into a well-written coming of age story. Take the time to read it, I certainly wasn't sorry that I did.
Goodreads review by Michael A. Cox on June 13, 2015

The Friendship Stones
Alan Black hits a home run with his book, The Friendship Stones. Its poignant story set in the Ozark Mountains in the early 20th century, brings to mind the life and stories my father lived while growing up in the southern North Carolina mountains. It is a life that today most of us do not know as we are accustomed to many luxuries and technology. Mr. Black brings an appreciation of what it means to cherish every little thing in life while appreciating the beauty of the world about us. It is set in a time of simplicity and hard work, and its main character, LillieBeth, accepts this with humility and determination to follow the lessons she has learned in life, both at church and from her family. Even in this simpler time, the world is flawed and the antagonists come in different characters. The suspense and tension they bring keeps the reader on edge and turning pages.

I highly recommend this excellent book and suggest all readers should continue reading the books of The Ozark Mountain Series.
Goodreads review by Nancy Livingstone on Jan 26, 2015

The Granite Heart
Heartwarming Historical Fiction
Alan Black takes us back to the 1920's, to the Ozark Mountains, and back into the world of twelve year old LillieBeth Hazkit, who tries to live by the teachings of God, but finds life can sometimes be confusing, brutal and too unforgiving to always accept that God has a plan for all contingencies. Her strange hermit-like friend has been killed, her teacher has lost her job through no fault of her own and the impoverished mountain town becomes a colder and less friendly place for someone with a heart as big as LillieBeth's. The archaic and small-minded double standards set her teeth on edge and she is determined to stand strong and be heard, no matter what. The men who murdered her friend and raped her teacher have been captured, but enroute to the county seat they escape and kill one man while injuring her father. To LillieBeth, justice must be done, plain and simple and she and her former teacher, Susanne Harbowe set out on an impossible mission to hunt down and capture these monsters.

Told from Susanne's point of view, LillieBeth's story takes on a new depth as she makes her mark on the hearts and minds of those who know her. Alan Black has created a warm and inviting tale that places the reader back in time, to a place so remote, it's almost as if the rest of the world does not exist. Simple joys, complicated pain and a loss of childhood innocence shake LillieBeth's world and harden her heart, while forcing her into the world of adults.

Alan Black creates a world filled with history, rich in detail and well-developed characters that worm their way into your heart and mind. That I could feel LillieBeth's feelings and see what she saw is the mark of an amazing author who deserves to be read.
Amazon review by Dii (TOP 500 REVIEWER) on August 22, 2014

The Heaviest Rock
Strength of character and a easy manner to it that catches you and keeps you ...
This series is one of the most enjoyable ones I have read. It has heart, action, humor, strength of character and a easy manner to it that catches you and keeps you right there through till the end. Can't wait for the next one 'wiggles on' for those of you who don't know what this means I guess you will just have to get the book and find out for yourself, big hint it is so worth it !!!
Amazon review by Tammie on March 2, 2015

The Inconvenient Pebble
Always great
The author has developed a great character who we as readers want to follow. I'm not into the religious part but it really makes the main character who she is and what she does. I hope the author has a lot more of this story for us to read.
Amazon review by Dave R. on July 4, 2015

The Jasper's Courage
Anger, Retribution, and Fulfillment
Once again, five times in a row in this series, Alan Black has roped me into a story that has filled my belly with anger, flooded my mind with a desire for retribution, and then filled my heart to overflowing. Unlike many series that seem to fall away from their origins, this book delivers on the promises of the first four books. It makes me want to be more courageous.

LillieBeth Hazkit is caught up in more problems than a seventeen-year-old girl should ever have to deal with, but that is like life. Our problems do not come at us one at a time. LillieBeth has the courage and fortitude to face her attackers head on, inspiring the readers to take a stand in their life.

Unusual problems? Not hardly! Read a paper. What was happening in 1925 Ozarks is going on around us today. This book should appeal to all ages, races and creeds. I could hope for more in a book, but I couldn't ask for better.
Amazon review by NonStop on November 11, 2015

The King's Rock
Saying Goodbye to LillieBeth with the perfect end to a Wonderful Series
Alan Black brings LillieBeth Hazkit's tale to an end with the final book of the series, The King's Rock. After watching LillieBeth grow up, this is a bittersweet finale, but perfectly timed, because she is now an adult, still set in her ways, not very flexible and on a mission that could be her last in life as she knows it. LillieBeth's horses have been stolen and she is determined to retrieve them and bring the thieves to justice. With a reluctant Leota at her side, their journey will take them back to Arkansas, the place Leota ran from to escape the clutches of her father. Will the journey give Leota the strength to face her fears and the man who has made her life a living hell? Will LillieBeth show Leota the kind of trust and faith she so sorely needs to grow as a person? Will they find

and retrieve the horses without unnecessary bloodshed? How far will LillieBeth go for justice?

Life is always in flux and LillieBeth's is now at a crossroads as she must determine which path to follow and listen carefully to what her heart is telling her. This is her time, these are her decisions to make, will she make the right ones? Her future lay in the balance, as do the futures of those she cares about…

Alan Black made me feel good about saying goodbye to LillieBeth, not "happy" good, but assured that she is on the right path for the rest of her life and has also pointed the way for those she has called friend. Mr. Black slips into the voice of LillieBeth and has given her a hard-headed personality, limited filters for her thoughts and a strength of character that few could rival. His ability to create a world that breathes will have his readers walking the dusty roads, feeling the raw heat and humidity and believing you are there in the Ozark Mountains of the early twentieth century. This is a series that will stay with me for a long time to come!
Amazon review by Dii (TOP 500 REVIEWER) on December 30, 2015

Chasing Harpo
Loved this book!
Alan knows how to write to engage the reader. Chasing Harpo had me laughing in some parts and on the edge of my seat in others. He has obviously researched the mannerisms of Orangutans and is able to describe the apes point of view with ease. The characters are believable and the writing style flows well. Great read.
Goodreads review by Amanda Mackey on February 08, 2014

A Cold Winter
What a horrible day.
In a bleak, one-woman show, Alan Black takes us through the hardships of surviving a cold, hard winter. You could almost freeze reading every page...and that's not even mentioning the wolves. I hope tomorrow's a better day for Libby.
Amazon review by Daryl Russ on December 7, 2014

How To Start, Write, and Finish Your First Novel
Are You Just Itching to Write a Novel?
Have you ever read a book and thought, "I didn't see THAT coming," or "Thank goodness I dragged myself through the first 30% because the last 70% was fantastic!" ??????? Or, how about, "I could write better than that!" or "I wish I had the guts to do what these people have

done…" ????????? Truth, I would be clueless where to start, I see myself as having a mazillion ideas and be running willy-nilly across the ages, no patience, no real plan, and worse, no organization…totally me.

Listen up budding authors, experienced authors, or anyone who knows someone with that "author" potential, the ever versatile Alan Black has gone all non-fiction on us and written a book on how to write a book that is fun, entertaining and full of great ideas, plans and Mr. Black's own sense of wry humor. How to Start, Write and Finish Your First Novel made so much sense to me, that I was in awe of his thought process and advice! Don't get me wrong, this is NOT Writing for Dummies, but a logical, and easily understood method to produce YOUR first novel! Mr. Black's suggestions and easy manner, while admitting the importance of baby steps is difficult to adhere to, the odds of creating a quality piece of work would be greatly increased!

Is the genre you choose NOT the current rage? Are your ideas NOT 100% original? If your writing is good, your plot well-paced and the very best you have to offer, following Alan Black's method could make you the next author to watch for or at least an author with talent and the ability to tell a story that people WANT to read! Take a look at Alan's list of novels, impressive and varied, but each one is well-written, entertaining and well-edited, he must be doing something "write." Yeah, yeah, I sound like an infomercial, but heck, even I would have the guts to express my writing abilities to the world after reading How to Start, Write and Finish Your First Novel, of course I would have Alan Black review it!

I think what Alan Black is trying to do is to give a future writer a firm foundation to take the leap from and he does it well!

I received this copy from Alan Black in exchange for my honest review, and no, it did not color my opinion.
Amazon review by Dii (TOP 500 REVIEWER) on July 2, 2015

Lightning Source UK Ltd.
Milton Keynes UK
UKOW06f1825240716

279132UK00010B/280/P